Book Three of The Hidden Houses

CLAN FIANNA

GUARDIANS

FIANNA

DiANGELO

BY
Brendan Myers

NORTHWEST
PASSAGE
BOOKS

Clan Fianna
Book Three of The Hidden Houses

Copyright © 2013 by Brendan Myers. All rights reserved.

This second edition is copyright © 2014 by Brendan Myers.
All rights reserved.

ISBN: 978-0-9939527-0-8

Published by
Northwest Passage Books
Gatineau, Quebec, Canada

For all enquiries, please visit
brendanmyers.net

"Clan Fianna" is a work of fiction. Any character's resemblance to any actual person, living or dead, is purely coincidental.

Other titles in The Hidden Houses series:
Fellwater
Hallowstone
The Seekers

~ Acknowledgements ~

In April and May of 2014, the Fellwater series of novels was the subject of a successful fundraising campaign on Kickstarter.com, a popular internet-based crowd-funding platform. More than five thousand dollars was raised from 144 supporters to pay for professional editors and designers.

I wish to thank all of my project backers for their generosity and support, not only with their money, but also with their time promoting the project. In particular, I wish to thank these outstanding benefactors and world-builders, each of whom donated $100 or more to the project:

Carole Martin
Ben Rossi
David LeBer
Gary Gibson
Laurent Castellucci
David LeClerc
Ezekiel Zong-Han Azib

I also wish to thank my designer Nathaniel Hebert, and my editor Jordan Stratford. Writing the books of this series, then re-writing, crowd-funding, editing, and re-publishing them, became my de-facto training course in creative writing and self-publishing. These two fine gentlemen did more than simply provide professional services. They also became part of a team. I am grateful to them for their confidence in this project, and their friendship.

Dedicated

to everyone who has been to Tartarus

and come back again.

Clan Fianna

~ Prologue: Autumn in Fellwater Grove ~

The silhouette of a woman dropped down the face of the rocky ridge, as swift and subtle as a whisper. One startled robin took to the air; the heavy fog, and a hooded cloak, concealed her from all other eyes.

A body lay on a narrow stone shelf at the foot of the ridge. The woman bent over it, taking the pulse, testing the breath, brushing away a beetle that scuttled over the blisters around the mouth.

"Stay strong, Livia," said the hooded woman. "Help is on the way."

She heard the snap of fallen twigs breaking under someone's feet. She pulled her hood over her head, and drew her cloak around her. Three steps to the side, and she vanished in the fog.

Eric Laflamme burst out of the bush. He ran to the body, and shouted out loud: "She's here! I found her!"

The hooded woman smiled, and quietly slipped away.

Brendan Myers

Clan Fianna

Clan Fianna

~ 1 ~

Donall MacBride's cloak and kilt flapped in the October breeze.

The twisted tree branches that formed the main gate to Fellwater Grove parted before him. His companions stood by his side, proud and alert, their armour polished, their weapons tied with peace ribbons. The red and gold leaves of autumn fluttered about them. Yet after a while they shifted their weight on their feet, and fidgeted with impatience.

"Is it their official policy to make us wait half an hour like this?" complained Donall.

"So it would seem," answered Aeducan.

"I bet they're making us wait to show that they can control our situation, make us do what they want us to do," said Ciara.

"Like keep us waiting!" Maread said.

"Well, if I have to wait two minutes longer, I'm going to get a sandwich," said Finnbarr.

A sentry on a platform on the top of the ridge shouted down to them: "A banner approaches! The ambassador is here!"

"About bloody time!" swore Donall. He and his companions stood themselves up a little straighter, and checked each other's readiness with a quick glance.

"Don't let him speak first," Ciara advised Donall. "This is our land. We take the initiative here."

The gate was formed of a mesh of branches and vines from two trees planted on each side. Of their own accord, they bent back to admit the DiAngelo ambassador and his party.

The ambassador himself walked in the lead: a bald and heavyset man with a severe face, and a Roman senatorial toga over his shoulders. He held hands with a woman in a white silk gown and purple sash, and raven-black hair piled in a bun behind her head. Two assistants carrying banners flanked them. One carried the red banner of the DiAngelo, with its white angel holding an hourglass. The letters "K" and "P" stood on each side of the angel: the signature of House DiAngelo's membership in an organization called The New Renaissance.

The other banner bore a black tree, also standing between the letters "K" and "P", and with a triple spiral in its roots, on a background of gold and red vertical stripes; and this was the banner that held Donall's attention. Behind the two flag bearers came an entourage of guards in Roman centurion armour, each carrying carbine assault rifles. Two olive-green military vehicles brought up the rear. Their eight huge wheels, pointed edges, and slit-like windows, jarred uncomfortably with the organic lines of the gate. The Brigantians glanced at each other nervously when they saw it.

As the ambassador approached him, Donall spoke quickly. "I recognize the banner of the House DiAngelo," he spluttered, "although I am curious to see it stand next to the banner of the Brigantians of Northumbria."

The ambassador, visibly annoyed at not having spoken first, said, "On behalf of His Lordship, El Duce, Grandmaster of House DiAngelo, First of the Guardians, and Apostle of the New Renaissance, I greet you, and I present myself as His Lordship's ambassador to the Brigantians of Fellwater."

Donall resisted the urge to roll his eyes. "Do we have to be that formal?"

"Yes," was the ambassador's stern reply. "Formality ensures that everyone knows exactly what they are doing. Formality prevents the kind of surprises that create scandals. Wouldn't you agree?"

Donall sighed. "You might be right."

Ciara shot a critical glance at Donall.

The ambassador returned to his script. "Let's try again. My name is Kendrick McManus, knight of the Brigantians of Northumbria, and this is my wife Livia Julia McManus, of House DiAngelo. I present myself to you as the ambassador of His Lordship El Duce of House DiAngelo, First Apostle of the New Renaissance."

"I am Donall MacBride, chieftain of the Brigantians of Fellwater. This is my guard captain, Aeducan, and my summoner and shield maiden, Ciara DeDannan."

Donall offered a handshake to Kendrick, but Kendrick kept his arms straight down at his sides.

"So, you're a Brigantian?" Donall asked. "I was expecting someone a little more Roman."

The ambassador turned his head to the woman at his side and said, "Our first snub of the day." The woman smiled.

"The first snub of the day," Aeducan interjected, "was the fact that your honour guard brought such provocative weapons into our land." He pointed to the modern machine guns carried by the ambassador's entourage.

The ambassador snuffed with disdain. "By contrast, your guards are carrying weapons that have been obsolete for centuries. And three of them are women."

The six Brigantians let out a momentary splutter of outrage. "The Brigantians respect the fighting spirit no matter what shape of breast it dwells in," Donall objected.

"I *am* a true Brigantian," insisted the ambassador, indicating the banner with the tree. "So was everyone in the whole line of my fathers, going back to the goddess Brigid, the Flaming-Arrow, just like you. That is why His Lordship selected me for this mission. But let us not make this occasion more unpleasant than it needs to be. Let me present you with my diplomatic papers." He held out his hand and the woman at his side put a scroll in it, which he then handed to Donall.

Donall acknowledged the papers with a nod, looked over them briefly, and handed them to Ciara. Then he took the book that Aeducan had been carrying and said, "Let us offer you this welcoming gift. It is a copy of the history of Fellwater Grove and its people, written by every herald of our clan since we first arrived here, more than five hundred years ago."

Kendrick accepted the book and passed it to his wife without looking at it.

"We hope it will help you understand our point of view," Donall continued, "so that relations between your people and ours will be–"

"Peaceful?" Kendrick finished for him. "Well, I should like peace between us as well. But that depends on you."

"You are the one bringing guns and armoured vehicles into our grove."

"You are the ones who killed Lady Emma DiAngelo," Kendrick retorted.

"No, we didn't," Donall growled, and he put his hand on his sword handle. A soldier in Kendrick's honour guard saw him do it, and stood ready.

Kendrick saw that he had found a soft place in Donall's character, and smiled with the knowledge. Then he waved his soldier back and said, "You don't want me here. And since we are already off-script, I don't mind saying that I don't want to be here either. But I am under orders, and we can both make the best of it. Consider the opportunities for mutual benefit. And, of course, consider your alternatives."

Donall looked at the Roman soldiers with their guns,

and then he looked to Ciara, asking with his glance what she thought of the idea. Ciara's gentle hand on his arm told him to let Kendrick have his way for now. He released his grip on his sword.

"We have prepared our guest house for you and your wife," Donall offered, in an effort to appear friendly. "It has room for some of your entourage, too. But we did not expect there would be so many of you."

"That's all right," said Kendrick. "We have field tents and our own supplies. And your grove is two hundred acres. We will surely find a quiet corner where we can set up camp, and stay mostly out of your way."

Donall looked to Ciara again, who shrugged and thus indicated Kendrick's suggestion was probably for the best.

"All right," Donall agreed. "There's a clearing in the arboretum that may be suitable. My guard captain will show you the way." Then Donall turned to Aeducan and spoke in a low voice, hoping the ambassador would not hear. "I want at least five pairs of eyes watching their camp at all times. And double the guard at the gates, and at the well."

Aeducan nodded, and led the ambassador's party to their camp site.

As the ambassador departed, Donall turned to Ciara. "Go into town and tell Miranda to get back here right now."

"A word of advice first?" she offered. "When a diplomat says he wants to do things by the book, then it's best to do things by the book."

Donall sighed. "You're the lawyer. You would know. But I think this whole thing is a mistake. I don't want to be remembered as the chieftain who opened the gate to our home and let a team of DiAngelo soldiers dance right in."

"Try not to let it get to you, lover," Ciara consoled him. "We will find a way to dance them out again."

~ 2 ~

By early evening, the sun painted the scattered clouds gold and red and purple, reflecting the fiery shades of autumn on the trees below. A cool breeze made the small torches that burned in their iron sconces struggle and strain to stay alight. Those who were not patrolling the ridge or standing guard in other places gathered in the mead hall. By far the largest building in the grove, it was really three roundhouses that had been built together in a row. Tonight the large open floor in the middle house was occupied by ring of tables. A feast of wild turkey was laid before everyone, and clay chalice full of wine came with every plate, and long sticks of freshly baked bread, still warm from the oven.

Donall MacBride sat in the high seat, with Ciara DeDannan to his left and Aeducan to his right; and next to them sat the best of the Brigantian fighters, Síle, Maread, Finnbarr, and finally Eric, the most recently initiated member of the clan.

"Once again," said Donall, as he shambled to his feet while carefully ensuring he did not spill his cup, "let us drink to the health of our mightiest warrior, Eric The Red, I mean Eric Laflamme, sorry you look like a Viking to me, who shall be armed and armoured like a man for the first time today!"

Everyone cheerfully but tiredly raised their wine-cups and toasted Eric, who smiled and shook his head.

"That's got to be the fifteenth time in the last hour you toasted me."

"Well, Eric, my son my lad my trout, you deserve it! You protected Lady Caitlin, last of the House Corrigan, at great risk to yourself. You stood up to Heathcliff Weatherby Wednesday, of House Wessex, at a time when no one else would. And most recently you negotiated an alliance between our clan and the Wessex-men, under their new Lord Protector, Algernon Weatherby, who is a much more reasonable fellow. Even as recently as a hundred years ago, none of us could have imagined such co-operation between us. Well, it seems to me that such effort deserves a reward. Now, Eric, my good and faithful man! Stand up!"

Eric stood. From a wooden box that sat on the table near his place, Donall revealed a dagger in a hand-crafted leather sheath, and held it out for Eric to take.

"Our tradition, from ancient times," Donall explained, "teaches us that a boy becomes a man when he receives his first weapons. Your father should have done this for you when you turned sixteen, but since he didn't, and since I'm the chieftain of this clan, it falls to me. So take this weapon. Take it as a sign that you are a man now. And though you are descended from ordinary men, and not from the gods as we are, nonetheless I declare you are no longer an outsider. I declare you are a full and proper member of the Brigantians of Fellwater. Let all the

Hidden Houses and all the Secret People acknowledge it!"

Everyone in the mead hall enthusiastically cheered his name: "Hail, Eric Laflamme! Hail, Eric Laflamme! Hail, Eric Laflamme!"

Eric got down on one knee, but Donall raised him up again with a gesture, and the observers giggled among themselves.

"You don't have to do that, Eric. We're not that kind of clan!"

"Sorry," Eric mumbled, as he got back to his feet, which caused the assembly to laugh again.

Ciara produced a carved wooden chalice from a decorated wooden box. Carved with the intricate Celtic knotwork lines and the totemic icon of the tree and spiral, Eric recognized the chalice as the same which Miranda once put in his safe–keeping.

"It was also the ancient custom of my clan, the DeDannans," Ciara explained, "that the lady of the house showed a guest that he was welcome by offering him a dram of mead. And so, I offer this to you. Drink, and be welcome." As she spoke she filled the chalice with mead from a nearby bottle, and then and offered it to Eric to drink. He grinned proudly, and gladly drank. Ciara hugged him and kissed both his cheeks.

The assembly cheered for him again, and various friends came forward to take a turn to welcome him.

When almost everyone had congratulated Eric and pottered back to doing whatever they were doing before, Eric wandered over to Donall and Ciara, who held up a drinking horn for him. They toasted each other and drank, and contemplated the festivities of the hall together.

Ciara said, "I think you are the first person in three hundred years to be given honorary membership in a Hidden House like this. It's a very rare honour."

"I don't know what to say!" Eric gushed.

"Then, say 'thank you!'" Ciara suggested.

"Thank you!" Eric laughed with her.

"It's we, who should be thanking you!" Donall laughed.

"I've only one question, Donall," said Eric.

"Oh? Let's hear it."

"It seems like everyone knew you were planning to do this today."

"Yes, they did," Donall confirmed.

Clan Fianna

"So I wonder why Ildicoe isn't here. And neither is Miranda"

Donall sighed and drank deeply from his drinking horn before answering. "I don't know. I certainly invited them."

"Now that I think about it," added Ciara, "we haven't seen either of them here since the election."

Donall wasn't in the mood to talk of such things. "Ildicoe went off on some mission, and I have no idea what Miranda's doing. But come back to the feast. Let's have some fun!" he decided, with a friendly thump of Eric's shoulder.

Then he moved to the centre of the room and clapped his hands to get everyone's attention. "This is a heroic hall! So where are the bards! Where are the singers! Let's have some proper revelry!"

From the loft above him a man with the red and green of clan Gaelach on his kilt called out "I am here, I am here."

"Excellent!" laughed Donall, and the world laughed with him. "Come give us a song!"

A table was moved out of the circle to allow the bard and two of his companions to stand in the middle, where everyone could see and hear. The audience clapped and stomped their feet and joined in the chorus, and drank like lords and swore like sailors, and delighted in the good things in life.

Before the song was over, the curtains of the main door were pulled open by a hand from outside, and then a tall figure in a maroon hooded cloak entered. The clapping and foot-stomping ceased. The wife of the DiAngelo ambassador drew back her hood. Her hair was tied in a bun above her head, as before, although now a few ringlets dangled down over her temples and ears. Her cream-coloured Roman stola fitted so elegantly it seemed she had been poured into it; and the gold cords that wrapped around her waist and under her breasts glittered in the torchlight of the hall. If the eyes that watched her enter were not openly hostile, neither were they friendly, and she saw she was not welcome.

"I am Livia Julia McManus, of house DiAngelo, wife of ambassador Kendrick McManus," she announced herself.

Donall, who up to that moment had been evaluating her from afar, set down his wine-cup on the table with an authoritative thump, glanced at Aeducan, and tipped his head in Livia's direction. Aeducan understood the signal, and he stood and casually strode to the centre of the ring of tables, as the bards stepped out of his way.

"Here in this hall," Aeducan challenged her, "we believe that someone who interrupts a bard in mid-song brings a lot of bad luck upon her head. Surely your Brigantian husband would have taught you that?"

"He did," she answered. "He also taught me that when a guest arrives in a heroic hall such as this, she is offered a drink and a seat by the fire before she is asked her business."

A murmur quietly arose from the crowd, as people whispered to their neighbours that their visitor might know a thing of two of the Brigantian ways.

"Our ways require that we must be good hosts. That is true," Aeducan returned, "but they also require that guests must be good guests! And good guests do not make demands."

A quiet wave of barely-suppressed approval for Aeducan's move was momentarily heard.

"I made no demands," said Livia. "I gave you my name, and stated a fact."

Donall cracked a small smile on one side of his mouth. Seeing it, Ciara whispered something in his ear.

Aeducan grimaced and continued. "Above our heads, hang the shields of the greatest of our heroes since we established this grove. That one is the shield of Lughair MacBride, great-grandfather to our chieftain, who by himself took down three frost giants in the Battle of the Ice Storm, not long ago. And there hangs the shield of Dubhdarra MacCool, the greatest DeDannan fighter of his time, and the only person to duel with Miyamoto Musashi, the great samurai of House Kami, until they both called it a draw. Every man and woman here can name every shield that hangs in this hall. If you can name just one, I shall be satisfied."

Livia knew that everyone expected her to fail. She also knew the rules of this game required Aeducan to give her a fair chance. She stepped into the centre of the circle, taking her time, evaluating each shield, and the faces of those who watched her. She pointed to one. "That one, I am sure, is not yours."

A wave of surprised snickering came from the audience.

"In fact," Livia smiled, "I don't see your shield anywhere at all. No stories of your deeds have reached us in the court of House DiAngelo. Perhaps your shield will never hang here."

The snickering changed to laughter.

"My shield, if you would like to know," said Aeducan, as he recovered his honour, "will not hang there while I still live. For all the shields that hang here are the shields of those who have gone into the west. That is what one must do, to earn the greatest honour. That, too, is a fact that your Brigantian husband should have taught you."

Now Livia stepped back, pulling her hood over her head again, and spoke her last piece.

"I came tonight to tell you that our camp is now set, and that the ambassador requests the honour of your chieftain's presence at his breakfast table tomorrow morning, if it should please you. I bid you good night."

As she turned to leave, Donall stood and called out to her. "Well done, Livia Julia McManus, well done. Very well done. Come forward please."

"Chieftain MacBride!" Livia flustered.

"You have an arrow for a tongue," he said appreciatively. "Why don't you have a seat here, beside our good man Eric? We have set this feast in his honour tonight, so the place by his right hand is a place of honour too."

Donall stretched an inviting hand toward an empty seat next to Eric. The Brigantians nodded their approval, and some of them started clapping.

Livia sat, gingerly at first, and kept the hood of her cloak over her head, as if she wanted to hide in it. She leaned over to Eric and said, "They're clapping for me, even though I lost the debate. Are they gloating?"

Eric said, "It's not about winning or losing. It's about showing what you're made of."

"That's it exactly," said Ciara, as she filled a cup of wine offered it to Livia.

Livia smiled, almost against her will.

"Besides," Ciara continued, "there's no point having you camp on our land, if we don't talk to each other, at least once in a while."

"In which case," offered Livia, "I hope you will accept my husband's invitation to breakfast tomorrow."

"That will be for Donall to decide," Ciara informed her.

"You let your husband make your decisions for you?" Livia balked.

"Actually, *I* make all of *his* decisions," smiled Ciara in return. "Why do you think you are sitting here right now, instead of walking back to your camp?"

Livia grinned.

Ciara leaned into Livia's ear, hoping that no one nearby would hear her next words. "If a time should ever come when your husband and my man stop talking to each other, then maybe you and I can start talking to each other."

Livia smiled. "You've played this game before."

Ciara looked around the room, and indicated two men arm–wrestling, a fiddler who had climbed on the shoulders of the guitarist to play the next tune, and a woman who was aggressively fondling and kissing her man. "With this hairy-legged lot," she grinned, "I play it every day."

~ 3 ~

After the feast and celebration, half the revelers sauntered up to guest rooms in the loft, or outside to the other roundhouses in the grove, to find beds in which to pass out. The other half were already asleep on chairs or benches somewhere in the hall. Donall was in the kitchen, and up to his elbows in dirty dishes. Eric sat by the fireplace, a cup of hot coffee in his hand, a tired but satisfied expression on his face. Livia drank the last of her mead in a long gulp and accidentally knocked her cup to the floor when she tried to set it down.

"So! Eric of the clan Brigantia. What's your story?" she said, as she pulled a chair next to him.

"My story?" asked Eric.

"Tonight's festival was all about you. So what's your story?"

"They made me an official member of the clan today," Eric smiled. "I'm no longer an outsider. It feels like coming home, after being away for a long time."

Livia suddenly saw him differently, and the cheerfulness of her demeanour was replaced by sternness. "Oh! You're *that* Eric. The one who escaped from Carlo's house the night it burned down."

Eric realized that it was very possible that Livia was a close relative of Carlo's, and his smile disappeared too.

"I was there, that night," he confirmed. "Someone told me that Carlo's mother died in that fire. Is that true?" he asked.

"Her name was Emma DiAngelo. Take care you never forget that."

Eric tried to remember to breathe. "I'm sorry."

Livia shifted her chair to face him directly. From inside a fold in her cloak she produced a large wooden cup, carved with intricate fine spirals, knot work lines, tree branches and strange animals, all turning around and inside each other. Some of the figures were slowly moving, and they looked upon Eric as if they could see him.

"Do you know what this is?" asked Livia.

"It's a chalice," Eric replied.

"It is an ancient Celtic lie-detector. It breaks into fragments if someone tells a lie in its presence, and it mends itself again when it hears the truth. So if you lie to me, I will know."

Knowing what he knew about the culture and supernatural abilities of the Secret People, and some of their treasures, Eric believed her.

"Tell me this, and tell me honestly," Livia ordered him. "Did you start that fire?"

Eric looked at the cup, a lump forming in his throat. Then he looked Livia in the eye and said "No."

Livia studied Eric's face carefully, looking for any sign of hesitation or uncertainty in his expression. Meanwhile, the cup in Livia's hands remained intact.

"You're telling the truth," Livia determined, and Eric breathed easier. "But you're holding something back."

"I did not start the fire. But I was there when it happened. Katie smashed an oil lamp on the floor. It was a spur-of-the-moment thing."

Livia continued examining Eric's mind with her gaze. "That's not it. There's something else. You told her to do it, didn't you?"

"No."

"Then you were glad she did it."

"I didn't hold her back, if that's what you mean. Those people made our lives hell, for months."

Livia paused. She glanced at the cup in her hand, which was still entirely intact. The animals on its face settled into restful postures.

From the kitchen, Donall and Ciara put down their dishes and moved to the archway, to see what was happening.

Livia took a moment to think before speaking again. "You still love her, don't you."

Eric nodded. Then he looked Livia in the eye, showing no fear, and said, "But I didn't start the fire."

Livia leaned back in her chair. "You're telling the truth. I believe you." And she returned the cup to the fold of her cloak.

Eric let out a deep breath of relief. He saw that Donall and Ciara were still watching, and he waved to let them know that all was well, and that they need not intervene.

"Tell me," said Livia, "what was she like?"

Eric didn't expect that. "What do you mean, what was she like?"

"Well," Livia shrugged, "what did she look like?"

"What do you want to know that for?"

"Just curious."

Eric sighed. "The spring of this year was a bad time for everyone, and I don't really want to talk about it," he muttered, and sipped his coffee.

Livia still wanted to talk. "What was Tara like?" she prompted him.

"She was still a baby, when she died," Eric recalled, without raising his eyes.

Livia nodded, and then ventured a more provocative statement. "Some say that Carlo DiAngelo was the real father, not you."

"I know," said Eric. "Perhaps he was. But Katie didn't want Carlo. She wanted me. So, I might not have been the real dad, but Tara was my child, nonetheless."

Livia considered Eric's words for a moment, and then reached for Eric's fingers and said, "Do you think you will ever fall in love again?"

"Why are you asking me these things?" said Eric, as he tried not to let his annoyance show.

"I just thought that if you could fall in love again, after what you went through, then that would be like a proof of concept for me. If you could fall in love again, so could I."

Eric looked down to Livia's hands, where they slipped into his own. Then he looked to her face, which did, he decided, resemble Katie's face, quite uncannily. He was not sure what she was doing, and so he dared not move his own fingers, lest he accidentally give her the wrong impression, though he did not know what that might be.

"Do you think you'll ever fall for someone again, like you fell for her?" Livia asked again.

For a moment, Eric's mind drifted to thoughts of Ildicoe Brigand, the woman with whom he shared an adventure last summer.

"Oh, someday, maybe," he said. "I don't know."

"Well," said Livia, as she squeezed his hands affectionately. "It is an honest answer. I respect that."

Then Livia playfully pinched his chin, as if he was only a boy, and whispered something in his ear, and smiled at him. Before Eric could respond, she stood and announced to everyone: "Thank you all for a surprisingly fun evening. I'm a little drunk now, so I'm going back to my camp. Good night, good night, good night!"

Donall chuckled under his beard, and Ciara playfully swatted him with a dishcloth for it.

Eric wished her good night in return, and then went back to drinking his coffee. Livia took his cup without asking him for it and finished it herself, and then staggered out of the hall and into the night.

~ 4 ~

After midnight, Síle wandered out of the mead hall, in the direction of the grove's arboretum, where she lived in a treehouse. As she was in no hurry to get home, she followed the light of the fireflies, and paused to listen to the howling of distant coyotes. She kicked up a pile of leaves, and laughed and danced as wind swirled the leaves around her. When she arrived at her treehouse she paused at the sound of someone stepping through the undergrowth. She crouched low, and crept ahead to see what was happening. Soon she saw a person in a long hooded cloak, carrying a flaming torch, walking slowly through the woods. She followed the figure to a small clearing near the cliff-like face of the ridge which encircled most of Fellwater Grove. In that clearing waited another cloaked figure. They spoke to each other in low voices, with their faces close together. Then the sound of a third pair of boots storming through the woods could be heard. The new intruder was evidently in a hurry, entirely unconcerned about who might see or hear him. Síle crouched lower, as the third figure passed by; at the same time, she saw one of the original figures pull his hood lower, and retreat into the darkness. His companion, however, could not escape before the third figure arrived, and pulled him away by the wrist, as a parent might take a child out of a playground for breaking some rule.

As they passed near the place where Síle hid, she got a brief look at one of their faces. Recognizing who she saw, she became more than a little bit angry. She stood up and let herself be seen, with her sword at the ready, and the many layers of her clothes flying in the breeze.

~ 5 ~

Aeducan asked Maread to watch over the ambassador's campsite. She perched herself in a hunter's tree stand, half way up a tall pine tree, close enough to observe the camp but far enough away to be unobserved, or so she hoped. The post was covered in a military camouflage net, although the net probably offered more psychological comfort to its occupants than real concealment from the eyes of others. There she watched the centurions set up the last of their tents, light fires in metal braziers to cook their meals, and do all the other late night comings and goings. There wasn't much to see. Maread spent much of her time texting.

When Maread saw two cloaked and hooded figures arrive at the camp, one of them pulling the other along by the wrist, she became curious. She took up a pair of binoculars and tried to see who they were, but they entered the largest of the tents in the camp before she could glimpse either of their faces. The sound of an argument followed the visitor's arrival, and although she was too far away to hear the details, she could clearly recognize a male and female voice loudly exchanging accusations and insults.

Maread leaned back and got comfortable in her perch. From a satchel she produced a thermos full of coffee. She sent a text message to Aeducan: "sentry duty tonight is going to be interesting."

After giving assignments to the warriors who were still sober enough to do sentry duty, Aeducan returned to the mead hall to find it almost empty. Donall sat on a chair by the fire, and Ciara sat in his lap, both of them with their backs turned to the door. Everyone else who he could see was asleep on their chairs or on the floor. The loudness of their snoring made Aeducan wonder how anyone could get any sleep at all. Aeducan cleared his throat to get his chieftain's attention. Ciara jumped up, genuinely startled, and pulled her bodice and chemise back on her shoulder. Donall slowly twisted his back to see who had arrived, although he winced in pain to do so.

"I'm sorry, but now that this ambassador has set up his camp, we might need some more people on patrol," Aeducan told them. "I was hoping that at least one of you might be available."

Donall sighed long, and looked over to Ciara with a question on his face that he didn't need to put into words for her to understand.

"You're the chieftain, you decide," Ciara answered him.

"How many eyes have we got on their camp right now?" Donall asked Aeducan.

"Just Maread's," answered Aeducan, "and mine, when I join her."

"I suppose that will be enough for now," Donall decided. "They won't do anything stupid on the first night. They'll dig their trenches and go to bed."

"I thought you wanted more people watching them," Aeducan recalled.

"Yes, I did, but we can deal with that tomorrow," Donall dismissed him.

Aeducan didn't leave. "When you appointed me captain of the guard, I swore an oath to protect the grove, and its people. That oath is very important to me."

"I know it is," said Donall. "But that doesn't mean other people can't take the night off once in a while." Then he reached out to Ciara's thighs to pull her back into his lap again. Ciara laughingly let herself fall into his embrace, and Aeducan could no longer see what he knew they were doing.

"Right," Aeducan unhappily excused himself. Once outside the hall, he gave himself a moment to survey the grove: the paths that ran from the mead hall to the other roundhouses, and the stone circle, the well of wisdom, the arboretum, the gates to the outside world, and the other landmarks he had come to love, and had sworn to protect.

A shadow passed over his head, barely visible as a black silhouette against the grey–black clouds. It reminded him of the giant falcons which had attacked the grove in the summer of the year. He made a mental note to ask Algernon Weatherby if any of his people were still using the falcon cloaks they captured from Heathcliff last summer. Then he trudged toward the arboretum, to take his turn standing guard over the ambassador's camp.

~ 6 ~

Finnbarr had been assigned to sentry duty on the ridge. After about an hour or two, he left his post wandered back to the mead hall in the hope of finding a thermos of hot tea, or a flask of whiskey, or even an extra cloak to take the chill off the night. His shift wasn't finished, but he didn't care; and he had a retort ready for Aeducan if he was caught wandering from his post. His attention was drawn to the sight of something crossing the green near the stone circle.

Finnbarr crept closer, and saw a cloaked man carrying another person in his arms, a drunk friend home from the night's festivities, he supposed.

"Safe home!" he laughed.

The figure turned and acknowledged Finnbarr with a silent nod.

~ 7 ~

The sun did not rise the next morning. The sky merely changed from featureless black to overcast grey. A morning mist turned all the trees into shadows in a wash of light.

Donall had invited Eric to attend the breakfast with the DiAngelo ambassador. Eric donned a tunic and kilt in the Brigantian tartan. He mounted his heaviest woolen cloak that he could find upon his shoulders, to keep warm in the autumn wind. He buckled his new honorary dagger on his belt. Then he found a small mirror with which to admire his outfit. It was the first time he wore the livery of his new tribe, and he wanted to do them proud.

"Katie would have been proud," he mused aloud.

Donall, Ciara, and an honour guard gathered in the great stone circle at the centre of the grove. Donall was carrying a banner-pole from which hung the tree and triskele crest of the Brigantians of Fellwater.

"I don't much like being summoned like this, here on our own land, but let's hear what these people have to say," said Donall.

"Miranda would shit a brick of she was here," said

Clan Fianna

Finnbarr.

"Well, she's not here," Donall reminded him. Then he turned to Eric and said, "Eric, I want you to come with us because this ambassador is going to think you're still an outsider. And that will piss him off. And that will amuse me to no end."

Eric grinned. "I get it. If my presence makes him uncomfortable, we might have an advantage."

"I'm also naming you the official herald of Clan Brigantia," Donall added. "That way, he has to deal with you, whether he likes it or not. Anyway, you're probably a better negotiator than me."

Eric grinned with pride.

"This has been a pretty good couple of days for you, Eric! The honours just keep coming!" Aeducan said. Eric blushed.

Donall wanted to get back to business. "Aeducan, since you're the captain of the guard, you get to carry the banner," he said. Aeducan gladly accepted the banner from him.

"Everybody ready?" Donall asked them all. Everyone answered in the affirmative. He finished with the tribe's battle call.

"Truth in our hearts!" he declared.

"Strength in our arms!" they all answered him.

"Fulfillment of our oaths!" Donall said again.

Together they cheered, "Raaah!"

Donall smiled, and gave them the sign to march to the DiAngelo camp. The band of seven left the stone circle and followed the path, over the rises and falls of the land, through the cathedral–tall trees, and into the mist.

"That was the first time I got to recite the charge with you guys," Eric observed with a smile.

"Fates be willing, it won't be the last," Donall winked.

~ 8 ~

The DiAngelo ambassador's camp was in an area of the arboretum where most of the trees were young saplings, not much taller than the tents which the DiAngelo had set up. In the centre of the camp stood the tallest of their tents: a large rectangular affair in the style of a Roman military commander's field post. On either side of the main tent stood the two light armoured vehicles that the DiAngelo brought with them, each parked at an angle to directly face anyone who stood before the main tent's front flap.

One of the sentries sounded a horn when Donall and his party came close enough, to alert the camp. Kendrick McManus emerged almost immediately, wearing the embroidered purple toga of a Roman of senatorial class, and a serious scowl on his face.

"Good morning," Donall started to say. "We are glad to accept your invitation to—"

"Shut up," Kendrick snapped back.

A very surprised Donall looked to Aeducan and to Ciara and back. "What? Didn't you invite us here today!" he said.

"Where is my wife!" demanded Kendrick.

"Isn't she here with you?" Donall asked.

"She is not," Kendrick spat back.

"That makes no sense," said Donall. "She walked back here to your camp late last night, after drinking with us in the great hall."

"She might have left your hall, but she never arrived here!" Kendrick retorted.

The news shocked every member of the Brigantian party, and they looked around each other to see who else was surprised too.

"Well, she's not passed out with the other drunks, I can tell you that," Donall informed Kendrick. This earned for him a nudge in the ribs and a judgmental look from Ciara.

"This is on your head, Brigand," Kendrick threatened, "if you don't find her and bring her back to me, right now."

At a hand signal from Kendrick, the sentries pointed their vehicle's mounted machine guns at the Brigantians.

"What is he doing here!" howled Kendrick, when he recognized Eric.

"Eric Laflamme is the official herald of the tribe. He is part of my diplomatic party. He has a right to be here."

"He's an outsider," Kendrick snarled. "And he started the fire that killed a matron of House DiAngelo! I would have him locked in the chthonic prisons forever!"

"I did not start that fire!" Eric insisted. "And I said as much to Livia last night, and she believed me!"

"You are on a first-name basis with my wife after only one night? The cheek of it!" Kendrick barked at him.

Clan Fianna

"Your wife came to my hall last night to invite us to breakfast with you today," Donall explained sternly, "Then she stayed to hear the bards for a while, and then went back to your camp. That is the truth of it."

"And I'm telling you she did not come back to camp," Kendrick reiterated. "So either you're lying to me, or she is still out there somewhere!"

Donall looked to Ciara again. Ciara gave him a worried look of his own, and then said to Kendrick, "I'll form a search party right away."

"I have already formed my own search party. And if any of your people get in my way, I will assume you are hiding her."

"You'll have full access to the whole grove, and everything in it."

"That's right, I will," Kendrick hissed. He turned and stomped back into his tent.

Donall eyed the Roman centurions with their machine guns and decided it would be a good idea to retreat. With a hand signal he ordered the party to return to the stone circle. When they were out of sight of the DiAngelo camp, he breathed a sigh of relief.

"That went well," said Maread.

"It would not have been worse if a dozen Firbolgs came and crapped all over his tent," remarked Finnbarr.

This brought a soft chuckle from everyone, but Donall remained circumspect. "We better find his woman before anyone else does."

"In a fog like this?" Finnbarr said. "She could be holding a twenty-foot sign saying 'Here I am!', and we wouldn't find her."

"Aeducan, pull some guards off the ridge and form a search party. Síle and Maread, you go look any place where she might have come to harm. The river. The well. The caves in the ridge. All our most sensitive places. Finnbarr, you check the perimeter outside the grove itself, and take somebody with you. And Eric, try to retrace her steps after she left the great hall. You were one of the last people to talk to her before she disappeared."

Finnbarr put his hand on Eric's shoulder and said, "Last night, I saw somebody carrying somebody in his arms, from the stone circle to the old part of the arboretum. Maybe it was her.

Try looking around there first."

"Thanks, I will," Eric agreed. "Did anyone else see or hear anything unusual?"

"No, nothing," Síle quickly replied, and looked away.

"All right. I'll get started," Eric declared, and he headed on his way. This was his first serious job as a full member of the clan, and he did not want to let his new chieftain down.

~ 9 ~

The thickness of the mist did not help. Eric could not see further than a few meters in any direction. The sounds of creaking tree branches and raven calls seemed to come from everywhere around and above him, all at once. Sometimes he heard the voices of other search parties calling out Livia's name, but they too echoed from every direction. He even came upon a bed of tall grass where a pair of deer lay sleeping. As soon as they smelled him, they lurched to their feet and bounded off, disappearing quickly into the glowing white atmosphere. The sound of their hoofbeats echoed from left and right and behind and before him.

In a cluster of willow saplings that grew near the edge of a pond, he found a discarded torch, covered in mud. He felt he was on the right track, and kept going.

His path meandered over a gently rolling landscape, thick with old hardwoods. A pair of fallen alders served as a bridge over a shallow creek. The white glow of the mist faded to grey, and the echoing voices of the other search parties shrank into the distance.

A crab-like creature, disturbed by the noise of Eric's passing, scuttled up a tree, and out of sight. A shadowy thing that might have been a large rat, but for its glowing green eyes and its wide row of smiling shark–like teeth, rustled nearby. Then it pounced toward Eric in a swift and single bound. But a shrubbery in its path caught the creature in its branches, which wrapped themselves like tentacles around the animal's neck and legs. It struggled and cried out, but the plant pulled it into its roots underground, where it was heard no more.

Eric tried to reassure himself that help would not be far away if he had to call for it. Nonetheless, he was now in a part of the grove he had never explored before.

As he moved along the path, the atmosphere darkened

further on his right hand side. A brief foray in that direction showed him that the path was now running parallel to the ridge that encircled most of the grove. This gave Eric a bit of hope, as he now knew that if he became lost he could follow the ridge back to the more familiar places. The slope of the ridge was very steep here: almost as vertical as a wall, much like the walls of the gorge near the village of Fellwater itself. Eric doubled back to the path, and continued following it, thinking that if Livia came this way last night, she would probably stay close by the path.

Eric began jogging. The twigs and low branches whipped at his shoulders and head, but he ignored them. He had a plan now. The path he followed soon swung up to the foot of the ridge, and the mouth of a shallow cave. It had the right kind of shape and depth to provide the shelter that Eric thought Livia would have looked for. It was a short climb up the face of the ridge, perhaps as high off the ground as Eric's shoulders, so it was probably dry. Eric grasped the outcroppings of cedar roots and the stone handholds, and pulled himself up. In the hollow of the cave, not far from the mouth, he found a sleeping woman bundled up in a blue cloak.

"Livia!" he called to her. He pulled himself up the rest of the way into the ledge and touched her shoulder. Livia did not move. He called her name again, and pulled back her hood from her face.

Then he saw that Livia's skin was bone–white, and her lips were spangled with purple blisters. Eric pulled back his hands by reflex, and gagged involuntarily, and Livia's head flopped into Eric's lap when he let it go. She was asleep, and her breathing was loud and laboured. A thin trickle of blood dribbled from her nose and from some of the blisters around her mouth.

"Wake up, wake up!" he urged, but she remained asleep. Eric began to fear for her life.

As gently as he could, Eric rolled her into his arms, and carried her back along the path, toward the healing house, shouting for attention the whole way: "She's here! I found her! I found her! Hey, over here!"

~ 10 ~

"Poison!" bellowed Kendrick.

Livia's sleeping body had been laid out on a bed in the

healing house. Around her stood Neachtain the healer, and Eric, as well as Donall the chieftain, and the ambassador with two of his guards.

"Poison," Neachtain repeated. "My guess is that she drank somnaweiss, perhaps mixed with nightshade, monkshood, belladonna, or maybe henbane."

"Flying ointment?" suggested Eric.

"What?" barked Kendrick.

"The plants you mentioned. They're ingredients in the mixture that mediaeval witches used to make themselves hallucinate. They'd rub themselves in it, and then they thought they could fly."

"Well spotted," approved Neachtain.

"Somnaweiss is one of those weird plants that grow in magical places like this grove. It puts people to sleep."

"What do you know about such things!" Kendrick sneered.

"I have a degree in history," Eric said.

"You have a degree in shut the hell up!" Kendrick snapped.

Neachtain stepped between Eric and Kendrick, and tried to diffuse the aggression. "Livia is alive. That's what matters. The poison will not kill her. But it will keep her asleep for a long time."

"How long," Kendrick demanded.

"That depends on how much she drank," Neachtain explained "Judging by the boils around her mouth, I'd say she drank enough to sleep for a week, maybe more."

Kendrick gazed upon his wife's sleeping form, with a cold and unreadable face.

"Take her back to my camp," he told Neachtain, without looking up.

"Or, I could take her to a hospital?" Neachtain offered.

"No hospitals. I don't trust them."

Neachtain looked at Donall, and shrugged helplessly.

Then Kendrick spun around on his heel and pointed an accusing finger in Eric's face. "You are responsible for this!" he roared.

"Me?" Eric protested. "I'm the one who found her!"

"You found her because you knew exactly where she was!" Kendrick accused.

"No!" Eric protested again.

"You were the last person to see her before she left the hall. And I have two witnesses, including your chieftain, who say she was seen talking intimately with you, and drinking something from a cup you gave her. Isn't that right, Donall?"

Donall was standing by the doorpost, trying not to get involved in the argument. At Kendrick's insistence, he admitted, "I did see her drinking from Eric's cup, yes."

"I didn't give it to her," Eric countered. "She took it from me!"

"She sat beside you at the table most of the night!" Kendrick continued.

"Yeah, she did, but–"

"You are the one who found her body less than an hour after the search began!"

"I followed the clues and made the most logical conclusion I could make with the information I had, which was–"

"Enough!" Kendrick grabbed one of Neachtain's herb cabinets and flung it violently to the ground.

"Hey, what the hell are you doing!" Neachtain shouted.

Kendrick motioned to his guards to pick the cabinet up again, but left Neachtain to gather most of the bottles and jars of things that were now strewn around the floor. Then he resumed interrogating Eric.

"Here's what actually happened. Last night my wife came to your hall to invite you to a simple ordinary breakfast. Then you offered her hospitality, and she accepted, knowing that you would be offended if she refused. But you sat her beside Eric, who hates House DiAngelo, who poisoned her, and then followed her."

"That's not what happened, I swear!" pleaded Eric, to Kendrick and to Donall.

Donall's face had been growing longer as Kendrick explained his theory. "Everything he said fits the evidence, Eric."

The blood began draining out of Eric's face. "This is all just speculation!"

The ambassador finally acknowledged Eric directly. "As far as I'm concerned, outsider, that's what happened, and it's up to you to prove that I'm wrong."

Eric shook with surprise and frustration. "You can't shift the burden of proof like that! It's not logical!"

Kendrick turned to the whole room and boomed: "Now listen to me! All of you! If she doesn't wake up, any chance of peace between your people and mine will be gone forever. Do you hear me! Gone!"

Donall eyed the ambassador's personal guards, and suddenly remembered how well armed the ambassador's camp was.

"And get rid of the outsider!" Kendrick ordered Donall. In return, Donall glared at him, but said nothing.

Kendrick ripped the flap over the door right off of its pegs and stormed out of the healing house with his guards in quick-step behind him.

When Kendrick was far enough away, Eric turned to Donall. "You don't seriously believe him, do you?"

Donall folded his arms. "I'm not saying I do, but his theory adds up."

"But everything he said is just circumstantial! That's not evidence!"

"It's enough to make me doubt you," Donall asserted.

Eric was so shocked he could only gasp incoherently for a moment. When he found his tongue again he asked, "What are you doing, Donall? You've known me long enough to know I'm not capable of something like this!"

"What I'm doing, Eric," Donall sighed, "is whatever it takes to avoid a war. Now I'm not the diplomat that Miranda was, but I know the meaning of the word 'realpolitik'. So do you. So I have to banish you from Fellwater Grove."

"What! Banish me! But I didn't do it!" sputtered Eric. "The person who actually *did* do it is still out there! No one in the grove is safe–not the ambassador, not even you– until we find out who really did it."

"What do you want me to do, Eric? You saw the hardware he brought with him!"

Eric did see the hardware in the DiAngelo ambassador's camp, and he pursed his lips regretfully. He looked to Neachtain the healer for support, but Neachtain only shook his head sympathetically.

Donall leaned out the door and shouted for Aeducan and Maread. When they arrived, he told them, "Take Eric home."

"I've got some things in the guest house. Can I–"

"No. You are not welcome. Stay away," Donall snapped

at him. He stomped out of the healing house, and out of sight.

~ 11 ~

Miranda stood in her back garden, wearing a hooded cloak to keep the autumn breeze at bay. She held a bouquet of heather and trilliums in one hand, and a whiskey flask in the other.

Before her stood the tallest and widest tree in her garden; and she faced the side where the trunk of the tree, from the roots to the lowest branches, looked like the head of a bearded old man. The roots of the tree spread out from his beard, and his hair became its branches and leaves. His eyes were closed, and his expression peaceful. Miranda placed the flowers into niches formed by the ridges of the old man's brow and beard, and she poured a sample of the whiskey into a cracked wooden bowl that sat on the roots, just below the cleft of the old man's chin.

"Happy birthday, Old Hobb," she said to the tree. Then she stepped back, sat down on the grass, and tried to find the sense of serenity that the old man in the tree appeared to embody.

A pair of goldfinches fluttered among the branches, followed by a nightingale. They perched a safe distance from Miranda, but they sang to her, and Miranda decided that was the sign that Old Hobb was listening.

"I've got some news that you're not going to like," she confided. "I'm going back to Scotland soon. I've been forced out by the DiAngelo, at last. Donall is the new chief, and he's made Aeducan the new captain of the guard. I trust them both; I'm sure they will take care of you. But as for me: I don't know if I will ever return."

A knocking sound at her garden gate attracted her attention, and frightened the goldfinches and nightingales away. Miranda turned and was greeted by a tall and middle-aged smiling man with a bushy grey-black beard, a leather jacket, and wiry grey-black hair falling down to his shoulders.

"Miranda Brigand?" he asked.

"Yes, that's me," Miranda confirmed.

A woman with grey-streaked black hair and a red bindi mark on her brow stepped out from behind the man, and spoke next. "And are you also known as the lady Cartimandua, of House Brigantia? Descendent of Brighid, the Flaming Arrow?"

This made Miranda hesitate for a moment. She narrowed her eyes and evaluated the visitors, even as two more people came down her front path to her door.

"There are few who know that name," she said.

The visitors clasped their hands together in a prayerful gesture. Then the man said, "My name is Ramanujan Bhattacharya, this is my wife Satya, and our daughter Kuvira."

A girl in her early teens, with wavy black hair, a denim jacket, white tights, and black boots, greeted Miranda next. She had an unsettled, almost hunted look on her face, and although her greeting was polite and formal, still her eyes searched their surroundings. Ramanujan and Satya, by contrast, looked tired.

"Is it safe to speak?" asked Ramanujan.

Miranda was suspicious, but she nodded and opened the garden gate to them. "Come in," she invited them, and she led them up the steps to her back deck, and then through the French doors that opened to her sitting room. Satya removed her shoes at the threshold, and she urged her distracted and nervous daughter to do the same. Miranda put two more small logs on the fire in her stove, and went to the kitchen to put the kettle on.

"I'll have tea for you in a minute, if you'll have it," she offered.

"Thank you," replied Satya.

Kuvira's eyes darted around the room, and she tried to speak to her parents without Miranda hearing her. "Are you sure we will be safe here?" she asked.

Satya answered with sternness. "This is the woman who defeated the Ice Giants and the Wendigo in battle, in the Great Winter Storm of 1998."

Kuvira saw Miranda slicing bread on her kitchen counter, and said, "She's a great warrior? She's a housewife!"

"She's a Brigantian chieftain!" Ramanujan corrected him. "In this world no one is ever who they appear to be. You know that."

When Miranda set a tea tray before them, along with a plate of olive oil and fresh bread for dipping, Ramanujan began his story.

"It's difficult to admit this. We are—we once were—members of House Arjuna, from the branch that took care of the hidden ashram near the Indian Bazaar, in Toronto, do you know it?"

"The one behind the restaurant on Gerrard Street? I

know it," Miranda nodded.

Satya continued the story. "Last month the head of our ashram, Raj Purana, declared his official allegiance to something called The New Renaissance, and its leader, El Duce of House DiAngelo. And then this morning, he told us we all had to do the same."

The mention of the New Renaissance made Miranda's smile fade from her face, leaving a serious frown behind. "I take it you said no?" she speculated.

"Absolutely we said no!" Ramanujan confirmed. "I'm not swearing an oath to a man I know nothing about! This isn't the dark ages anymore!"

Satya leaned forward and said, "A representative of that front group of theirs, the Guardians, came to the ashram to witness our vows of loyalty to the leader of the New Renaissance. I told them I wanted to know more about him before I swore an oath to him. The representative gave me some pamphlets and a book, but then he shouted at me for not trusting him, for staying inside my 'comfort zone', whatever that means, and not letting go of 'negative thoughts', and having a closed mind and a young soul. A young soul! I was just asking questions!"

Satya calmed herself as her husband gently took her hand and whispered something in her ear. It fell to him to continue the story. "Raj Purana told us that if we didn't swear loyalty to El Duce, then he would banish us from our House."

"So you stood by your questions, and he banished you," Miranda guessed.

Ramanujan confirmed her guess with a nod.

"Satya and I helped build the ashram, more than a hundred years ago!" Ramanujan related, as he did his best to contain his frustration. "It's been our home ever since! But he wouldn't listen to reason. Well, all things must pass, as the teachers used to say. So we went to our chambers to pack up our possessions,"

Satya finished the story. "But that man from the Guardians, I give him too much credit by calling him a man, he decided we were taking too long. And he sent the kshatriyas to throw us out. And who did he think he is, to give orders to our fighters like that!"

Miranda sighed sympathetically, and shook her head.

"We went to a few other freeholds, looking for help,"

said Ramanujan. "They all said they didn't want to get involved. Even the djinni dervishes over in Hammertown– famous for their hospitality– they turned us away too. Which brings me to the reason we are here. We have come to ask you for asylum in Fellwater Grove."

Miranda bowed her head and stroked her brow thoughtfully for a while. She looked out the glass doors to her garden, and to Old Hobb, and bowed her head again. When she sensed that her guests were getting anxious for a decision, she asked, "Why do you need asylum? Are the kshatriyas still following you? Do they know you are here?"

From another part of the cottage suddenly came a loud banging sound, possibly made by a hammer on a door, followed by the shouting of several angry men.

"I'd say that's them, right now," said Kuvira.

Miranda stood and pointed toward a door that led to a different part of the house. "Go down that hall and turn to the right. You'll find a circular room with a stone floor, and a fire pit in the centre. Hide in there."

The four members of the Bhattacharya family dashed down the hall and into the room that Miranda had indicated. Resembling a gazebo, or even a Celtic roundhouse, its walls were made of floor–to–ceiling windows set between heavy, ornately carved wooden pillars. A conical ceiling with a smoke–box at its summit formed the ceiling. Kuvira stuck her head around the corner and said, "There's nowhere to hide in this room!"

"It's the safest part of my house. Honestly. Just close the door behind you and stay quiet," Miranda whispered back.

The banging was coming from a door in one of the modern extensions on either side of the original log cabin. When Miranda reached it, she found three tall and muscular Hindi men wearing serious faces, and the black and blue uniform of the Guardians. One of them, she noted, tried to hide a fighting hammer behind his back. Another was fitting tiger–claw blades between his fingers, but quickly removed them when Miranda opened the door. Miranda saw this, but gave them no sign that she saw it.

"Can I help you?" asked Miranda.

"Good morning," replied the tallest of the three. "We are from The Guardians."

"And?" Miranda asked.

"We saw some suspicious people enter your back yard not long ago, and we'd like to search for them."

"You're not the police," Miranda replied.

"That's true," said the leader, as he put a foot on Miranda's threshold. "But we would like to have a look around anyway. Can we come in?"

Miranda didn't like his foot in her door. "No."

The two other Guardian footmen bullied their way into Miranda's house anyway, while the third one pressed an official-looking document into her hand. "Your permission would have made it easier for us, but we don't really need it." Then he, too, pushed past her and entered the house.

The three men split up and searched different rooms and hallways in the cottage and its extensions. Miranda stomped after the lead man.

"You have no right to come in here!" she ranted after him. "Get out! Right now! Do you hear what I'm saying? Do you know what the police will say when they hear that three big men forced their way into a single woman's house?"

The man totally ignored her, until she stepped in front of him and stopped him from looking in the room where the Bhattacharya family were hiding.

"Ma'am, this will all be over in less than a minute if you let us do our jobs," he said, tersely but professionally.

"Get out of my house!" Miranda repeated.

"The people we are looking for are potentially very dangerous. It's very important that we find them."

On the other side of the door, the Bhattacharya family leaned on the wall near the door, in the hope that they would not be noticed if the door suddenly swung open. The room was perfectly circular, and clearly offered no hiding places. Ramanujan and Satya held each other's hands. Kuvira stood defensively behind them.

In the hall, Miranda stood firm. "All right then, what did they do. Did they kill someone? Steal something?"

"They are members of a large and well-organized terrorist group, with a criminal agenda, and we need to question them."

"A terrorist group called House Arjun, maybe? Or did you mean The New Renaissance?" said Miranda. The man's reply caught in his throat: he was genuinely surprised to hear Miranda call his bluff. Miranda then stepped out from in front of the door she was protecting, and then deftly floated around and behind him, so that he could clearly see the tree-and-triskele crest carved into the door in raised relief.

"Brigantia!" he whispered to himself, as he realized exactly where he was, and what house he had invaded.

"Rakshasas! Over here!" he shouted, which brought his two companions running, with their hammer and tiger claw weapons drawn. Their heads had taken the form of Bengal tiger heads, and their uniforms had become suits of iron chain mail with armoured plates. When they saw the symbol engraved on the door, they too understood the truth of where they were. They perked their ears, alert for danger.

"Who are you–" the lead man started to say, until he discovered that Miranda was no longer in the hallway with him. His brow furrowed with thought for a moment, and then he turned to his companions and the task they had come to complete.

"In here," said the lead man. From under the collar of his uniform he drew up a hood over his head, and then swept it down again; then he, like his companions, bore the head of a tiger. He grinned with his tiger teeth, anticipating a successful hunt just beyond the door. Carefully, he turned the knob and pushed the door open.

Inside the room, the Bhattacharyas began looking for another way out. Kuvira and Satya examined the windows, to see if they could be opened, or punched out. Ramanujan looked around for something he could use to barricade the door.

When the door opened, the three Rakshasas did not see the gazebo attached to the cottage. Instead they saw a narrow city alleyway, with industrial recycling bins and graffiti-covered brick walls.

"A Seven League Door!" marveled the lead rakshasa.

Meanwhile, Miranda cleared her throat to get his attention. They turned around and saw that she had become a Celtic warrior, in full armour, with blue spiral war-paint on her hands, her face, and her legs. A bright yellow-white glow shined from her flesh. With three swift and precise strokes of her short sword, she disarmed the two Rakshasas and tripped the third one so that he staggered backwards through the door and on to the alleyway. Then she wheeled upon the two that she had just disarmed, poised her sword to strike at the throat of the nearest one, and hissed, "Now get out of my house."

They looked at each other, and ran.

When Miranda was satisfied that the two Rakshasas were gone, she went to the first one, who she had kicked through her Seven League Door. He still lay on the ground, near a stack of cardboard boxes. She grabbed him by the collar and lifted him to his knees and growled in his face: "My house is *nemeton*. Do you know what that means?"

The Rakshasa did not answer. He was still dazed from his fall, and confused by his new whereabouts.

"It means," she informed him, "that no violence is allowed within its bounds. That's a tradition even Carlo DiAngelo will respect. If you break the peace in my nemeton, other clans will feel free to break the peace in yours. Is that what you want?"

The Rakshasa still said nothing, but it was clear in the expression on his face that he understood her perfectly.

Miranda threw him back to the ground again and returned to her house.

The Rakshasa struggled to his feet and wondered aloud, "Where is this? Where did you send me?"

"You're in downtown Toronto, about a mile from the ashram of House Arjun. Now go home."

She crossed the Seven League Door back to her own house, and shut it behind her.

At home, she leaned on the door and caught her breath. The blue spirals faded from her skin as she calmed down, and the hero-light faded. She hung her sword belt on its display mounting on the wall, and untied the warrior-braids from her hair. Then she knocked on the door to the gazebo and opened it, to let the Bhattacharya family know they were safe.

Kuvira jumped out first and gave Miranda an enthusiastic hug. The others emerged next, elated and grateful, with their hands clasped in a prayerful gesture toward Miranda, to show their thanks.

"Let's wait for a few hours, just to be sure you aren't being followed anymore," said Miranda. "Then I'll take you to Hallowstone. There's not much more I can do for you here."

Another knocking on the front door caused the Bhattacharyas to fret for their safety again, but Miranda assured them the Rakshasas would not have returned so quickly. They stayed by the door to the gazebo anyway, just in case. Miranda took up her sword again and went to see who was knocking now.

Eric entered the cottage and Miranda hugged him affectionately. "Lucky you didn't show up two minutes earlier," she said.

"Actually, I saw two guys coming out of your house. Two guys with tiger's heads. They were in an awful hurry."

"I offered lunch, but they ran away. Tell me, Eric, what's wrong with my haggis!" Miranda joked.

Miranda called out to her other guests to invite them to meet Eric. The Bhattacharyas emerged from the gazebo again, but before they got too close Eric whispered in Miranda's ear, "There's a problem at the grove."

"There's always a problem at the grove," Miranda said. "Well, come and have a cuppa, and tell us the story."

"Can we speak privately?" Eric whispered again. "It has to do with that ambassador from the DiAngelo."

Miranda could see on his face that he was scared of something, so she guided him to the gazebo. Ramanujan Bhattacharya overheard part of what Eric said. "The DiAngelo? My friend, you and I may have the same problem."

Eric felt a little less worried. Miranda made introductions all around, and then sat everyone in her sitting room again. "All right, what's happening," she asked.

"Last night," Eric related, "someone poisoned the ambassador's wife. She's in a coma now."

Eric did his best to describe everything that happened, including how he found Livia's comatose body, and the argument with Donall in the healing house.

"Now both the ambassador and the chieftain think that I'm the one who did it. So I've been banished from the grove," he finished.

Ramanujan sat back and cradled his teacup in his fingers. "You've been banished from your clan; my family and I have been banished from our ashram. Meeting you here seems auspicious."

Miranda perked an eyebrow at his words, but said nothing.

"Miranda, you've got to talk to Donall," Eric pleaded.

"Oh, I talk to him, but he's the chieftain now. These things are his decision to make," Miranda replied.

"There has to be proof somewhere that I didn't do it!" Eric tried again.

"You must admit, the proof against you is rather

strong," Miranda said.

Eric's face began to drain of blood again. "We have always trusted each other. Why don't you believe me?"

"I do believe you," Miranda reassured him. "I don't see what I can do about it."

Eric sighed. "It's not right, that I should be punished for something I didn't do. And for what? Political stability?"

"I know. It's not right. And I don't like it either," Miranda agreed. "We all have to live with the consequences of everyone else's actions. Even the old gods had not the power to change the past."

"Fellwater Grove is where the most important events in my adult life happened. And the people of the grove are my only friends. And this fairy-tale world you live in, with its weird animals, its trees that attack people, its pools of water that mess with your mind: even with all those things, it's where I feel most like myself. I can't imagine what life would be like without it."

Ramanujan leaned forward to make his own contribution. "All things must pass, my friend," he offered Eric.

Satya added her own piece. "And you have ask yourself, why do you want to win back the friendship of someone who threw you under a bus?"

"I don't just mean Donall. I'm also thinking of everyone else, too."

"You're thinking of Ildicoe," Miranda smiled.

Eric smiled a little bit in spite of himself. "You too, Miranda. I will always be grateful to you."

"I understand," nodded Ramanujan. "After one is Awakened, no one can live the same way again."

"Actually," said Miranda, "Eric has not undergone the Awakening. And he never will. His ancestors were ordinary people; his soul is an ordinary soul. The Awakening would do nothing for him."

All three of the Bhattacharyas made small noises of surprise. "He's actually an outsider?" marveled Kuvira.

"He's not descended from the gods, like we are," Miranda informed her.

Ramanujan looked at Eric again. "Strange that I did not see that," he remarked.

Eric perked his ears, but resisted the urge to say something in reply.

"He's not an outsider," Miranda explained. "He has a

foot in both worlds. And that's what makes him important. As you know, our world is fading away. People like you and I are fading with it. Some day soon, this whole world will belong to ordinary people, like him. And I have to believe that people like him will be able to take care of it."

Ramanujan and Satya nodded knowingly. Kuvira, however, grew worried.

"Mom? Dad? What does she mean, the world is fading away!" insisted Kuvira.

Ramanujan sighed unhappily. "Do you remember, we went to India last year to find the place where I was born?"

"I remember," said Kuvira. "They tore the old ashram down, and they built a factory."

"They make bobble-heads there now. Shaped like little Bollywood dancers. Bobble-heads!" added Satya.

Eric turned to Miranda. "So is that why you brought me into the clan? You wanted to see if someone like me could handle living in your world?"

"At first I gave you a chance for Katie's sake," she replied. "Then I made you part of my circle for your own sake. You're smart, and a loyal friend. Such people are worth keeping."

Eric was grateful for her praise, and showed it with a smile, and a friendly touch on her hand. "I'm glad you think so. But what about Donall? He probably thinks I'm a criminal."

"Yes, well," sighed Miranda, as she let go of Eric's hands, "he's the chieftain now. He has to do what he thinks is best for the grove."

"What, like throw me out? But I didn't do it!"

"If you want to prove your innocence that badly," Miranda suggested, "then you are going to have to put on your big girl panties–" Eric smiled against his will, "–face your situation, and do something about it."

Eric sighed; he knew she was right.

Miranda paused before continuing. "I'm sorry to say I can't help you. I have another mission. I can't tell you about it, not yet. But I have to finish it before I can do anything else."

Eric nodded, reluctantly accepting. "I'm on my own."

"I'll give you this piece of advice, though," she added. "Find the cup that no poisoner will touch. That cup will tell you the truth."

"Of course! The poisoner is certainly not going to

poison himself," Eric reasoned.

"Something like that," Miranda winked. "Now I should probably ask you to go home. If Donall finds you here, it wouldn't go well."

Eric pursed his lips and said nothing. He pulled on his coat and left the house, and slammed the door behind him.

Miranda turned to the Bhattacharya family next and said, "Now let's see about getting you somewhere safe."

A short while later, the Bhattacharyas were sent on their way to Hallowstone through Miranda's Seven League Door. Miranda wrote a letter of introduction for them, to deliver to Algernon Weatherby, in the hope that he could grant them asylum.

Alone, she collapsed on the couch in her sitting room, drank the last of her tea, and gazed up to the ceiling, where the face of a man was carved into the wood of the beam that held up the ridgepole. His hair, beard, and flesh were made of oak leaves, and his eyes were knowledgeable and kindly. His good gaze gave her no comfort.

She threw her teacup across the room, and it smashed into fragments on the wood burning stove. Then she picked up a lamp from a side-table near the couch, and from underneath it she grabbed a small black electronic device, no larger than her thumb, with a small flashing red light.

"I hope you're happy with what I did for you today, you bastards!" she shouted into the device. Then she put it back where she found it, and slammed the lamp back on the table.

Less than a heartbeat later, Miranda's phone rang. She picked up the handset and shouted "What!"

"Yes, Cartimandua," said the voice on the other end of the phone line. "You have done well."

~ 12 ~

Eric took a longer route from Miranda's house to his apartment, along a boardwalk on the river's edge as it passed through the village. He was not in a special rush. When he got home, he slouched down on his couch and cuddled his cat Ganga in his arms.

"The cup that no poisoner will touch. What does that mean?" he wondered aloud.

Eric surveyed his apartment. The boxes of Katie's

possessions and Tara's baby things, which once covered an entire wall of living room, was gone now, and replaced with bookshelves. Most of their things had been redistributed to friends or sold in a yard sale, and he kept only the items with the most sentimental value. The process was slow. Some of Katie's clothes still hung in his closet, and a box of Tara's toys still sat beside his couch. Now such things were the last mementoes of his life among the Secret People.

Eric gently picked Ganga off his lap and set him down on another couch cushion. Ganga made an irritable meow, and trotted off. Next Eric searched around his apartment for anything that might be useful for sneaking into the forest after dark. Dark clothing. A flashlight. The dagger. A camera for evidence.

As he put these things together, someone knocked on the door. His first thought was that someone had come from the ambassador's camp, to punish him. His heart began pumping a little faster. He checked through the peephole and saw a handsome young couple, both wearing buttons that announced their membership in a local environmentalist group. He relaxed somewhat, and opened the door.

"Good evening, sir," said one of them. "We're just checking to see if you received your package of new energy-efficient spiral-coil lightbulbs for your home."

"No, I haven't," Eric told them. "But I'm not carrying much cash right now, so—"

"Actually, they're free," one of the canvassers asserted, and handed Eric a box containing a dozen of them. "If you fit these into all the lights in your home, you should notice a big drop in your hydro bill. You'll be using less power, so that the power plants won't have to burn as much coal. Saving electricity means saving the earth!"

~ 13 ~

That afternoon, Aeducan stood in the middle of a circle of Brigantian fighters and Wessex cavaliers. As the captain of the guard, it was his responsibility to assign them their patrol routes around the grove for each day. He sent Síle to the arboretum, for which she was grateful. Maread was sent to watch the ambassador's camp, for which she was indifferent. Finnbarr was given the ridge to patrol, for which he complained.

At the perch overlooking the ambassador's camp,

Clan Fianna

Maread and Aeducan settled in for what they hoped would be an uneventful afternoon. As the afternoon began fading into twilight, they heard the same unhappy voices coming from the biggest tent in the ambassador's camp. Although this time they were not arguing, Maread could tell by the tone that they were still cross with each other.

"A house divided," Aeducan quipped.

"I want to hear what they're saying," Maread rejoined. As she climbed down from the tree stand, Aeducan grabbed her shoulder to stop her for a moment. "Stay safe, don't be long," he warned.

"I'll be fine," she reassured him. Then she silently dropped to the forest floor, and crept closer to the camp.

She crouched behind a thicket and listened. The argument definitely included a female voice. It sounded like the voice of Livia Julia, the ambassador's wife, but it was strained and gravelly, as if she was very sick. The argument soon intensified to a more aggressive pitch, and then she heard someone walkaway. Maread retreated quietly.

A bright blue-white light picked her out of the shadows of twilight. At first she tried to scuttle away, but the light followed her. She ducked behind a tree that looked big enough to hide her. Kendrick's commanding voice followed the light, saying: "Come out, come out, wherever you are!" A second spotlight fixed upon her.

Maread decided that there was no point in hiding, and she trusted that Aeducan would jump in to help her if necessary. So she emerged from behind the tree, shielding her eyes from the lights.

About an hour later, Maread returned to the hunter's stand. Aeducan was impatiently tapping his hand on his seat as he waited for her.

"So, what did you hear?" he asked.

"I heard nothing," she replied. "There was nobody there."

"Really? I heard at least two people arguing. Very loud, very angry. Or was the ambassador just watching reality TV?"

"I heard nothing," she repeated in a monotonous voice. "There was nobody there."

Aeducan gazed at her for a moment, confused by her incongruous report. He shrugged his shoulders. "Well, let me know if anything else happens here. I have a meeting with

Donall, and I've got to go."

Maread nodded. "Okay, see you at the feast tonight."

After he was gone, Maread scanned the camp with her binoculars, looking for anything that might be worth reporting. When the sound of the arguing voices reached her again, she whispered to herself the refrain "I heard nothing, there was nobody there. I heard nothing, there was nobody there."

~ 14 ~

In the evening, when Eric decided it was dark enough, he headed out toward the grove. As he crossed the old stone bridge, he saw something moving among the trees of the park, across the river. It was tall, it seemed to have four arms, and a strangely shaped head. A low and drawn–out roar emerged from a deep and heavy throat, followed by the sounds of fleeing drivers.

Eric knew he was probably going into danger, but he assumed it was connected to the grove, and his investigations.

Before he could get too close to it, Eric encountered a team of six men wearing the uniforms of the Guardians: a white military jacket, black trousers, and a blue beret. Most of the men held ropes or nets; one of them carried a heavy crossbow.

"Please stay back, sir," one of them told Eric. "We have the situation under control."

"Your situation is a gorilla with four arms," Eric replied with a smile. All six of the men turned to face him when they heard that remark. This allowed Eric to see that under their jackets they wore the shining steel armour of Roman centurions.

The man with the crossbow had a familiar profile: dark hair, streaked grey at the temples, and a precisely shaved goatee.

"Brigantian," Paul Turner to his companions. "He can see this thing just as well as we can. Now keep on top of it!"

The centurions were annoyed, but they went back to following the creature again. By that time it was on the other side of the park, and so they had to jog to catch up.

"Okay, Eric, you're right, it's a creature from the Hidden World," Paul admitted, "And it's dangerous. You probably should go home."

"Let me call the clan then," Eric offered, as he reached for his cellphone.

"No need. We're here to catch it, sedate it, and take it back where it belongs before it hurts anybody."

Clan Fianna

At that moment, however, the creature roared angrily, and one of the Centurions came flying through the air, as if he had been hit by a truck.

Paul grimaced, and then handed Eric his crossbow, and a handful of bolts. "Okay, listen. These bolts are coated with somnaweiss oil, to put it to sleep. But you might need two or three hits before it works. Don't get too close to it. If you have a clear shot, take it."

Paul unsheathed a Roman gladius from a scabbard on his belt, and ran after the creature. Eric smiled, almost against his will, and followed him. When Eric was close enough to see what the creature really was, he stared at it unblinking for a heartbeat or two, until Paul cuffed him on the shoulder to bring his mind back to the job.

The creature was a little taller than Eric, and its flesh was a mottled pink and grey, with tufts of black hair growing in patches on its legs and chest, and all four of its arms. The head resembled that of a gorilla, though its two upper fangs protruded from its lips and curved in toward its jaw. The four centurions who surrounded it were trying to fling ropes over it and pull it off its feet, but the creature was able to bat them away.

Eric saw a chance to loose his crossbow bolt at the creature, so he lined up the shot, squeezed the trigger, and let it fly. The bolt struck the creature in the shoulder, causing it to roar out painfully, and then look to see where the bolt came from. Seeing Eric for the first time, it cocked its head to one side and made a loud gruffing noise. Suddenly it seemed to Eric that the creature might be thinking: it might be wondering who Eric was.

It stomped toward Eric angrily, but Paul slashed at the tendons in its lower leg with his sword. The creature screamed, fell to one knee, and swiped one of its muscular arms at him like a club. Paul ducked out of the way.

By that time, Eric had scrambled on to a nearby park bandshell, where he had a better angle for shooting. Though his hands were shaking with stress and fear, Eric managed to pull the wire back and lodge a new bolt into the slot, and aim.

"Take the shot!" Paul bellowed at him.

Eric took the shot. The bolt struck the creature near its navel. It swung its arms at Paul and the other few centurions a few more times, and then it slumped to the ground, no longer able to walk.

"Good job!" Paul exclaimed. He took the crossbow

back, loaded a third bolt into it, and shot it one more time. The bolt pierced the creature's pectoral. It threw back its head and screamed again, which gave two of the centurions a chance to throw a rope over its neck. It made one last flailing attempt to ward off its attackers and pull itself away, but soon its arms slowed, and slowed some more, and then fell uselessly to the ground.

"That did it," Paul declared. Then he said to one of his companions, "Call for the truck."

Eric kneeled down close to the creature's face. It flared its nostrils when it smelled Eric getting closer. Then its eyes drowsily opened, and its lips curled into a snarl.

"What is it?" Eric asked.

"It's called a Gargantacore," Paul told Eric. "They're about as smart as a horse, or a dog. You can teach them to do tricks, sometimes. But they're very aggressive, and they can't talk."

Eric stood again and said, "Miranda once told me that the gods of ancient times were all just people, once. Is it the same for creatures like this one?"

"It is, I'm sorry to say," Paul confirmed. "This thing here was a man, once upon a time. But back in the mythic age, he and his people fought a great war with the gods, and they lost. They were imprisoned in caves, the deepest caves anyone could find, all over the earth. Maybe it was the darkness that changed them. Or something else–I really don't want to know. But this is what became of them. And now they're no better than animals."

A pickup truck arrived on the scene. Paul, the truck driver, and the centurions pulled the gargantacore by the ropes and the net into the truck.

"Where are you taking it?" asked Eric.

"Back to Tartarus, where creatures like him belong. Don't know how he got out. But it's easy enough to put him back in."

"Tartarus? Isn't that in Greece?"

"It is. But there are caves all over the place with gates that take you straight there." Then Paul changed his tone. "Eric, I know I'm not your favourite person in the world. But there's still a place for you among the Guardians if you want it."

Eric thought about the place he once had among the Brigantians, and his hope for winning that position back. He didn't wish to be rude to Paul either. "Not today."

Paul sighed with disappointment, but accepted Eric's answer. "Well, if you change your mind, you know where to find us," he concluded, and jumped into the back of the pickup truck with the other Guardians and the heavily sedated gargantacore. He tapped on the roof of the truck to let the driver know he was ready to go, and they all drove away, leaving Eric to stand alone again.

~ 15 ~

Donall sat on a stool near the fireplace in the Brigantian Great Hall. In a semicircle around him sat Ciara DeDannan, Aeducan MacBride, and Algernon Weatherby. Donall was gazing blankly into the fire, and his friends gazed upon him, as they waited for someone to say something about Livia's condition.

Algernon remained thoughtful. "Have any of you asked exactly *why* the DiAngelo want a diplomatic mission here in your land? They already have a house in town. Why aren't they just sending messengers like always?"

Aeducan thought he had an answer. "I've been thinking about nothing else since they got here. Especially since I counted at least sixteen centurion guards. All of them armed with C7 assault rifles. And they're sitting on a pair of Light Armoured Vehicle Mark Three's, each with a twenty-five millimeter chain gun on the turret, and two mounted 7.62 millimeter machine guns."

"I didn't know that you knew about military stuff," Ciara marveled.

"I don't," Aeducan admitted. "I took photos of everything and emailed them to Miranda. She was in the Princess Louise regiment a few years ago. She knows about these things."

"Good call," Ciara praised him.

Aeducan wanted to finish his point. "Let's face the facts. That camp is not a diplomatic mission. It's a forward operating base. They're here to kick us out."

An unhappy murmur of acknowledgment arose from everyone in the group, followed by silence, as everyone contemplated whether Aeducan's words were true.

"We don't really know what they want," Algernon reminded everyone. "All we know is that they're camped here in the grove, and they're heavily armed. We can make educated guesses, based on those facts. But if you really want to know what someone wants, the best way to find out is to simply ask him. So let's invite him to dinner."

"Isn't it obvious what they'll say!" laughed Aeducan.

Algernon smiled. "Always treat people as if they are who they appear to be. And then, let them surprise you."

Ciara addressed Donall with her next words. "Time for a decision. What does the chieftain want to do?"

Donall had been listening, and he sometimes nodded to acknowledge something that had been said, but he had been keeping his thoughts to himself. When the silence was getting too uncomfortable for the others to bear, he spoke. "I've never been very good at politics. I don't even like politics! I like actions. A man's word doesn't always tell you where he stands. But you can always count on his deeds."

"I know you don't like politics," said Aeducan, "but you have to deal with these people, and you have to make a decision. That's what it means to be chieftain."

Donall looked at Ciara before speaking again. "This armed camp they have on our land. They're calling it a diplomatic mission. So, let's be diplomatic. Let's invite them to dinner here tonight. Lay before them the finest food we can make. Bring in the best bards to entertain. Show them some proper Celtic hospitality! But let's have a few guards of our own, armed with bows, watching from the loft above."

"This is a very risky strategy," observed Algernon skeptically.

"I know," Donall agreed. "But I don't want that McManus fellow to think he can push us around so easily. I want him to think we can fight him, if we have to." Donall then turned to Ciara and said, "Ciara, will you go and deliver the invitation?"

"Of course, but why me?" she asked.

"Because he sent his wife last night to deliver his invitation, so it seems somehow fitting that I should send my shield–woman to deliver my invitation. It shows a bit of trust, or at least some symmetry."

Aeducan chuckled. He stopped when Ciara gave him a dirty look, and an elbow in his ribs.

"Besides," Donall added, "you are better at this diplomacy stuff, than me. I will have to rely on you to do most of the talking at the feast tonight. You too, Algernon, if you are willing. And tonight, at the feast, I want both of you to find out what Kendrick McManus really wants."

"I think we have a plan," Aeducan concluded happily.

"One more thing," Donall added. "Ciara, when you are at their camp today, don't eat or drink anything."

~ 16 ~

Eric was no more than two blocks from the place where he encountered the gargantacore when three black cars, each with the badge of the Guardians on their doors, careened down the road toward him. They stopped in front of him, blocking his way. Six more men emerged from them, dressed all in black, except for the blue Guardians beret. From the lead car stepped Carlo DiAngelo.

"Eric Laflamme," Carlo began. "Truly, it warms the heart to see you again, after all this time, after all we had been through together."

"Yeah, well, I can't say I'm happy to see you either," Eric sighed.

"I recently heard some distressing news about a distant cousin of mine. Livia Julia McManus."

The blood drained out of Eric's face. "I didn't do it!" he burst out.

"I am also reliably informed that you are no longer under the protection of the Brigantians," Carlo finished.

Eric reached back to steady himself against a nearby lamppost, and he glanced at each of the Guardians surrounding him in the hope that there might be a way he could slip away. But they saw what he was thinking, and took the initiative. Eric was grabbed again by two of them, handcuffed behind his back by a third, and then pounded in the stomach by the fourth.

"It's time for you to take responsibility for the death of my mother," grimaced Carlo. Then the four Guardians stuffed Eric into the back seat of one of the Guardian vehicles. Eric shouted at them that he didn't do it, that he has rights, and that Carlo can't abduct him like this. But once he was shut into the back seat of the range rover, no one could hear him anymore.

~ 17 ~

Maread was sitting on a stool just outside the entrance of the

Brigantian Great Hall, keeping watch. When she saw Kendrick McManus approach, she put her head in the door and warned everyone inside that the DiAngelo ambassador and his party had arrived. Four men accompanied Kendrick, all dressed in Centurion armour, and Kendrick himself was dressed in a purple toga, indicating he held the rank of a senator. Maread welcomed them and held open the blanket that covered the door. No one in the ambassador's party acknowledged her presence at all, except for one of the centurions, who gave her his torch to hold. When they were all inside, a very irked Maread flung the torch into a nearby rain barrel, before following them in and taking her seat.

Donall stood welcome the ambassador and his party. "A very good welcome to you, Ambassador McManus. I hope that by sharing this meal with us, we can give our relationship a much better start."

"Yes, well, we shall see," Kendrick snorted.

"As you know, Mr. Ambassador–" Ciara began.

"Kendrik," he told her. "You lot don't seem to care about formalities anyway."

Ciara gritted her teeth for a moment before speaking again. "As you know, the responsible party has been banished from the grove. And when we found some of the ingredients of the poison in the guest house he was using, we decided to strip him of his membership in the clan."

"He should be disenchanted as well," Kendrick added. "but I shall be satisfied with banishment, for now."

"If you would like to take your seat?" Donall invited him, indicating a place made ready for him.

Kendrick nodded, and everyone sat down. Kitchen–witches from the wings of the great hall carried plates of roast mutton, spiced lamb, mascarpone, and various greens, and baskets with more bread. The Brigantians began eating as soon as the food was placed on front of them, but the four DiAngelo centurions looked to Kendrick, waiting for him to eat first. Kendrick, who had not yet taken his seat, looked at Ciara and stated bluntly, "It is an ancient Brigantian custom, is it not, that the lady of the house offers a cup of mead to the guest, to show that the guest is welcome?"

Donall rolled his eyes.

"It is," Ciara confirmed. She took her own wine–cup, walked around the table to Kendrick and offered it to him. Kendrick snatched it from her hands, and drank deeply, without making eye contact with her. Then he looked up to the ceiling, breathed for a moment, and savoured the taste.

"It's a local cabernet sauvignon, is it not? Niagara region?" he asked.

Donal was impressed. "It is," he replied.

"Well, you could cook with it, if you had nothing else available. Still, the fact that you have wine at all is very civilized of you. I think this evening might go well," he pronounced, and he handed the cup back to Ciara, again without looking at her. Ciara caught the cup before it spilled its contents on her bodice. Kendrick sat and began eating, and then his companions started into their own plates too.

"It has been many years since we have had a guest from our cousin-clan in Northumbria. I trust that the six freeholds of the region are still strong?"

Kendrick did not answer right away, but drank from his wine–cup first. "I'm afraid we have only five left, now. The smallest of them, the sanctuary near Sunderland, was abandoned, and the site now lies beneath the A690 motorway."

"That's terrible!" Donall said, genuinely surprised.

"Not really," Kendrick replied. "We ensured that our people owned most of the surrounding land. So when the government bought the land to build the motorway, we made a lot of money. It was a very lucrative arrangement."

The Brigantians who heard his words froze with astonishment. Algernon dropped his fork. Ciara put her hand over her heart. Kendrick went back to eating, as if his words were quite casual and ordinary. When Kendrick saw the effect his remark made on his hosts, he declared, "Our Hidden World has been growing smaller and smaller for at least three centuries, maybe more. You know this, and I know this. Our homes and livelihoods are threatened by the whitewash of modernity as much as yours are. We had to make difficult decisions, such as choosing which of our freeholds are worth saving, and which are not."

"They are all worth saving!" Ciara blurted out.

"Philosophically, that's fine, fair enough," Kendrick replied. "But in practical terms, it's just not possible. We all understand that triage is an acceptable way to manage resources in a crisis. We all accept that strategic retreat is sometimes necessary to win a battle. This is the same thing."

"It's not the same at all," Ciara countered sternly.

"These freeholds are all that remains of the Mythic Age. They are the last places on Earth where we can be who we truly are. If they disappear, we disappear."

The Brigantians bowed their heads, contemplating Ciara's words.

"You speak the truth," Kendrick conceded, "but what should we do? Shall we feast here in this hall, and hide from the outside world, as if that was the only way we can save ourselves? Shall we fight futile battles that we know we cannot win? I think not. For we are descended from the gods! As a Brigantian myself, I am descended from the same goddess that you are. And yes, she gave us beer-making and poetry and all those things. But she was also a blacksmith, so she also gave us industry, and hard work, and clear-headed thinking. And that bestows upon us great responsibility."

"Responsibility for what?" said Donall.

"For doing whatever it takes to save our world," Kendrick answered, leaning forward in his chair.

"Well, if your plan involves sacrificing a finger to save the hand, you can count us out," Ciara declared.

"If the plan involves sacrificing a finger to save the whole body, and a hundred other bodies, then that's the plan you choose." Then he sat back in his chair, satisfied that his point was made, but he added one more observation anyway. "The money we made when the government bought our land helped to pay for the Guardians public relations work. A fair trade."

Ciara shook her head.

"You don't have to like what is right," Kendrick told her. "But let's get back to the point. The real problem we are all facing is the decline of civilization. I'm not just talking about our disappearing Hidden Kingdom. I'm talking about everything. The collapsing economy. The deadlocked political system. The feeling of hopelessness, pessimism, and denial, that has taken over the minds of good people. That's what El Duce is worried about. That's what you should be worried about too."

Ciara pursed her lips and looked away.

"So you and your New Renaissance are here to save the world. Is that it?" Donall asked.

"Yes, we are," was Kendrick's confident answer. "We are an alliance of Hidden Houses, under a unified leadership. Our mission is to reverse the decline of civilization. To restore mankind to greatness. My clan, the Brigantians of Northumbria, joined it a few years ago. I am here to invite you to join us too."

~ 18 ~

In the newly renovated DiAngelo mansion, Eric sat in a wooden chair, awaiting the return of his captors. Duct tape and handcuffs kept him secured to the chair. Shouting for someone from outside to come and help had proven useless. Save for a few thin beams from distant streetlights in the windows, he sat in darkness, and but for the sounds of passing cars he sat in silence.

When he counted a hundred cars passed by outside, someone finally creaked open the door. The sound of hard heavy footsteps on the wooden floor echoed in the house. Next Eric heard the scrape of a chair on the floor, and then the footsteps stopped just behind Eric's head. Eric's heartbeat picked up, and the adrenaline in his bloodstream tingled the muscles in his arms and legs. The visitor planted his chair in front of Eric and sat facing him, with an expression of tightly controlled anger on his face. They regarded each other silently for a moment. There was no point in struggling: Eric knew this man would not let him go. When he spoke, his Mediterranean voice was as dulcet and silky as ever, but his words were straight and grim.

"Eight months ago, my mother died, here in this very house," stated Carlo.

"I know, and I'm sorry," Eric replied.

"She died in a fire," Carlo continued, "started by you."

"I didn't start that fire." Eric insisted. "Katie did."

"Isn't it convenient that she's not here to bear witness." Carlo asserted.

"That's because she's dead too," Eric sternly reminded him.

"Indeed, I wonder whose fault that is," Carlo insinuated.

"Yours," Eric answered him, "for driving her to depression, after you killed our child."

Carlo inhaled sharply, and his brow narrowed, and his fingers clenched into fists. Eric tried to brace himself for a beating. Carlo spoke again only after he had calmed himself. "I'm not interested in playing games with you," he declared.

"Well then, get to the point," Eric said defiantly.

A small smile tugged at the corner of Carlo's mouth for

a moment. "You know, some of my associates actually admire you, Eric. The way you pretend you're not afraid, when it's clear that you are. The way you stand up for the people you care about, even when those people take you for granted, and then abandon you. You remind me of a little dog I once knew, that used to lick his master's hands with love, even when the master caned him with a yardstick for doing it."

Eric struggled against his binds for a moment.

"I know you don't want to believe me when I tell you that your friends don't care about you," Carlo continued. "Nevertheless it's true. They don't. Just this morning, you were accused of a crime you say you did not do. But does your chieftain order an investigation? Does he even listen to your side of the story? No, he simply banished you. And does Miranda Brigand do anything to help? No, she just sent you home again. What about Ildicoe Brigand, or whatever name she's using now. She wants nothing to do with you anymore either. And as for your lover Katie Corrigan, given the choice between staying with you and killing herself, she actually chose to kill herself! I wonder what kind of a man you are, that your friends would abandon you so easily."

"She didn't kill herself," Eric retorted. "She just fell."

"Just what do you think she was doing, standing so close to the edge of the gorge like that? You both grew up in this town. You know that locals don't accidentally fall in the river. Tourists do."

"What do you want, Carlo," Eric sighed.

"I want you to sit here and think about how alone you truly are," said Carlo. "I want you to sit here, and count the hours while your friends do absolutely nothing to help you. They know you're here. I told them myself! And they're not coming to get you. I want you to sit here and think about that. I want you to think about Emma DiAngelo, a matriarch of my house, a far better human being than you could ever hope to be, whose life was cut short eight months ago, right here, in a fire started by you."

"I didn't do it!" Eric insisted.

"You started that fire, destroyed my home, killed my mother, and you've never taken responsibility for it! You've been protected by Miranda Brigand far too long. But now it is time for you to face justice."

"This isn't justice. This is revenge!" Eric countered.

Clan Fianna

"That's what everyone says about justice, when they face the sharp end of it," Carlo scoffed at him.

"If this was justice, you would have to prove my guilt before you punished me." Eric shouted, as he got more frightened. "Justice and revenge are two different things. You can't have them both at the same time!"

"Do not lecture me about justice!" Carlo scorned. "You've been running free, under the protection of that Celtic rabble for far too long. And I've had to stand back and do nothing but watch. Well, I refuse to let you humiliate me anymore! It's time you answered for your crime!"

Eric was frightened. "What are you going to do?" he demanded to know.

"You will be taken from here to Domus Eleutherios. There you will– get a trial." Carlo seemed reluctant to admit this fact. Seeing the relief on Eric's face, he added, "You will be found guilty, and then you will be punished. You're a student of history, so I assume you know what we did to criminals in the old Roman Empire?"

Eric knew. His muscles grew tense again.

Carlo moved to leave the room. With mock affection he said, "Goodnight, Eric. Sleep well."

~ 19 ~

"There's a lot you could gain by joining the New Renaissance," Kendrick McManus explained to Donall and the other Brigantians.

"We already have everything we need," Donall countered.

"Do you?" Kendrick crooned doubtfully. "I have a talent for observing people. Sensing their motives and interests. Figuring out what they want. For example, look at that woman over there," He pointed to Maread, who was sitting by herself in the wing of the mead hall where the Brigantians kept their trophies, quietly reading a book. "Her head is covered in dreadlocks and rings, she's wearing combat boots, and lots of studs on her belt and bracelets, and T-shirt from a heavy metal concert. Everything about her image says, 'I wanna kick your ass.' But she's also reading a first edition of Tolkien's Lord of the Rings. And she's struggling with it, too. I bet she dresses tough to hide the fact that she can't read."

Mared briefly looked up from her book to glare at Kendrick, and then shift her chair so that she would face her back to him.

Kendrick chuckled and then pointed to Finnbarr, who was sipping a glass of wine and gazing at Síle, and said, "Now look at this fellow here. He's a little easier to figure out. Right now, what he wants is for that fine young lass over there, the one dancing by herself in the corner, to come over and sit in his lap for a while."

Across the room, Síle was completely unaware that anyone was talking about her. With two small oil lamps hanging from short chains in her hands, she weaved every limb of her body in delicate hypnotic shapes, and so transformed the music of harp and fiddle and flute into visible movement and form.

Finnbarr admired her dancing for a moment, and then grinned shyly to Kendrick and said, "Am I that obvious?"

"Not only that," Kendrick continued. "I sense that you are also wishing that you were about six inches taller, and a little more buff on the shoulders, and a better dancer, because you think that's what will win the lady's affection."

Finnbarr tried to laugh it off. "Actually I thought I would win her affection with my charming personality and razor sharp wit!"

"That's exactly what I mean," Kendrick concluded. "You're a short and wiry fellow, not especially tough. The bird with the book over there could beat you in a fair fight nine times out of ten. And you're certainly no fashion model. So you probably rely on your social talents to get the girls to follow you to bed. But you haven't got any girls in your bed. So you probably have no social talents either."

Finnbarr laughed, as did most everyone who heard that short exchange. But when everyone finished laughing, Finnbarr got up and discretely left the hall. And Kendrick smiled, convinced that he was right.

"As for you," Kendrick said to Donall. "It's easy to figure out what you want. Fellwater Grove is a two hundred acre freehold hidden inside a large public conservation park. With the New Renaissance as your backer, you could have the entire park. And you could expand it into the surrounding farmland, and into the village, too. That music festival you host every year around August could attract ten thousand people, and the bards of your clan who perform there would be international stars. And your

Clan Fianna

warriors wouldn't have to use swords and spears and bows anymore. We would arm them with proper modern equipment. Just think, you would command soldiers and fighting vehicles like the ones I brought with me. The New Renaissance offers you that. In fact it offers you *more* than that."

"Like what," Donall doubted.

"The New Renaissance actually has a larger, more serious purpose," Kendrick related. "There was a time, many centuries ago, when there was hardly any difference between these freeholds of ours, and the outside world. We walked proudly among mortal men, unencumbered by the Celtic mist that hides us from outsider eyes. And the people knew us for who we are, and they looked to us for knowledge and leadership. We can be the leaders and teachers of men once more. The New Renaissance integrates the people of our hidden world into the institutions of the outside world. It's much bigger and more important than this freehold, or any one of us individually. It's going to shape the future of society. And you can be part of it."

Donall had to admit to himself that he was intrigued by Kendrick's words. Aeducan's ears certainly perked at the suggestion of modern weapons for the Brigantian warriors. The bards, quietly performing on harp and fiddle and flute in the loft above, eyed each other and imagined themselves on a larger stage.

Only Algernon Weatherby was visibly skeptical. He wiped his mouth and cleared his throat, and spoke slowly and measuredly. "Several years ago, an ambassador from El Duce came to my castle in Hallowstone, and made us a very similar offer. My nephew accepted it, on my behalf. But not long after that, people began to disappear, first in twos and threes, and then entire families, until eventually the whole village was empty. And we found them in the catacombs, working as slaves, with their minds drugged into a waking dream."

"I heard about the unfortunate events at Hallowstone," Kendrick acknowledged. "I assure you the New Renaissance had nothing to do with it."

"No?" Algernon balked. "And yet the products manufactured by my people in their slavery somehow ended up in the basement of the local Guardians Hall."

"We sent people to investigate that bold accusation, and they found no evidence. The basement of the Guardians Hall was entirely empty. And where is the woman who made the accusation in the first place? She was summoner for Miranda, wasn't she? What was her name? Ildicoe something? But no one has seen her in months."

Algernon studied Kendrick with a critical eye, trying to decide whether Kendrick was lying, or whether someone had deceived him.

"Now, as our hidden world slowly but relentlessly dwindles into oblivion," Kendrick finished, "we can keep throwing accusations at each other, and remain divided among ourselves. Or, we can unite, for our mutual protection and survival."

"We are well protected, here in our grove," Donall declared. "And as you can see by the meal we have laid before you, we are doing more than merely surviving."

"Indeed you are, at the moment," Kendrick agreed, but then he ominously added, "but how long do you think your prosperity will last?"

Before Donall could answer, Finnbarr burst back into the hall, breathless from running.

"Gargantacores! Three of them! Right now!"

The warriors watching from the loft above looked to Donall for an order to join the defense. Donall turned to Aeducan and said, "Have we got enough people on the ridge?"

Finnbarr ran up to Donall and said, "They're not attacking the ridge! They're in town!"

Now Donall was worried. "Where exactly?" he asked.

"By the school!"

Most of the Brigantians jumped to their feet and reached for their weapons, and so did the DiAngelo guards who accompanied Ambassador McManus. But the ambassador himself remained blasé.

"You're unprepared, aren't you!" he said.

Donall turned to Aeducan and said, "Captain, take a reccee squad and go to the village to see what's happening."

"Maread, Finnbarr, Síle, you're with me," said Aeducan. The three of them got up and followed Aeducan out the door.

As soon as they were gone, Ambassador McManus sipped his wine, leaned back in his seat, and declared, "By the time your reconnaissance team reaches the village, they will discover that the Guardians have already rounded up all the gargantacores, and taken them back to wherever they came from."

Donall did not greet this news kindly. "The job of ensuring that that the creatures of our world stay in our world belongs to whatever Hidden House controls the nearest freehold. In the case of village of Fellwater, that means us. So why are your people doing *our* job?"

"Because you and your people are clearly *not* doing your job!" the ambassador shot back.

"Is that so?" Donall stated between clenched teeth.

"For instance, it appears you have more sentries standing over my camp than you do standing over the village itself," Kendrick idly observed.

"What did you expect? You brought an army with you!" Donall growled.

"I had to. Didn't you hear? There's a wild gargantacore running loose out there!" was Kendrick's reply.

Donall rose to his feet, although with some difficulty, as his old injuries tended to pain him when he was angry. "Are you implying we can't defend our own land?" And he gripped the hilt of his sword, on his belt.

Ciara stood and put on a gentler face. "What he means, you understand, is that we don't know why you had to bring so many warriors with you." Then she helped lower Donall gently back into his seat.

"I didn't want to tell you this right away," Kendrick offered. "It's a little bit embarrassing, to be honest. But given the report of gargantacores sighted within the wards of the village, perhaps it's best I tell you now.

"Back in the Mythic Age, as you know, our ancestors fought creatures like those, and their masters. The DeDannans fought the Fomorians, the Olympians fought the Titans, the Djinnis of Arabia fought the Ghouls. And we won those wars, and we locked our defeated foes in the chthonic prisons, deep beneath the surface of the earth. You know those stories already. But now, as our world shrinks and fades away, so do the walls of those prisons weaken and crumble. And now the prisoners are breaking free. You have seen this already. You teamed up with the Ojibway to fight an incursion of Wendigo and Frost Giants not more than twelve or thirteen years ago, did you not? Did you ever wonder why those creatures were not safely frozen under the ice, where they belong?"

Donall glared at Kendrick, angry at what he perceived

to be yet another insult to his intelligence. Ciara put a hand on his thigh to remind him that she could do his talking. "We thought it had to do with climate change and global warming," she replied.

Kendrick laughed. "Well, it's your right to stick your head in the sand, if you want to."

Donall sat back and considered Kendrick's words. "If what you say is true, I don't see how the guardians can help us. Most of them are outsiders, are they not?"

"Most of them are, yes," explained the ambassador. "However, each and every outsider who passes the Guardians test is enchanted, so that they can see and remember the things of the Hidden World. And it happens that there are more of them in the village than there are of you here in this hall. If only one of them notices something unusual, he'll call the auxiliaries to deal with it. So you can bet that if the news of tonight's attack on the village has reached this hall, it has surely reached the Guardians too."

Donall considered Kendrik's claim for a moment. "So that's why you want us to join your movement. It isn't really about culture and leadership and all that. It's really about a war."

Kendrick nodded, and said, "Take a few days to think about it. But the sooner you join the movement, the better. For all of us. You need us, and we need you."

~ 20 ~

The four Brigantian warriors arrived at the school, and found that a black-clad team of Guardian Auxiliaries had already arrived. Armed with crossbows, they watched over every window, poised to launch their bolts at anything that might emerge from the school. Others were examining a side door in the building which had been torn off its frame and tossed nearby. Paul Turned was tying a line of yellow "CAUTION" tape across the entrance to the school yard, and urging a small crowd of people to stay back.

"We heard shouting! And howling! Like some kind of animal!" said someone in the crowd.

"How did that happen to the door?" said someone else.

Paul noticed the arrival of the Brigantian warriors, and he glared at them for a moment. Then he turned back to the crowd and said, "Everyone stay back, please. We've got a job to do here."

"Just tell us what's happening!" insisted someone else.

"I need you to stand back, for your own safety," Paul repeated.

A bearded man wearing three coats, a hand–knitted woolen touque, and winter boots that were probably too big for him, handed Aeducan a photocopied pamphlet and said, "It's an alien invasion, man! They're experimenting on the kids in this here school! The leaders of the world have been hiding the truth from us for years!" The pamphlet was advertising a protest rally planned for the following day.

"Wasn't that Harvard Willie?" said Maread.

"I think it was," Aeducan replied. So he jogged after him, caught his sleeve and asked, "What happened here today?"

"Whoa, you mean, you don't know?" replied Harvard Willie. "It was like, man, you should have been here! Seven of them, or maybe eight, and they were twice as tall as me, and– and– and they just started running around and screaming, breaking windows and shit."

"What were they?" asked Maread.

"Giant apes, man, giant apes! With four arms! They come from outer space. There's photos of them all over the internet now."

"There are?" said an incredulous Aeducan.

"Dude, look around! Everybody's got a camera!" laughed Willie, and he pointed to a boyfriend and girlfriend pair who held up their cellphones to photograph themselves together, with the broken school door in the background. Then Willie rejoined the crowd to distribute his pamphlets.

Maread wondered, "Do you think the Celtic Mist will affect people's photographs? Or just the way people see them?"

Before anyone could answer, someone from among the Guardian Auxiliaries was heard to shout "Cut the power!", and then the lights inside the school went out. The Guardians with the crossbows snapped to a more alert posture.

"Everybody, go home, please! For your own safety!" Paul pleaded again.

"Arms at the ready," said Aeducan to his companions. The four Brigantians unsheathed swords and brandished spears.

A moment of breathless silence passed. Someone in the crowd laughed uncomfortably. Then two gargantacores burst out of the school through a classroom window, and a third stormed out through the damaged door. Shards of broken glass, wood, and metal exploded in the air. The crowd of onlookers scattered and ran for safety.

Aeducan unsheathed his sword and said to the team, "Let's go."

The Brigantians charged toward the nearest gargantacore, ready to meet it in battle. Before they got anywhere close enough, however, the Guardians unleashed a barrage of crossbow bolts upon all three of the monsters. The creatures howled angrily, and then they fell, groaning and whimpering, and finally snoring, tranquilized and asleep.

Aeducan stopped running just at the place where the nearest creature fell. He lowered his weapon, and looked at Paul.

Paul smirked, and saluted Aeducan with two fingers. Then he said to one of the other Guardians, "Okay, bring up the trucks. Let's get these things out of here."

The Brigantians put away their weapons and looked at each other, puzzled and annoyed.

"Well, I'll be fucked," Aeducan whispered.

"We better tell Donall about this," said Finnbarr.

"Yes we should," said Aeducan, "but first I want a word with that pompous proud-smiling weasel, Paul Turner."

~ 21 ~

"Well, do you believe him?" Ciara asked Donall.

"About what?" Donall asked.

"Do you think the chthonic prisons are weakening?"

Donall took a moment to think about it, and when he answered he said, "It's possible."

"I think that if he's right, all of us will be in serious danger," Ciara reasoned.

"I don't trust him," Donall declared. "In fact I don't like him. He says he's a Brigantian, but he talks like a DiAngelo."

"Well, I don't like him either, but he's here now, and he brought an army with him, so we have to deal with him," Ciara reminded him as gently as she could.

Donall sighed, and let his anger pass. "Well. Enough of this sad talk! The ambassador is gone now, so let's have some music! The problems of tomorrow can always be put off to tomorrow. Let's do something fun!" And he looked around the hall and found that it was mostly empty. The sentries in the loft above had gone back to their cabins or back home, and the musicians were packing their instruments into their cases and wishing each other goodnight.

"One more, before you go, would you please?" he called up to them. The musicians shrugged their shoulders in a mock expression of weariness, and opened their instrument cases again.

"Dance with me?" said Ciara, as she got up from her seat, and Donall smiled.

The harper began plucking the chords of a Robbie Burns love ballad, and then the bouzouki player and the fiddler joined them. Donall was about to ask them to play something more energetic, but Ciara cradled his face and said, "It's late, it's the end of the night, everybody wants to go home. And I just want you to dance with me." So Donall nodded, smiled to the musicians, and took his hand in her hand, and her waist in his arm, and danced her slowly into the centre of the floor, as the musicians caroled the first lines of the song. And Ciara smiled happily.

Half way through the song, Donall let her go, and ambled a few steps away to lean on the back of a chair. Ciara moved swiftly to his side, full of worry.

"It's the old wound, from this past summer," said Donall, indicating the scar near his kidney, where Paul Turner had stabbed him. "Every once in a while it bleeds again. I got Neachtain the healer to look at it last week, but all he could do was patch it up, and tell me to take things easy."

"How is it tonight?"

"It's not bleeding, thank the gods, but it's been paining me all day."

"Oh, you big crybaby," she grinned, and stroked his arm affectionately. Donall grasped her hand and kissed it.

"Thank you, Ciara," Donall told her.

"For what?"

"For being so good tonight, at the feast. For handling the ambassador so well. For making sure I didn't sheath my sword in his head. Tonight would have gone far worse without you."

Ciara smiled, then lifted his arm over her shoulder to take part of his weight off his feet, and kissed him. "Anything for you, my man."

Donall drew Ciara closer to kiss her brow and caress

her breasts. "We'll see about those preparations, like you suggest. But we'll see about them tomorrow."

Ciara slid her fingers into his tunic, and kissed him again, and said, "You're my chieftain."

~ 22 ~

The four Brigantians marched up to where Paul was issuing orders to various parties through his phone. When he saw the four warriors approaching, he snapped his fingers to summon several Guardian Auxiliaries to his side.

"Here we go," Finnbarr muttered.

The Guardians, with Paul at their head, met the Brigantians just on the edge of the schoolyard. "As you can see," said Paul, "we have the situation under control."

"As we can see," Aeducan retorted, "you've got it under control all too well."

Paul was puzzled. "What the hell does that mean?"

"It means tonight's incursion had all the marks of a well-rehearsed piece of theatre," Aeducan accused him. "The gargantacores took the stage, and you met them right on cue. And the audience was in the right place, at the right time. So who directed this show? Was it Carlo? Was it you?"

"Whenever something bad happens in this world," Paul ruminated, with a condescending chuckle, "there's always somebody who will say it's a conspiracy."

"That's because, sometimes, that's what it is," Aeducan countered.

"What did you come here for? To accuse me of training the gargantacores to attack on command?"

"We're here to remind you that Fellwater belongs to us, not to you, and not your New Renaissance either," Aeducan declared, as he took a step forward. "We have kept this town safe from the Hidden World for hundreds of years. We don't need your help."

"Apparently you do," Paul replied, "because we rounded up and dispatched these gargantacores before you even showed up!"

Some of the last bystanders, who had run to a distance to be safe but remained close enough to watch, began taking pictures of the altercation between Paul and Aeducan.

"Fellwater village is ours now," Paul declared. "So go

home to your hidey-hole in the woods. It's way past your bedtime."

Aeducan drew his sword. "I'll put you to bed for an insult like that!" he shouted.

In response, the Guardians who surrounded Paul raised their crossbows.

Seeing the weapons drawn, the other three Brigantians produced their two-handed fighting-spears, drawing them from the space beneath their cloaks as if their cloaks were larger on the inside than the outside. The combatants paced around each other in a wider circle, while the last bystanders retreated to a safe distance to watch.

Paul threw off his trench coat, revealing his Roman centurion's armour. He drew his gladius and uttered his ultimatum: "If you go back to your grove, right now, this will end peacefully and we be friends again in the morning."

"You think you can take over our lands and treat us like children, and just get away with it as easy as this!" Aeducan shouted.

"The real question," Paul shouted back, "is, do you want to start a war?"

Aeducan kept his sword pointed at Paul's face, but he considered Paul's words for a moment. He checked his left and his right, to see what his companions might be thinking. All of them were poised and ready to attack, but Maread subtly shook her head, just enough to let Aeducan know it would be unwise to start a fight. Finnbarr tilted his head to indicate the witnesses standing not far away, some of them filming the standoff with the cameras on their cellphones.

"Not today," smiled Aeducan, and he sheathed his sword.

The guardians lowered their crossbows, and the Brigantians lowered their spears.

"All right," said Paul, as he sheathed his own sword. "Now, everybody, let's all just go home."

"Our chieftain will hear of this," Aeducan grunted, "and so will all the allied clans." He and the other Brigantians began walking away.

"The allied clans!" Paul laughed. He looked to his companions, and quietly laughed, "They're a rabble of half-wit Celtic tribes and Indian bands, singing and fattening themselves in that stone circle of theirs, telling stories of how they stood up to the legions of Rome armed with pointed sticks and sharpened rocks! They're history's perpetual losers. They've given nothing to civilization, and they never will. We built the Pantheon in Rome when they were still learning to count to ten!"

Aeducan was still close enough to hear Paul's insults. He whipped his sword out again and roared with anger. The muscles on his body hardened and grew, while blue and green spiral tattoos appeared on his skin, and a yellow-white light radiated from his head and breast. He launched himself on Paul with a ferocity that surprised everyone around him, and his first blow landed directly on Paul's chest and sent him flying across the playground.

The guardians raised their crossbows again, and so Síle, Maread, and Finnbarr joined the fray, screaming a battle-cry and glowing with hero-light that outshone the streetlights above. Maread spun her fighting-spear in a deadly whirl, which disarmed one of the Guardians instantly, and flung a second one face first into a flower bed. Finnbarr deflected a crossbow bolt with his spear head, then leapt into the air and landed behind the Guardian who shot at him; then he brought that man to the ground with a swipe of the blunt end of his spear across the back of the man's knees.

Síle knocked another one unconscious by hammering him in the forehead with the shaft of her spear. The last remaining Guardian fired on her with his handgun, but with a dance-like spin she dodged it, and with an impossibly quick twist of her wrist she caught a second bullet in her bare hand and deflected it to the earth. Then she darted to the man who shot at her and easily disarmed him with a wheel kick, and sent him sailing out of the fight with a spear hit to his belly.

Aeducan ran to where Paul had fallen, but Paul was back on his feet again, sword drawn and ready. Aeducan's attack was fast and savage, yet graceful and elegant, his footwork as swift and precise as dancing, his blade rung with music as it clashed with Paul's gladius. Yet he could not land a solid wounding blow; Paul's swordsmanship was efficient, effective, and just as fast.

Two more Guardians, armoured as Roman centurions, emerged from the hall, to come to Paul's defense. But Síle and Finnbarr dispatched these new opponents with ease as the hero-light blinded them.

Maread, meanwhile, knocked out one of the Guardians

who she had previously defeated, just as he tried to get up again and fire another shot from his crossbow. Paul and Aeducan paced around each other, blocking and deflecting each other's exploratory strikes, and looking for a new opening for a more forceful attack. But by then the four Brigantians had defeated all the other Guardians, and Paul discovered that he was now fighting four angry Celtic warriors by himself.

He was saved by Carlo DiAngelo, whose car arrived at just that moment.

"I see it takes four of you to defeat one of us," opined Carlo. "Well done!"

Maread set her foot down on the chest of a nearby unconscious centurion. "Yeah. Your guys are really tough," she said.

"Fellwater belongs to the Brigantians!" Aeducan growled at Carlo. "It's been our home for hundreds of years."

"I'm sure the local Ojibway people would say this land has been their home for thousands of years."

"You want to join this fight?" Aeducan threatened.

"I am unarmed," Carlo declared, with his hands open in front of him. "But I don't have to fight you because I've already defeated you."

"What? Look around here, you blind blue-blooded moron!" shouted Aeducan. "See how many of your men lie unconscious on the ground here! Men that we put down!"

"Actually, it's you who should look around," Carlo replied. "For you might have won this battle," he smiled, "but you will not win–"

"The war?" Aeducan cut him off with a laugh. "Such a cliché!"

"The story!" Carlo retorted. "For we will control the story of what happened here today. We will decide what people see and hear, and we will shape how they talk about it. The side that controls the story wins the war!"

With a sweep of his hand, he indicated the group crowd of onlookers who hadn't run away when the gargantacores broke out of the school. Most of them were still holding up the cameras on their phones, and the Brigantians suddenly understood Carlo's meaning. The people whispered amongst each other both excitedly and fearfully about what was happening, and some moved to help the fallen Guardian centurions. Some thought that the Brigantians, still glowing with their hero-light, were spirits, or faeries, or demons. Some thought they came from the same place that the gargantacores came from; some thought they were gargantacores in disguise.

Sirens from distant police cars grew louder. Paul stepped off to one side, and placidly lit a cigarette.

"I'll fight the DiAngelo any day of the week, but I'll not fight the people," Maread told her companions, as she deflected a pop can thrown at her by someone in the crowd.

"Back to the grove," Aeducan ordered.

Together, the four warriors took off into the sky, running as if on solid ground over the treetops and houses of Fellwater village, away from the angry crowd.

~ 23 ~

"You did what!" Donall fumed.

The four Brigantians had returned to their Great Hall. Donall was dressed only in his trousers, since he had been summoned from his bedchamber when the squad arrived. Ciara leaned on the frame of the bedroom door in the loft above, wrapped in a bed sheet; she, too, was very unhappy to be disturbed.

"We had to fight them!" Aeducan insisted. "They're moving into our territory. We have to show them the village is still ours!"

"Did it ever enter your head that we cannot win a war against them!" Donall shouted. "They've got a squad of infantry– modern infantry– sitting in our own back yard. All they need is one excuse, and they'll swoop in here, and our home will belong to them."

Aeducan kept his eyes fixed on his chieftain, but he pursed his lips and sighed.

"Carlo DiAngelo may be our enemy but he's a smart enemy," Donall reminded everyone. "He makes plans. He gathers allies. He's patient and careful. You have to respect that kind of enemy. When you disrespect your enemies, you lose the war. Every time."

"Well, what are we supposed to do then!" Maread burst out.

"Tonight, we do nothing!" Donall decided.

"Nothing!" all four of the squad exclaimed.

"I'm sure the ambassador will give me an earful of it in

Clan Fianna

the morning. He'll probably demand your banishment, too. So I'm re-assigning the four of you to Hallowstone."

Almost simultaneously, the four members of the squad shouted in protest. "But they started it!" said Maread. "What if there's another attack while we're gone!" said Finnbar. "You can't do that to me!" said Síle. Aeducan gaped in dumfounded silence.

"Enough!" Donall exasperated. "My decision is made. Take one of the flying curraghs and be on your way before the ambassador wakes up."

Aeducan, Maread, Síle, and Finnbarr slouched out of the hall. Just before leaving, Aeducan paused and told Donall, "You know, back at the Gathering of the Clans, I voted for you."

Donall pursed his lips. "I made you the captain of the guard."

The two men regarded each other coldly for a moment, before Aeducan grumbled something under his breath and slipped out the door.

When the four warriors were gone, Donall exhaled tiredly and looked up to Ciara, who was still standing by the bedroom door.

"What?" Donall asked her. She only stared at him.

"I know that sending them up north might not have been kind," Donall explained. "But I have to avoid anything that might antagonize the ambassador. I'll summon them back when things settle down. Besides, they don't have enough people up in Hallowstone anyway. It's the best decision. You know it is. For everyone."

"You're the chieftain," Ciara replied, and she slipped back into the bedroom.

~ 24 ~

Eric spent the night bound to the chair in the empty and cold DiAngelo mansion. His muscles ached from being unable to move; his head swam from lack of sleep, and he desperately needed to urinate. Twisting his legs and waist in his binds brought no comfort. When he heard loud tromping footsteps enter the house, he lifted his head to see who it was, though it took an effort. At least four, possibly five, DiAngelo centurions stood around him.

"We were just getting to be friends again, Eric," intoned

Paul Taylor. "Now I hear you poisoned a friend of mine."

"I heard the same thing," Eric tried to say between a yawn he couldn't suppress.

"You say you didn't do it?" Paul asked.

"Of course he did it," said Carlo, as he strode into the room. "No one else could have done it. And he's always hated us."

"That's not true," Eric protested, but he was so exhausted that he couldn't raise his voice.

"The Archon will be the judge of that," Carlo declared.

The centurions untied Eric from the chair. When Eric told them he needed to urinate, they carried him to a bathroom and pushed him inside, where he almost hit his head on the sink.

"Two minutes. Clean yourself up," Paul barked at him. When the two minutes were up, the centurions pulled him out and took him to the front door, where he saw a Roman carriage and two chariots waiting. There was no point in struggling or resisting. There were more centurions around the perimeter, with daggers in hand; and Eric was too tired to do anything anyway. The centurions shoved Eric into the carriage and locked him inside. Eric felt strangely glad to have been put there: the cabin had room for him to stretch and lie down, and the rough wooden boards of the carriage floor became the most comfortable bed he had ever slept in.

Although wooden shutters covered the windows, Eric knew the carriage had become airborne when the noise of the wind picked up, and the sound of the horse's hooves on the road abruptly stopped. The carriage swayed a little in the wind, almost as if he was on board a riverboat instead of a carriage. The gentle rocking relaxed him, and drifted him almost to the edge of a sorely needed sleep. But the thudding of the wheels on the ground, and the shouts of the centurions in the chariots that escorted him, jarred him to full wakefulness again. He had arrived at his destination, wherever it was. Someone flung the carriage door open, filling the cabin with light, and roughly grabbed his shoulder and pulled him outside.

Eric found himself in what appeared to be a small plaza, with a cobblestone pavement, rectangular in shape, and perhaps as large as a soccer field. Roman style villas sat along the edges; their whitewashed walls and red clay shingles shone brightly in the late morning sunlight. Eric's handlers hustled him toward the largest building in the square: a great temple, with

Clan Fianna

tall Doric columns supporting a large triangular pediment, decorated with images of classical heroes. The largest of them was an angel holding an hourglass, which Eric recognized as the heraldic sign of the house DiAngelo. Yet Eric was not allowed any time to marvel at the scene. The centurions pushed him forward, and they shouted at him to "Shut up!" whenever he complained, or said anything at all. In a final effort to escape, which he knew would be futile he but wanted to try anyway, he twisted himself out of the grip of the centurions at his side, and tried to dash across the plaza.

He got no further than five steps before Paul Turner himself caught him under the elbow, sending him spinning to the ground. With his hands still cuffed behind his back, it was easy for the centurions to manhandle him to his feet again and drag him into the temple.

The main temple space was a large round atrium, lined with tall stone columns on the sides, high enough to support several tiers of balconies, where various people watched Eric's arrival. A large stained glass mosaic in the dome of the ceiling, laid out like the firmament of stars, illuminated the atrium with soft blue and gold light. Statues and busts of Roman heroes and gods watched from their niches. In semi–private alcoves along the walls of the room, he could see various well-dressed women and men sitting at tables, playing various card games, betting on roulette wheels, drinking fancy cocktails, and smoking from cigars or from hookas. Most of the men he could see had at least one bikini-clad woman hanging on his shoulder, although some were attended by muscular young men in silk loincloths. At the far end of the temple stood a massive statue of Eleutherios, bare-chested and bearded and smiling, with clusters of grapes and leaves in his hair, and his pinecone-topped scepter in one hand.

Before the statue stood a platform, as high above the ground as Eric was tall. Three cloaked and hooded figures sat enthroned upon it, and they stood as Eric was shoved to the ground before them. The one in the centre pulled back his hood, revealing that he wore a gold mask, with a judgmentally frowning face. His voice boomed from all around, as if it came from the statue of Eleutherios instead of from behind the mask.

Is this the person of Eric Laflamme, here before us?

"It is," Carlo answered on Eric's behalf.

We have heard of this one. We find it– interesting– to meet him at last.

Eric attempted to raise himself to his feet and say something, but a centurion kicked him to the ground again. "This is an archon judge who came directly from the court of El Duce himself," Carlo chastised him. "You're lucky to be judged by him."

"I'm telling you, Carlo, I did not kill your–" Eric pleaded once more, but he was interrupted by the archon judge.

Speak only when you are permitted to speak, outsider!

One of the cloaked men at the archon's side stood and gestured toward Eric. A long length of black cloth whipped out of the man's sleeve and wrapped itself around Eric's mouth and neck. In the space of a heartbeat, Eric was effectively gagged and silenced. Carlo smirked with satisfaction.

In the name of our leader, El Duce, and in accord with his good and wise laws, I declare this special tribunal is now in session. Carlo DiAngelo, Patrician of House DiAngelo for all of Ontario, state your charges against the accused.

Carlo gave a sidelong contemptuous glance at Eric before speaking. "Honorable judges! Members of this House! I have brought before you this infamous outsider, Eric Laflamme, who until recently was under the protection of House Brigantia. I accuse him of starting a fire which destroyed my home in the village of Fellwater, and which killed Emma DiAngelo, Matriarch of House DiAngelo, and my mother!"

Murmurs and whispers arose among those watching from the balconies and alcoves. Some of them left their gambling tables to find a seat with a better view of the events unfolding below.

Carlo continued his deposition. "Further, I accuse him of poisoning another matriarch of my house, Livia Julia McManus, the wife of Kendrick McManus, who is our ambassador to the Brigantians of Fellwater. Livia remains unconscious, and if she should die before the poison can be cured, I shall accuse Eric of murder."

More whispers filled the atrium. The three archons gazed down dispassionately.

Eric Laflamme, how do you plead? Guilty, or not guilty?

The gag around Eric's mouth unwound itself and fell around his neck and shoulders, allowing Eric to speak. "I'm innocent!" Eric declared. He then tried to explain himself, but the gag sprung up and tightened itself around his mouth again.

Clan Fianna

Patrician Carlo DiAngelo, as the plaintiff in this case, do you wish to make a statement at this time?

"Lord Archon, the charges against this boy are deeply serious. And his continued obstinate denial of his responsibility only shows how he does not care about the suffering endured by me and my family. I therefore demand that the court should classify him as a Dangerous Offender, and presume him to be guilty unless he can prove his innocence."

Eric struggled to speak and to break free of his handcuffs, but a nearby centurion kicked him to the ground again, as Carlo continued speaking.

"We don't know what he might do if he is allowed his freedom between now and his trial. And I, for one, am not willing to risk the safety of my family on an outdated legal technicality."

The archons paused for a moment to consider Carlo's words, while the observers debated among themselves and rolled new cigarettes.

The suspension of the presumption of innocence is not without precedent, in cases such as these. Therefore the accused shall be presumed guilty, and the burden shall fall upon him to prove his innocence.

"Thank you, Lord Archon," Carlo smiled. Eric continued to struggle uselessly against his bonds, while two centurions picked him up and dragged him toward the door.

The accused shall remain in the custody of House DiAngelo until the trial itself begins. We have spoken. Justice has been done. This tribunal is now adjourned.

~ 25 ~

The village of Hallowstone had been cleaned of the weeds and rubbish that had cluttered it for years. The timbreframe houses were inhabited and loved again, although a few were caged in scaffolding for more comprehensive repairs. Gardens that once bulged with dandelions and burdock had been mulched and planted with vegetables, tree saplings, and the many flowers of autumn. In a garden park near an impromptu outdoor carpentry workshop, Algernon Weatherby smoked his briar pipe and answered questions from a small group of teenagers.

"My dad always talks about something he calls the Hidden Reality. Is that what you mean when you talk about those elements and forces and things?" asked Kuvira Bhattacharya.

"Not exactly," Algernon explained. "There are several ways that we who live in the Hidden World talk about what makes us who we are. For instance, Kuvira, most of the members of your house say that the whole world is a thought or a dream inside the mind of a cosmic consciousness. And so we are like many beams of light reflecting from the many facets of a single gem. Those of you whose family comes from the Celtic tribes, with all those names I can never pronounce, most of your elders say you are descended from ancient heroes, who drew their power from the land, the sea, and the sky. And then there are some old families like the Seraphim, the Merovingians, and our old friends the DiAngelo, who say they are descended from saints, and prophets, and angels, placed here on earth by God, many ages ago. Finally, in my own lineage, House Wessex, and a few other enlightened houses–" Algernon grinned, and some of his listeners chuckled politely "–we say we are formed by a concentration of elemental forces, governed by laws of reason. You can read the movements of these forces in the stars and planets, and in mathematics too. It's quite a fascinating study."

"Then who are the gods? Why do some people around here say they are descended from the gods?"

"The gods, as far as anyone knows, were just the first people to discover these sources. But otherwise, they were the same as you."

"The same as me?" asked Kuvira, incredulously.

"Well, they were a little taller," Algernon chuckled.

The four warriors from Fellwater had arrived as Algernon was speaking, and had been listening to his lesson. Maread asked a question of his own: "So what do you think, Algernon? Are the four sources really just the same thing? Or is one of them the truth, and the others just interpretations?"

Algernon turned in his seat to see who had addressed him, and he smiled gladly, but decided not to answer.

"Good morning, my friend," he greeted her. And when he saw the three others, he said. "Goodness, there are so many of you now, coming to hear an old man talk stuff and nonsense!"

Aeducan grinned and said, "Sorry, but we didn't expect to be here today. Our chieftain asked us to come up and help out."

"What he really means," said Maread, "is that our

chieftain would rather ignore a problem than face it."

"Oh?" asked Algernon, as he puffed on his pipe, "What problem is he not facing?"

"That he doesn't know what he's doing!" blurted Maread.

Algernon studied Maread from over the top of his glasses, and then he addressed the circle of teenagers who sat around him. "Why don't we leave it at that for today?"

Algernon's audience thanked him and dispersed. Algernon filled some more tobacco in his pipe, and invited the four warriors to walk with him up the cobblestone path to the castle.

"He's impossible!" Síle complained. "Our territory is being slowly taken over by the DiAngelo. They even planted an army in our grove. In the middle of the oldest part of our forest!"

Aeducan filled in another detail. "They were right on top of things when a pack of gargantacores invaded the village. But that's our job! Not theirs! Ours!"

Finnbarr finished the story. "Finally, when we stood up to them, Donall banished us to here!"

"It seems like all he wants to do is feast and drink and hear the bards tell stories about old victories," Aeducan added. "He doesn't want to do his actual bloody job!"

Algernon considered his words for a moment. "The head of a great house seldom leads a simple life," he ruminated. "When I became Lord Protector of House Wessex, all I really wanted to do was work in my observatory, discover the secrets of cosmology, alchemy, philosophy, and expand my knowledge. A worthy goal– but I had responsibilities. So I gave to my nephew the job of handling the day to day affairs of this freehold."

"Heathcliff Weatherby," volunteered Maread.

Algernon confirmed her guess with a nod. "And like my good friend old Prospero, I was too busy with my books to notice that he had taken my chain of my office away."

"Do you think that's what's happening to Donall?" asked Finnbarr.

"I'm rather fond of your chieftain," he declared. "In the past he has been solid, reliable, strong. He comes from a very troubled country, if you understand my meaning, and he's done a lot to put it behind him. I'm proud of him. But I can't say I'm surprised that he would rather live up the good life, than mire himself in another war."

Aeducan asked, "What do you think we should do?"

"Why, show him the truth, of course," Algernon offered. "The Sacred Truth is an old Celtic idea, after all. It's part of that battle cry of yours. Curious that you needed me to remind you about it."

Aeducan endured Algernon's good-natured chastisement with a smile. "Well, we're not scholars like you are."

"We're the blunt object that our smart people throw at the enemy," Finnbarr chuckled.

Maread asked, "So we just have to show him the truth? Make him look at his reflection in the Well of Wisdom? It worked for Paul Turner. Mostly."

"Donall must look at himself, but he must look around him, too. This past summer, Eric Laflamme led me out of my castle and showed me the village, as it really was. As my nephew prevented me from seeing it. No single hero saved us all. But many heroes saved each other. That seems to me a very happy ending. By the way, that fellow Eric is a clever one. He's helped you out once or twice before. You should think about getting him to help you now."

The four Brigantian warriors balked at the thought of soliciting Eric for help. "Can't do that. He's been banished," Aeducan informed him.

"Banished?" asked Algernon. "Whatever for?"

"He poisoned the ambassador's wife!" explained Aeducan. "Right in the middle of the mead hall. The same night that you were there with us. By the gods, you think you know someone, and you think he's honourable, but as soon as no one is looking, you find out who he really is."

Algernon drew another breath of smoke from his pipe thoughtfully. "Did you see him do it? Did anyone else see him do it? And at the time he was supposed to have done it, wasn't the hall still full of people who might have seen him do it?"

"Most of us were asleep," Aeducan reminded him.

"Ah, but if most of you were asleep, surely that means some of you were still awake," Algernon proposed. Aeducan conceded the point by gazing to the ground. Algernon finished by saying, "It sounds to me like there's a few questions about his crime that no one is asking."

Aeducan shook his head. "I don't know, it seems to me

Clan Fianna

no one else could have done it. He had motive. Anyway, Donall believes he's guilty. So he's probably guilty. What more do we need?"

"You need the truth, of course," Algernon answered him. "But the truth, presented naked and without any fanfare, is so rarely persuasive on its own. It has to be dressed up in flashing colours, before most people notice it. And even then, it must compete with other players: the insidious half-truth, the convenient explanation, the gratifying lie. You can look a plain truth in the face, but if you don't know how to look, you won't know what you're seeing."

The four warriors contemplated Algernon's words for a moment, until Finnbarr suddenly blurted out, "Actually, I saw him do it."

Algernon and the others looked to Finnbarr.

"Well, I didn't exactly *see* him give her the poison," Finnbarr explained. "I saw him carrying Livia's body across the green, toward the place where he found her the next day."

"I thought you said it was too dark to see who it was," Aeducan questioned him.

"It was just light enough," Finnbarr clarified. "Besides, he's the only one of us who wears an olive-green trench coat."

"I suppose that settles it then," said Aeducan.

Algernon took off his hat and shook his head with disappointment.

As the four Brigantians contemplated this revelation, they heard the unlikely squeaks and whistles of the song of a whale, somewhere in the distant sky. They looked, and saw two enormous blue whales, each with a boat suspended on ropes and cables beneath it, like a dirigible. Kuvira Bhattacharya, who had gone to help out at the carpentry shop, ran up to Algernon and excitedly exclaimed "Flying whales! Can you see them? Flying whales! Carrying boats full of people! This place is amazing!"

Algernon was skeptical. "Is anyone else from the Brigantian Grove coming to visit today?" he asked.

"No, not to my knowledge," answered Maread.

"It's the DiAngelo!" whispered Síle.

"I think it's too far away to tell, for sure," doubted Aeducan.

"I know it's them. I can hear the whales, calling us, warning us." Síle said.

Finnbarr asked, "Warning us?"

"They say they had no choice. They say that they're sorry."

As the whales approached, the boats they carried were recognized as Roman galleys, and their occupants were seen in Centurion armour. There was also a platform on the whale's back where two centurions were loading a ballista. The first bolt streaked down and smashed one of the windows in the castle.

All four of the Brigantians drew their weapons.

"Good thing that you're here after all!" exclaimed Algernon.

A second ballista bolt slammed into the front doors of the castle, smashing them open. Meanwhile, many of the Wessex-men who had been working at the carpentry shop ran to their houses, and emerged with crossbows and muskets, to fire on the approaching Roman galleys.

"Algernon, what's in the castle that they might be going after?" asked Maread.

"My nephew Heathcliff," Algernon replied. "He's still locked up in the catacombs. This is a jailbreak!"

"The only place they can land is the castle courtyard. Let's get there first," Aeducan ordered. Algernon put a hand on his sleeve before he could run off.

"If you have to choose between protecting the castle and saving someone's life, then save the life," he said. Aeducan nodded, and then joined his companions.

When the first of the galleys hovered over the castle, almost level with the castle's highest tower, the Romans began dropping small clay pots into the castle courtyard. The pots broke to pieces when they hit the ground and splashed a foul–smelling oil all around them. Then the centurions in the other galley prepared to loose a volley of flaming arrows on the courtyard.

"Quick, get inside the castle!" shouted Finnbarr.

"No! The fire will trap us inside!" Aeducan countered.

The four of them ran across the courtyard, now slick and slippery with oil, and dodged the bombs that were still being dropped on them from above. Finnbarr slipped and fell on a puddle of oil, and then shrieked with horror when the first of the flaming arrows hurtled his way. Síle jumped in front of him and blocked as many of the arrows as she could with her cloak. They clanked and broke when they struck her, as if her cloak was made of solid stone. But when her cloak caught fire she threw it off, as far from the oil–saturated ground as she could. Some arrows flew over her head and landed behind her, and they ignited a wave of fire that roared upwards and toward them like a storm front. Finnbarr grabbed Síle around her waist, and with a burst of superhuman strength he ran with her in his arms across the courtyard, out of the way of the rushing flames, and jumped into a water fountain.

"Thanks, but don't ever do that again!" Síle told him.

Maread, meanwhile, had drawn a bow and was aiming for the crew of the boats suspended beneath the whales. Some of the men were prodding the whale with cables and pikestaffs, to make it move the way they wanted it to go. As they scrambled to protect themselves from Maread's arrows, they let go of the cables, thus allowing the whale to twist in its harness and float away. When one of the centurions saw what she was doing, he aimed the galley's ballista directly at her. Maread dodged out of the way, and then dodged a second ballista bolt fired from the other galley. More flaming arrows rained down. All she could do was deflect them with her cloak or dodge them. The strategy distracted the galley crews enough to allow Síle, Finnbarr, and Aeducan to dash to safety. She joined them as they huddled behind a nearby wall.

"Any of you badly hurt?" said Aeducan.

Finnbarr was bleeding from a head wound which he received when he fell in the fountain. He smiled. "Head still attached to my body, captain!"

"Síle?"

Síle was carefully cutting off the arms of her tunic with a dagger, to see how badly she was burned. "I'm all right," she said, although the stress in her voice revealed she was in a lot more pain than she was willing to admit.

"Maread?"

"Never mind me. Just call the play," said Maread.

"All right. Let's get to our own boat, and try to fight them in the air!" Aeducan suggested.

Aeducan peeked around the wall to see where the centurions were. One of the galleons hovered directly above the castle. A team of centurions swung down on ropes, smashed the upper floor windows, and broke into the castle.

"Now that's weird," he remarked. "Why jump inside a burning castle?"

The other three warriors leaned out to see what

Aeducan was looking at, and furrowed their brows with confusion.

A new voice from behind them said, "The fire was set to stop you from following them!"

Aeducan turned to see who was speaking, and saw a woman standing there, in the leather armour of a Celtic warrior, and a cloak and shawl patterned in a blue and black tartan. Her flesh, though visible only around her elbows and knees, was painted in blue and green spirals. She also wore a long black hood on her shoulders and head, which concealed her face in a deep shadow, leaving only an occasional glint of light where her eyes should be.

"It's the Bann-Shee!" Síle whispered.

Maread quavered a little bit when Síle named the stranger that way. "the herald of death!" she said.

"Who are–" Aeducan began to ask the hooded warrior–woman.

"You need to get inside the castle, find out what the centurions want, and rescue anyone who might be trapped there," the bann-shee told them.

"Through the fire?" Maread balked.

"There's no other way," countered the bann-shee. "Follow me." Then she galloped through the flames and into the castle.

The Brigantians looked at their battlefield and considered their options. Above them, the centurions were moving their second galley into position to drop a second team into the castle. Across the road, Algernon arrived, with a team of cavaliers armed with muskets. Their fire kept the second galley at bay.

"The Wessex-men are giving us covering fire. If we're going into the castle, we have to go now," Aeducan told the team.

"Whenever a bann-shee appears, at least one witnesses dies," declared Síle. "That means if we run through that fire, one of us– one of us will–"

Finnbarr put a hand on her shoulder, and she squeezed it worriedly.

Aeducan clapped Finnbarr's back to rouse his courage, and then did the same to Síle and Maread. "If I am going to die today, then I want to die on my feet, with my eyes open. That's a warrior's death. How about you?"

The others nodded, and got to their feet.

Finnbarr wanted to reassure Síle. "It's all right to be afraid, Síle."

Mairead came to Síle's defense, saying: "Of course she's afraid! But that doesn't mean she won't do it. She's a Brigantian!" Then Mairead playfully punched Síle in the shoulder.

Síle looked at the fire, and tried to remember that she was a Brigantian.

Aeducan shouted to Algernon: "Get your fighters into the castle through the catacombs! Try to cut off their way out!"

"What are you going to do?" Algernon shouted back.

"We're going to run through the fire!"

~ 26 ~

Donall set up a table of tea and coffee and bowls of bread and fruit near the middle of the stone circle, the largest feature in Fellwater Grove. A runner had been sent to the DiAngelo camp to invite the ambassador to breakfast. Donall guessed that the ambassador would have learned about the previous evening's fight between Paul Turner and Aeducan. A good faith gesture of hospitality, Donall imagined, might help lessen the anger that the ambassador must surely have been feeling.

The runner returned, with a message that said the ambassador and a small party of representatives would join them shortly. Donall summoned Ciara to join him, and asked Neachtain the Healer to take the place normally filled by the captain of the guard.

"Where is Aeducan, anyway?" asked Neachtain.

"I've assigned him to Hallowstone for a while," Donall informed him. "The other three in his squad, as well."

"So who is handling the patrol assignments?"

"I'm doing it myself," Donall answered, and he sat down at the table and picked a strawberry to eat.

"This morning I noticed there was nobody standing guard at the main gate," Neachtain observed.

Donall finished his strawberry before speaking. "Well there should have been. I assigned one of the Wessex cavaliers who is helping us out. I didn't get his name," Donall replied. "Said his family came to Canada from Northern Ireland during the famine. Well, I'm from Belfast, myself. We had a great old chin-wag, so we did."

Ciara wasn't in the mood for social niceties. "If there was no one at the main gate last night, even for ten minutes, then the DiAngelo could have smuggled in another of their war machines and we wouldn't know."

"We've got people watching their camp, too," Donall argued.

"Since you sent our four best warriors away, I don't know if we have enough," Ciara stated. Donall only shrugged his shoulders.

Time seemed to pass more slowly as they waited for Kendrick McManus to arrive. Neachtain paced around the stone circle and contemplated the clouds. Ciara took up a fire poker and drew spirals and other designs in the ashes of the fire pit. Donall ate more of the fruit on the table, and re-arranged them to make it look like he had not eaten as much as he had.

Kendrick marched over the crest of a low hill and into the stone circle. The cold and serious grimace on his face told Donall that the breakfast offering would be no help to him at all. Kendrick was accompanied by four of his soldiers, as usual; and although they were not apparently armed, their presence nonetheless reminded the Brigantian party of who had the upper hand. Donall welcomed him, and motioned to invite him to sit at the table, but Kendrick remained standing, and spoke first.

"You know, the reason we have a diplomatic mission here is to prevent incidents like the one that happened last night," he began.

"Of course it is," Donall agreed, "But I can't always be responsible for–"

"Yes, you can," Kendrik interrupted him. "These are your people, and one of them is your captain of the watch. If you, his chieftain, can't control him, then something is seriously wrong with your team."

"The thing that's seriously wrong here," Donall raised his voice, "is that your people seem to think we can't manage our own affairs on our own lands!"

"You can't," Kendrick pronounced cooly.

Donall resisted the urge to spit an insult at Kendrick for that statement. So he gripped the back of a chair to contain himself, and said, "Even if that was true, it wouldn't be your problem. For this is not your land."

"But it *is* our problem," Kendrick countered. "It's

Clan Fianna

everyone's problem. Yours and mine, and that of all the Secret People. I've already told you the reason why."

"You say the chthonic prisons are weakening," Donall recalled. "I concede that might be true. But if you look after things on your lands, and we look after things on ours, then incidents like what happened last night won't happen again."

"The weakening of the chthonic prisons affects all of us," Kendrick countered. "There is no Hidden House able to handle this crisis alone. The New Renaissance is the only serious coalition of Hidden Houses with the ability to face down this crisis professionally. But we can't succeed– we will surely never succeed– when irascible hotheads like your captain get in the way!"

"As I heard the story," Donall replied, thinking that he was about to play a winning card, "it was your man Paul Turner, who baited my people into a fight, and who unsheathed his sword first."

"He had to defend himself! Outnumbered four to one, he was!"

"Only because my team defeated six of yours to get to him!"

"This is getting nowhere," Kendrick declared. "You're only lucky none of my people died, or else the peace treaty between us would be broken."

"I've been training my people for many years in a nonlethal fighting style. We don't have to kill a man to neutralize his threat. We are true warriors: we trust the strength of our arms, over the calibre of our rifles." And to make his point, Donall nodded toward the four guards who surrounded Kendrick.

"Well, that's evidently true," Kendrick chuckled, "since I'd estimate the calibre of your rifles to be nearly zero."

Donall narrowed his eyes. "What do you mean by that," he said.

"You're still fighting with swords and spears!" Kendrick answered. "It's ridiculous! You're the Brigantians of Fellwater. A house that's famous among all the Secret People as a warrior clan! Descended from the Celtic gods! Warrior gods! And your best weapons are sticks and stones!"

"We have better weapons enough in store, if we need them," Donall attempted to lie.

Behind Donall, Ciara and Neachtain exchanged worried

looks with each other.

Kendrick saw right through it. "No, you don't."

Donall pursed his lips and thought for a moment before speaking again. "What do you want, Kendrick? Is it just to recruit my clan into this coalition of yours? If that was all, why bring such a heavily armed escort with you?"

"My guards are equipped as necessary for the protection of the diplomatic staff," Kendrick told him.

"Don't give me a talking point. Give me an answer! You know, many of my people are saying you brought the big guns because you mean to take Fellwater Grove away from us. By force. And after last night's incident, I'm beginning to agree."

"Donall, as I already told you, there's an epidemic of escaped prisoners from Tartarus happening out there! My guards are here to protect me from them. I dare say, they're here to protect you too!"

"We can protect ourselves, on our own territory!"

"No, you can't."

Ciara decided this was a good moment to interrupt. "All right, boys, why don't we all have a twenty minute caucus meeting, and come back to the table when we've all cooled down a little. Kendrick, help yourself to the tea and coffee here. Donall, let's go for a walk."

Kendrick looked at Ciara and then back to Donall and said, "Your shield maiden is very wise. Send a runner to let us know when you're ready to talk again." He picked up the fruit bowl and strode casually off in the direction of his camp.

Donall watched him go, and then turned to Ciara and said, "What did you do that for?"

"He was five seconds away from ordering his guards to shoot you, right here. I mean, you all but accused him of being a liar."

"He *is* a liar," Donall pleaded.

"He's a damn better liar than you are. 'We have better weapons in store' –What were you thinking!"

"I was thinking that the man's an ass, and I want him out of our land," Donall stated definitively.

"Right now he has more firepower, and more resources than we do. You can't go after him with a full frontal assault. You have to slide in the back door, quietly, patiently. You have to get him to want the same things you want. And then you won't have to attack him."

"What I want, Ciara, is to get him out of our land. Then we can feast and drink and make music and love all day and all night, just like we used to do," Donall told her.

"Then we have to show him it's in his interest to leave," she smiled, and caressed his cheek, and playfully tugged his goatee. Then she turned to Neachtain and said, "Would you kindly ask Kendrick to come back to the table again tomorrow?"

"Whatever you're planning, I hope it works," Neachtain sighed, and trundled off to fetch the ambassador.

~ 27 ~

At a signal from Carlo, two centurions grabbed Eric by the elbows and led him out of the temple, into a long stone corridor that was more like a tunnel than a hallway, followed close behind by Carlo himself Eric gave them a token struggle, but he knew it was useless; the most he could demand was to walk on his own. Carlo rolled his eyes and allowed it, but the two centurions stayed on each sided of him.

"I don't understand you, Eric," said Carlo. "I understand that you hate me, but poisoning the ambassador's wife? What were you thinking!"

"I didn't do it!" Eric repeated, as he had done so often before.

"Are you calling me a liar?"

"I'm calling you grossly misinformed," Eric replied.

Near the end of the corridor, the two centurions thrust Eric into a round stone cell. Featureless and empty, but for a single incandescent light bulb in the ceiling, Eric balked at the absence of anything to prevent him from escaping.

"This is a holding cell? Where the hell is the door!"

"It's a prison with no bars, no gates, no walls, and no towers. But still, no one escapes," Carlo stated, as he removed Eric's handcuffs.

"Is that because you personally stand guard over me the whole time?"

Carlo made a quiet patronizing chuckle. "You want to know how it works? Turn around and look."

"Where–?" Eric began to ask, as he turned around to look. Instantly, Eric was no longer standing in the little round cell on the side of the long stone corridor. Instead he found himself stepping through a revolving door, and into the brightly lit lobby of a decadent hotel, richly appointed with marble floors, mahogany and walnut furniture, high ceilings hung with crystal chandeliers, and tall landscape paintings framed in solid gold. Near where he stood was a decorative mirror, in which he saw that he was now dressed in a tail-coat tuxedo and silk bow tie. Three or four clusters of similarly well-dressed people stood around the front desk or the bar or a fireplace, drinking martinis and discussing business plans. A five piece chamber orchestra was performing Vivaldi in a suite next to a grove of potted trees.

From somewhere in the air above, Eric could hear Carlo's crooning voice speaking to him.

Imagine a prison with comfortable chairs, elegant decor, and a fully stocked bar. Imagine a window with a good view of the sea, Imagine good news in the mail every day. Money in the bank. A sexy woman in your bed. Your enemies reduced to poverty. In a place like that, you wouldn't want to leave. You wouldn't call it a prison! You would call it your home. You would think that life is good.

An elderly gentleman with a little round head and glasses was the first person to notice Eric's presence. He seemed both surprised and glad to see him, and he called Eric's name and toasted his good health. Others soon did the same, as excited whispers spread; some approached to shake his hand, some to kiss both his cheeks, some to shyly wave from a distance as if they were too scared to speak to him. All seemed to admire him for some reason; but Carlo's voice continued to narrate a different reality.

Every day that you stayed there, your muscles would weaken, your mind would dull. Your spirit would slowly fade away, like a fire that no one is feeding anymore, until all that remains are faint glowing embers. But you wouldn't notice this. The waning of your soul would be so gradual, so measured, you would never detect the difference one day to the next.

The small crowd of well wishers and admirers parted and turned their attention to a newcomer, approaching from across the lobby. Eric immediately knew who she was by the sound of her high heels clicking toward him across the marble floor. But when she glided into view, with her little black dress swinging round her knees and her embroidered red scarf playing with her hips, and her blood-red hair falling in unruly curls round her breasts, Eric let out a burst of astonishment and glee.

Clan Fianna

"Katie!" he exclaimed happily.

"Of course it's me, silly! Who else would it be?" And she picked up her pace to reach him sooner, and placed her lips proudly upon his in a warm and loving kiss. She wound her arms over his shoulders and let her hair fall upon him, while the small crowd of onlookers smiled and applauded them. She took his hands next, and Eric saw the glint of a diamond ring on her finger.

"Happy anniversary, my love. And thank you for six wonderful years!"

Eric wanted to believe what he was seeing, but his mind was disbelieving. "Katie, how can you be here? You fell from the cliff–"

"That was seven years ago. You found me at the bottom of the gorge, and carried me to safety, and looked after me until the ambulance came, remember? You tore your shirt to make a bandage, and you stopped the bleeding. The paramedics said it probably saved my life."

It seemed he did remember. The glass of a nearby mirror dimly reflected a memory of Eric carefully tying a splint on to one of Katie's legs, and then heroically carrying her in his arms, out of the river and up a stone stairway. Eric's gaze shifted between the mirror, and Katie's face, with her freckles and loving eyes. The memory in the mirror was a memory of him as he might have been, and as he wished he was. He felt the strain of carrying her, and the fear that she might die, and the pride in being her salvation. But he also felt smaller and sadder, when he thought of how different his actual life had been, where no such heroics happened. The voice of Carlo DiAngelo spoke again, this time in a more mocking, condescending tone:

Soon, like everyone else, you will forget the life you had before you came here, You will embrace this dream world, because you will want it to be real.

"I've got to get out of here," Eric apologized to Katie, and he quick-stepped toward the nearest exit. Katie caught his hand before he got far.

"Where are you going, Eric?" she pleaded.

Eric let himself be pulled toward her, and let himself kiss her one more time, but then he closed his eyes and turned away. "Nothing here is real, Katie. This place, these people. They're not real. Not even you."

"Of course I'm real. What a thing to say! On our

wedding anniversary!"

For a moment, the shadows playing in the glass of a window reflected a vision of Katie and Eric's marriage ceremony, in the stone circle of Fellwater Grove, surrounded by their friends, and with little Tara, who was a toddler, just barely able to walk, clinging happily to Eric's leg.

You will work hard to make this dream a reality. You will fight to stay inside it, with what little fire you still possess. And every time that you win, you will shackle yourself with another chain. So you see, this is a prison that needs no gates or fences or towers. For the strongest prisons are the ones the prisoners build with their own hands.

"Everything here is an illusion!" Eric shouted at the ceiling, in the hope that Carlo might hear him.

The small crowd of sycophants and admirers laughed lightly; one woman was heard to say, "There's that famous sense of humor of yours, Professor Laflamme!"

Eric took Katie's hand. "Come on, Katie, let's get out of here," he said. Katie smiled, and allowed Eric to lead her to the door.

You see, young master Laflamme, you are already growing attached.

On hearing Carlo's statement, Eric stopped abruptly, and looked at his hand, which tightly clasped Katie's hand.

"My God, Carlo's right," he told himself.

Katie was still gazing upon him with admiration, although with puzzlement as well. Eric reached around her neck to play with her hair, and then closed his eyes, and reached deep into his mind, trying to remember something. He placed himself in the memory of the time when he sat by the edge of the sacred pool in Fellwater grove, and slipped a braid of Katie's ruby hair into its water, and said goodbye.

"I had to let go of you once before, and now I have to let go of you again," he whispered.

"Eric, you're making no sense," Katie complained.

"I'm sorry, Katie. I love you, and I always will, but I have to let you go. Because– you died."

"Don't be silly, Eric. I'm alive! I'm right here!" Katie objected.

"No, you're not here, you're an illusion, just like everything else in this place. You are a memory now, Katie. And this place we're standing in is a dream. A good and beautiful dream, but still, only a dream, and nothing more. I have to let you go and wake up from this dream, before I'm caught in it forever."

When Eric opened his eyes, and all the people that surrounded him vanished, and the chamber musicians vanished. Katie, too, had vanished, although for a moment Eric saw her reflection in the mirror, standing in his place.

The mirror itself vanished, and the furniture disappeared too, and potted trees, and the paintings, until only the walls remained, austere and silent and expectant. The only movement came from the revolving hotel door, though its glass and all the windows were now blackened. So he took a last look around, and walked into the revolving door.

The lights dimmed, and the walls retreated to the horizon, and the ceiling fell into to the sky, and the floor faded to grey. Eric found himself standing on a jagged platform of cold grey stone, with an abyss all around him, and rough stone walls like cliff faces just beyond his reach. A dim blue-white light from above glared upon him, though he could not tell how high above him it was. As he got used to the light, he could see what looked like claw scratches on the ledges of the walls, seemingly left there by some titanic creature trying to climb to the light. He saw the platform he stood on was carrying him down, slowly down, toward what seemed a bottomless blackness. The distant sounds of people crying out in loneliness or despair surrounded him, with voices gone raspy and low for having cried that way for a very long time.

~ 28 ~

Aeducan, Mairead, Finnbarr, and Síle faced the courtyard of Hallowstone Castle, now completely filled with flames. Algernon's cavaliers still held off the second galley of Roman centurions, but even with that protection, the Brigantians could not retreat.

"Run through the fire? You'll be killed!" Algernon warned.

"We have to do it! There's no other way!" Aeducan hollered.

"All right then, I'm with you," agreed Mairead.

Aeducan smiled. Then he jumped in the fountain to drench himself in the water, to protect himself from the flames.

The other three did the same, and when they were ready, they lined up together, across from the castle door.

Aeducan called out the first line of the Brigantian battle charge: "Truth in our hearts!"

"Strength in our arms!" the other three replied.

"Fulfillment of our oath!"

"Raaaah!"– they shouted together.

They charged into the fire. Their eyes stung with smoke, and their lungs choked with it. Their feet scalded, though the stones had not been burning long. Through the smoke, the tears, and the squinting, it was almost impossible to see where they were going: each had to trust that their feet knew what to do. Hot burning oil splashed in their steps, sometimes flinging small licks of flame on each other, singing and scalding their exposed flesh.

Each knew to keep running, lest the flames grasp them and burn more fiercely. First one, then another, then all four howled with the heat in their lungs and the air all around them; two nearly tripped but recovered before planting their bare hands on the blistering cobbles below; and one almost blindly ran into a wall. All four of them emerged on the other side, into the castle's main feasting hall, mostly unscathed, and panting for breath. Maread and Aeducan were still wearing their cloaks, and they both gave them to Síle and Finnbarr to cool themselves with the water that still drenched them.

"We just ran through fire!" exclaimed an exhilarated Aeducan. The four of them shouted for joy and bashed each other's arms playfully.

"Brigantians!" called a scratchy voice from across the hall. They turned and saw the bann-shee, beckoning them to follow her. When all four of the Brigantians acknowledged her, she darted into a side passage and was out of sight again.

"Maybe she knows the way," Síle suggested, and the four of them ran down to see where she had gone. They found themselves at the head of a long corridor, with various side passages branching from it. The shadow of the bann-shee beckoned to them from the far end, and they followed at a full sprint, only to find themselves at the fork of another corridor, facing the same shadow at the far end once again.

"Is this really a good idea? Following the lead of a bann-shee?" said Finnbarr.

"Got a better idea of what to do?" said Maread.

"I'd rather fight the DiAngelo," said Finnbarr. "Them, I understand. The bann-shee, on the other hand–"

"–is being more helpful than you are, right now," Maread admonished him.

"Let's keep going," said Aeducan.

At the end of the third corridor, they came to a spiral stairwell, and met three centurions coming down from above. The centurions had the advantage of a clockwise–spiraling stair, which made it easier for them to reach their sword arms around the central pillar. The Brigantians had the advantage of surprise, and they pulled their opponents down and knocked them out, and dragged them into the corridor and locked the stairwell door behind them.

They followed the stairs down and reached the catacomb level. There they found three more centurions, clustered around the door of a prison cell. A bang echoed from the door, magnified to a deafening din as it echoed off the stone walls, and a bright flash momentarily dazzled everyone's eyes. When the Brigantian's senses returned after a heartbeat or two, they saw that the centurions had blown up the lock on the cell door, and the prisoner from the cell was being carried away.

"Algernon was right! It's a jailbreak!" exclaimed Maread.

"That's right, you Scottish whiskey-swilling sheep shaggers! I'm free! And I'm going home! Tally-ho!"

Heathcliff Weatherby Wednesday saluted them with a flourish, slamming the wooden gate closed.

Finnbarr sprinted forward, leaped up, and crashed feet first through the gate, allowing the Brigantians through.

"Fixed that for you," he grinned to his companions.

Heathcliff was not hard to follow: his celebratory whooping echoed down the catacomb corridors, telling the Brigantians exactly which fork in the tunnel to take. Or so they thought, when they came to a fork where his laughter seemed to come from two or three different directions at once.

"His footsteps!" Maread suggested. The floor of the catacomb was mostly covered in dust, and the footsteps of the centurions were easy to see. But at the next fork in the catacombs, the footstep path branched off in three directions at once.

"Oh, he's playing with us now," Finnbarr smirked.

"Wait–" Síle stopped him. "I think I can hear the

Wessex-men coming in from the other entrance." Then she dashed down toward where she thought the Wessex-men might be. The other three shrugged at each other and followed her. Síle was correct: they soon met a small team of Wessex cavaliers, in their frilly collars and steel breastplates and pantaloons.

"Did you see them!" Aeducan frantically asked them.

"They broke Heathcliff out of the dungeon!" Maread added.

"No, we didn't see them," one of the Wessex-men replied.

"Is there any other way out of here?" asked Síle.

"Behind us is the entrance by the foot of the hill. Back that way is the castle entrance. There's more catacombs that go deeper down, but no one knows where they go."

Aeducan made a decision on behalf of everyone. "Well he has to get to the surface somehow. His getaway boat is up there. So let's try to cut him off outside."

"Right," agreed the Wessex-man, and the entire team ran for the nearest exit.

Once they were under the blue sky again, the sight that greeted him was a jubilant Heathcliff, dancing in a balloon basket, which was lifted by a pair of levitating dolphins up to one of the waiting whale-borne galleys.

"Haha! Free again! Thank you, my friends, for such a thrilling chase. You've been wonderful! But I'm free as a whale now, and I'm going home! Adios, auf wiedersehen, goodbye!" He threw the ballast sandbags out of the basket at them, and laughed, and waved his hat, and laughed again, while the Brigantians and Wessex-men only watched with clenched fists. Aeducan angrily flung a stone at him, but it harmlessly bounced off the basket, and Heathcliff laughed again.

~ 29 ~

A short distance away, around the back of a cottage, the bann-shee watched Heathcliff board one of the Roman galleys and regain his freedom. She also saw the Brigantians catch up to him, just slightly too late. She relaxed somewhat, and gave her attention to the teenage girl who was hiding nearby. She pulled back her hood and let her ginger hair spill out.

"Thank you for coming to get me," the bann-shee told Kuvira, "I'm sorry that I could not do more to help."

Clan Fianna

"What's going to happen now?" asked Kuvira.

"I'm going to follow them, and see where they go. Take this–" she reached into a pocket on her belt, took a small piece of lapis lazuli, carved in the shape of a Neolithic warrior–queen, and gave it to Kuvira. "Keep this close. If they come back here again, hold it and call for me three times, and I will hear you, and I'll come if I can."

"That's amazing! Thanks!" Kuvira marveled. A heartbeat later she grew skeptical. "What if it doesn't work? What if you're too far away? What do we do then?"

The bann-shee sat down on a nearby stone, and borrowed the token back from Kuvira for a moment. "Well, this little warrior is only a piece of stone. But this little piece of stone was once part of a mountain, and she still has the soul of the mountain inside her. And she has the beauty of the sun inside her, and the darkness of the night, and the speed of the wind, and the strength of the sea. All those things are right here, inside this little piece of stone. So if you call to me, and I'm too far away to help you, then I want you to hold this little warrior in your hand as tight as you can, and imagine that you are just as strong and fast and brave as she is."

"Will that really work?" asked Kuvira.

"It will," the hooded warrior replied. "Because the soul of the mountain that lives in this little piece of stone also lives inside you. It's in me, and in you, and everyone you know, and all the animals, and trees and clouds and raindrops, and every living thing in the whole world."

"All of them?" Kuvira marveled. "What about things like spiders, and snakes, and poison ivy?"

"Even in those things," the bann-shee confirmed. "If you close your eyes and breathe deeply and touch the earth, you will find that everything you see is part of you, and you are a part of all that you see." Then she handed the figurine back, and clasped Kuvira's hands tightly around it.

"My dad talks like that sometimes," Kuvira remarked, as she looked at the little figurine that the bann-shee gave her. Then she asked, "How will I see all that with my eyes closed?"

The bann-shee chuckled and answered, "Well you might not see it at first. But if you keep looking, and remember to breathe, then you will." Then she stood up and straightened her hood. "I've got to go now," she said.

Kuvira tugged her sleeve and asked, "One more thing.

Why don't you want anyone to know that you were here?"

The bann-shee paused before departing and reluctantly answered, "Because if the men in those boats up there knew I was helping, they would attack us all the more. So I need you to keep this secret between us, just for now. Before you can tell anyone that it's me, there's something I have to do, to set things right."

~ 30 ~

The pedestal carrying Eric eventually descended into a wide cavern, with a high round ceiling that curved down to become its walls. Soft blue-white light streamed in from cracks in the walls shaped like jagged prison cell bars. As the pedestal settled into the surface of the floor, Eric found that a thin layer of water slicked every surface, making everything shiny, yet treacherous to walk upon. Echoes of water droplets, and the lonely cries of distant creatures, surrounded him, and the smell of moss and mushroom spores.

Tip-toeing over to one of the cracks in the wall where the light came from, Eric looked and saw that it was an open window to a small chamber, brilliant with light, and Eric had to squint to see. When his eyes adjusted he saw a man-sized scorpion creature, clicking its pincer-mouth and scrabbling with its pincer-hands to reach him.

Eric instinctively ducked away; his heartbeat and breath accelerated. When he calmed down, he looked again. This time, he saw the creature was actually just looking for something to hold on to, so that it could reach the lights on the ceiling.

Eric began to think about this a little more. He looked into the bars of another nearby cell, and saw that it held a gigantacore, much like the ones which had attacked the village on the previous day. It was lying on its back on the ground, plaintively grasping toward the ceiling of its cell, where five spiral lightbulbs filled the space with blue–white light. In every place he looked, he saw monsters of various shapes and sizes, some alone and some in small groups, all hypnotized by the light s on the ceiling of their cells. Some were desperately climbing the walls to reach the light, like drug addicts desperate for a fix. Others were content to lay down and stare at it, and coo softly to themselves, as in a trance. Some slept peacefully, with smiles on their faces.

A low rumbling noise from some distance away startled Eric, and he crouched down to the edge of the floor, although there was nowhere to hide. Light streamed into the catacomb from a short distance away: a huge stone gate was opening, and whatever was on the other side was illuminated by the same dim blue–white light that filled the cells. Across the way, some of the lights behind the cell bars went out; and cries of rage and despair suddenly echoed from them. The stone walls of those darkened cells folded back, allowing whatever was within them to emerge into the main catacomb.

It was twice as tall as a man, and its flesh was rough and scaled like a reptile; bone plates stuck out down the length of its spine from its neck to its tail. Its hands were lobster claws and its head was a reptilian beak, with bulging bloodshot eyes. Spittle oozed out down its chest and to the floor.

The creature frantically scanned the area, sniffing and seeking something. At first it made for Eric, following his scent in the air. It spat a stream of greenish fluid from glands in its mouth, which splashed close to Eric. Its scent was so foul that Eric had to suppress the urge to vomit.

The creature saw the light from the gate that had opened across the catacomb. It let out a screech and dashed toward it; the vibrations from its heavy footsteps caused small pebbles and stones to dislodge from the ceiling and clatter on the floor. A second similar creature followed it, and then a third, and a fourth; Eric eventually counted fifteen of them. The wall of the cell that they came from folded shut again, and the gate on the other side of the catacomb began to close.

Eric decided that as long as the creatures were following the light, he was probably safe; and that if he followed the creatures, they might lead him out of the prison. It was a risky move, but it was preferable to sitting on the cold wet floor and doing nothing. So he dashed ahead, and slipped through the gate just before it became too narrow to let him pass. He rolled a nearby stone in the way, to block the doors open, just in case he needed to get back in.

The next chamber resembled the chasm through which Eric had arrived in this underground vault: a roughly circular pit with stone walls, with an unfathomable abyss below, and a dazzling light shining from an endless height above. But this one was massively larger. He had emerged from but one little cave in a wall of hundreds, perhaps thousands, of similar caves, carved into the side of the wide round abyss. Some were barely small enough to contain a single animal, some were as wide and tall as houses. A rough and restless wind whipped around from above and below, pelting everything with dust. The cries of thousands, perhaps millions, of unseen creatures, was thicker than the air. Howls of rebellion and of mourning echoed from everywhere and nowhere, above and below, and all around.

The creatures Eric followed here were tromping along a narrow ledge, toward the source of the hypnotic blue–white light, now shining from inside another nearby catacomb. Some scrambled a little faster than they should, and one of them lost its footing and slipped, and plummeted to the abyss below. Whether it fell to its death, Eric could not tell, since its cry only merged with the perpetual harrowing that already saturated the darkness. Eric picked his way along the ledge carefully, as the stones here were slick and slippery with dust. Yet he also kept his distance: for although the creatures were entranced by the light, still he did not think it wise to get too close to them. As he waited for them to get a little ahead, he braved a glance to the abyss below.

There he saw an absolute depth, beyond blackness and beyond darkness, an absolute nothingness without beginning or end. The clouds of dust and fog that spiraled around, and the points of light from the caves below, faded into grey, and then into black, like the iris of a cold unblinking eye. As Eric gazed into the abyss, so did the abyss gaze into him, seeking his darkness.

New voices reached him from the swirling wind. He heard his childhood schoolmates laughing at him for placing third in some race, many years ago. He heard his parents chastizing him for staying out too late at night. He heard a professor at his university dismissing his class comments for being too simple. He heard his landlord blame him for the bedbugs in his room. He heard Carlo's voice too, from the previous day, reminding him of how Katie tried to kill herself, instead of stay with him. Every reason anyone had ever given him for why he was useless and a failure flooded up from the abyss and into his ears.

Eric felt the strength draining from his arms, and became fearful that he might fall. He forced himself to look away from the edge of the abyss, and to focus on something at the same height as the ledge he sat upon. The voices of judgment still surrounded him, and it wasn't long before he felt compelled to look down into the abyss again. This time he heard Katie's voice, chastizing him for spending more time with his homework than with her. She criticized the fact that he hadn't thrown out old socks and T-shirts that were full of holes. She told him to take a shower more often. Eric heard the voices of other women he loved. Miranda dismissed him for being an outsider. Ildicoe angrily denounced him for having another woman's bite-marks on his body. Siobhan mocked him for being so easy to seduce, and for finishing too soon. Eric found himself shouting back to them, trying to explain himself, apologize to them, and promise to be better in the future. But they did not seem to hear. They persisted and lingered, and repeated their judgments louder than before, and always with the most terrible of words: unwelcome, undeserving, unworthy, uninvited, and unwanted.

Something about hearing these words made Eric pause, and sit up straight. As he did so, he briefly glimpsed a puddle of water on the ledge near him, which reflected Katie's face back at him. Though the light in the abyss was dim, she looked as lonely as he felt. The image reminded Eric of another pool of water, back in Fellwater Grove, where he saw her reflection before.

Another illusion, Eric realized.

As this thought took hold of him, the voices that berated him faded away. For now he knew where he was. This place had to be one of the chthonic prisons, where the gods confined their ancient enemies from the mythic age. Eric realized Carlo didn't tell him everything about what kept the prisoners from escaping. Not only a fantasy of bliss, but also a mountain of anguish and hope-crushing despair enervated them and held them down, as effectively as locks and bars on their minds. Eric could see the other prisoners now, hanging their heads out of their caverns, staring into the abyss, wailing and howling into the dark.

"Hey, all of you!" he shouted at them. "Don't listen to the voices! You do deserve to be loved! Everybody does!"

Over the din of despair, no one could hear him.

~ 31 ~

Around the feasting table in the Brigantian Great Hall, the leading women and men of the clan took their usual places.

Donall sat in his high seat with Ciara next to him on his right. Most other Brigantians sat in the kitchen or in the loft, as far from Donall as they could go without looking like they were deliberately avoiding him.

"I think I'll sell that car repair business to Gregory Morningfrost," Donall meandered to no one in particular. "I haven't gone to work there much since I became chieftain. But it's a good business. Honest work. Decent pay."

"He might not go for it," Ciara commented. "He's already got a job that he likes. He runs that paralegal firm."

"Then I'll sell it to George Medewiwin."

"George is a very old man, Donall!" Ciara objected. "He just wants to watch his grandchildren grow up. When you're that old, that's all you will want to do as well!"

"I don't have any grandchildren. Or any children. Although we could try making one tonight," he grinned at Ciara, as he petted her thigh.

"Not tonight, Donall, not tonight," said Ciara, as she brushed away his hand.

Donall's face fell, but he knew not to persist when she had made a decision like that. He took another bite of his bread, and wanted to enjoy it, but it gave him no pleasure. So he tossed his knife and fork on the table and climbed up on his feet, and raised his walking stick above his head like a conductor's baton.

"This is a heroic hall!" he half-shouted to everyone who could hear him. "So where is the harp, and where is the singer? Where is the teller of tales! Alas, for the mead cup, and the well laid feast, and the well dressed lady–" Ciara smiled, although she shied away from him "–always seem incomplete when the bards have gone away, into the darkness of night, as if they were never here!"

Around him, the few Brigantians who sat at their benches and stools raised a cup to toast their chieftain, but then they settled back to their conversations again. Disheartened by their lack of enthusiasm, Donall lowered himself back in his chair.

"What's happened to everybody?" he asked Ciara.

"Don't you know?" Ciara sternly replied. "You sent our four best fighters up to Hallowstone. And you banished Eric Laflamme. And then–"

"I had to send them away, you know I did!" Donall defended himself.

Ciara wasn't listening. "Most everybody else is either out there patrolling the ridge, or spying on the ambassador's camp. Or else they've gone home, because they can't stand the fact that all you want to do is sit in this hall, and eat!"

"I'm the chieftain!" Donall insisted. "I've done my time, standing guard on the ridge, and fighting the Fomorians, and all that. Other people can take their turn now. I've earned the right to just sit here and eat!"

"Just what do you think being chieftain means?" Ciara shrilled at him. "That you give the orders while everyone else does all the work?"

Donal relented a little bit. "No," he admitted. Then he sighed and tried to explain himself better. "You know, I wanted to be chieftain because I thought that would make everything simpler for me. Sure, I knew I would have to make tough decisions. But how was I to know I'd have to deal with someone like Kendrick McManus? Miranda never had to face a problem like him!"

"Oh yes she did," Ciara reminded him. "Many times. And when she was chieftain she took a turn patrolling the ridge just like the rest of us. When the Ice Giants attacked us back in 'ninety-eight, she was right there, in the middle of the fight. Right beside us. And that's why we followed her."

"I don't want to be compared to her," Donall shouted. He lurched himself to his feet, and glared angrily at Ciara, as a dozen more angry retorts clamoured in his mind. The other Brigantians began to take notice, and some put their cutlery down to watch what was happening. Donall winced as pain suddenly lanced his sides, and he crashed back into his seat again. He had to grasp the table to stop himself from falling on the floor. When he was steady again, he touched his old injury, and found that a spot of blood was welling up beneath his tunic.

Ciara saw the blood, and compassion grew on her face. "Where's Neachtain?" she said to whoever was nearest.

"I'll find him," answered someone from the kitchen, who then darted out the door.

Ciara crouched down to Donall's level, and helped him lift up his tunic and examine his wound.

"You might have told me it was this bad," Ciara gently suggested.

"I didn't want you to worry," Donall explained.

"Donall, it's getting bigger!" she observed. "When were

you going to tell me?"

Donall was finding it a bit difficult to breathe, so he whispered, "I didn't want to tell you at all. I didn't want you to feel sorry for me."

A sentry burst into the great hall, short of breath and looking a little scared. "The ambassador just sent one of his armoured cars into town! Something's happening!"

Donall looked up at Ciara and whispered, "Get Aeducan and his team back here. We have to deal with this, whatever it is, before they do."

Ciara stood. "It might be too late already, but all right. Are you coming?"

Donall tried to stand again, but could not. So he cast his face down, in the hope that no one would see his shame.

"Please take care of yourself, Donall," she whispered to him, and gave him a quick kiss on the cheek. Then she raced out the door, followed by everyone in the hall. When they were gone, Donall tried his best to sit upright in his chair. He looked at his food, still warm on the plate before him, and slowly pushed it aside.

~ 32 ~

Eric tried to rest, and recover his sense of where he was. As he looked around, he noticed that almost all the creatures he was following had climbed into another catacomb.

He scuttled after them, but leaned as far from the edge of the abyss as he could. The next chamber was wide and high, and lit by dozens of theatre lamps rigged to metal frames that straddled holes in the floor. The lamps focused a bright beam of blue-white light down into each hole.

Eric saw great giants of men and women with thin hair and leathery skin, basking in the hypnotic light. Some would reach up and try to touch the light, and then they would slink down again, and sigh.

The creatures Eric had seen earlier were following one such lamp, which was placed as a spotlight on top of a row of railway boxcars. An antique steam engine waited at one end, ready to pull the train away. Spotlight operators wearing sunglasses and industrial ear defenders were lighting a path for the creatures, and making sure none got distracted by the lights straddling the cells in the floor. The creatures followed the light up a platform and into the boxcars. Observing the whole scene from the steps of a passenger car at the front of the train was a man wearing a kind of tabard, with chain mail armour beneath it. He wore a gold mask, much like the ones worn by the judges at the tribunal. Occasionally one or more workers would approach him, seeking his approval for something they were doing. He would nod, and then direct them back to work again.

When all the creatures were all on board, the workers locked them in. The man in the golden mask boarded the passenger car, and the train started moving. Eric dashed to the train and jumped up to catch a hand–hold, before it got moving too fast. He nestled into what looked like an empty boxcar for the journey back to the surface of the earth.

The train ran through various narrow tunnels and rocky caverns, swiftly and uneventfully, but for the occasional bump when the train struck something on the tracks, or something jutting in from the sides of the tunnel. It travelled in darkness, and Eric was tempted to sleep, but he kept himself alert, for he did not really know where the train was going. Eventually it entered a wider tunnel, and then emerged to the surface, and Eric risked peeking outside. Night had fallen, and the sky was grey–orange, reflecting the street lights of a distant town or city. He could not pick out any familiar landmarks. Soon the train slowed to a stop, somewhere in the countryside, surrounded by farm fields. By the dim light of the orange sky, Eric could see that the boxcar he was hiding in was not fully empty. Some wooden crates were piled at the other end, and one of them was partially open, as the bouncing of the train had dislodged its lid. Unable to resist his curiosity, Eric opened it fully and looked inside. He found it full of flourescent spiral light bulbs. As he searched further, he found a shipping receipt: manufactured in nearby Royal Wyndham. The buyer was listed as "Guardians Hall 434".

As the meaning of this discovery unfolded in his mind, he heard the sound of an approaching helicopter, followed by the sound of the other boxcar doors opening. Eric pocketed the shipping receipt, then moved to the door of his own boxcar, to see what was happening. He saw four or five of the massive lobster-clawed creatures bounding toward the blue-white beam of the helicopter's powerful spotlight. Eric thought of everyone in Fellwater who had received a free package of light bulbs just like the ones he found on the train.

As the train workers shut the cars closed again, one of

them spotted Eric. Alarms shouted, whistles blew, flashlights shined in his face, and before Eric fully realized what was happening, three DiAngelo centurions tackled him to the floor.

~ 33 ~

Wearing a bathrobe and fluffy pink bedroom slippers, Miranda politely accepted the gift of a free box of lightbulbs from the environmental campaigners at her door.

Then she returned to her gazebo, where the door was propped open with a broom. Across its threshold lay a cottage garden and a cobblestone path in the village of Hallowstone. Ciara had gone there in search of the fighters whom Donall had sent away. When she returned, followed closely by her companions, Miranda asked them "Where's the fire?"

"We don't really know," Ciara admitted. "We just saw the ambassador's armoured cars head out of the grove and toward town, so we think it might be something big."

"More of those gargantacores, maybe?"

Ciara let herself be worried for a moment. "I'm not much of a fighter. I'm an artist. If those things show up, I plan to stay well behind these four people."

"We're artists too, you know," said Maread, as she tapped the sword sheathed at her hips. "Martial artists."

"But we mostly paint everything red," added Finnbarr.

Everyone chuckled at Finnbarr, but Aeducan wanted to be serious. "We saw the Bann-Shee today," he said.

"Oh?" said Miranda.

"She was actually helping us for a while. But I've heard the stories," said Aeducan.

Síle strayed to the window and looked outside. "Do you think she might have followed us here?" she trembled.

"You're quite safe from her in this house, I promise you," Miranda reassured her friend. Then she said to everyone, "It's true that wherever she goes, death often follows. But she is not always the one who kills."

"So she's a herald of death," said Maread.

"She's a herald of injustice," Maread clarified, as she took down a book from a nearby shelf and flipped through it, looking for something. "Sometimes she comes to protect. Sometimes, to grieve and to mourn. But sometimes, to punish."

Finnbarr said, "So we should stay out of her way?"

"Definitely stay out of her way," Miranda replied. Then found what she was looking for in her book: an illustration of an old woman standing up to her knees in a river, washing a blood-stained tunic, while a warrior watched her from behind a stand of ferns and tall grass. Miranda showed the drawing to everyone, and said, "But I'll tell you this. If you see her by a riverbank washing blood out of someone's clothes, and it looks like she's washing *your* clothes– then she has come for you. And there will be nothing you can do about it."

The discussion was interrupted by the sound of police sirens wailing somewhere in the town.

"We better go," said Aeducan. Then he turned to Ciara and said, "Did you bring any transport?"

"There's a curragh waiting for you just outside," she informed him.

"Perfect, thank you," Aeducan replied, and then he signaled for everyone to follow him to it.

Miranda caught Ciara just before she left. "Where's Donall? Why isn't he here?"

Ciara shook her head. "Back at the grove. Tending that wound in his side, and– doing nothing."

Miranda nodded gravely. "Strength in your arms," she blessed the team. Ciara smiled thankfully, and followed the others outside.

One of the Brigantian flying currachs hovered just above Miranda's front door. The four warriors had already hauled themselves on board, so Ciara grabbed one of the dangling ropes and Aeducan pulled her up. Together they flew over the town, looking for the DiAngelo's armoured vehicles, and following their likely route from the grove. Their attention was eventually drawn to a hockey rink just on the edge of the town.

When they got closer, they saw three tall and gangly creatures with huge claws for hands, sharp beaks for faces, and sharp plates of bone sticking out from their spines, all trying to smash their way into the building.

"Terrabiters!" shouted Síle.

"Bloody hell!" Finnbarr exclaimed.

"Those lights over there are probably the DiAngelo, on their way. So we have to take care of these things before they do."

Ciara, who was at the rudder of the curragh, warned

everyone to "Hang on!" Then she steered the currach in a sharp and fast fall, aiming to land as close to the arena as possible. When she was no higher above the ground than the roof of the arena she pulled up and hovered the boat in place, as the four fighters jumped to the ground and brandished their weapons.

Two of the terrabiters were trying to enter the arena through the windows, even though the flames poured out and scorched their scales. A third had climbed on top of the building and was smashing a hole in the sheet metal roof with its claws. Aeducan and Síle leapt up to either side of the one on the roof, and bashed it with their spears, knocking it to the ground. It screeched angrily and spat a blob of acid at them, but its aim was poor, as it was also struggling to stand up.

The acid splashed the metal roof and began dissolving it. Maread and Finnbarr confronted the other two creatures. Maread lightly ran up the plates on its spine as if they were a stairway, and stabbed the creature in the neck with her spear. Finnbarr, armed with a sword, slashed at his terrabiter's claw just as it reared back to pound the door. It turned to Finnbarr and screeched at him, and disgorged its acidic spittle at him, but Finnbarr dodged out of the way just in time, and slashed at the creature's other claw. His sword, however, was drenched in the creature's fast-acting acid, and so when it struck the chitinous plates on the terrabiter's wrist it bent on an angle, doing no damage. Finnbarr dropped it and cursed, as the acid dissolved the metal away.

Ciara, still piloting the currach just above the fray, noticed an elderly couple rushing out of the arena through a service door around the back. She maneuvered the currach down to their level, just in front of them, and urged them to climb on board.

"Come on! They'll get to you before you get to your car, so this is the safest place for you!" When they were safely on board, she guided the boat back up to a height again.

"What in the world is this!" exclaimed an elderly woman, as she gripped the gunnels of the boat.

"It's a traditional Irish skin boat," Ciara smiled.

"It's a miracle, is what it is!" her husband declared.

The creature which had fallen from the roof was now on its feet, but Aeducan was on top of it, plunging his spear into its throat, one of the only vulnerable places in its chitinous armour. The creature twisted itself around, and so Aeducan's spear–thrust missed, slicing a gash in its chest instead. The creature roared at him, and bashed him to the ground with a swipe from one of its claws. Aeducan tried to roll out of the way, but the creature had caught his leg and was holding him down. Then it raised itself up into the best position to pummel him into the ground.

Two arrows struck it from one side, one quickly after the other. They lodged in the bone of its head and its flesh just under one arm. The creature turned to see where the arrows came from, as did Aeducan, and they saw the silhouette of an archer, standing on the roof of the arena.

The Bann-Shee, who had helped them back at Hallowstone Castle.

The terrabiter spat a stream of acid at her, but she dodged out of the way, and loosed another arrow which struck the creature between the bone plates on its knee. This gave Aeducan the chance he needed to jump to his feet again, and finish the creature with a spear thrust into its abdomen.

At the same time, Síle ran to Finnbarr and tossed him a new sword. Together the two of them sliced at the creature's ankles and knees, while the archer on the roof of the arena planted a few arrows into its shoulder and neck, bringing it to the ground again. Looking around, they saw that all three of the terrabiters were now incapacitated or dead. So they lowered their weapons and relaxed a little.

Maread examined an arrow in one of the dead terrabiters. The head was shaped like a comet.

"These arrowheads look like fairy darts. The kind we make in our own forge," she mused.

Ciara guided the currach back down to the ground, to let the people out.

"I'll never forget the way you saved our lives!" said the husband, as he shook Ciara's hand.

"I'm sorry, sir, but yes, you will," said Ciara.

The sound of snapping trees and angry howling brought everyone's attention to a line of trees across the road.

"Get in your car and go home, please!" Ciara urged the two elders. Hearing the approach of new danger, they quickly did as she said.

The four Brigantian fighters made a defensive line around the entrance to the hockey arena. Three more terrabiters crashed out of the woods and ambled toward them. The

Brigantians braced themselves and readied their weapons.

This time the creatures avoided the hockey rink and went straight for the windows of an office attached to the arena. The fighters looked at each other, not understanding, and then followed them. The first creature to reach the windows smashed them away with its massive claws, and then stood up straight, and made a quiet warbling sound, like a bird purring over its children. It gingerly stepped through the hole in the wall where the window once was, followed by the other two, and parked itself in the floor. Those outside heard the sound of some furniture being shoved out of the way, but then silence. With their weapons lowered, the four fighters looked inside, and they saw the three terrabiters placidly staring into the lamps in the ceiling.

"Never seen them do that before," Síle remarked, and the others nodded in agreement.

"Brigantians! Get out of the way" shouted a strong voice from somewhere behind them. When they turned to look, they saw a squad of DiAngelo centurions marching toward the arena, followed by one of their light armoured vehicles. At the head of the column marched Kendrick McManus, his bronze breastplate shining in the reflected light of the burning arena.

"Captain, what do you want to do?" Maread asked Aeducan.

Aeducan thought for a moment, and then said, "We take those three terrabiters back where they belong. And we do it without Kendrick's help. This is our town."

Maread, Finnbarr, and Síle traded worried glances.

To Ciara, hovering in the currach above, Aeducan said, "We're going to need more people. So head back to the grove, and—"

Kendrick interrupted to say, "May I be of assistance?"

Aeducan turned to Kendrick and said, "We don't need your help, Kendrick, thanks for asking."

"Apparently you do," Kendrick insisted. "Five people in one flying bucket just isn't enough to move three terrabiters."

"We have resources of our own that we can bring in. Now stop wasting our time."

"I have resources right here," said Kendrick, and he tapped his hand on his LAV.

"The terrabiters are passive right now. No threat to anyone. So we don't have to kill them. We just have to take them

Clan Fianna

home."

"They could become violent again at any time."

"We're prepared for that, too," Aeducan told him, and nodded in the direction of the dead ones, lying on the ground nearby. "Didn't need your help for those ones. Not gonna need your help for these ones either. So I'll say it again: this is our town."

Kendrick looked behind him and said, "Gunner commander, take aim."

The turret on the LAV swerved to aim at the creatures in the arena. Aeducan and the other Brigantians found themselves directly in the line of fire. The warriors tightened their grips on their weapons.

"Docile as they may be right now, they are still a potential threat," Kendrick declared. "It's best to deal with them efficiently. Now, if you would kindly step out of the way?"

Aeducan folded his arms and said, "No."

Maread looked at Aeducan, and bit her bottom lip.

Kendrick didn't expect Aeducan to resist him. Aeducan's companions stood their ground with him, although Maread leaned into his ear and whispered, "What are you doing?"

Aeducan whispered back, "Taking back our town."

"I hope you have a plan."

Kendrick heard Maread's whisper and said, "Yes, Captain. I, too, hope you have a plan."

"It's very simple," said Aeducan. "We're going to stand right here, in front of this arena. If one of us dies because you tried to shoot the things behind us, then the peace between our houses will be over, and you will have a war. And you don't want that."

"Humph! Human shields. Protecting a dire-creature. Aren't you the brave ones. So, I guess we'll both just stay right here all night, and see who gets tired and goes home first."

~ 34 ~

A black limousine arrived on a country road near where the train had stopped, and Paul Turner emerged from it, along with two more centurions. They strode briskly over to where the train workers were holding Eric, and handcuffed him again, and stuffed him into the limousine, to take him back to Domus

Eleutherios.

"You know," said Paul, as he tried to pass the time, "I think you are the first outsider to see one of the chthonic prisons. In fact I think you're the first to escape from one."

Eric wasn't in the mood to talk. He acknowledged Paul's words with a nod, but then turned to look out the window.

"Either way, I don't know whether to congratulate you, or to lock you up again," Paul continued. Eric shrugged.

"Actually, I'm not sure why Carlo put you down there, in the first place. You might not have been found in time for your trial tomorrow."

Still staring out the window, Eric mumbled "I think that is exactly what he had in mind."

"Well, you did kill his mother," Paul stated.

Eric rolled his eyes, and turned back to the window.

Paul took Eric's silence for another denial of the charges. "Are you saying Carlo is a liar?" he asserted. "How dare you! He's a man of great integrity."

"A man can have the reputation of a saint and still be an asshole," Eric quietly retorted.

"Not him," Paul countered. "No one who knows him doubts his integrity."

Eric shook his head.

"Since we have about twenty minutes of time to ourselves here, I'd like to ask: how did you do it?"

"Do what?"

"Escape from the chthonic prison."

After Eric didn't answer for a while, Paul added, "Look, we all know that the prisons are weakening. Things are escaping all the time. If you could tell me about the holes you found, maybe we could plug those holes. Keep the bad guys contained. So an outbreak like what happened yesterday won't happen again. That might save people's lives."

Eric still didn't answer, so Paul leaned forward and asked the question he really wanted to ask. "I was wondering– what's it like down there?"

Eric didn't really want to answer. "It's difficult to explain if you have not seen it for yourself," he said.

"I'm a smart guy. Try me."

Eric closed his eyes, gathered his thoughts, and spoke slowly. "Imagine looking down into an abyss so black and deep that you could fall into it forever. Imagine hearing all around you

Clan Fianna

the voices of everyone you have ever hurt or wronged, even in the smallest way. Imagine those voices constantly lecturing you about every failure, every loss, every stupid mistake you ever made in your life. And now imagine those voices made you hate yourself so much that you want to throw yourself into that abyss. But you can't. Because you need initiative, and will, to throw yourself in. But the voices took that away, too. That's what it's like."

Paul was silent for a moment, and then forced himself to sound cheerful. "You escaped. Here you are. How did you do that?"

"I didn't escape at all," Eric reminded him, and he rattled his handcuffs.

Paul wanted to ask a different question. "I mean, you're out of the caves, out of Tartarus, back here on the surface of the earth again."

Eric returned his mind to the present and said, "On that train of yours. There are thousands of weird things imprisoned down there. But someone is putting them on that train and letting them out."

"Don't be silly," Paul laughed. "The train is used to catch the ones that escape, and bring them back down there."

"I saw them being loaded on the train with my own eyes," Eric insisted.

"First you say Carlo's a liar, now you say I'm blind? Really, Eric! Nobody will believe you!"

"The truth does not depend on what anybody believes," Eric asserted. "The truth is the truth."

"By the gods, Eric, you live in a sheltered world!"

"At least in my world, the difference between truth and lies has nothing to do with anyone's reputation," Eric concluded, and he faced out the window again.

"You don't know what the truth really is, do you, Eric? It's actually very simple. The truth is any statement about the way things are, that a powerful man successfully imposes on the world. The powerful man doesn't just study things as they are. He creates his own truth. And while people like you merely study that truth, he goes on to create another one. He doesn't wait for anyone's permission. He doesn't apologize for anything. The truth is what he says it is." After a pause, Paul added, "You can thank me now for answering all your philosophical questions."

Eric tried to sit up straighter to answer Paul's proposition. "When you speak of a powerful man, you mean someone like El Duce, I suppose?" he speculated.

"You should have sided with him, instead of with the Brigantians, while you had a chance," Paul confirmed. "The truth that he's creating is beautiful. That's why he's going to win."

"So what happens when this powerful man runs up against the limits of his power?" Eric asked.

"A truly powerful man acknowledges no limits to his power," Paul replied confidently.

"Not even the limits imposed on him by, for example, another powerful man?"

"Like who? Like Miranda?"

"Let's say there's another El Duce out there. And he's got his own Guardians Organization, and his own New Renaissance. What would happen they found out about each other?"

"Well then, the two of them would have to compete with each other, maybe even go to war."

"Is that what they wanted in the first place?"

"Obviously not. What they wanted was to be free."

"There, you see," Eric sat back, satisfied. "That's a truth that the powerful man didn't create on his own. It's a truth he was forced to accept when he ran up against the limits of his power."

Paul did not answer right away.

"That's what the chthonic prison is like." Eric reminded him. "I suppose Carlo was right, when he said it's a prison we all build for ourselves. So, you want to know how I got out? I remembered the one thing that the abyss could not take away from me. I saw it once before, when I looked in the Well of Wisdom. You've looked in the well yourself; you know what it reveals. Then I just stood up and walked away."

~ 35 ~

Kendrick paced left and right across the front of his LAV, glaring at Aeducan and the Brigantians. Aeducan's muscled arms stayed folded over his chest. Ciara hovered the curraigh just behind the four fighters, adding it to the protective line. The wind rustled stray leaves into little whirlwinds, and no one spoke.

Clan Fianna

The deadlock was broken by a flaming arrow, that flew from the bann-shee's bow and slotted itself straight down the barrel of the main gun on the turret of the LAV.

"Who the hell did that?" shrieked Kendrick.

In the time it took for him to speak, the bann-shee jumped from the roof of the arena to the top of a nearby tree, and balanced on a branch that looked too thin to hold her weight. She let fly another arrow, which sprouted into a streak of flame in mid-flight, and struck one of the two mounted machine guns, knocking it off its placement and to the ground.

"Fairy darts!" shouted Kendrick. "Return fire!"

At Kendrick's signal, the centurions took aim with their weapons and fired. Above them, the figure that the DiAngelo centurions were shooting at let herself fall behind the tree, and no one saw where she landed.

"Cease fire!" Kendrick ordered. "Get out there and find her!"

Some were reluctant to do so; they whispered the word 'bann-shee' among themselves, and clutched their weapons close. Kendrick had to grab his lieutenant by the collar and push him toward the tree, to make him search for her.

At almost the same moment, a fleet of range rovers and pickup trucks, emblazoned with the badge of the Guardians on their doors, arrived at the scene. Carlo DiAngelo stepped out of the lead vehicle, and Kendrick saluted him.

"Excellent work, McManus. We'll take it from here," Carlo told him.

"Sir," Kendrick saluted, and then said "we're under attack from an unknown enemy, and my men are searching for him."

Finnbarr said to Aeducan, "If you were looking for a way to end the standoff, this is probably it."

"Can't do that," Aeducan countered. "Not yet."

"But it's the fucking bann-shee!"

Another flaming arrow struck the second mounted machine gun on top of the LAV, smashing it away. This time it came from the roof of a curling club building, across the parking lot from the arena. The bann-shee mockingly struck a sexy pose and blew a kiss to Carlo, before leaping behind the building again, out of sight. The centurions ran after her, but found no one there.

Maread pulled on Aeducan's arm and said, "I think

we've made our point. It's our town again. The bann-shee is doing the rest of the work for us. And we can come back for the terrabiters later."

Aeducan relented. "All right, let's get out of here."

The four warriors jumped into Ciara's curraigh, and they floated away, toward the grove.

"Gunner commander," barked Kendrick, when he saw that the Brigantians were out of the way. "Have you removed the obstruction from your chain gun barrel?"

"Sir, yes sir."

To one of the centurions who had been searching for the archer, he asked, "Are any of our people still inside the building?"

"No sir."

Kendrick donned a pair of industrial ear defenders and said to the LAV commander, "Open fire."

Three bursts of bullets from the chain gun slammed into the three terrabiters, smashing their chitinous scales and killing them instantly, and destroying most of the office wall behind them. The four Celtic warriors, witnessing from above, gasped and shouted in outrage: "What the hell!" and "There might have been people still in there!" and "What did you do that for!"

Carlo wheeled on Kendrick and said, "Kendrick, you just gave me the worst ringing in my ears I've ever had in my life!"

~ 36 ~

The songs of crickets and frogs floated through the arboretum as the sun set. The stars emerged from behind wind–blown clouds, and the rainbow–coloured fireflies flew among them, making new constellations of their own.

"I still can't believe they shot the terrabiters," Maread complained.

"We killed three of them as well," Aeducan reminded her.

"We were protecting the town. The centurions were committing murder," she snapped back.

"Nothing we can do about that right now, not with Carlo on the scene," Aeducan sighed. "Let's just watch the camp."

Aeducan agreed with a nod, and then they both paused to survey the ambassador's camp again, from their perch in the hunter's stand. They sipped tea from a thermos that they shared between them.

Their idle conversation ended with the sound of someone in the DiAngelo camp coughing, retching, and whining miserably. This was followed by the sound of someone else, shouting.

"This is the second night in a row that there's been a row in the camp," Aeducan observed.

Maread held a finger to her mouth to quiet him, and leaned forward to listen more closely. She traced an idle finger along the point of her ears. And then she said, "I hear nothing. There's nobody there."

"No? I can hear it as clear as a bell," said Aeducan. "Two people in the ambassador's tent, having an argument. One of them is seriously ill. Probably the ambassador's wife. I think the other one is the ambassador himself."

Maread leaned forward, to try to hear what Aeducan could hear. "I hear nothing. There's nobody there."

Aeducan saw a painful look on Maread's face, and began to worry about her.

"I've got a hell of a headache right now. It just came on. The noise of the gun on Kendrick's LAV, maybe. Do you mind if I go home for a while?" she asked.

Aeducan sighed, then patted her shoulder and said, "All right."

"I'm sorry, Aeducan, I just can't– I can't stay out here tonight," she apologized, as she climbed down the ladder to the ground.

Aeducan watched her walk away, and then turned his attention back to the camp again. He folded his hands under his chin, and furrowed his brow in thought.

~ 37 ~

Overnight, photographs of the damage to the school and the arena spread around the village. The talk in the restaurants, social clubs, and internet boards was all about what might have happened. An angry former employee with a bomb. A drunk driver, crashing his truck. A meteor strike. The only point of agreement among all the different theories was that the

Guardians were somehow involved: the photographs placed their uniformed members at the scene.

By the following morning, the news reached Miranda, by way of two police officers who knocked on her door, and asked if she could identify some people in a photo they gave her. The photo clearly showed Aeducan and his team, brandishing their weapons, ready to attack someone or something outside the frame of the photo.

"Sorry, officers. I can't help you," she said. "What do you want them for?"

"Didn't you hear what happened to the school and the arena?"

"No, actually."

"If you do see any of these people, or see anything suspicious, don't approach them. Call us immediately."

When the officers moved on to the next house on her street, Miranda threw on a shawl and marched to the Guardians Hall, in search of Carlo, and some answers.

A small group of people were gathered in front of the rectory office next to the hall. One of whom was angrily demanding a meeting with "whoever is in charge". The office manager was doing his best to be polite.

"We know the Guardians were involved in the Okanagan Lake Monster coverup. So you might as well tell us what you know about the cave bears here in Fellwater."

"We aren't covering up anything," said the office manager. "We make all our activities public knowledge. You can even read our tax records online."

Miranda moved around them and aimed for the back door of the Guardians hall, and felt satisfied that no one saw her. But she did not count on Harvard Willie.

"Hey, look who it is, everybody! It's the Queen of those amazons that live in the forest! They rescued me from the giant monster flying things! She'll tell you that what I've been telling you all this time is true!"

Miranda suddenly found herself at the centre of attention. The leader of the monster hunter group said, "Who are you? And – Giant eagles? Really?"

"Well," Miranda tried to answer, "I do have a summer house near the conservation park, but I've never seen any giant eagles flying around it."

Harvard Willie instantly interjected with "That's

Clan Fianna

because they were falcons! They weren't eagles. They were falcons. I remember now."

All eyes turned back on Miranda again.

"What can I say, but–Harvard Willie's an interesting fellow," she told them.

"She didn't deny it!" Willie triumphed. "You all heard what she said. She didn't deny it!"

Before Miranda could respond, Heathcliff stepped out of the building and strutted over to her.

"Miranda Brigand! What a delight and a pleasure and a surprise to find you here," he cheerfully declared. To the other listeners he said, "Miranda is an old fighter. We go back a long way, together. I had no idea she was interested in joining the Guardians."

"I'm not," Miranda asserted.

"Well then, are you here to–oh I don't know–escort me back to my castle up north?" Heathcliff asked. "Alas, it's not nearly warm enough for barbecue parties in the back yard anymore. I'm happy to stay in Fellwater town."

Miranda said, "Let's talk somewhere private."

"Step into my office. Right this way," he invited, and he entered the Guardians Hall. When he thought Miranda might not be looking, he told a nearby Guardian auxiliary to "Stay close."

Inside the Guardians Hall, Heathcliff led Miranda to one of the old church pews that now ran along the sides of the room, and invited her to sit with him. But she remained standing.

"Okay, Heathcliff," she started. "I just had a visit from the police, who seemed to think four of my people are responsible for bombing a school and a hockey rink."

"Well, are they?" asked Heathcliff.

Miranda angrily slammed her fist on one of the pillars that held up the choir loft. The force of her blow shattered most of the light fixtures in the hall. An artist across the room, who had been painting a still-life, shrieked with surprise and ran away.

"Don't feign ignorance to me, Weatherby!" she threatened.

Heathcliff was genuinely startled by Miranda's burst of anger. He settled himself, then said, "There was an incursion of dire-creatures last night. They broke into the arena, on the west side of town. Your people interfered with our clean-up team."

"So you're punishing them?"

"Me, personally? No, not me," Heathcliff smiled.

Miranda leaned closer to Carlo and growled, "We have laws about interfering in the outside world. The Parliament of 1066. The Great Peace of 1820."

"I know all of those old laws, the same as you do," Heathcliff yawned.

"Then what the hell are you doing, with the police in your pocket?"

"You want the big picture? We're doing what we have to do, to survive," Heathcliff hissed.

Miranda smirked. "I know the chthonic prisons are weakening. But even if they all broke open, all at once, they are no threat to us. We beat them down once before, we can do it again."

Heathcliff shook his head disdainfully. "There's another animal in this world, more dangerous to our kind than all the things that our ancestors locked underground, all those centuries ago."

"Let's hear it then," Miranda prompted him. "What are you afraid of?"

Heathcliff leaned forward and said, "Mankind."

"Oh, don't be ridiculous," Miranda chortled.

"I'm being very serious," Heathcliff exclaimed. "I know that the Mythic Age has been over for thousands of years. But the Age of Man that's coming: it's going to be hell. Have you actually had an honest look at what humanity is really like? They've invented a hundred ways to kill each other for every one way to *talk* to each other. They've created a thousand ways to make money but *not even one* way to eliminate poverty. And the thing they love to do most of all is hurt each other and put each other down. Did you know that there are forty-five countries in this world that are war zones right now? Forty-five! Sure, there are lots of animals that hunt and fight and kill, but only one animal that has learned to hate. That animal is Mankind. We can't let that animal destroy our world."

"Is that all you can see in humanity? Humans are also the only animals that can do heart transplants, you know. Or put satellites in orbit around Mars. What about people who adopt orphans? What about—"

"Oh, some of them talk a good talk about loving your neighbour, following your dreams, and all that," Heathcliff interrupted. "But those ones spend most of their time worshipping movie stars and visualizing inner peace. You don't see them doing anything that would actually cause real practical changes. They think all you have to do to change the world is wish upon a star! So the festival of cruelty goes on. Now as far as I'm concerned, the people of the world are welcome to kill each other by the truckload, if that's what they really want. I don't care. But they're not taking me down with them. I'm going to survive."

Miranda shook her head. "That's what your New Renaissance is all about?"

"Let's just say humanity's free-range days are almost over. And it's for their own good."

Miranda stared at him for a moment before answering. "You're wrong, Heathcliff. There are good people in the world. Billions of them. And you cannot enslave them like that – I won't allow it! I will expose you. Then I will–"

Heathcliff interrupted her with a laugh. "No, you won't. That's the beauty of this deal you made with El Duce. You retire as chieftain of the Brigantians. You don't interfere with anything we're doing. You don't even tell anyone about our deal. And you don't set foot in Fellwater Grove ever again. In return, Fellwater Grove remains in Brigantian hands. Safe. Untouched. Protected. Well, protected from us, anyway. I can't speak for anyone else."

Miranda opened her mouth to speak, but no words emerged.

Heathcliff stood and brushed the dust from his tail coat. "By the way, it's too bad that your little friend Eric isn't part of the tribe anymore."

"What are you implying, Weatherby?"

"Isn't it obvious? If he's not part of your tribe, then who is protecting him?"

~ 38 ~

Eric spent the night locked in a holding cell, in the basement of a house near Domus Eleutherios. Narrow, windowless, and cold, still it had a bed and a toilet and sink, unlike his accommodations the night before. The following morning, he was handcuffed again, and taken back to the temple where the archon from El Duce was holding court. More people filled the balconies and galleries this time, and by their aristocratic costumes Eric surmised that nearly all of them were members of

House DiAngelo or their allies. Eric's arrival caused a quiet stir among them, and he could hear them murmur to each other about who they thought he was, or what they thought he had done. His vain struggles against his bonds seemed entertaining to them: one woman actually pointed and laughed.

The three judges stood on a platform before the statue of the god, with wry smiles frozen on their faces by their golden masks. The head judge stood and addressed Eric in a rumbling, foghorn voice.

Eric Laflamme, you are accused of the murder of Emma DiAngelo, the arson attack upon number 4 Julian Court, a DiAngelo property in the village of Fellwater, and the poisoning of Livia Julia McManus. In accord with the New Twelve Tables of the Law, if you are found guilty of these charges then you shall have done to you what you did to your victims: you shall be compelled to take poison, and then you shall be put into a fire, and burned until you are dead. Do you understand these accusations?

The gag around Eric's mouth unravelled enough to let him reply. "I understand you, but I plead innocence because–" but he could not finish speaking, as the gag muzzled him again.

Who shall speak on behalf of the plaintiff?

"Your honour, I shall speak for Carlo!" boomed a voice from the gallery. Heathcliff Weatherby Wednesday moved to Carlo's side. Dressed in the black top hat and red tailcoat of a circus ringmaster, and with three fresh daisies pinned to his breast, he doffed his hat to the three judges, and to Eric as well, although with a smirk on his face.

Who shall speak on behalf of the defendant?

The spectators murmured among themselves and looked around the room, to see if anyone would step forward. When no one did, they laughed.

"No one wants to take the side of a Dangerous Offender," Carlo remarked to Heathcliff.

"Besides, everyone knows he's guilty," Heathcliff chuckled.

Eric didn't know any of the rules of this court, and he was certain he wouldn't get a fair trial. But he thought that even if he lost, at least he would make himself heard. So he squirmed out of the muzzle and blurted: "I will speak on my own behalf!"

"This is your trial! You can't speak for yourself at your own trial," Heathcliff admonished. Then to the judges he said,

"Sirs, although no one has come forward to advocate for the defense, nevertheless the show must go on. Justice must be served."

The judges appeared to agree with Heathcliff.

Let the representative of the plaintiff come forward and state his case.

Heathcliff bowed to the judges, and then turned and addressed the audience watching from the galleries. "Eric Laflamme, outsider, is guilty of all charges. He had opportunity, he had motive, and most of all, he has a guilty mind. But to tell this story I must start at the beginning. Some years ago, House DiAngelo began recruiting outsiders a little more vigorously than they normally do. And one of the first people they found was the late Caitlin Corrigan, descendent of the goddess Morrigan of Ireland, last of the House Corrigan, and possessor of an untrained yet promising talent in clairvoyance. A perfect asset to the Guardians, and Carlo wished to train her to serve as the public face of the organization. But two individuals stood in the way. One was chieftain Cartimandua, of the Brigantians of Fellwater, who belligerently claimed Katie for her own house. The other obstacle was the accused who stands here before you, whose ancestors were people of no special importance. But he loved her, and he was good to her, so Ms. Corrigan chose to side with him. That fateful decision eventually cost her the custody of her child, Tara Corrigan. When she and Eric forcefully abducted Tara from her rightful legal guardians, namely my lord Carlo DiAngelo and his mother Emma DiAngelo, Eric started a fire which eventually destroyed the building."

Eric struggled against his chains and tried to shout out, but all he could do was rattle his chains and bite on his muzzle.

"In the ensuing chase to recover the stolen child, young Tara Corrigan met an unfortunate and unlucky death, at the hand of a Brigantian warrior."

Eric struggled again, since he witnessed Tara's death and he knew that Heathcliff spoke a lie. But the scarf around his mouth only gagged him tighter. Some of the observers in the gallery giggled among themselves at the sight of his struggling.

"Eric has always blamed the plaintiff personally, and the members of his house, for the death of that child. And he blames the plaintiff for the death of Ms. Corrigan herself a few days later, when she threw herself from the cliffs of the gorge, over the Grand river."

The noise Eric made by struggling against his chains began to annoy the judges. One of them made a conjurer's gesture, which summoned more chains to burst from the floor and hold Eric down tighter.

"That is the basic story. Now, to prove that my allegations are true," Heathcliff declared, "I have obtained an artifact from clan DeDannan, generously donated to us by their guard captain and my good friend, Amergin DeDannan. It will objectively measure the truth or the falsehood of any statement made by anyone here in this room today, by breaking into fragments in response to a falsehood, and mending itself if the liar comes clean with the truth. Honourable judges, and gentlemen and ladies, I give you the Cup of Cormac the King."

Paul Turner stepped forward, holding an ornately painted wooden box. Heathcliff took it and placed it on a table before the judges, opened it, and revealed a spherical glass case on a little wooden stand. The case contained a decorated wooden cup, which reminded Eric of the one that Livia brought with her to the mead hall. Although Eric could not be sure, as he was not close enough to see its details, he thought the knotwork animals on its face were poised in postures of alarm and warning. The audience in the galleries hushed themselves in its presence; some wondered at the cup like a treasure hunter, and some smiled like proud thieves.

"This artifact," Heathcliff explained, "was once used by the high kings of Ireland, many centuries ago, when they heard criminal cases. A most fitting instrument for a servant of justice, like a king. And may I say personally, I enjoy the irony of using a treasure of the Celtic tribes to convict this young man, who was, well, until recently, an ally of those same Celtic tribes. But we all set in motion the wheels of our own undoing."

Light laughter rose from the observers in the galleries above. Eric gazed upon the decorated cup, finding it familiar. It might have been the same as the one given to his safe keeping while he served as Miranda's arbiter of succession. But he was also worried that the cup might be ruse. Lie detectors, even magical ones, could be rigged to serve the interests of power instead of truth.

"Honourable judges, will you accept this treasure of the mythic age as a means to measure the guilt or innocence of the accused?"

The three judges conferred among themselves for a

Clan Fianna

moment, and then the lead judge leaned forward.

We shall. Please proceed.

"Now, Eric, tell these fine gentlemen," Heathcliff grinned, confident of winning the case, "Isn't it true that on the night of the fire that destroyed the patrician's residence in the town of Fellwater, you were on the scene."

"Yes," Eric answered.

"Why were you there?"

"Katie and I had gone there to get our daughter back."

The cup vibrated again, and cracked in half. A small gasp rose from the audience, and even the judges leaned forward to see what had happened.

"Ladies and gentlemen," Heathcliff confidently announced, "the falsehood that the cup has detected here, is Eric's claim that he is the father of Katie's child. But he is not the father. Not biologically, and not legally. In fact he and Katie had just lost legal custody of the child. Isn't that true, Eric?"

Reluctantly, Eric answered "yes."

The cup of truth mended itself again.

"Now, let me rephrase my question," Heathcliff continued. "Isn't it true that you were at the house that night, to help Katie remove the child from her lawful guardians?"

With a downcast face, Eric confirmed "Yes."

"Isn't it true that you were inside the house when the fire began?"

"Yes."

"In fact, isn't it true that you were in the very room where the fire was ignited, at the very moment the fire was ignited?"

"I was, yes."

"Now, isn't it true that you have a grudge against the plaintiff."

"What?"

"It's a simple question, Eric. The courts granted custody of Tara Corrigan to him, instead of to you. And you have always resented that, haven't you?"

"Well I wasn't thrilled about it, that's for sure."

"That's why you were in the house that night. To get Tara back. Isn't it?"

Eric eyed the cup with worry before answering, "Yes."

The cup remained unmoved. Heathcliff smiled. Then he stood tall above Eric and said, "That wasn't enough. You also wanted to punish him for taking Tara away from you in the first place. Isn't that why you started the fire?"

"I didn't start the fire!" Eric protested.

The cup in the glass case broke into another fragment again.

"What the hell!" Eric exclaimed.

Heathcliff's smile grew wider, and he even clapped his hands. "I think that says all that needs to be said about the charges of arson and murder."

"I didn't do it!" Eric howled, and the cup lost another fragment again. The audience in the galleries above laughed at him.

"Now, concerning the poisoning of Livia Julia McManus," continued Heathcliff, ignoring Eric's protestations.

Eric was still flustered by the previous line of questions. "Wait! I just told you the truth!" he shouted.

"Apparently you did not," Heathcliff chuckled, and with his words the cup mended itself again, and lay on its side. And the audience laughed louder.

"This is a setup," Eric mumbled to himself. And the cup broke again, causing the audience to laugh again.

Heathcliff ignored it, and continued with his questions. "On the night that Livia was poisoned, isn't it true that the two of you were talking intimately with each other for a while? Come now, don't just sit there. Silence will not save you. Answer the question. Were you and Livia talking intimately with each other?"

"Yes," Eric barked.

"You were talking about the night of the fire at the DiAngelo mansion, weren't you?"

"How did you know that?" Eric countered.

"Just answer the question!" Heathcliff demanded.

"Yes, we were," Eric admitted.

"Isn't it true that the last drink she had that night was from your cup?"

"She actually took the cup from me!" Eric told him.

"We don't need your editorial interpretation here. All we need is a yes or a no."

"Fine. Yes," Eric growled.

"Isn't it true that since you were named a full member of clan Brigantia that afternoon, you had access to everything in Fellwater grove? Including the kitchen, and the healing house,

Clan Fianna

where the herbs and potion ingredients were kept?"

"Probably, I don't know," Eric answered. "I was a full member of the clan for less than twenty–four hours."

"Isn't it true that the following morning, you correctly identified the poison as a concentrated dose of witch's flying ointment, mixed with somnaweiss oil?"

"That doesn't prove anything!" Eric countered.

Heathcliff continued. "And isn't it true that the cup with the wine tainted with flying ointment was found to have your fingerprints on it!"

"I wasn't drinking wine at the end of the night," Eric asserted desperately. "I was beginning to feel a little drunk, so I switch to drinking coffee."

The cup of truth broke into two pieces again. Another round of light laughter rose from the galleries. Eric flustered and pulled on his chains.

"Served to me by Ciara DeDannan, the lady of–" but Eric stopped, as he began to think that whatever he said would be useless, or even turned against him. He looked around the audience, desperate for help.

In one of the galleries, he saw a woman in leather armour and a blue-and-green tartan cloak, and a hood shadowing her face. Unlike the rest of the audience, she was not pointing and laughing at him, nor gossiping with her neighbours. She was only observing, silent and still. Her voice whispered to Eric from across the room, so that only he could hear it: *find the cup that no poisoner will touch*.

At first Eric was confused, and a little bit scared. Then he looked at the cup, in its glass case, and knew what to do. He raised himself as tall as he could and addressed the archon judges.

"On a point of order! Honourable judges, I'd like to call for a point of order!"

"Objection!" Heathcliff sneered. "The accused has been declared a Dangerous Offender, to be presumed guilty unless proven innocent. He has no right to declare a point of order! He has no rights at all!" Heathcliff wanted to make more angry declarations, but the head judge was looking at the Bann-Shee, who folded her arms and stared back.

The judge then turned to Eric and said, *We shall hear your point of order*.

Some of Eric's bonds loosened, to let him stand and

speak.

"Thank you," said Eric. Then he looked to the Cup of Cormac, and took a breath to give himself time to gather his courage. "My point of order is this. How do we know that this chalice really is the Cup of Cormac? It might be a fake."

The audience members murmured among themselves, trying to guess where Eric was going with this. Carlo smirked and shook his head, and Heathcliff rolled his eyes. Eric saw this, and felt emboldened.

"I say we take the chalice out of that glass case, and put it to a test."

"Objection!" said Heathcliff. "The case is there to protect the artifact, and to ensure its broken pieces don't go missing! This will only waste everyone's time!"

"Interesting that you didn't object to testing it. Only to removing the case. Perhaps it really is the Cup of Cormac, but the case is interfering with its function?"

"What possible reason could you have to think that?"

Eric had to think fast. "For one thing, the people who made it would not have kept it in a case like that. The Celts didn't have glass-making technology. The Romans did."

Again, murmurs and troubled voices rose from the audience. Heathcliff continued repeated the word "Objection, objection!" as if that was all he had to do to get Eric to stop talking. The judges, their eyes still on the Bann-Shee, silenced him by standing up and delivering their decision.

Remove the case.

Heathcliff looked up to the judges, and the head judge bowed his head, indicating that he wanted Heathcliff to comply with Eric's request. Reluctantly, and slowly, and resentfully, Heathcliff removed the glass case that contains the cup. In the unfiltered light of the temple, the lines and figures carved on the cup might seem to move by themselves.

Eric faced the cup and uttered the sentence which he hoped would save his life: "The cup which Livia Julia McManus drank from on that night contained coffee, and not wine."

With these words, the Cup of Truth mended itself completely. The audience in the galleries exclaimed their surprise. Carlo clenched his jaw to contain himself. Eric smiled, and almost laughed. He looked up to the woman in the long hood, but she was gone. Eric was on his own again. But he was no longer afraid.

Clan Fianna

"I think my point of order has been made, now," Eric concluded.

Heathcliff Weatherby, you may continue.

Heathcliff gave Carlo a worried look, and Carlo responded by shaking his head and looking away. So Heathcliff moved to the centre of the floor, closed his eyes for a moment to compose himself, and then asked Eric, "Did you set the fire that destroyed the DiAngelo residence and killed Emma DiAngelo?"

Eric uttered the simple word "no."

All eyes in the room turned to the cup which, as all could see, did not move.

"You're saying you did not start the fire?"

"That's right. Katie started it, actually."

Heathcliff looked back at the cup again, expecting it to break, but it remained intact and whole. Those in the gallery who once marveled at the cup now marveled at Carlo and Heathcliff, whose credibility was swiftly disappearing

"You must have been the one who poisoned Livia Julia McManus. You poisoned her, didn't you? It had to have been you. No one else could have done it!"

"I couldn't have done it, because–"

Heathcliff didn't let Eric finish. In the loudest voice he could raise short of obviously shouting, he addressed the judges: "Honorable judges, we know that the Cup of Cormac has been tampered with. Eric himself proved that. I therefore request that you disregard all the testimony we heard today, and adjourn until we can properly analyze and correct the truth-telling properties of this artifact."

The three judges conferred with each other, and then stood up, which everyone took as a sign that they should be silent.

All shall rise and hear the judgment of this tribunal.

Everyone rose.

Eric Laflamme, on hearing the case against you, and seeing how you fared when your words were measured by the objective test of the Cup of Cormac, we find the case against you is Not Proven.

A wave of surprised murmurs rose from the observers in the gallery. Carlo only stared at the cup, still intact and whole on the table where he placed it.

As of this moment, therefore, we release you from the custody of the House DiAngelo.

The chains restraining Eric immediately fell away, and scattered on the floor, with every link twisted and broken.

We have spoken. Justice has been done. This tribunal is adjourned.

With those final words, the three judges walked away. The observers in the galleries also began departing in twos and threes, gossiping and whispering among themselves as they went.

Eric massaged his wrists and neck, glad to be free of the manacles and chains. Carlo was looking at the platform where the three judges had been. He sniffed disdainfully at it, then took the cup and roughly shut it back in its glass case.

"I told you I was innocent," Eric offered.

Carlo glowered at Eric from under his dark brow for a moment, and then spun around and marched toward the exit, under a black cloud. To Paul, who was waiting nearby, he growled "Bring my car."

"Sir, your own policy forbids cars in the–"

"My car!" Carlo barked at him, and he slammed the door behind him as he left. Paul put the glass case over the chalice again, and packed it under his arm and followed Carlo.

"We all set in motion the wheels of our own undoing," Eric reminded Heathcliff. Heathcliff swallowed the angry retort that was forming in his throat, and stomped out of the temple.

Eric breathed deeply and let his shoulders rest. He was no longer a prisoner, and his enemy had been shamed and forced to retreat. The temple was now empty of people, and his footsteps echoed as if he stood in a cavern.

"So this is what it feels like to win," he said, and his voice reflected back to him in the empty space. The only ears that could hear him were the lifeless stone ears of the statues. He moved to the nearest statue and looked into its face, and imagined for a moment that it might acknowledge his presence. It stood in its cold pose, unblinking, and unmoving.

"Well, I suppose I should go," he said.

As Eric headed out of the temple, he passed a half-open side door that apparently led to a private function room. From down the corridor, Eric could hear Heathcliff vigorously arguing with someone.

"I don't care what Kendrick McManus said," Heathcliff's voice growled. "I am a scion of the oldest Hidden House in England. A descendent of the All-Father, Odin himself!

Clan Fianna

And I am not going to answer his preposterous accusations!"

Eric did not hear the rest of the argument very clearly. It seemed the DiAngelo ambassador had also accused Heathcliff of something, although Eric could not determine what it was. But when he heard Heathcliff mention his own name, and then heard another voice say, "We will handle him for you," Eric decided to leave.

~ 39 ~

In the stone circle of the Brigantian Grove, under a rolling overcast sky, Donall and Ciara and Neachtain stood by one side of the negotiating table, and Kendrick McManus stood by the other. Behind him, a few members of his honour guard, armed with their rifles, leaned casually on one of the LAVs. Fruit and tea and coffee was laid out on the table as before, but no one was touching any of it.

"Well, here we are again," Kendrick sighed. "Now are we going to talk about anything, or are we all going to stand here until one of us dies of boredom?"

Ciara began by asking, "We were wondering about the condition of your wife."

"She is stable, although she grows weaker every day," Kendrick stated tersely.

"We've a gift for her," Neachtain told him, and he placed a bottle of water on the table. "This is water from the spring at Rath Manannan, the freehold of the DeDannans of West Galway. It's been known to heal wounds and diseases. It might help with poisons, too. You never know."

At first, Kendrick was annoyed. "Are you trying to say we can't provide for her medical care on our own?"

This was not the response the Brigantians were hoping for, so Neachtain said, "We're trying to say, we want her to recover, and we'd like to help."

"I see it's done a load of good for your injury, Donall," Kendrick observed sarcastically.

"We didn't request it for my sake," Donall answered. "We requested it for your wife. So I didn't touch it."

Kendrick thought about it for a moment, and then closed the case and handed it to one of his guards. "Very selfless of you. I accept your gift."

Donall let out an unnecessarily audible sigh of relief.

Ciara looked at him and smiled. Donall understood what she was silently telling him: her way of negotiating was better than his.

"It may interest you to know, by the way," Kendrick added, "that the interfering wastrel who poisoned her in the first place was put on trial today, in the temple in Domus Eleutherios. It should be finished now, and I'm sure we'll hear about the verdict soon."

Donall acknowledged this news with a nod. "For a man whose wife might be dying, you seem remarkably calm."

"Yes, well," Kendrick mumbled. "What can I do, but surrender myself to Clotho, like a good Stoic."

"Shall we have a seat?" offered Ciara.

Kendrick agreed, and everyone sat down, although Donall and Kendrick eyed each other as they sat, both of them anxious not to crouch lower than the other. But Donall sat first, as his injury made him unable to sustain the little game, and Kendrick smiled.

"We'd like to start with some questions," Donall began, when he was comfortable. "We would like to know why you ordered the killing of three terrabiters who were posing no threat to anyone."

"The mere fact that they were inside the village itself constitutes a threat," Kendrick replied.

"Five people were still in the building, and they all died," Donall reminded him.

"Collateral damage. Unfortunate, but unavoidable," was Kendrick's casual reply.

Donall wanted to argue the point with him, but Ciara gently clenched his hand to restrain him, so he let it pass.

"We would also like to know," Donall asked next, when he had calmed down, "why several members of my house are wanted by the police." He produced from his pocket a police press release with the photo of Aeducan, Maread, Síle, and Finnbarr. "We found this on the OPP web site," he explained.

Kendrick thought quietly for a moment. "It says here that they're wanted as 'persons of interest', not as suspects for a crime. I'm not responsible for this, but I suppose I can find out who is. As a way of showing gratitude for the gift you offered my wife."

This time Donall looked at Ciara, and smiled.

"There, you see?" said Kendrick, as helped himself to some orange slices. "These meetings don't have to be so hostile

Clan Fianna

after all."

Donall and Ciara looked at each other; Donall with resignation, and Ciara with hope. Then Ciara asked Kendrick, "Have you any questions for us?"

"Yes, I do," said Kendrick, as he poured himself a cup of tea. "How would you like to re-negotiate the peace treaty between you and the DiAngelo?"

Donall and Ciara did not expect that at all. Ciara stared, wide-eyed and slack-jawed, at Kendrick; and Donall stared at Ciara, hoping for a sign to show him how best to react. Neachtain sputtered his tea and dropped his cup.

"Look, we all know that the treaty isn't working," Kendrick stated. "You have even sent away some of your best people to prevent conflict with us. That captain of yours, although he can be prudent, also has a very short fuse. One of these days it will burn out, and everything will explode. What if there was a way to have peace between us, that was based on respect instead of fear? Wouldn't that be preferable to things as they are now?"

"I'm listening," Donall stated, although he was still skeptical.

"Or, what if we amended the treaty to say that the armed forces of any of the Hidden Houses, yours or mine, must come under the authority of the chieftain of the freehold in which they are stationed. That would mean that my infantrymen, and both of my LAVs, would be yours. Yours to command. Just think about it."

This proposition aroused Donall's interest. Under the table, Ciara put her hand on his lap, to try and remind him not to get too excited. He brushed her off.

"Also," Kendrick continued. "Our treaty currently says that you have to deliver one hundred firkins of water from your magic well to the DiAngelo, every seven years, as a condition of continued peace. What if we got rid of that clause altogether? So that you wouldn't owe us anything? It's clearly an extortion threat anyway."

Ciara was intrigued, but said nothing.

"You might want access to some of our resources," Kendrick continued on. "As you may know, the New Renaissance, through its public front organization, The Guardians, is able to wield some considerable influence over key players in the outside world. The government, for instance. The media. The police. A few big businesses, too. What if we offered you access to that network of influence? Imagine whispering a few words into the ears of a corporate executive, and two weeks later finding yourselves the proud owners of a newly privatized Grand River Conservation Park. Your territory could increase from two hundred acres to, oh, I think around nine square kilometers. You could even keep part of it open to the public, and run it as a business."

"You're really willing to put that on the table?" Ciara marveled.

"I'm putting it on the table!" Kendrick smiled, and he slapped the table. "And that's not all. You've got some fine musicians in your clan. I've seen them perform at the local summer festival. We could arrange recording contracts for them, with the big labels. Get them on the radio, and on TV. Get them performing in a stadium, before an audience of fifty thousand. Our network has contacts in almost every important sector of this country's economy. You would be able to get almost anything you want, for yourself and for your whole clan. Just think about it."

Donall smiled. Ciara was still skeptical. "I presume you would want something in return for all of that?" she asked.

"We would like to make my embassy a permanent mission," Kendrick informed her. The Brigantians bristled a little at the proposition, but they let Kendrick continue speaking. "I hope you agree that my occupation of a small corner of your two hundred acres is preferable to the DiAngelo constantly threatening you with destruction. By the gods, I just can't imagine the constant psychological stress you people must be under, all the time!"

The fact that Kendrick was a major part of that stress was not lost on Donall. He gritted his teeth and glanced to his companions, looking for a sign that they knew what he was feeling.

"Anything else," he growled.

"Well, there is one other thing, actually," Kendrick told them, and then he nonchalantly sipped his tea.

When Donall could not wait any longer, he said, "Well, go on, what do you want?"

"You know, this really is delicious tea," Kendrick ruminated. "I suppose I have not been grateful enough for your hospitality."

"Well," Donall offered, without enthusiasm, "we can certainly give you the recipe."

"We are all good Celtic warriors here," Kendrick sang, as he finished his tea. "I'd much rather be drinking mead around a fire, same as you. I've been working as a diplomat for El Duce for a few years now, but it's not the same as doing battle with the Fomorians by day, and feasting like heroes by night. That's a proper life for a warrior."

"If what you say is true about the weakening of the chthonic prisons," Donall trifled, "then we may have many days like that to come."

"So, if I understand you right," Ciara cautiously stated, "you're saying what you want in return for all those things you offered, is to join our war band."

"Oh, no, no, those things are just what I want for myself!" Kendrick corrected her. "My superiors want something else. I just hoped you would let me have a few personal perks on the side."

Ciara sighed. "Just tell us what El Duce wants."

Kendrick took another sip from his teacup, and then leaned forward and said, "What my lord El Duce wants is for you to swear an oath of allegiance to him."

All three of the Celts immediately jumped to their feet, although Donall winced in pain to do it. "You want me to hand over the sovereignty of my freehold to you!" he hollered.

"Don't think of it that way," Kendrick soothed. "Think of it more like a strategic alliance."

The three Brigantians began shouting all at once. "You can put any fancy name on it that you want, and you are still asking for our submission!" argued Donall. Neachtain, who had remained quiet so far, crushed his teacup in his hand and shouted "You want us to give up our land? Our children are born here! Our ancestors are buried here!" Ciara hollered something in her native Irish which few others could understand.

"You will remain chieftain of the Brigantians, of course," Kendrick reassured Donall, with a voice that rose above the din. "You will swear your fealty to El Duce, and in return El Duce will grant you authority to rule your clan in his name. Nothing would change, really. I will serve as merely the representative of His Lordship, and offer advice and analysis from time to time."

"You mean you would tell us what to do, in our own

house!" Donall protested.

"I mean I would offer advice and analysis," Kendrick corrected him. "You would be free to disregard it, if you wished, of course. But the consequences of ignoring my lord's wise council would be– well, depending on how important it was, it could be anything. But it would certainly include the immediate withdrawal of all the benefits of membership in the New Renaissance."

"Benefits like peace," Neachtain insinuated.

Kendrick smiled, but said nothing. His guards chuckled among themselves, and one of them patted the hull of the LAV that he was leaning on.

"This is exactly the same deal that the English forced on the Irish five centuries ago, and it didn't work then, and it won't work now!" Ciara protested. "And none of our people will accept it."

"They don't have to," Kendrick countered. "It's not their decision to make." Then he pointed to Donall. "It's his."

Donall's gaze glanced back and forth between Ciara and Kendrick, hesitantly.

"Just think about it," Kendrick crooned, before Donall could say anything. "You could have command of my army. You could get very, very rich. You could influence the law. In fact you could have that arrest record of yours entirely wiped clean away, gone forever. Just think– you could visit your native Belfast again."

"You've read my rap sheet!" Donall accused, as his hands clenched and unclenched and clenched again into fists.

Kendrick turned his attention to Ciara. "As for you, my fine lady, remember how you were forced to sell your house, when you lost your job? You could buy it back again. You could transform the attic into an art studio. You could build a labyrinth garden in the back yard, just like you always wanted. You could see your paintings hanging in the National Gallery, in Ottawa."

"How did you know I sold my house?" Ciara demanded.

Kendrick ignored her and turned to Neachtain next. "And you, good sir, you never wanted to study nursing, right? If I'm not mistaken, you originally wanted to study astronomy. But someone convinced you that you'd never get a job with that. What if you had a chance to study anything you wanted, at any university in the country? Or in the world? Oxford. Cambridge.

Clan Fianna

The Sorbonne. Just imagine, looking through the best telescopes, and discovering planets orbiting faraway stars that no one has ever seen before."

"I'm perfectly fine as the healer for the Brigantians," Neachtain asserted, although his voice was quiet and low.

"How do you know all these things about us?" Donall demanded to know.

Kendrick shrugged Donall's question away. "Almost everyone in the Hidden World has a special talent or two," he said. "My talent helps me get into people's heads."

Donall and Ciara leaned back defensively.

"Don't worry, I can't read your minds," Kendrick reassured them. He laughed. "Well, actually, I can. But still, don't worry. Most of your thoughts are not very interesting."

Donall clenched his fists under the table and gritted his teeth. Ciara took his hand and squeezed it, partly to remind Donall not to get angry, but also to quell her own growing annoyance.

"This talent of mine has served me well, in the diplomatic corps," Kendrick ruminated casually, ignoring their reaction to his words. "But you know, I wasn't always a negotiator. I grew up in a not-very-nice part of Scarborough. College was a joke so I didn't bother with it. I joined a gang, I sold drugs, I stole cars. I made a lot of money. Then I joined the Guardians. I found them by stealing one of their cars. They took me to the Brigantian freehold near Sunderland, back in England, where I had my Awakening. I served as their summoner for a while. Now I work in the New Renaissance diplomatic corps. I make even more money now than I did as a car thief. I get to travel the world. I married a very sexy bird. If El Duce can do that much for me, he can do all that and more for you."

Both Ciara and Donall sat back in their chairs, staring at Kendrick.

Kendrick wiped his mouth on a napkin, and stood up to leave. "Don't make your decision today. Think about it for a while. Talk about it with your people. Oh, and Donall, I'll leave one of my rides here for you, in case you want to borrow it for a test drive."

With that last comment thrown over his shoulder, Kendrick tossed Donall the keys to the LAV, and then he and his entourage hiked back to their camp.

~ 40 ~

In the square outside the temple of Domus Eleutherios, Eric stepped out and faced the sun. A cluster of people stood nearby, most of whom, as Eric recognized, had been in the audience during his trial. He spread his arms wide and twirled around in a circle, partly to savour his freedom, but also to rub that freedom in the noses of everyone who doubted him. Some of them made quiet cussing sounds and turned their faces away. Some rolled their eyes, and some chortled like annoyed aristocrats. Others tipped their hats in a respectful salute, acknowledging Eric's unexpected victory. To these, Eric smiled and saluted, but he did not linger. Seeing what looked like familiar buildings in the distance, and a gravel path that looked like it was heading toward those buildings, he started walking away.

Once out of the square and into a wooded area on a riverside, Eric recognized that he was actually near the middle of the city of Royal Wyndham. The tall buildings in the distance were familiar apartment towers and church steeples, and across the river he recognized a century-old residential area. Domus Eleutherios, he surmised, occupied a plot of land on the south bank of the Swift River, between a golf course and the university arboretum. He wondered if anyone ever wandered into Domus Eleutherios by accident, but then remembered that the Celtic Mist would quickly quell the memory of it.

The rustling of some branches just behind him caught his attention, and when he turned to look, he saw a man clad all in black, and with tiger's head, crashing through the trees toward him. He held claw-like metal blades between the fingers on his closed fist, and plates of metal armour on his shoulders and arms. Eric recognized him as probably one of the same men he saw fleeing from Miranda's house. When he tried to back away, he bumped into a second tiger-headed man, similarly prepared for a fight.

"Who are you people!" Eric shouted.

"We're your new personal trainers," one of them grinned. "Compliments of House DiAngelo."

Eric didn't need any other reason to start running. He pushed one of the rakshasas out of his way and dashed as fast as he could down the path toward what he hoped would be a more public place, where he might find help, or where the rakshasas might not follow him. There wasn't much room for him to dodge away. Old maples and oaks lined the path on both sides, and a riverbank lay to the right, while a steep tree-covered uphill slope lay to the left. The rakshasas chased after him, easily able to cover more ground by leaping through the air than Eric could cover by running. They landed in front of him again, and Eric instinctively howled with surprise. Then he ducked off the path, hoping that they would not leap after him in a space more thick with trees. This, too, was futile: there were at least three, possibly four, rakshasas chasing him now. They pounced ahead at ground level, deftly dodging the thicker trees and crashing right through the saplings. Eric desperately picked up a stone and threw it at one of them, but his target deflected it with his hands easily, and growled at him.

Eric picked up a thick fallen tree branch to defend himself, and raised it over his head just in time to block a strike from one of the rakshasas. He tried to strike back, but the creature deftly dodged and blocked his every swing. In a powerful counter-attack the creature knocked the branch into the air and caught it in his own hands. He broke it in two pieces with his knee, and flung them away.

Eric started running again, this time toward the water, hoping that he might be able to find safety amid the nooks and corners of the residential area on the other side of the river. By the time he was up to his knees in the water, the rakshasas had both jumped in front of him, and he reflexively ducked away from the splashes they made.

Eric ran again, down the length of the river. He hoped that the water would slow his pursuers down. One dashed back to the shore and from there leapt ahead, blocking Eric's path yet again. The other caught up to Eric from behind and grabbed him by the back of his collar, and threw him into the water. Eric struggled to get away, fearful that they would hold him under the water and drown him. With both of his assailants standing over him, they threw him back into the water every time he stood up. Eric realized they were playing with him, but that realization made him no less frantic to get away. When one threw him down, he tried to grab at the arms of the other to take him down too. The first time it worked, however, they only got angry, and they slashed at him with their tiger claw blades. Then they threw him down into the water again, and held him there.

They might have drowned him but for a stone that bounced off one of their heads. Eric was able to reach the air again when the two rakshasas turned to see where the stone came from.

On the bank of the river stood the hooded woman he had seen in the temple, loading another stone into a sling–staff. The rakshasas hissed at her, and then one went to attack her while the other thrust Eric back into the water again. Eric grabbed his attacker's arms and tried to swing the creature into the water with him, using his weight to pull his attacker down. It didn't quite work as Eric hoped, but it created enough of a distraction to make the second rakshasa look to see what happened, only to receive a stone from the bann-shee's sling in his right eye.

Half-blinded with blood and tears, it leapt out of the water to attack the warrior, but she easily sidestepped him, and tripped him with her sling-staff just before he reached the ground, so that he landed on his head. He did not get up again. The rakshasa that stood over Eric did not see this, but continued wrestling with Eric. A stone from the sling-staff impacted the back of his head, caused him to lose his balance momentarily and fall. It was just enough to let Eric roll out of the way and run to the bank again. The fallen rakshasa in the river inhaled water and panicked: he stood up, unsteadily, and coughed and heaved to expel the water from his lungs.

The bann-shee grasped Eric's wrist and started running. Eric kept up her pace as best as he could, but eventually slowed and gasped for breath. The warrior looked back to see that they were not being followed, and then let Eric's wrist go.

"You did well today, Eric Laflamme," the bann-shee whispered.

Eric was still leaning on his knees, panting for breath. "You killed those people, didn't you!"

"Some of them," she replied.

Eric was afraid now. "Who are you!"

"A friend," she replied. "I'm here to help you get out of here." She removed a small leather pouch from her belt and handed it to him. "Take this. But don't open it unless you have to," she warned him.

"Why, what's inside?"

"The wind," she replied. Then she glanced back down the path and saw that the two rakshasas were running toward them, so she took a stand to intercept them.

"Why are you helping me?" Eric asked.

Clan Fianna

"Run, Eric!" she admonished him, and she loaded a stone into her sling-staff. Eric decided to do as he was told.

Although Eric thought he knew where he was, he had never explored this particular riverside path before. Unfamiliar with the terrain and its obstacles, he did his best to avoid rocks that could trip him, or branches that could lash his face. Risking a quick look over his shoulder, he saw that the bann-shee had just plunged the blunt end of her sling-staff into a rakshasa's neck, causing him to choke, and possibly killing him. One of them broke away from the melee to chase Eric again. He had a good head start, but he also knew they could outpace him easily. So he dashed ahead again. Coming to an area where the slope on his left was not so steep, he climbed up and entered the golf course. There he hoped that the rakshasas would not follow him.

As he sped across the green, much to the annoyance of several golfers, the rakshasas emerged from the trees and leapt into the air, aiming to catch him. Eric darted to one side, so that the rakshasas would not land directly in front of him. He bumped into a parked golf cart and apologized to its driver, and then pointed at the rakshasas and pleaded that he was under attack.

"Those are just a pair of stray cats. Are you on drugs, or something?" replied the golf cart driver.

Eric remembered that the Celtic Mist would cause people to misinterpret the sight of the rakshasa, and so the driver could be of no help. This was still the case even as one of them pounced ahead and landed on the canvas roof of the golf cart, ripping it in two.

"Wow. Really angry cats!" The driver marveled.

Eric was on the run again. Most of the golfers were watching him now, and a few were reaching for their cellphones. Whichever way Eric turned, one of his pursuers pounced ahead, at just the right angle to land exactly where Eric wanted to go. Finally Eric sped toward a part of the golf course where he thought the course bordered one of the city's main roads.

As he rounded a copse of trees, he found a chain link fence barring his way. The rakshasas were only a heartbeat behind him. Eric unravelled the knot that held the leather pouch closed, and pulled it open with his fingers. Immediately, a strong jet of air streamed from the pouch, and Eric almost dropped it, partly from the force of the wind, and partly from surprise.

All around him, a fierce whirlwind rose up, and shook

nearby tree branches and whipped the dust from the ground. He struggled for a moment to get a better grip on the pouch. Soon he found that he could control the strength of the wind by controlling how widely he held the pouch open. The two rakshasas hesitated briefly, as they evaluated Eric's move. Then they ran a few steps and leapt high into the air again, apparently hoping to vault over the top of Eric's whirlwind and catch him in the centre. His two hands holding tightly to the lip of the leather pouch, Eric pointed the whirlwind at them, and caught them in its grip. They spun around helplessly in a circle, rising high in the air, and then the wind flung them away in opposite directions, over the crowns of trees and the rooftops of nearby houses.

Once they were out of sight, Eric closed the pouch again, and the whirlwind subsided. The pebbles and pinecones and bits of rubbish fell to the earth, although a cloud of dust still remained in the air. Feeling out of danger for the moment, Eric examined the pouch more closely. It seemed ordinary enough, like something that one would find in any leather crafter's workshop, perhaps something made with a discarded scrap from another project. But he saw that near the lip of the pouch, someone had embossed a symbol he had never seen before. The symbol was only three lines: two were dark ovals like menacing eyes, and the third rounded over the eyes like a hood over a face.

~ 41 ~

Aeducan, Síle, and Finnbarr strode purposefully across the green from Aeducan's house to the chieftain's mead hall. As they walked, Síle said, "Maread looked really rough this morning."

"She got that headache during her shift on watch, last night," Aeducan explained. "Then she didn't sleep much."

"She'll be all right," said Finnbarr. "Let's find out what Donall wants."

Arriving at the great hall, they found two Wessex-men standing by the door as honour guards, dressed in doublets and breeches and starched ruffs around their necks. They saluted and lifted their pikestaffs out of the way so that the three Brigantians could enter. Before crossing the threshold, Aeducan paused.

"Now why has Donall got the Wessex-men standing guard here, instead of his own kin?" Aeducan wondered.

"Hey, I don't mind," said one of the Wessex cavalier

guards. "He's paying us well enough."

"He's paying you!" Aeducan marveled. "Where's he getting the money from?"

"The arboretum," the guard informed him. "He's selling the wood to a lumber yard."

Just as the guard finished speaking, the sound of a chain saw could be heard in the distance.

"He's selling the trees!" Síle sputtered, and then she roughly threw the blanket off the entrance to the great hall and stormed inside, followed by the other warriors.

Donall sat on his high seat, with one hand gripping a mead horn, and his other hand clutched on his sword pommel.

"Donall, have you lost your mind! Stop it! Right now!" Síle demanded. Aeducan and Finnbarr lined up beside her, with arms crossed.

"Stop what?"

"Cutting down the trees!"

"The grove needs money," Donall replied defensively.

"The grove is one of the last pieces of forest untouched by human hands since before Europeans came to this country," Síle fumed.

"We need money!" Donall insisted again. "That's what buys the coal for the blacksmith forge. And the grain for the bakery. And all the stuff we can't make here on our own. And now that it's the twenty–first bloody century, I'm getting these old houses wired up for electricity! So we need to make wise use of our resources."

"Wise use? Of our 'resources'? Some of those trees are Grandmother Trees. They have memories going back to the mythic age!" Síle raved.

Donall looked to Aeducan and Finnbarr for support, but found none.

"And you're chopping them down!" added Aeducan.

"It's not like I'm chopping them *all* down," Donall protested. "Just the mature maples and other hardwoods. Don't exaggerate."

"One tree cut down for no good reason is too many," Síle declared.

"Our grove is the most sacred place in the world for a great many people, including me," Aeducan summed up. "You can't just–I don't know–make decisions like that. Without telling anyone."

"Yes I can," Donall asserted, as he leaned on his sword to stand up. "I am the chieftain. I worked hard to become chieftain. And all of you voted for me. That makes it my responsibility to decide what's good for the clan. Not yours, not anyone else's."

Síle glared at Donall for a moment, and then marched out of the hall, tearing down the blanket over the door as she left.

Finnbarr shook his head, and followed her out.

Donall looked to Aeducan and said, "What's the matter with them?"

"What do you think!" Aeducan grunted. "I would follow them out myself, but I swore an oath of loyalty to you, as your captain."

Donall sat down again and put his face in his hands. "I had to do it, Aeducan," he sighed. "I knew the clan wouldn't like it, but it had to be done. Desperate times, and all that."

"Exactly who are you trying to convince?"

Donall looked at Aeducan, his brow furrowed. Then he changed the subject. "I called you here because I've an assignment for you," he said.

Before he could say what the assignment was, his attention was diverted by a commotion from outside. Donall leaned on his sword to stand, and hobbled to the door to hear what was happening. Aeducan, similarly diverted, reached for his sword, ready to unsheath it.

~ 42 ~

Eric bought a single can of beer from the LCBO, "for the fairies" as he said to the cashier, who laughed politely in return. Then with the beer hidden in his trench coat pocket, he caught a bus back to Fellwater, and its conservation park. He followed the old hidden trails and narrow paths that he had used since he was a child to avoid paying his admission ticket at the front gate.

At the clearing before the main entrance to the grove, Eric poured some of the beer on the stones, as that was the traditional way to ask the stones to roll back and reveal the gate. But when nothing happened, he started shouting for Donall, or Miranda, or just about anyone to open the way for him. He poured out the rest of the beer on the stones, and they remained still. The stones had rejected him, and he was still an outsider.

Clan Fianna

Eric threw his empty beer can aside in disgust, and trudged away. When he thought he was far enough away from the gate, and out of the sentry's field of view, he doubled back on his path, and followed the ridge along its base to a part which he thought might be easy to climb.

Although Eric had been climbing the stone cliffs of the gorge since he was a boy, climbing the ridge to Fellwater Grove was not easy for him. The stones of the ridge knew friend from enemy, and they resisted him. Handholds would crumble into pebbles under his fingers. Dust clouds would fall from upper ledges and sting his eyes and lungs. Footholds would suddenly break free, as if they were not strong enough to take his weight. And the higher he climbed, the more dangerous these obstacles became. First a wash of pebbles, then a flight of fist–sized rocks, and then boulders as big as his head or bigger, fell toward him. Several times, Eric had to jump aside or drop down to the forest floor again to avoid a collision that might have killed him.

He remembered the leather pouch that the bann-shee gave to him. Carefully, he untied the drawstring and opened a space no bigger than his finger. A light breeze then swirled around him, and it dissipated the dust thrown down by the ridge, and pushed around some of the smaller pebbles with it. Carefully, with the pouch in his hand, Eric ascended the ridge one more time, using the wind from the pouch to deflect the falling stones.

When he reached the top of the ridge, he was bruised, and one of his arms was bleeding from a cut, and his glasses had fallen off. But he was inside the grove.

The sentries on the ridge were waiting for him.

The sentries brought Eric to the mead hall, where Donall received him with his sword unsheathed.

"Donall, I'm here to warn you–"

"What the hell are you doing, Eric!"

"Those monster attacks!" Eric breathlessly reported. "They're not random!"

Aeducan and the cavalier sentry immediately grabbed Eric by both arms and held him back from the chieftain.

Donall stepped forward, pointing his sword at Eric's face. "You can't come back here, Eric! I already told you!"

"Listen to me!" Eric pleaded. "Those chthonic prisons– they're not weakening. Someone is opening them! Someone is deliberately letting everything out!"

Still holding Eric firmly, Aeducan looked to Donall and said, "Donall, if that's true–"

Donall unhappily sheathed his sword and said, "I hope you have proof of this."

"I saw it with my own eyes. I can show you the entrance to the tunnel. And there's going to be another attack tonight!"

Aeducan said, "The least we can do is send someone to check it out."

Donall sat back in his chair again and said, "There are two possibilities here. One is that Eric is telling the truth, in which case I'd have to accuse someone of conspiracy. And I don't want to do that. The other is that Eric is so desperate to get back in the clan that he'll say anything. And that seems to me much more likely."

"I'm telling the truth, Donall. I don't care if you kick me out again. It's still the truth!"

"Either way, you can't be here. The ambassador is holding the sword of Damocles over my head. And he'll let it fall if he sees you." Then he motioned to Aeducan to take him away.

As Aeducan dragged Eric toward the gate in the ridge that was furthest from the ambassador's camp, Eric pleaded with him. "I'm telling you, someone is setting all those monsters free! I've been there, I can show you!"

"Even if you're telling the truth, it doesn't mean you're innocent of Livia's poisoning," said Aeducan. "More important than that: how the hell did you get in here, anyway?"

"I climbed over the ridge. With the help of this thing."

Eric fumbled in his pocket for the leather pouch that the bann-shee had given him. Aeducan snatched it away.

"I'll have that," he said. But when he saw the symbol embossed upon it, his voice grew more stern. "This has the mark of the bann-shee. How did you get it?"

"The bann-shee?" Eric exclaimed.

Aeducan pushed it back into Eric's chest. "She'll kill you to get it back, so you can have it!"

The vines and branches of the gate twisted open, and the sentries shoved Eric down the passage leading out of the grove.

"Now go home, Eric," Aeducan told him with finality. "Don't ever come back here again!"

~ 43 ~

Síle and Finnbarr were not far away, and they saw Aeducan send Eric out of the grove. They joined Aeducan to watch the gate close.

"I hope, for all our sakes, that Eric is wrong," said Aeducan.

Síle had a faraway look on her face. "He has been to a dark place. And soon that darkness will find us," she whispered.

"Snap out of it, Síle," interrupted a voice from behind them. All turned to see Donall, hobbling toward them on his walking stick. "Eric's warning is a desperate attempt to get himself back in the clan. Nothing more. Ignore him. And besides, there's something else I want you to do. Something far more important."

"You want us to help chop the trees in the arboretum?" Finnbarr cheeked. Aeducan elbowed him in the ribs for it.

"It's about Ciara," said Donall, in a softer voice. "I don't know where she is. She left around mid-day to take her turn to patrol the ridge, like always. But then she disappeared. And with all the wilderlings that have broken out of the underworld lately– well, anything could have happened. I'd like you to find her."

The three warriors looked at each other and considered his request. Some widened their eyes with worry, some sighed with resignation. Then Aeducan took the lead. "Síle, check the arboretum. Finnbarr, the ridge, and the paths leading to the village. I'll talk to the sentries, see if anyone saw anything. Then I'll check the riverside. Meet at the stone circle in an hour if you don't find her."

The warriors dispersed.

"Please find her!" Donall called after them.

He turned away from the warriors, ashamed to let them see his feelings. He let his sword fall to the ground, and he grasped the barbed vines and iron branches of the gate, and squeezed them and shook them until his fingers turned white. He looked out, between the posts of the gate, down the path to the outside world, searching for any sign that Ciara might be coming back, although he knew there was no such sign to be seen. A nearby sentry on the ridge walked by without turning his head to look, and did not break stride as he passed.

~ 44 ~

Eric knocked on the door of Miranda's cottage. Although he remembered that she refused to help him the first time, he hoped that she would be more willing to help with a problem that affected everyone. When no one answered his knocking, he peered into the windows to see if she was home. White lace curtains were drawn inside most of the windows, making it hard to see anything. He wandered around to the garden behind the old log cabin, and found that Miranda was sitting cross-legged on the ground before Old Hobb, cradling a glass of wine in her hands.

Eric cleared his throat, to politely announce his presence. Miranda invited him to join her with a friendly wave.

"I'm always happy to see you, Eric," Miranda said to him. "But I still can't help you."

"This time it's not about me," Eric replied. He told her everything about what he saw in the chthonic prisons, and the organized way in which the creatures imprisoned there were being deliberately set free.

"If you're a witness to that, then the guardians are probably trying to find you," Miranda concluded for him.

"I know," Eric agreed. "They caught me again when I escaped on the same train. They put me on trial for killing Carlo's mother, and poisoning the ambassador's wife. But the judges gave a verdict of 'not proven', and then they let me go. I didn't know that was a verdict you can get in Roman law, but I'll take it."

"It's not Roman law, it's Scottish," Miranda noted. "That's it's curious, isn't it, that they would say 'not proven' instead of 'not guilty'. I would guess they didn't want to admit that you might be innocent."

"I know they're still out to get me," Eric told her. "Two men with tiger heads attacked me when I left the temple. Maybe the same ones I saw here in your house, a few days ago."

"Rakshasas," Miranda named them. "Warriors from the Secret People of India. But not the honourable ones, I assure you. The honourable ones show their real faces." Then Miranda turned away from Eric for a moment, and closed her eyes.

"There was a woman, whose face I could not see, who protected me from them. And she gave me this," said Eric, and

Clan Fianna

he showed Miranda the leather pouch containing the wind.

"That mark near the lip is the mark of the Bann-Shee," said Miranda. "Please tell me you didn't steal that, because if you did, she'll kill you too."

"No, she gave it to me," said Eric.

"She will probably want it back, so don't lose it."

"Who is the bann-shee? Why would she help me?"

As Miranda shared her wine with Eric, she said, "The Bann-Shee is a ghostly woman who follows old Irish families, and who cries when someone from that family is soon to die."

"Is she one of you? One of the Secret People?"

"Probably, but no one can say for sure."

"She killed some people to protect me. I don't know how I feel about that," Eric admitted.

"I'm an old soldier, Eric," Miranda related, as she leaned back in her chair. "Soldiers like me sometimes have to go to places like Dieppe, and Passchendale, to kill people to keep other people safe. How do you feel about that?"

"I know what you're saying, but– I've never seen it happen right in front of me before," Eric admitted.

Miranda nodded. "Well, that does make a difference," she said.

"Do you suppose the bann-shee would let me thank her?" Eric asked.

Miranda smiled, and then said, "It's best if you just don't interfere with her. She lives by her own rules, and no man knows what those rules are."

Eric was still worried about his safety, so he said, "Those guys with the tiger heads– rakshasas? –They're still out there, looking for me. Can I hide here for a while?"

Miranda shook her head sadly, "I'm sorry, I can't let you stay here very long. In fact there's not much of anything I can do for you."

"Why not?"

Miranda sighed and closed her eyes, and tried to keep up a steady composure, but Eric could tell that she was distressed about something. He reached out to touch her shoulder, but she shied away, and smiled as if nothing was wrong.

"Oh, you know, I'm not as young as I used to be."

"I don't understand," Eric responded. "Last spring you fought two people to a standstill in a straight-up sword fight.

Then after that you sky-dived without a parachute from one of those flying skin-boats of yours, to capture one of those giant falcons. Today you say you are feeling old? I don't get it."

Miranda smiled again. "I know that I sometimes act two thousand years younger than my real age, but– there are just some things I can't do anymore."

"Miranda, I need your help!" Eric pleaded.

Miranda tried to smile, and pretend that her words and her feelings were in accord. She could see that Eric didn't believe it.

"There's not much I can do for you that I haven't already done," Miranda sighed.

"You haven't done much of anything!" Eric accused.

"I know. I haven't. You're right. But listen," Miranda eyed the lamp that concealed the listening device planted there. Then she led Eric into the kitchen. She turned on the water in the sink to create a wash of background noise. Then she whispered into Eric's ear, "I know someone else who can."

"You do?" Eric blurted happily.

Still whispering, Miranda told him, "The old library. Tonight, after sundown. That's where you will find her. And don't be late."

Eric nodded, and hugged Miranda to show his gratitude.

"Now go on home, before anyone sees you here," Miranda recommended. Eric hugged her again, and made his way home.

~ 45 ~

In the guest house in Fellwater Grove, Maread sat on the bed, with her legs crossed beneath her, and her elbows on her knees, and her hands cradling her head. The smoke hole in the roof was covered, and the blankets over the door were drawn tight, to let in as little light as possible. She massaged her temples and rubbed her eyes, and cried aloud to the soul of the earth about what she would trade to make her headache go away.

A bright shaft of sunlight suddenly fell upon her, and she cowered away from it. "Close the door!" she whimpered, and the door was closed again.

"I'm not in any state to go on patrol today, captain," she apologized.

"I know, it's all right," replied a woman's voice.

Maread sat up and uncovered her eyes to see who was speaking. "Who are you? Oh shit!"

Beside Maread's bed stood the Bann-Shee. Maread scurried across the bed as far away as possible, and pressed her back against the wall. The bann-shee passed her hand over a nearby candle, and brought its flame to life.

"Don't be frightened," whispered the bann-shee.

"Is it me?" Maread stuttered back. "Am I the one fated to die?"

"We are all fated to die," the bann-shee replied.

Maread tried to find a nearby weapon, but her eyes squinted painfully in the sharp lines of light that slipped past the door and into the roundhouse. "What do you want with me?" she pleaded.

"Come to the old library, tonight," said the bann-shee. "Someone will meet you there, who can help take the stones out of your head."

Maread was confused. "Stones in my head? What do you mean? Is that why I've been in pain all day?"

The bann-shee was mow moving toward the door. "The old library, just after the sun has set," she repeated.

"At sunset the library will be closed," Maread objected.

"That's never stopped you before," sang the bann-shee. Then she stepped out of the roundhouse, and out of sight.

~ 46 ~

Aeducan had questioned almost everyone he could find who might have seen where Ciara had gone, but no one had any firm answers. She had done her shift on patrol, as usual, but no one saw where she went when her shift was finished. Aeducan trudged to the stone circle, where he had agreed to meet the others if the first hour of searching had proven fruitless.

When he entered the circle and planted himself on a bench by the fire, he looked up to the sky. There he saw the banshee, seated on top of one of the trillithons. In a panic, he jumped to his feet again, and brandished his spear.

"Get away from me, doom-crier!" Aeducan shouted at the bann-shee. "It's not yet my time to die!"

"That is not for you to decide," the bann-shee replied.

Aeducan tightly gripped the shaft of his fighting-spear,

with the tip of the blade pointed at the bann-shee's heart. "If I must die today, I will die with my blade ripping out the heart of whoever killed me!"

"Brave words, warrior," the bann-shee praised him. "If you want to die fighting, then you will die fighting. But if you want to live, then go to the library, tonight after dark."

"Why, what's happening there?" Aeducan demanded, confused.

But the bann-shee stood and backflipped off the trilithon, and was gone.

~ 47 ~

Finnbarr had searched around the ridge of the grove, and did not find anything that would help point the way to Ciara. He sat on a platform, near a place where he could overlook the ambassador's camp. Beyond it, in the distance, he could see the arboretum, from whence he could hear the sound of chainsaws and the engines of the trucks that carried the trees away. From a pocket on his belt he took up a flask and drank a swig of whiskey.

The bann-shee was standing just behind him, and she called his name. Finnbarr turned and saw her, and was startled for a moment, and then he sat on the ground and started quietly laughing.

"Well, I suppose I had a good run at this life. Can't complain. Didn't get to do everything I wanted to do. But who does, eh?"

The bann-shee did not answer, and her silence made it harder for Finnbarr to maintain his veneer of good cheer.

"If it's not too much trouble," he asked, "maybe you could let me say goodbye to a few people first?"

The bann-shee whispered, "The old library, after sundown, tonight."

Finnbarr was baffled by this instruction. "Is that where I'm fated to die? If there's nothing I can do about it, then–maybe you can tell me how it will happen? So I can be–you know–ready?"

"What makes you think it's you who will die?" the bann-shee told him.

"Because I'm the only one here! Look around!" He swept his hand at the ridge and the grove below, to show that there was no one else close enough to see her besides himself.

Clan Fianna

When he turned to face her again, she was gone.

~ 48 ~

In the arboretum, Síle confronted a man with a chainsaw, just as he was about to slice into the base of a mature alder tree, one of the last in the forest that was still full of the green leaves of summer.

"Hey! Hey you! Who hired you! Whose in charge of this!" she demanded. The worker pointed toward a man wearing a hardhat and a reflective vest. Síle stomped toward him, and when she recognized him she gasped, "You!"

"Yes? Can I help you?" said Kendrick McManus.

"I knew this had to be your idea!" she fumed.

"Actually, it was Donall's idea," Kendrick informed her. "Your chieftain was impressed by the story of how we in Northumbria sold one of our freeholds to save the other four. So we made a deal. I hire all these workers, and supply the vehicles and equipment, and in return, when I sell the lumber, you will get a royalty."

"I don't want a royalty, I want my trees," she shouted back.

"These trees are not just yours, my dear. They belong to everyone."

"That doesn't mean you can just cut them down like this!"

"Everyone will benefit when we sell them," Kendrick reassured her.

"It's not to *my* benefit!" she screamed at him, and then she ran away, too angry to continue arguing about it. When she was far enough away she slowed to a walk, and wandered among the thinned forest where stumps of varying sizes lay between the saplings and yearlings that the lumberjacks spared. It was her land, but it was also strange, and foreign. The bird calls that reached her ears were few, and the rabbits and chipmunks fled from her. The noise of the chainsaw was distant, but still louder than the bubbling of the streams, and louder than the wind in the branches above. Twigs and small branches crunched under her feet. She kicked the discarded tin cans in patches of bare soil where soft grasses and wildflowers used to grow. She held out her hands to feel the air, and touch the leaves of autumn as they fell around her, and caress the occasional sapling branch. But this communion gave her no comfort as it used to do. The sight of all the jagged stumps, with their splinters and sharp angles, felt to her like voices violently silenced from speaking. Some of them still bubbled with sap, and some of the sap ran red.

Síle sat on the ground, and pushed her fingers into the soil, and lent her voice to the land that it might cry through her. She squeezed shut her eyes, and threw back her head to face the sky. Her weeping echoed from the stones of the ridge, and followed the trails and paths of the grove to the roundhouses and riversides.

When she was nearly spent with exhaustion, she opened her tear-filled eyes again, and saw the bann-shee, seated on the earth as she was, just before her, and almost close enough to touch. Síle scuttled away, more from surprise than from fear, until she backed into a stump and could retreat no further.

"Who are you!" Síle whimpered.

"A friend," answered the bann-shee.

"You're a bann-shee. A bringer of death! If you're here, it must mean I'm going to die."

The bann-shee shook her head. "No, we are not spirits of death, although death often follows us."

"Then– what are you?"

"We are a secret among secret people, a sisterhood of the spirit. We are women who tried to win our battles by following the rules, but found that the rules were written against us. So our only remaining choices were to fall into despair, or to fight our battles by some other means."

Síle began to worry that the bann-shee had come to punish her for something, and she pushed her back on the tree stump, in a vain attempt to scuttle further away. "Then what do you want with me!" she cried.

Then the bann-shee pulled back her hood, and revealed to Síle her smiling and loving face.

"Miranda?" exclaimed Síle.

"Yes, it's only me. And I'm here to invite you to join us," Miranda replied. From under her cloak she produced a folded blue and black cloth, and placed it on the earth before her.

Síle unrolled it, and found herself holding a bann-shee hood of her own. And as she gazed upon the hood and thought about what it meant, she asked, "But– why me?"

"Because I heard you calling me," answered Miranda.

"What? I didn't call you!"

"You did," Miranda asserted again. "Just now. You were keening."

"Keening? What's that?"

"It's is the cry of a mother whose children have died, or the lament of a woman whose love was never returned. It's the frustration of a girl who is told she can't be beautiful because she's too big, or told she can't be smart because she's too beautiful. It's the anguish that you feel in your heart when you are sent away for doing the right thing, and made invisible by the indifference of others. It is the sound of the endless loneliness of the soul. That is the sound you made, just now, when you saw what those men were doing to your trees. When a woman cries like that, it resonates in the hearts of other women who have cried the same way. And that is how you called me."

When Síle was able to speak again, she asked, "So you– as the bann-shee– you come when people cry like that?"

"I'm not the only one," Miranda replied. "We come as a witness to suffering, not as a cause. But we sometimes come to protect those who suffer, when their sorrow is so deep that they keen with it, like you did."

"You want me to join you?" she stammered.

"I'm sure more questions will come to you. And they will be answered," Miranda reassured her. "For now, I want you to promise some things to me."

Síle nodded.

"I want you keep this a secret between us. People fear the bann-shee, and if our enemies knew that the bann-shee is only a woman, and not a spirit, then they will want revenge. I want you to promise that you will become the bann-shee only when you have no other way to do what must be done. For the bann-shee is powerful, but her power comes from sorrow, and vengeance. Such things can take over your life and kill the best part of you. I want you to promise that you will never fight because you hate something. But you will fight because you love something. I want you to fight with all your courage, all your rage, and all your pain, but I want you to fight in the hope that you'll never have to fight like that again."

"I will," Síle promised.

Miranda rose to her feet, and added: "One last thing. Go to the library, tonight, after the sun has set. A few more answers are waiting for you there."

"Will you be there too?"

"I have other business, I'm afraid," Miranda replied. "But I will not be far away."

Síle nodded, and then stood and hugged her tightly. Miranda gazed in her eyes to wordlessly express her hopes and her fears for Síle's future. Then she strode away, into the woods, and soon vanished behind a distant tree.

Síle stood where Miranda left her, and contemplated the bann-shee hood that she held in her hands. She thought of how many stories she had heard of the bann-shee, and how they had frightened her when she was a child. Now that she could become the bann-shee, those stories suddenly seemed comforting, and empowering.

The sound of a distant chain saw disturbed the peace of the forest again, and Síle glared coldly toward the quarter where it came from. She donned her hood, and her face vanished into a shadow, but for a small glint of light for her eyes. She walked toward the sound of the chainsaws, then ran, then cartwheeled, then leaped into the air, high above the treetops, and vanished in the sunlight.

~ 49 ~

Fellwater's public library was a a century old Edwardian red brick building with a round arch above its front doors and a triangular tympanum above that arch, and tall wide windows all around. Inside the main floor the books were kept on creaking brown–black wooden shelves almost as old as the building itself. Eric went to the space near a back corner of the library, and found an old table, with a small podium at its head. He recalled how he once used to imagine that this table was where the town council had its meetings, and that the town council was secretly a cabal of mystics and sorcerers. Today, the table would serve him as an out-of-the-way corner where he could wait until nightfall, and meet whoever it was that Miranda said would help him.

While waiting, he browsed through the sections of the library that seemed dark and scary when he was a schoolboy. Here, most of the books were heavy hardcovers bound in cloth or leather, with their titles pressed in tarnished silver and gold. At first he sought books that might prove useful for his Master's degree research, but soon he let himself pick the books that seemed to call out to him. Here he found an unexpected fact about a faraway place; there he found a memorable line of poetry; in this one a beautiful plate illustration; in that one a scribbled note in the margin left by some reader from many years ago. With books in his hands he let his mind imagine. Then he reasoned about what he imagined. The afternoon slipped away.

A quiet sound reached him from around some corner, ending his private moment. He followed it down the darkened aisles of library. He came upon Ciara DeDannan, curled on a cushion on the floor, with her hair uncombed and wild, and her face in her hands.

When Ciara recognized Eric, she grew suspicious, and tried to quell her weeping. "What are you doing here?" she questioned him.

"Miranda sent me. She told me that I would meet someone here who would help me prove my innocence. Maybe she meant you."

"I can't help you, I can't help you," Ciara sobbed. "I'm no help to anyone."

Eric crouched down to meet her at her own level. "What happened to you?"

"I left the grove!" Ciara confessed. "I can't take it anymore! The soldiers, always watching me in all the shadows, waiting for me to screw up! The constant fear of attack."

Ciara looked up at Eric, revealing how red her eyes had become from her crying.

"I know exactly how you feel," Eric offered.

"Everybody thinks you did it, Eric," she suddenly scolded.

Eric sighed with exhaustion. "Except that nobody saw me do it. Nobody has actual proof that I did it. All they have is some circumstantial evidence and a lot of peer pressure. But now that you've left the grove, why should you care what everybody thinks?"

This made Ciara think for a moment. She rubbed her eyes and sat up more straight. "All right, Eric. Innocent until proven guilty."

Some of the tension dissipated from Eric's shoulders. Only then did he realize his shoulders had been tightly clenched for days.

Ciara looked around the library, and noticed that she

and Eric seemed to be the only people still in the building. "So, Miranda told you to come here and meet someone who could help you? Someone told me the same thing."

"Who was it?" Eric asked.

"Actually, it was–" but Ciara didn't finish her thought. The knock of a pair of boots on the creaking wooden floorboards approached from along the stacks and corridors of the library. Eric and Ciara looked to see who approached, and saw Maread, with her wild blonde dreadlocks barely contained under a headscarf, and a sympathetic expression on her face.

"I've been listening for a few minutes," Maread said. "I think it was brave of you to leave the grove, and– and I don't want to go back, either. I'm leaving, too."

Ciara jumped up and hugged her friend, and kissed both her cheeks, and thanked her. Then Maread let her go, and frowned at Eric. "What's he doing here?" she asked Ciara.

Before Eric could answer, all heard the front door of the library open and close, and another pair of footsteps approached. The three companions grew hopeful, and turned to face whoever was approaching. A moment later, Aeducan rounded the stacks and joined their growing circle.

"Ciara, you're safe!" he exclaimed happily. He saw Eric, and he paused. "Eric? What the hell!"

"He's here for the same reason we are," Ciara replied. "Waiting for someone."

"Donall banished you, Eric. You don't belong among us anymore," Aeducan asserted.

"Banished without cause or evidence," Eric said.

"My chieftain said you did it. His word is good enough for me," Aeducan concluded.

Ciara took a step forward and said, "But not for me. Not anymore."

Both Aeducan and Maread wheeled on Ciara, with shocked looks on their faces.

"Ciara! You're his girlfriend!" Aeducan stammered.

"I've left him," Ciara explained. "He's lost his hero-light. No one will admit it because they don't want it to be true. But it is. He was glorious, once. We were going to do amazing things together. And I knew where I belonged. But I can't do it anymore! He hides in his mead hall, and tells stories about his glory days. He won't take proper care of that bleeding wound in his ribs. He just rolls over whenever that ambassador tells him to. And then he let those guys cut down the trees. I was his summoner and his shield maiden, and his lover, for a long time, so I should be the first to say it. Donall MacBride is not my chieftain anymore." Then she buried her face in Maread's shoulder, so that no one would see the tears that everyone knew she was shedding.

"He's not my chieftain anymore either," Maread declared, and she held Ciara a little tighter.

Aeducan sighed, and looked critically at Eric, and then plaintively to the two women, and then back to Eric again.

"I swore an oath to protect and follow him," Aeducan insisted. "I can't just abandon that so easily. I know he's made some bad decisions lately– there, you heard me admit it– but someone has to stand up for him. And I'll not have it said of me that I broke my promises."

"The way I see it," Maread told him, as she loosened Ciara's embrace, "I swore my oath not to one man, but to the whole clan, and to the earth, and the sea, and the sky. My loyalty is to the truth that is in our hearts. And the strength in our arms. And–"

As Maread was speaking, the others heard the library door open again, and another pair of footsteps across the groaning floorboards approached them.

"Someone told me I had to–" announced Síle, but then she noticed that Ciara was crying in Maread's arms, and that Aeducan seemed to want to keep Eric away from the two women. So she asked, "What's happening?"

Ciara let go of Maread and embraced Síle, saying, "I've left Donall, and I've left Fellwater Grove," she wept.

"So have I," Maread added.

Síle was astounded. "You too?" she asked Aeducan.

Aeducan shook his head. "Donall might have lost his hero-light," he explained, "but he is still my chief."

"Eric!" marveled Síle. "I suppose I should have known you were here. I saw your shadow."

"My shadow? You mean the one that you say lives in mirrors and things, and watches over me?"

"No, just your shadow, on the bookshelf. It's getting dark outside, it's easy to see in through the windows," Síle grinned. "So, why are you here?"

"I was told that if I came here tonight, I would meet someone who can help prove my innocence," Eric explained.

The front doors opened again, and the old floorboards of the library brought Finnbarr to the table. When he saw how many people were gathered there already, he grinned mischievously and said, "It looks like I'm fashionably late."

"So did the bann-shee tell you to meet her here too?" Aeducan asked him.

Eric's ears perked at the mention of the bann-shee.

"Yes, she did," Finnbarr confirmed. "One of us here tonight is going to die. Hilarious, isn't it?"

"Hilarious," Maread drawled.

Eric smiled, and decided not to tell the others who had sent him to the library.

"Does anyone know who we are supposed to be waiting for?" asked Ciara. Everyone shook their heads and muttered, "No".

"Well," said Aeducan, as he sat himself in a chair at the table, "what shall we do while we wait?"

Maread picked a book off a nearby shelf and said, "We're in a library, we could read something."

Finnbarr suggested, "Let's start with a Samuel Beckett play. *Waiting for Godot.*"

Most everyone laughed uncomfortably. But Maread became cross. "Don't knock it, Finnbarr. I was Awakened in a library like this one."

"You were?" Finnbarr marveled, genuinely surprised.

"That ambassador was right about me, you know. I have dyslexia. When I was in school, I'd lose my temper and throw books across the room because I could not read them. Can you imagine what it's like to not be able to read? Can you imagine looking at street signs, shop fronts, computers, everything– and all the letters just scramble around before your eyes? But there was a book that Miranda showed me, here in this library. I didn't open it for a month. I was afraid of it. But then I tried it. And the words just came together, and I understood them. For the first time in my life I held in my hands a book that I could read and understand, without anyone's help! Now, look at this library we're standing in. Thousands of books. Thousands of stories, voices, people's lives! And I still have difficulty sometimes, but now when I hold a book in my hands I can hear the words speaking to me, and I am not afraid."

No one responded for a moment, as they contemplated the sound of all the books in the library, whispering their stories.

Finnbarr smiled. "Would you believe me if I told you I was awakened when I fell in a pool of water?"

"You did not," Síle challenged him.

"I did!" he repeated. "Eric was only the *second* man in history to break into the grove by climbing over the ridge. I was the first. I was twenty-one years old. That ridge had been there for ever, but no one had any idea what was on the other side. The Mist kept it hidden. But I wanted to explore! I climbed it in the middle of the night, and couldn't see where I was going. I tripped on my way down the other side, and fell into the Well of Wisdom. Life is just a great big joke sometimes, you know?" he concluded, with a happy smile.

"How about you, Ciara?" asked Maread. "Since we're waiting here, why not tell us how were you awakened?"

Ciara sighed. "I was awakened in an art gallery."

"An art gallery!" laughed Finnbarr. "What, surrounded by outsiders?"

"I was working for a branch of a big law firm, and I was sent on a business trip to Ottawa. I had an afternoon off, so I went to the National Gallery. And I remember standing before the works of Lawren Harris and Emily Carr, and thinking to myself, why am I working in law? I research precedents and develop arguments to help the clients– I like those kinds of puzzles, but– but what does that tell the world about who I am? Sometimes we protected the innocent, but sometimes we protected the guilty. I'm sure of it. Some of the partners in the firm cared more about winning than about justice. But art isn't about winning and losing. It's about– I don't know– trying to create something that will make life meaningful."

"That's how I feel about books," Maread observed.

"So that's why you quit your job at the law firm," Finnbarr said.

"I didn't quit," Ciara said. "I wrote a memo to the partners, saying that we should take on more pro-bono cases, and stop representing guilty clients. They fired me. I lost my house. But maybe the gamble paid off, in the end. Because, here I am!"

"That's beautiful," Eric praised her.

Síle, who had been anxiously clenching her fingers and pursing her lips while Ciara was speaking, suddenly stood up and said, "I came here tonight because I hoped to find someone who could help me protect the trees. I still want to do that but–

but you're right about Donall. If the two of you will not follow him anymore, than neither will I."

Ciara and Maread opened their arms to invite Síle into them.

Aeducan was shaking his head with profound disappointment. "I don't believe this. Three of you, in the same day. In the same hour!"

"I have to!" Síle snapped at him. "My Awakening happened in a forest, a lot like the one in our grove. So I feel like I can't follow a man who would cut them down."

"Awakening in a forest. That's beautiful. Can you tell us the story?" Finnbarr asked her.

"It was a school trip to Algonquin park," she related. "Some friends and I stole some canoes in the night, and went off by ourselves. We came to some rapids in the river, and I got separated from the rest of them. I was only thirteen years old."

"You were thirteen!" marveled Ciara. "Most people Awaken in their early twenties!"

"That's why she's so wonderfully weird," Finnbarr grinned. Maread glared at him, and he stopped laughing.

Síle continued her story. "Well, I spent the whole day alone in the forest. You think you're safe up there, because there's paved roads and ranger stations and stuff, but you're not. There's bears and wolves and snakes and things up there, you know? The wilderness begins only ten feet away from wherever you're standing. Anyway, at night while lying awake, afraid of being killed, or lost forever, I suddenly felt like all the trees and grasses and everything were talking to each other, and all saying the same thing: I'm alive, I am here, I'm alive! It was like the voice of a child at play, then it became the voice of a grandfather telling the story of his life, then the voice of a mother telling her children that she loved them, that she loved all of us—"

Subtle tears grew in Síle's eyes, and she tried to hide them by bowing her head, but Maread saw them, and she embraced her sister lovingly.

"I wish I had a story like that," Eric lamented.

"Maybe you do," Ciara told him.

"I don't have a god for an ancestor, like all of you do," Eric related. "I can't suddenly change my clothes into armour, and pick a weapon out of the air as if I was carrying it with me the whole time. How do you people do that anyway?"

"I think it's weird that you can't," Finnbarr grinned.

Clan Fianna

"How do you live like that?"

As the others chuckled, Eric thought about it for a moment, and then said, "Actually, maybe I do have a story. I met a woman once, and I fell in love with her. One day she asked me if I believed in soul mates. I said no, I don't. So she left me. Then she fell into trouble, and Miranda helped me find her again. She took us both to Fellwater Grove. We discovered this hidden world of yours together. We fell in love with each other again. And we had a child together. Actually, she had the child, but– we were going to be a family. Then the child was taken away from us. So we went to bring her back. We made it to the edge of the grove, we were almost safe! But our child was taken away from us again. And the woman I loved– she died."

Ciara put her hand on Eric's shoulders affectionately.

Aeducan had no sympathy. "It's easy to love a woman who is dead, Eric. You never argue with her about who left the toilet seat up. You don't ever see her without her makeup on. And you never worry about whether she's gonna leave you for another man."

Maread furrowed her brow and inhaled sharply, but resisted the impulse to say something.

"Why are you running him down like that?" Ciara scolded Aeducan. "You've lost a friend or two in your life, haven't you? Don't you know what it feels like?"

"He's been living in grief for what? Eight months now? Nine? Long enough to have another child. And that's long enough."

"My story isn't over yet!" Eric argued, and all eyes turned back on him. Eric took a deep breath before continuing. "One day, many months later, someone showed me an image of what my life might have been if she had lived. It turned out to be an illusion, and I was actually trapped in a cave. I looked down. It was dark, and black, and bottomless– it was like a kind of eternal nothing. But it was a Nothing that was somehow a Thing. It got inside my head. I could hear the voices of everyone I had ever failed. I heard all the reasons why I, too, am Nothing. That's what hell is, you know. Hell is what it feels like to be Nothing! But I stood up. I looked away from the abyss. I saw her reflection in a puddle of water. I remembered who she was, and who I am. I suppose that's the nearest thing to being rescued by a ghost, isn't it? Even so, I had to let her go. If I didn't let her go I would have been trapped in that cave forever, staring at

Nothing. So I let her go. That is how I found the way out."

Finnbarr had been staring out the window through most of Eric's story. "Can't we find something more cheerful to talk about while we're waiting?" he complained.

Maread roughly shoved Finnbarr in the shoulder, almost knocking him off his chair.

"You've been quiet, Aeducan," Ciara observed. "Why don't you tell us a story?"

The others also prompted him to contribute a story, but he waved them off. "I don't want to," he told them.

"At least it will pass the time," Síle urged him.

Aeducan pursed his lips and stared at Eric before speaking. "I don't want to tell my story while this outsider is still sitting at this table with us!"

"This isn't Fellwater Grove, you can't kick him out!" Ciara objected.

"Not after he told a story like that!" Síle added.

Aeducan was adamant. "I'm sure he was told to come here, just like we were. But that doesn't mean I have to be nice to him. Now let's just sit here and wait until whoever we're waiting for arrives."

Eric slapped his hands on the table. "Okay, Captain, what do I have to do to get you to trust me? Tell me. I'll do it right now."

Aeducan inhaled deeply and raised himself to his full height, which was almost a head and a shoulder taller than Eric. "I want you to prove to me, right now, that you're not the one who poisoned the ambassador's wife."

"You seem to have made up your mind already, no matter what I might say."

"You know, there were witnesses!" Aeducan barked at him. "Ciara said she saw Livia drinking from a coffee cup that you gave her. Finnbarr said that he saw you carrying Livia's body to the place where she was found."

"No he didn't!" Eric contradicted. "Finnbarr said he saw *somebody* carrying a body, but it was too dark to see who it was!"

"He definitely said he saw you, Eric," said Maread, as she let go of Ciara's embrace. "We all heard him."

"Finnbarr!" Eric rounded on him.

"I did see you carrying her to the arboretum. I know what I saw," Finnbarr informed him.

Clan Fianna

"See!" said Aeducan triumphantly.

Eric turned to Finnbarr and said, "You say that you saw me? How far away were you?"

"I don't know, across the green?"

"What was the weather like that night?"

This time, Finnbarr looked to the floor and answered quietly. "It was overcast."

"So, was there enough light to see anything?" Eric asked.

"No," replied Finnbarr, and he fell silent. Aeducan's smile fell away.

Ciara leaned toward Finnbarr and said, "What's the truth, now? Did you see him, or not?"

"I saw somebody carrying Livia across the green that night," Finnbarr related. "It had to have been Eric. Who else could it have been!"

"Did you actually see my face?" Eric insisted.

Finnbarr slumped into one of the chairs surrounding the table and mumbled the word "no."

Everyone let out a sigh of exasperation.

"Damn it, Finnbarr! You might have just fingered an innocent man!" Ciara berated him.

"The truth that's in our hearts, Finnbarr! Remember the charge!" Maread chastised him.

"Why did you do that to me!" Eric demanded.

Finnbarr studied the floor. "I did it for Síle!" he confessed.

"For me?" Síle balked.

Finnbarr looked at Síle, but pressed his hands on his head, as if trying to stifle a headache. "Remember the night when the ambassador came to the mead hall? He said that what I want is to be closer to you. He was right. I think you're the most wonderful, amazing woman I've ever met. You're so free and beautiful. A child from a fairy tale. I joined the Brigantians because I wanted to know you, and be closer to you."

Síle shifted herself from one foot to the other, and crossed her arms. "What does that have to do with Eric?" she demanded.

Finnbarr saw that he wasn't impressing anyone, so he returned to his story. "So the next day Kendrick came up to see me when I was on patrol on the ridge, and he offered me this–" Finnbarr reached into his pocket, produced a small glass phial containing a pink liquid, and placed it on the table. "It's a love potion. Mixed with some of my blood, and some of my– well, you know."

Síle wrinkled her nose in disgust.

"He said I could have it," Finnbarr concluded, "if I told everyone that it was Eric who I saw."

Everyone's gaze suddenly turned very judgmental, and Finnbarr shifted uncomfortably in his chair.

"I didn't think it mattered much," he pleaded in his defense. "By that time, Eric was already banished."

But most everyone else was concerned about another point in Finnbarr's story. "Did you ever try to use that potion on me?" Síle demanded.

"No, I never got the chance," Finnbarr admitted.

"Is that the only reason you didn't use it? You didn't get a chance?" Maread fumed. "Do you think that just because you have a crush on someone that therefore she owes you something?"

Finnbarr looked to Síle and said, "I just wanted you to notice me!"

"If you use it on me, I'll kill you!" Síle growled at him.

"Actually, if I use it on you, you will fall in love with me forever," Finnbarr said. But no one laughed with him, and his grin quickly faded away.

Aeducan roughly turned Finnbarr's chair around to face him, and said, "So you made a bargain with Kendrick McManus, and traded your honour to get laid."

"Well, I'm not the worst!" Finnbarr shot back. "Look what Donall did to the forest!"

"This isn't about him, Finnbarr!" Eric countered angrily. "Your lies ruined my life!"

"All right, okay!" Finnbarr conceded. "I admit, it might not have been you I saw that night. It could have been anyone."

"Well, that's a start," Eric accepted.

Finnbarr put his hand on Síle's shoulder. An expectant, apologetic look possessed his face. Síle pushed his hand away, and moved to stand on the opposite side of the room, with the table between them.

"I'm sorry," Finnbarr mumbled. Síle only stared at him with pursed lips.

Aeducan turned to face Eric again. "All right. So Finnbarr might not have seen you that night. But that's not enough to save you. What about all those herbs and things that went missing from the healing house, and that were found in your room?"

"I didn't put them there," Eric testified.

"So they got in your room by themselves?" Aeducan pushed him.

Eric did not have an answer.

"I don't know if I can explain how those herbs were found in Eric's house," Síle said, "but I know that there was someone else around the grove that night."

All eyes turned to Síle. "What did you see?" asked Eric.

"You know that I live in a treehouse in the arboretum?" Síle narrated. "Sometimes I see things out there that no one else sees. Strange animals, strange lights at night, moving shadows. That night I came across two people in some kind of secret meeting. I went out and followed them, to see who they were. Someone sneaking into the grove at night is a big problem, for all of us."

"It's a serious breach of security, is what it is," Aeducan remarked.

Síle continued her story. "By the time I got close, someone else got there too. He argued with one of the other two. He was really angry about something. Then they all left. One of them pulling the other one by the arm. Then I got to see who two of them were."

"And?" Eric prompted her.

"They threatened to set fire to all the trees, if I told anyone I saw anything," Síle asserted.

"Now that they are cutting the trees down anyway—" Ciara reminded her.

"Damn them!" Síle cursed. "All right! It was the ambassador, and his wife. That's who I saw."

"Really!" Eric interjected with surprise.

"I don't know who the third man was. I assumed that he was just one of their guards."

"That person might have been the one who poisoned his wife," Ciara speculated. "Maybe he planted the evidence against Eric in the guest house."

"It's possible," Síle agreed.

"This is just speculation without evidence," argued Aeducan. "It doesn't prove anything."

"All the evidence against me was speculation," Eric

countered. "Yet you were happy to believe it."

"This has nothing to do with me," Aeducan snapped back. "Stick to the facts!"

"All right," Eric announced. "Let's do that. Here are the only facts we know. At the end of that night, Livia Julia McManus left the mead hall by herself, and no one saw where she went. Until Síle found her and her husband at a secret meeting with a third person. And after that, Finnbarr saw someone carrying someone else back to the arboretum. Now, we can make a few educated guesses based on these facts. For instance, we can assume that Livia was dragged back to the ambassador's camp by the ambassador himself, where someone poisoned her, and then someone carried her to the place where I found her the next morning."

"You don't know that that for sure," Aeducan reminded him. "All you've got is a theory."

"True," Eric acknowledged, "but that is the simplest and most logical theory, given the facts we have. Even so, we can assume nothing about who Finnbarr saw, or who was the third person at the secret meeting witnessed by Síle. So I'd like to ask you all: did any of you see or hear anything that might tell us anything more?" he asked.

Maread immediately answered, "I heard nothing. There's nobody there."

"You heard nothing?" Eric asked her. "Then did you see anything?"

"I saw nothing," she repeated. "There's nobody there."

"Nobody where?"

Maread suddenly had to stop and think for a moment. "I don't know," she eventually realized, with some surprise.

"I've heard you say those exact words several times, now," Aeducan mentioned.

"I heard nothing, there's–" Maread started to say again, but she caught herself before finishing the refrain. "I suddenly have that headache again."

"I think you did see something," Eric theorized. "Maybe something you were not supposed to see."

"Maybe, but I – I can't think," Maread complained. She pressed her wrist against one of her temples, and then she got up from the table, to wander out of the room. Eric stood in her way.

"I need you to remember what you saw!" he told her.

"Let me do it," said Aeducan. Gently he guided her

hand down to her side, and then held her head in his hands and said, "Remember the first time you told me you saw nothing? We were watching the ambassador's camp. You said you wanted to hear what those people were arguing about. So you went down to the camp, and–"

"I saw nothing," Maread repeated, but a tear formed in her eye as she spoke.

She closed her eyes and tried to remember, as Aeducan asked. "I went down to their camp– and I tried to get close– and then– and then– there was a light–it went right in my eyes–and then–oh, my head! I can't believe how fast this headache came on! I need to sit down for a while."

Maread slumped to the floor, and crouched into a little ball, with her arms tightly wrapped around her legs. Aeducan crouched down next to her, and tried to prod her for more, but she no longer responded to him. He tried calling her name, and rubbing her shoulder, but she remained still. Even her eyes, although open, did not move. Only her breath and her heartbeat showed that she was still alive.

Síle, seeing how Maread had suddenly withdrawn into her mind, rushed to her sister's side. She held Maread's shoulders, and fearfully called Maread's name a few times, as if calling to her from a distance. Then she looked into Maread's eyes, and told the others what she saw: "By the gods, she's been implanted with a telepathic wall."

"What's that?" asked Eric.

"It's like a kind of hypnosis," she explained. "Except that you can't just hypnotize her out of it. You have to go inside her mind to break it down."

"Maybe the person we're waiting for can help her," Aeducan speculated.

"Will she remember everything then?" Eric asked.

Aeducan pointed a finger in Eric's face and said, "Oh, shut it, you noisemaker! Can't you see she's been hypnotised!"

Ciara stepped forward. "I've got an idea that might help," she offered.

Everyone snapped around to face her. Aeducan stood and faced her directly: "Anything!" he demanded.

"I don't know if this is important, but– when Maread was telling us about how she was Awakened by reading a book, well I thought to myself, isn't it interesting that the bann-shee sent us to a library!"

"Maybe the book that awakened her is somewhere around here!" Aeducan exclaimed happily. "Síle, you're her sister, do you know what book it was?"

"Probably her favourite book when we were growing up. We read it together, almost every day, when we were little girls. Mom and dad took it away from her when she turned twelve. They said she was too old for it."

"Maybe there's a copy in this library," Eric suggested.

"There has to be!" Síle exclaimed. She left the table and dashed to the children's section. Aeducan and Ciara picked up Maread and carried her along.

"I don't understand why we have to stop reading children's books when we grow up," Síle mused aloud, as she searched. "Adult books turn people into salesmen, accountants, and clerks. Children's books turn us into heroes."

"What book was it?" asked Eric.

"This one," Síle declared proudly, as placed before Maread a dusty, leather-bound, plate-illustrated edition of the faerie tales of the Brothers Grimm. Síle crouched beside her sister and opened the old tome to the first page of text, while the others gathered around her.

"The first story in the book was her favourite," Síle explained, and she began to read aloud "Once upon a time there was a king who had two daughters, each more beautiful than the other–"

"The book says the king had twelve daughters," Aeducan corrected her.

"I'm reading the story!" Síle jibed, and she pushed his hand off the page.

Maread's eyes were fixed on the page before her, but made no sign to show that she knew what was happening.

"Once upon a time there was a king with two daughters. They slept together in a hall where their beds stood close to one another. At night when they had gone to bed, the King locked the door and bolted it–"

Still, Maread made no movement. Síle suppressed a frustrated sob, and moved her hand to close the book. Her hand was stilled when she heard Maread's soft voice whisper the lines together with her: "–But when he unlocked it in the morning, he noticed that their shoes had been danced to pieces, and nobody could explain how it happened."

Maread looked around the room, as if she wasn't sure

how she got there.

"You're back!" Síle cried, and hugged her sister roughly!

"I feel a little strange," Maread reported.

"How's your head?" asked Aeducan, as he touched her temples carefully.

"Well, I've a pounding headache but– actually, my headache feels like it's going away now," she reported, and she tousled her hair and rubbed her eyes. Then she noticed the books that were sitting open in front of her.

"Why are we in the kid's section?" she asked.

"We had to find the book that Awakened you. This one, right?" asked Síle, as she tapped the Brothers Grimm.

Maread cast her gaze away, but all could tell that Síle was right.

"You had a wall in your head," Aeducan said to Maread. "That wonderful book helped break it down."

Maread looked to Síle and said, "Don't tell Mom and Dad."

"I promise," Síle replied, and she held up her hand with her baby finger extended. "Pinky swear!" she laughed.

Maread giggled, and wrapped her own baby finger around Síle's. She pulled her close into another hug.

Eric was about to prompt Maread to say if she remembered what she saw when she scouted the DiAngelo camp, but Ciara put a hand on his shoulder. "Wait until she's ready," she advised him. Eric nodded, and returned to the table in the reading area. Maread followed him.

"Oh, Eric! I framed you! I put those poison herbs in the guest house. I remember now," she whispered.

"You did it?"

"I wasn't myself. It was like– I was just watching someone do it, but I was watching through that person's eyes. My eyes!"

"That's an effect of the telepathic wall," Ciara explained. "It allowed Kendrick to control her mind for a short while."

Eric wasn't happy about it, but he tried to sound forgiving. "Then it wasn't really you who framed me," he said.

"I remember more now," Maread continued, as her concealed memories returned. "On that first night, in their camp, I did hear something. There were people there. I remember now.

Just like who you saw, Síle– I saw the ambassador and his wife. She did get back to their campsite that night."

"So the ambassador lied to us," Ciara remarked. "We should have expected that."

"They were talking about who Livia had seen in the forest," Maread continued. "The ambassador was very angry. He thought his wife was a spy. Then a third person arrived. I didn't see who it was. There was some more talking. Then I think some furniture was thrown around and broken. Someone went out the back door of the tent, and put on a falcon cloak and flew away."

"Falcons!" Aeducan whistled. "I saw one of them flying over the grove that night."

"Aeducan, what the hell!" Eric blurted. "You've been insisting that I'm guilty all this time, and yet even you saw something that you didn't tell anyone about!"

"I thought it was one of the Wessex-men, going home," Aeducan explained. "Those falcon cloaks are theirs, after all."

Eric gazed sternly at Aeducan for a moment, and then decided it wasn't worth the trouble to chastise him any more. So he turned to Ciara and said, "I saw Paul Turner using a falcon cloak, once. It might have been him."

"I don't think so," Maread replied. "Because, although I couldn't hear everything that they were saying, I definitely heard the ambassador shouting two people's names."

"Whose names?" asked Aeducan.

"Your name, Eric," answered Maread.

"I suppose that makes sense," Eric stated. "Livia and I had been talking that night."

"The other name was Carlo DiAngelo."

"Interesting," Eric mused. "Okay, I have new theory about what happened. When the feast in the mead hall was over, Livia went to the arboretum to meet someone. The ambassador followed her. But they met Síle on the way, and the ambassador threatened to destroy her trees if she told anyone about what she saw. Then Livia and Kendrick returned to their camp. A short while later, Carlo DiAngelo arrived."

"He's probably the third man I saw in the forest," Síle contributed.

"I agree. Then the three of them argue for a while," Eric continued. "Somewhere in there, Carlo slips the poison into Livia's teacup. Maread probably heard the sound of Livia knocking things over as the poison took effect."

Clan Fianna

"Why would Carlo do that to her?" asked Ciara.

"Probably for the same reason that Kendrick hypnotized Maread, and threatened Síle with burning her trees. To protect a secret from getting out. You see, Carlo has always blamed me for the death of his mother. I think he poisoned Livia to make sure she would never vouch for my innocence. That way, no one would stop him from getting his revenge."

"Why would Livia vouch for your innocence?" Aeducan scoffed.

"That night at the feast, she wanted to know who started the fire in Carlo's house. And she had some kind of magical chalice with her, which she said would break if I didn't tell the truth."

Maread interrupted Eric to say, "The Cup of Cormac the King!"

"That's who has it!" Ciara exclaimed. "Niall DeDannan told me it was stolen!"

"Anyway," said Eric, "I told Livia that I didn't start that fire. And because the chalice didn't break, she believed me. So maybe she went and told Carlo, but he refused to accept it."

"So you're saying that Carlo poisoned Livia to keep her quiet, and then framed you for it, so that Donall would banish you from the grove. And then Carlo could lock you up in the underworld. So it's all about you." Ciara summarized.

"I think it's all about him, really. But I was able to escape, because someone is opening those underworld gates and letting everything out."

Aeducan clapped his hands in mock applause. "It's an interesting theory, but you have no way to prove it."

Eric thought for a moment. "Actually, I think I *can* prove it. But I will need all of you to help me." When Eric was sure that he had everyone's attention, he said, "We need to go to the temple of Domus Eleutherios, steal the Cup of Cormac, then confront Carlo with it, and get him to confess."

"That's a ridiculous plan," Aeducan grumbled.

Eric disagreed. "It's an excellent plan! We can even question him about who is opening the chthonic prisons at the same time."

Finnbarr was the first to agree with him. "I like this plan!" he exclaimed. "It's totally insane, and it will probably get us killed. Let's do it!"

"It's risky, but it sounds like an adventure!" grinned

Maread.

"I'm up for it," chimed Síle.

"Me too, but let's not pretend Carlo will confess to anything easily," Ciara warned. "He is as dangerous with a smile and a handshake as a warrior with a sword."

"Seriously, guys," added Finnbarr, "I really would like to help, if you're willing to forgive me for, you know, everything."

Síle glared at him, and said nothing.

Before anyone answered him, the sound of new footsteps approached them from the other side of the library. Everyone looked to see who it was, but they saw only a shadow on the floor, cast by someone unseen.

"Maybe this is who we were supposed to wait for, after all," Aeducan wondered aloud.

Finnbarr gripped the handle of a dagger and said, "Or maybe this is how the bann-shee takes her victims."

The source of the footsteps rounded a bookshelf and revealed herself. She was dressed for adventure: a long autumn jacket full of pockets, and two rucksacks full of oddments, one on each shoulder, their straps crossing between her breasts. On her head she wore a knitted winter touque that contained all her hair, and the shafts of her boots were painted with flowers.

Eric happily called her name: "Ildicoe!"

Ildicoe smiled. "I heard your plan, and I like it. Count me in."

Everyone welcomed her in. "Wonderful to see you!" said Maread. "Where have you been?" said Aeducan. "Come join us, come join us!" said Síle. "When did you get here?" asked Ciara.

Ildice decided to answer Ciara's question. "I've been here for an hour. Waiting."

"So, you're not—"

"No, I was sent by the Bann-Shee, the same as you."

"Then why were you hiding?"

"I saw Eric come in. I heard about the reasons for his banishment. I wanted to be sure he didn't do it."

"We still don't know that," said Aeducan.

"Yes, we do," Ildicoe declared, and she strode over to Eric and hugged him, and kissed both his cheeks.

Finnbarr cleared his throat and said, "Get a room."

Ildicoe let Eric go, and the two of them smiled at each

other. Then Ildicoe looked to the rest of the group and said, "Listen, I have to tell you: I found the Tartarus gate that the DiAngelo opened. The same one that Eric found, I think. And I was told that if I came to the library tonight, I'd find some people who could help me close it."

"How did you find it?" asked Eric.

"I move around, in my life, as a summoner for the Hidden Houses in this country. I hear things. Rumours. Whispers in secret meetings. Notes passed between school boys under the table. I began to notice a pattern. So I followed the smell of it, and it took me underground."

"We've got a plan now, to try and stop them," smiled Eric.

"Only one thing remains," said Maread. She turned to her man and said, "Aeducan, are you in?"

Aeducan's eyes moved thoughtfully from one person to another, taking his time to think. Eventually he shook his head and said, "No. I'm staying right here, to wait for whoever we're supposed to be waiting for." He dropped himself in a nearby chair and folded his arms.

Then Eric began to laugh. Finnbarr looked to his neighbours and began to laugh too, but mostly because he did not know what to do. Maread gently swatted his arm to stop him from laughing. The others looked among themselves with puzzled eyes, wondering what Eric was laughing at.

"Oh, she was brilliant!" Eric laughed. "She didn't tell us who we're waiting for, so that we would have to figure it out for ourselves! And now I know who it is!"

"So who are we waiting for," Aeducan grunted.

Eric spoke quickly. "Us! We've been waiting for *each other*. It's really that simple. And now, here we are."

"That can't be it," Aeducan objected. "I was not sent here by just anyone. I was sent by the Bann-Shee! We're probably waiting for her."

Eric insisted he was right. "Look. Each of us was told to come here to wait for someone who can help with something. For example: Ciara, you came here because you didn't know what to do about Donall. You wanted to leave the clan, right? Well, Maread and Síle have already helped you do that."

Ciara's eyes widened a little, and she grasped Síle and Maread's hands tighter.

"Maread's problem was the telepathic thing in her head.

We dealt with that now, too."

Maread smiled. Eric felt flushed with excitement.

Finnbarr said, "I came here to search for Ciara. Donall said she was missing."

Eric gestured toward Ciara and said, "Here she is!"

Aeducan rolled his eyes.

Síle stood up and said, "I think Eric is right. I came here looking for someone who could help me protect the trees in the grove. I can't do it by myself. But maybe with the five of you helping, we could– we could do something!"

"We can close the Tartarus Gate together, too," added Ildicoe.

Eric said, "I was led to believe that I would meet someone who could help me prove that I'm innocent. And tonight some of you have helped me with that, too. So it all fits. We're not here to wait for a saviour. We don't need a saviour. We have each other."

"We have each other," Ildicoe agreed.

"We also have bigger problems here. None of you believed me because you thought I was guilty of a crime. Maybe you will believe me now."

"You think someone is deliberately opening the chthonic prisons, and letting everything out," Aeducan remembered. "That's ridiculous. Why would anyone do that? Everyone knows how dangerous they are."

"I think they released the monsters so that they can be the ones to save us from the monsters," said Ildicoe.

"Don't be absurd," Aeducan chortled.

"I'm serious!" Ildicoe countered. "I've been around the world a few times now, and one of the things that's the same everywhere is that politics is theatre. It's a blood sport, to be sure, but it's also nothing but a show. When you see one group raised up and another put down because someone made a new law, or when you hear someone telling us of another terrorist group, another economic slowdown, and he says we all have to make sacrifices or die, well, its tragic and terrible, and it's also a performance. So you have to ask yourself: who is he performing for? What does he want you to see? What is he hiding backstage? And if we get caught in the act– make no mistake, it's an act– then what will we do? If you want to understand politics, those are your questions. Because politics is theatre. And that's all."

Clan Fianna

Finnbarr furrowed his brow. "You're saying that those gargantacores and terrabiters were let loose on us for the sake of someone's entertainment?"

"I'm saying they were let loose so that the Guardians could be seen rounding them up and catching them. The story of what's happening in Fellwater is getting around. Lots of clans now believe the Guardians are the only people who can protect them from the next attack."

"They must have been preparing this for years," Síle marveled.

"I'm still not convinced," grumbled Aeducan. "If somebody is opening the caves, we will need an army to close them."

"Maybe not," said Eric. Aeducan made a puzzled face. "Because of something I heard Heathcliff say, last summer," Eric continued. "He said that the village of Fellwater was chosen as the site of an experiment. Phase Two of The Magnum Opus, he called it. I think he was referring to what's happening now. So if I'm right, then they're probably not opening *all* the prisons. They're opening only one of them, somewhere nearby, just to see if they can control what comes out."

"If you're right, then I don't want to imagine what phase three is," mused Finnbarr.

"If it's only one cave they're opening, then the seven of us might be enough to close it," Ciara reasoned.

"I don't know, Eric," Aeducan doubted. "You talk a good talk, but what, really, can we do?

Maread swatted his shoulder. "Why are you being so difficult?"

"Because this outsider might be a criminal," Aeducan loudly contended. For Ciara's benefit, he added: "And I will not abandon my chief!"

"What have you got to lose?" asked Maread.

"The peace!" Aeducan answered directly. "We've trespassed on their lands, and we almost started a war that way. And this time, they've got an armed camp right in our home. If we're caught, their retaliation would be fast, and bloody."

"That sounds like Donall talking," Maread grunted at him. "I'm not taking orders from him anymore."

"Neither am I," added Ciara.

Síle moved to stand by her sister and said, "And neither am I."

Maread squeezed her sister's hand affectionately.

Finnbarr looked to the three women and said, "If you three are starting a new clan, then I would like to join it. If you'll have me. I'm a good fighter; I can be useful."

Ciara and Maread looked to Síle for a decision about Finnbarr. Síle took the love potion on the table and threw it out the window, where it shattered on the asphalt.

"Now you can join," Síle told Finnbarr. He happily stood to take his place next to Ciara.

Maread intercepted him and said, "You're on probation."

"What do you mean?" Finnbarr flustered.

Maread roughly pulled him aside by the arm to speak privately. "My little sister lives in a world of her own most of the time. And sure, it makes her a little bit weird. But it also keeps her happy. And I won't have you or anyone else take that away from her."

"I guess I've been warned," Finnbarr smirked.

Maread responded by throwing his arm down and sending him back to the rest of the group.

"Eric," said Ciara, as she stretched out a hand to him, "In my new clan, you're innocent until proven guilty."

Eric took her hand and said, "In that case, I accept your invitation." He took his place beside Maread.

"What about you, Captain?" Ciara asked Aeducan, as she offered her hand to him. "Won't you join us?"

Aeducan struggled for a while before answering, "I don't think I can. I'm sorry."

"Please!" said Maread. "We've been a team for a long time, you and I. It wouldn't be the same without you!" And she, too, offered him a hand of invitation.

Aeducan shook his head. "My place is at the right hand of my chieftain."

Maread closed her eyes for a moment, then reached for Aeducan and pulled him into an embrace. "I know you are doing what you think is right, but I just– I just–", she said, and then she lost the words.

Aeducan smiled modestly. "I promise you this much. I'll never raise a weapon against you. Any of you. Not even you, Eric. You have my word."

"If you ever change your mind about joining us," Ciara offered in return, "we'll be here."

Clan Fianna

Aeducan nodded, and thanked her. Then he said, "I suppose I should go back to the grove, now. Donall might need me for something." As he stepped away, his footsteps and the creaking floorboards echoed in the empty library. When he was half way to the door he turned back one last time and said, "There's a name in the old language for a small band of warriors like you, with no lands and no chief and no tribe."

"Outsiders?" Eric asked.

"Fianna," Aeducan informed him.

"That's what we are, now," Ciara declared. "We're the Fianna."

"It feels like we've been Fianna for quite a while now," ruminated Maread.

Aeducan nodded to Maread, almost apologetically, and then stepped out of the library, and into the night.

Maread slumped into one of the chairs around the table. "He was my best friend," she grieved.

Ciara put a hand on Maread's shoulder. "We have to respect his decision. We have to let him go."

"I know, but–" Maread sighed. "Like you were once so sure of Donall, I was sure of Aeducan. I can't imagine life without him."

"This is a change of topic," said Eric, as he looked out a nearby window, "Did anyone else notice that the village has lost power?" He strode to the front door and looked out the windows. "Yes. All the shops across the road are dark. Most of the street lights are dark. In fact it looks like only the library has–" and then he interrupted himself. He looked at a nearby reading lamp, and then he shuddered. For he saw that the light bulb within it was a spiral coil. As his glance frantically scanned the room, he saw that every reading lamp by every chair, and every ceiling fixture above him, and every wall sconce in every corner, and every socket in the chandelier above the table, held a spiral-coil bulb.

They heard the low and heavy sound of something slow-moving and monstrous, tromping down the road toward the library.

"Everyone! Turn off all the lights!" Eric shouted, running around the library and switching off everything. "They're attracted to the light! That's how the Guardians control them. They follow the light!"

The others soon joined Eric, in switching off all the

lamps and overhead lights in the library. As the library was a single room, not much larger than the ground floor of an old manor house, it should not have taken long. But the warriors soon found that they were switching off lights that someone else had already switched off a moment earlier.

"They're switching themselves back on again!" shrieked Maread.

Eric switched off the front stairwell light and then watched the switch. True to Maread's warning, in the time it took for whatever beast was approaching them outside to make one footfall, the switch clicked itself back on again. So he tried breaking the lightbulbs with a broom handle. Seeing his precedent, others did the same, by throwing chairs at them, or ripping them out of their fixtures.

"Who else knew that we were coming here?" Ciara shouted, as she broke a reading lamp by smashing it on a table.

"Only the one who sent us here!" answered Maread, from the other side of the library.

"The Bann-Shee!" howled Finnbarr fearfully. "Maybe she sent us here to die!"

"No, she didn't, she couldn't have," Síle shouted back.

"How do you know?" Finnbarr asked.

Síle had to think quickly. "Well, she's been helping us all along! She was there, at the arena, when we were fighting the terrabiters! She was there in Hallowstone, when they broke Heathcliff out of the dungeon!"

"Yes, she was!" Ciara realized.

"Maybe she knew this thing was going to attack tonight, and she wanted us to be in the right place to fight it!" Síle concluded.

Everyone in the library took to a window to see what new remnant of the mythic age was tromping down the road to kill them. It was a giant, as tall as the street lamps, and with limbs as long as a fully grown man. Its knotted flesh seemed eerily illuminated by the light of the two lamps on either side of the library doors. Its rough cow-hide loincloth and tunic, tied in place by ropes and metal cables, hung with bear skulls and moose antlers: animals the giant had recently eaten, and their blood still stained the giant's arms and legs. It planted itself by the front steps of the library, blocking everyone's escape. It wielded the trunk of an uprooted maple tree as a club, and it bashed the ground violently, cracking the sidewalks and setting off car alarms with the vibrations.

"We've killed all the lights in here. Why is it still coming!" hollered Maread.

"We didn't kill the lights on the outside!" Ciara hollered back.

"I told you," cried Finnbarr, "one of us here is going to die!"

Maread, now clad in her battle armour, unsheathed a sword. "Not today!" she fumed. Her hero-light began to glow from her flesh. Then she pulled the front doors open and placed herself between the giant and the library. But some of her bravado drained away when she saw how tall the giant was.

"Whoa! Never fought one of these guys before!" she suddenly remembered.

Síle and Finnbarr ran out and joined her, with their fighting spears ready.

"Now's your chance!" Finnbarr cracked, and Maread gave him a worried smile.

Hero-light emanated from the fighters on the steps of the library, as they stood ready to meet the giant in battle.

~ 50 ~

Still inside the library, Ildicoe turned to Eric and said, "Is there another way out of here?"

"Through the basement," Eric told her, and the two of them dashed away to find the stairs and the basement doors. Once they were outside, they saw their friends doing their best to keep the giant from getting too close to the library. They knew that one good strike from its club would damage the building beyond repair, along with the books inside. The giant would reach for them with its huge hand, or swing at them with its club, to force them out of the way. As one warrior dodged out of his attack, two more were ready to jump between him and the library again, and the giant could get no closer to his desire.

"So this is all just theatre, right?" Finnbarr shouted at Ildicoe.

"Theatre of cruelty," said Maread.

"Theatre of the absurd," Síle added.

"Then we better put on our own show before the audience gets here!" said Ildicoe.

By the time Eric and Ildicoe emerged from the library's basement, Maread, Síle, and Finnbarr had broken the two exterior lights on each side of the library doors, darkening them permanently. As soon as they did, the giant roared angrily. Now he saw the three warriors not as a nuisance, but as a threat. He crashed his club down at them with real anger, and missed, crushing the roof of a car instead. Other nearby parked cars immediately triggered their anti-theft alarms. His second swipe also missed, as Síle was able to leap out of the way just in time; the giant's club knocked over a street lamp and sent it flying down the street.

Eric looked to a nearby hardware store, and then asked Ildicoe, "Can you do that thing that Miranda can do with locks? Open them by snapping your fingers?"

"Yes, why?" Ildicoe answered.

"Quick, follow me!" he replied, and then he ran to the hardware store, with Ildicoe close behind him. She tapped the lock twice and snapped her fingers. Immediately, it unlatched and the door swung partially open.

"What are we doing?" Ildicoe said.

"These monsters are attracted to the lights, right? Let's make a light of our own!" Eric grinned.

Ildicoe laughed. "Perfect! You find some batteries or something. I'll put together the biggest lamp that I can."

Eric dashed to the warehouse in the back of the shop, where he found a gas generator, and decided that it was better than a battery. A battered orange jerrycan of gas sat by the door and he filled the generator from it, spilling a lot on the floor in his haste. Then he hoisted it on to a child's toy wagon and rushed it back outside. Meanwhile, Ildicoe found a trouble lamp housing, and she screwed a spiral-coil bulb into it. Thinking that whoever handled this might not want the giant to get too close, she attached it to a broom handle with some duct tape. Then she picked up an extension cord, and followed Eric back to the street.

"Where the hell did you go!" shouted Maread at Eric and Ildicoe. But when she saw them assembling their makeshift monster lure, she understood right away.

"Let's get in that truck over there!" Maread called to her companions, as she pointed to a black pickup truck parked in front of a convenience store. Ciara reached the truck first, and she unlocked it and started the engine with a tap on the locks and a snap of her fingers. Ildicoe helped Eric load the generator into the cargo bay in the back. The others followed last, and they made sure that the giant was following them, but also that he didn't get too close. Eric pulled the generator's starter cord a few times, and the generator spat and rumbled and then roared to life. The trouble light at the end of the broom handle sang out with a powerful chord of blue-white music. Ildicoe held it up for the giant to see. The giant's expression changed from fury to fascination, and it reached out to touch the source of his bliss.

"Floor it!" shouted Síle to Ciara, in the driver's seat. The truck sped ahead, almost throwing those in the cargo bay into the street. The giant dropped his club and chased them, growing more hopeful and more impatient as the light remained just slightly out of reach, no matter how hard it ran after the truck. Vibrations from the thuds of the giant's footsteps shattered the windows of nearby houses, and caused onlookers watching from behind their doors to scurry away.

Finnbarr turned to Eric and said, "Look at us– we're baiting a giant! Nobody ever believes this sort of thing."

"Look at his face!" shouted Eric, over the din of the generator. "You'd think he was a drug addict!"

"Who knows what they did to him to turn him into this!" Maread agreed.

When they were almost outside of the village, they heard the siren of a fire truck following them.

"There's the guardians!" Finnbarr decided.

"Right on time!" Maread declared. Around a corner came a fire truck, one of Kendrick's LAV's, and a few of the Guardian's other vehicles.

A loudspeaker from the fire truck blared out a command to slow down, or a warning about how much danger they were in, but over the noise of the sirens and the generator in the back of the truck, none of the Fianna could hear it. They laughed and waved at the fire truck and kept driving. They passed a pair of dumbfounded Mennonites in their horse carriage, and waved joyously to them too. They passed a few oncoming cars, who swerved out of the way of the giant's pounding feet. The Fianna felt like they were finally winning, and they laughed and whooped like happy children let out of school early.

Then they came to a corner where several Guardians vehicles blocked the road. Several Auxilliaries jumped from the fire trucks, armed with crossbows that Eric presumed were laced with somnaweiss to tranquilize the giant. But they were watching the Fianna, not the giant, so Eric wondered if they had something else in mind. Then Kendrick emerged from one of the Guardian's range rovers, followed by a Guardian carrying a television camera.

Eric and Finnbarr took defensive postures beside Ildicoe, who was still holding the trouble lamp that fascinated the giant.

"Didn't your mother tell you not to approach stray animals?" Kendrick remarked, as he waved his walking stick toward the giant.

Eric confronted him and said, "We know all about how you control these creatures with the these lights. And we know these monster attacks are not random! They are planned, deliberately planned, by you! And now, we can control the monsters, too."

"Sure you can," Kendrick smirked.

"We can! Look!" Eric grabbed the broom handle that held the trouble lamp, and waved it from left to right. The giant followed its movements with his eyes and his fingers, still half hypnotized by its glare.

Kendrick turned to the cameraman and asked, "Are you streaming this live, or are you just recording?"

"Just recording, sir," said the cameraman. "We're setting up the live stream as quick as we can."

Kendrick gestured to another of his Guardians, who immediately ripped the camera off the man's shoulder and smashed it to the ground.

"What the hell!" hollered the cameraman.

"Now go," Kendrick ordered him.

"I hope the Guardians are paying for that," the cameraman muttered, as he returned to his car.

"Now it's just us," Kendrick smiled. He ordered his guardians to deal with Ildicoe's trouble lamp. The Fianna readied their weapons, preparing for an attack. But one of the guardians simply shot the bulb of the trouble-lamp with his crossbow, which was all he had to do. Ildicoe covered her head to protect herself from the falling glass shards, then threw the useless light down to the ground and shut off the generator.

Kendrick smiled, and started to say something, when the giant roared angrily at the loss of his light. He swatted the man who shot it, and sent him sprawling away, over the roadside ditch and over the wire fence into a farmer's field. Kendrick's first reaction was nervous laughter, but the giant took at swing at him next. He ran for the protection of the LAV.

"Shoot it, kill it!" Kendrick shouted. But as the LAV turret swung around to take aim, the giant was back on his feet, and had pushed the fire truck out of his way, in a rush to reach Kendrick. The fire truck rolled off its wheels and on to its side. Its frightened occupants clambered out and ran for the fields. Just as Kendrick got behind the LAV, and its turret was ready to fire, the giant pushed it aside too, and rolled it into the ditch. Although it landed on its wheels, the gunner lay sprawled on the ground; he had not escaped in time, and the roll broke his neck.

Kendrick saw his dead LAV commander, and then ordered the auxiliaries: "Call the air corps!" Then he dashed for his range rover, jumped in, and sped away.

One of the remaining Guardians was heard saying, "I didn't sign up for this. I'm getting out of here, too!" He ran for his car, and the last remaining guardians ran with him. No one wanted to be the next target of a giant's wrath.

Ciara was prepared to drive off, too, but as Síle pointed out, the giant was ignoring them. It was only going after the Guardians. When they were gone, the giant heavily pounded his chest and roared out a last warning, and then turned and tiredly tromped over to the truck. It grunted and snorted at the Celts standing there, prompting Ciara to get back in the driver's seat and tell everyone to grab hold of something. But then the giant sat on the ground again, and picked up the broom handle with the broken trouble light between its massive fingers. He held it before his eyes, and made a kind of low-throated whimpering sound.

Ciara saw this, and decided she didn't need to race the truck away. The other Fianna let out long sighs of relief.

"Hey there!" shouted Eric at the giant. "Are you all right? What's your name?"

Finnbarr stepped in front of Eric and said, "No point in talking to a giant. When they get this big, they also get stupid."

But the giant heard Finnbarr's words, and its eyes narrowed on him.

Little man! What nonsense you have heard about giants!

Finnbarr spun around and stepped back, completely surprised by the giant's rumbling rocky voice. "Fuck me, they can talk after all!" he gulped.

Maread nudged Finnbarr and said, "Who is the stupid

one now?" Finnbarr blushed.

"Maybe you should apologize, eh?" suggested Ciara.

"Umm– how do you apologize to a giant?"

"Same as you would to anybody. Tell him you're sorry!"

Finnbarr took a defensive step back, and then hollered up to the giant, "I'm sorry! I'm sorry for saying that giants are stupid. I guess I haven't met all that many giants before. I had no idea."

The giant grunted back, which Finnbarr decided was a sign that his apology was accepted. "Well, he didn't kill me," he whistled with relief.

The giant looked to Eric next.

And you, little man! You are brave to ask for my name! But you grieve my heart. For no one has spoken my name in a very long time. And now, I do not remember what it is.

Eric gaped and stuttered with surprise before speaking. "You've actually forgotten your own name? How long has it been? Decades? Centuries?"

Síle stepped forward and said, "Is it because of the light? Is that why you can't remember?"

The giant looked again at the broken trouble light in his fingers.

The light. It was so beautiful–it was so beautiful–

"Do you know where your home is?" asked Ildicoe. "Do you know where you came from?"

The giant looked off to the horizon to the east, and then the west.

My home? My home is not this land. I have never seen this land before. I do not know these trees, these hills. And they do not know me. My home must be very far away.

And then he looked back to the broken trouble light again.

I could see my home on the other side of the light. My mountain! My friends! My land! All there, waiting for me.

"The light is a prison!" Eric offered. "Those people were using it to control you! But you're free now!"

The light was my friend.

Eric looked to his companions, and then shouted to the giant, "We could be your friends!"

Finnbarr and Síle, who were standing closest to Eric, suddenly looked on him strangely. "You can't make friends with a giant!" Finnbarr admonished him.

"Why not?" Eric asked.

"Because–" Finnbarr began, but he didn't really have an answer. So he blurted out the first thing that came to his mind: "Because– think of how much they have to eat!"

The light was my only peace, in this faraway strange land. The light made me happy.

"No, the light was an illusion! It was keeping you a slave!" Eric told him. "But we're real! We can help you!"

The giant turned his furrowed eyes and glowering glare toward Eric. He clearly did not like to be contradicted.

"I think it's not a good time to try and argue with him about the light," Ildicoe recommended.

"Okay, in that case," Eric thought for a moment, and then said, "If you don't remember your name, what would you like us to call you?"

The giant's expression softened, and it looked off to the horizon again.

The only name I want is my own name, the one I was given when I was born. A man is nothing without his own name.

The Fianna looked quizzically at each other. None of them knew how to help the giant with that.

Eric spoke for them all when she said, "Okay. We will try. But first, maybe you would like us to take you some place safe, where you can rest, and eat?"

The giant nodded.

"Where did you have in mind, Eric?" asked Ciara. "We can't take him to Fellwater Grove."

The Fianna considered bringing him to George Medewiwin, who lived in a freehold in a First Nations reserve. They considered Ciara's former clan, the DeDannans, who had a freehold on Lake Huron. They even considered going as far as Hallowstone, although it was seven hundred kilometers away.

As they were talking, they heard the sound of a helicopter approaching from the village, and when it was almost directly overhead, its spotlight flashed out. The beam scanned the area for a moment, and then fixed itself on the giant.

The light, the light! I can see the way home!

The giant rose to his feet, and reached up to the light with his hands. The five Fianna called out to him to look away, and promised to take him somewhere safe, but the giant ignored them. Eric tugged on one of the stray rope ends that hung from the giant's loincloth, but the giant batted him away, and reached up to the light again. The helicopter turned around and slowly flew away, over the farmer's fields. The giant followed it. His walking stride was faster than Eric could run. Soon Eric's friends called upon him to give up and come back. Eric did so, reluctantly.

"It's all right, Eric. At least they're not taking him back to town," Ildicoe consoled him.

"We have to find his name! We have to take him home!" Eric urged.

"I know what you're doing, Eric. But you don't have to fight *every* battle. Come on, let's return this truck to where we found it, and go home."

"Go home?" asked Síle. "Donall will have closed the gates of the grove against us by now. We don't have a home any more." When Maread touched her shoulder, Síle fell into her arms. Finnbarr saw them holding each other, and looked to the ground.

"You can all stay at my apartment tonight," Eric volunteered. "There's room enough, although it will be crowded."

"Thanks, Eric," said Ciara. Then to everyone else she said, "Come one, everyone, let's go before the guardians come back."

~ 51 ~

In the early hours before the sunrise, Eric stopped fighting his insomnia. He got out of his bed, careful not to disturb Ildicoe who slept beside him. In the living room, he regarded the strange, otherworldly friends asleep on his floor and on his couch. And he wondered at the string of events that brought them here.

Once upon a time, they were the leading warriors of a proud and strong Celtic tribe, dwelling in a magical grove hidden deep within a forest. What history they must have seen! What adventures they had! Yet today they were five tired and lonely people, perhaps the last of their kind. Once they feasted in grand halls, with the shields of their ancestors around them. Now they slept in a bachelor apartment in a low-rise building in an ordinary village in an unimportant country.

Eric looked out his window and saw Miranda leaning

Clan Fianna

on the low wall of the old stone bridge, throwing breadcrumbs to a flock of gulls. Eric dressed and went out to see her.

"How did your meeting at the library go?" she asked him cheerfully.

Eric laughed and shook his head. "Nothing like anyone expected, but I suppose it went very well."

"Did you get help proving your innocence?"

"I did. Well, almost. I got help creating some reasonable doubt. And that's a start."

"Glad to hear it," Miranda smiled.

"Thank you," Eric told her.

"For what? I didn't do anything."

"For bringing us together."

"You did that on your own."

Eric was skeptical. "The others were under the impression that they were sent to the library by someone called the Bann-Shee. You wouldn't know anything about that, would you?"

Miranda only smiled, as she tossed another breadcrumb to a passing gull.

"I see," said Eric. "Then I won't tell them that I was sent to the meeting by you."

Miranda looked at him like a little girl with a secret. She offered Eric some crumbs for the birds. You saved the town from a giant! Well done! Have a biscuit."

"I suppose we did save the town," Eric grinned.

Miranda put her hand on his wrist and said, "How are you holding up?"

"What do you mean?" Eric asked.

"You spent a night in the underworld, in one of the chthonic prisons. That can't have been easy."

Eric sighed. "I'm trying not to think about it. There are more important things to do."

Miranda gripped his arm a little tighter. "I know what the abyss can do to you, Eric. I have seen it, too."

Eric looked at her again,

"There are very few people who have escaped the gaze of the abyss," Miranda continued. "Those who do escape come out of it with a powerful drive to save the world. They think they need to prove themselves worthy again."

"I'm not trying to prove anything," Eric countered. "Someone is opening those prisons and we have to close them again! It has nothing to do with me."

"You can't save the world, Eric. Not by yourself."

"Then what am I supposed to do?"

"Just go home, Eric," Miranda whispered in his ear. "Let me and the other Brigantians deal with the troubles of the Hidden World. You're only an outsider, after all."

"You've never called me an outsider before."

"Just enjoy the park, and the morning sunrise, and this bonnie stream below this bridge. You don't need to fight anymore, Eric. Your part in the story is done."

"Miranda, this isn't like you. What's the meaning of this!"

"Just gaze into the water, Eric. Gaze into the water, and be at peace."

Eric leaned over the stout wall of the old stone bridge, and saw that below him there was no river, but the deep black nothingness of the chthonic abyss, ringed with its torrent of cold rain and grey dust.

Eric shrieked involuntarily, and turned back to Miranda, but found Carlo standing in her place, laughing at him. He tried to run away, but saw Heathcliff and Kendrick guarding one end of the bridge, and Siobhan Summercraft and Paul Turner guarding the other.

The wind from the abyss gusted up, and blew around them all, flapping their hair and clothes, and ripping away their skin, turning them into laughing skeletons, tearing at Eric's youthful flesh until he was left a naked and shriveled old man.

~ 52 ~

Eric awoke from the nightmare with a gasp. Only when he felt assured of his body did he look to see where he was. He found himself in his bathrobe and bare feet, lying on the ground just past the foot of the old stone bridge. What few stars could be seen though the glare of the streetlights twinkled above him. The old oaks and maples of the park shivered their brown and yellow leaves in a light October breeze. Eric shivered with them.

As he stood up to return to his apartment, he saw a crow's feather float down through the air, and land on the grass before him. Looking up, he saw Ildicoe sitting in a tree branch above him, holding a candle lantern in one hand. She was wrapped in a warm heavy cloak.

Clan Fianna

She gracefully slipped off the tree branch and landed on her feet just before Eric. He embraced her warmly, and touched her face, as if to reassure himself that she was real.

"Ildicoe," whispered Eric.

Ildicoe guided his fingers to her temples, to allow him to remove the scarf and cap that hid the thick mane of crow's feathers which grew upon her head.

"You are the only one who can see my feathers uncovered," she told him. "You're the only one I trust."

Eric stroked her feathers, kissed her gratefully, and thanked her for returning to him.

"Where have you been?" his voice more urgent than he intended.

"I had to go and set something right," she replied. "I think you know what it is."

"The opening of the underworld," Eric said. She confirmed this with a smile.

Eric's next question was delivered in a serious tone. "Did you see the darkness? Did you see the abyss?"

Ildicoe nodded gravely. "Yes, I saw the darkness. And I heard the echoes, and the voices. And I know that you did too. I can see the darkness still upon you. That's how I knew you were telling the truth."

Eric involuntarily stepped back. "I'm not still having a nightmare, am I?"

Ildicoe laughed. "No, love, you're awake now. And it's really me. Look at my face. It's really me." She removed her cloak and clasped it around Eric's uncontrollably shivering shoulders. Eric stepped back into her arms. He held her there, and thought of what more she might have meant by the word 'love', and by the word 'awake'.

"Those who escape the abyss always end up taking a piece of it with them," Ildicoe explained. "It gets inside your mind, and it never goes away. I'm sorry to have to tell you this, but you're going to have nightmares like the one you had tonight, for the rest of your life."

"Every night?"

"No, thankfully, not every night. But often. I have them once a week."

Eric closed his eyes, and tried to accept this new fact. Then he said, "I'm very glad you're back."

~ 53 ~

When Eric awoke in the morning, the others were already up. Finnbarr was in the kitchen cooking some omelets and breakfast sausages for everyone, while Ciara was using Eric's computer.

"Ah, there you are, at last!" Ciara cheerfully.

"What time is it?" Eric yawned.

"Almost noon," she informed him. "We all slept late."

Eric moved to see what Ciara was doing on his computer. "How did you figure out my password?" he asked her.

Ciara laughed. "I didn't have to. The Hidden Houses have a Hidden Internet. It's a sector of the Deep Web, the part of the net that isn't catalogued on any search engines. I'm using it to call in some favours."

"So there is some benefit to being a former lawyer, eh?" said Finnbarr from the kitchen. Ciara laughed again.

"Over the next few hours, some packages will arrive. Try not to let the couriers frighten you," Ciara told Eric.

"Why would a courier be frightening?" Eric asked.

A knock sounded at Eric's door, and when Eric opened it, he found himself face to face with a troll: wide-shouldered, green-skinned, wart-covered, frazzle-haired, red-eyed, and wearing a Canada Post uniform.

"Package for Eric Laflamme?" grunted the troll, between two huge fangs that jutted up from his jaw and almost into his nose.

Eric only stared with his mouth open.

The troll put the package into Eric's hands, and then handed him the electronic register and said, "Sign here please."

Eric signed the register without taking his eyes off the troll's brooding Neanderthal brow.

"Have a nice day," the troll gruffed, and walked away.

Ciara picked the package out of Eric's hands and said, "That should be the grappling hooks."

~ 54 ~

That same afternoon, more refugees arrived in Hallowstone. Three tall and muscular men from House Songhai gathered around Algernon Weatherby in the courtyard of his castle. They described how their freehold near Niagara Falls pledged its allegiance to the New Renaissance. Their angriest and most outspoken member, Ibrahim Nefzawi, was a tall and sharp-featured man with a razor-thin goatee, and a richly embroidered turban.

"They said the gates of Tartarus are weakening," he ranted. "They said that what happened in Fellwater might happen to us next. They said they would protect us, keep us safe, respect our ways. We are only a small freehold, and we have children among us too. We are not enough to protect our madrasa from even a single desert wraith by itself. And so I signed El Duce's treaty. The very next day fifty men set up their tents in our soccer field. They pushed our eldest scholar around, and laughed at his lectures right in front of the students. Those Guardians say they are so much more enlightened than the rest of us. Yet they don't know how to say 'hello' without sneering."

Algernon puffed on his pipe and considered Ibrahim's situation. "So the three of you are looking for asylum, here in Hallowstone?"

"All of us. Sixteen in all."

As Algernon considered their request, Ramanujan Bhattacharya jogged toward them, gasping for breath.

"Is something the matter, Rama?" asked Algernon.

"Oh, the first problem is that I am not a teenager anymore!" he wheezed. "The second is that there is another whale boat in the sky! The DiAngelo are coming back!"

"Please don't tell them we are here," Ibrahim pleaded.

"Get inside the castle," Algernon advised him, and the three Djinnis dashed away. Ramanujan followed them.

The galley of Romans came to land near the castle courtyard, and a squad of centurions climbed out of it, along with Heathcliff.

"Uncle Ally, the prodigal nephew has returned!" Heathcliff laughed, with open arms and an unconvincing smile.

"So I see," Algernon replied. "And you brought a few of your new friends with you."

"My personal bodyguard," Heathcliff grinned. "Can't be too careful these days, what with the doors of the underworld breaking open, you know. It's the end of the world, I tell you!"

Algernon knew Heathcliff had come in force for another reason. "The hospitality of my castle is always open to those who come in peace."

Heathcliff smirked at his uncle's real meaning. "Well, you see, there's a little sticking point in what you've just said.

And I don't mean the implication that I might not have come in peace. Which we will talk about later. I mean the point about the castle being yours."

"Is that so?" Algernon inquired, with a piqued eyebrow. "Kindly explain."

"It's like this," Heathcliff began, as he picked a flower in the garden, sniffed it, then dropped it on the ground and stepped on it. "It occurred to us that we never did have a second election to make you the head of our house again. And I never did officially resign. So, I know it's a tiny little technicality of law, the sort of thing only lawyers and neurotic people care about, but it means that, officially speaking, I'm still the Lord Protector of Hallowstone and of House Wessex. And not you."

Algernon shook his head. "You can quote all the laws you want, but you have lost the moral authority to lead our house."

"You don't need moral authority to be a leader in a democracy," Heathcliff laughed back. "You just need enough votes."

"Just what do you think democracy is, young man?" Algernon lectured him. "You can't just tell people what to do. You have to listen to them, talk with them, care about them. It's a contradiction of logic for a people to vote away their own freedom!"

"It's not my fault if the people wish to vote for a tyrant. But if that's what they want, then I want to be that tyrant."

A cold wave of horror washed over Algernon. "There are older forces in this world, written on the wheels that carry the sun and moon through the sky, which make every man who enslaves his fellow-man a traitor to his people, and a traitor to himself!"

Heathcliff was unmoved. "I'll take that as your acknowledgement that I am Lord Protector," he said. He turned to his centurions. "Gentlemen, lock him up!"

Two centurions quickly surrounded Algernon, and roughly manhandled him toward the castle doors.

"Put him in the same cell where you found me!" Heathcliff ordered. To the other centurions he said, "The rest of you: let's go for a walk into town. With all hell breaking loose from Tartarus, it's time to proclaim some emergency laws."

Two columns of centurions marched down the cobblestone road that led into the terraced village. Heathcliff strode confidently between them, and he twirled his walking-stick and waved happily to everyone they passed. The first few Wessex-men they encountered only stared in dumbfounded surprise. The second cluster of them pointed at Heathcliff and whispered among themselves. The third small group of Wessex-men loudly mocked and berated him: "It's Heathcliff! The usurper! He's back!"

Without needing any prompting from their leader, one or two centurions would break out of their column to punish a nearby protester. They shoved the weaker ones by the scruff of their neck back up the hill to the castle courtyard. The stronger ones were clubbed in the head or thumped in the groin, and left lying on the ground. When the Brigantians and Wessex-men at the outdoor carpentry workshop bellowed more hurtful names at Heathcliff, the centurions kicked over their workbenches and broke their tools on the stones. A Wessex cavalier armed with a sword tried to break through the weather-front formed by the centurion's columns, but he was repelled by the heavy blows of the centurion's maces. In the eye of the storm, untouched by the turbulence an arm's length away, Heathcliff stood on a bench and unfurled a scroll, and began to read from it.

"In light of the present security situation of both real and apprehended danger to the freehold of Hallowstone Castle and village, I, Heathcliff Weatherby Wednesday, the lawful Lord Protector of House Wessex and Castle Hallowstone, do hereby enact the following emergency measures."

From a window in a half-finished house, young Kuvira Bhattacharya could see almost everything. She grasped the little stone figurine which the bann-shee had given her, and squeezed it in her two hands, and whispered into its head.

"Fairy-woman of the moor, the wolves are howling at the door! Fairy-woman of the fen, come, we need your help again!"

~ 55 ~

The negotiating table was now set up in the middle of the mead hall, instead of the stone circle, as it was raining outside that day. Donall sat on his side of the table, flanked by Aeducan on his right and Neachtain on his left. Across from him sat Kendrick, who was casually smoking a cigarette; his usual retinue of four centurions surrounded him. No one else was in the hall, and the silence of their absence caused Donall to shift uncomfortably in his chair.

"It seems to me, Donall, that you have little real choice," Kendrick crooned. "Your grove is almost entirely surrounded by wilderlings from Tartarus. You rely on hired cavaliers from House Wessex to patrol your land, instead of your own people. And while they believe that they owe their freedom to you and your people, still their gratitude is not a bottomless well. On top of that, your new business venture, selling lumber from your arboretum, is not bringing in as much cash as you had hoped. And now, some of your best fighters, and your own shield-maiden with them, have deserted."

Aeducan cast his eyes to the floor.

"Finally, if I may say so, I think you are not telling me the whole truth about your own physical health," Kendrick finished, and he tapped his ribs, to show that he knew about Donall's worsening wound.

Donall's breathing was now slightly laboured; he could not inhale without causing himself a small degree of pain. He did his best to keep his demeanour calm.

"I can still stand, and hold my sword. I am still a warrior," Donall assured him.

"So you are," Kendrick agreed, "but how long do you think you can continue like this?"

Donall looked to Aeducan, to indicate that he should do the talking on behalf of the Brigantians for a while. Aeducan exchanged a glance with Neachtain.

"Tell us again what you are offering in return," Aeducan stated.

"Donall shall remain chieftain of the Brigantians, of course," Kendrick announced, after a drag from his cigarette. "Every current member of your clan shall become honourary members of the Guardians, with all the privileges that will be due to them. All of you can, of course, freely come and go in Fellwater Grove. And in any freehold that has joined the New Renaissance. Incidentally, that includes the pleasures of the temple at Domus Eleutherios. Think about that for a minute."

Aeducan leaned back in his chair, and glanced at Neachtain again before speaking. "That sounds like a good deal. Except that it's mostly symbolic. Can you offer anything more practical?"

"We are also prepared to give complete amnesty to any

member of your clan who has broken the peace with the DiAngelo in the last thirty-six months," Kendrick added.

"All of us?" Aeducan questioned him.

"With some exceptions. I have been instructed not to extend this amnesty to those you have exiled, or those who have recently renounced their membership. It's a reasonable condition; I hope you agree."

Aeducan wondered whether Kendrick knew about what happened in the library on the previous night.

"So that will include people like our former chieftain, Miranda Brigand?" he asked.

Kendrick nodded. "It will. But it will not include banished outsiders like Eric Laflamme."

"I see," Aeducan acknowledged.

"You will also be glad to know," Kendrick droned, between pulls on his cigarette, "that the land itself shall remain in Brigantian hands."

Donall was pleased to hear this. "Ambassador," he said, though he had to cough painfully as soon as he spoke, "I would like to discuss your terms with my people for a while. In private, if you don't mind."

Kendrick nodded. Then he snapped his fingers, and one of his aids laid a scroll on the table, along with an inkwell and a quill.

"I trust you will make the wise decision," Kendrick smiled. "I will be at my camp."

Before Kendrick disappeared out the door, Aeducan asked him, "One last question, Ambassador. How is your wife?"

Kendrick did not expect Aeducan's question, so he paused before answering, "She is awake, but she is severely ill. She can't get out of bed, she's in constant pain, and she can barely speak. But it seems that she will live. Thank you for asking."

When the ambassador and his entourage departed, Donall let out a long and tired sigh, and cradled his forehead in his fingers. "Can one of you bring me a bowl of water please?" he asked, and Neachtain went to the kitchen to fetch it. Donall wiped his hands down in the water to clean them, and then splashed a handful of water on his face.

Neachtain regarded Donall dispassionately for a moment, and then turned and left the mead hall without saying anything.

Donall watched the blanket over the mead hall door settle back into place after Neachtain had flung it open on his way out. Then he shifted himself to face his guard captain and said, "Aeducan Brigand, my good brother-in-arms. I think you might be my last real friend in this world."

"I think that will depend on what you do with this treaty," Aeducan told him, in a soft but direct voice.

"What do you mean?" Donall asked.

Aeducan stood and picked a candle from a nearby shelf, and pinched the wick in his fingers to light it. Then he placed the candle beside the treaty on the table.

"Here you have a candle, and here you have a quill. And between them you have this treaty. You understand my meaning now?"

"I see," Donall reluctantly affirmed.

Aeducan sat in the chair that Kendrick vacated, put his elbows on the table and folded his hands under his chin.

"There's got to be another choice here," Donall pleaded. "We've got more allies than just the Wessex-men. We can get more help!"

Aeducan was growing annoyed. "There might have been more choices a week ago. But you pissed them away by drinking in here, and ignoring what was happening out there!"

Donall didn't notice Aeducan's ire; he was still imagining other options. "Maybe the Orenda Nation can help patrol our lands. Maybe Clan Cymru, or Clan Gaeleach, can send some people."

"Even with their help, how long do you think we can last?" Aeducan challenged.

"Long enough to show the ambassador that we don't need his help," Donall confidently answered.

"A week. Ten days. That's all," Aeducan sternly corrected him. "And only if the other clans don't have their own problems. Look, Donall, you are still my chieftain. But I need you to make a chieftain's decision. Pick up that treaty, and sign it, or burn it. Don't put off this decision any longer. Do it before the ambassador runs out of patience, and makes your decision for you."

Donall took the treaty in his hands, and held it beneath his nose to gather its scent. He closed his eyes and whispered, "I wish Ciara was here."

"Donall," Aeducan prompted him. "The quill, or the

candle."

Donall made his chieftain's decision.

~ 56 ~

Seven hundred and two kilometers south–east of Hallowstone, Miranda Brigand sat in her living room near her wood–burning stove, attaching clean new strings on to her guitar. From the ceiling above came the sound of angry voices in a village street, and the crack of wood and steel upon bone.

She heard Kuvira's voice desperately whispering: "Fairy-woman of the moor, the wolves are breaking down the door! Fairy-woman of the night, come and put the wolves to flight!"

Miranda put the guitar down and climbed the wrought-iron spiral stairs to the loft above her kitchen, and retrieved a small chest from behind a panel in the wall behind her bed. She took the chest downstairs and opened it, and smiled to find inside it the long hood of the bann-shee. Blue and green spirals grew upon her arms and legs, and her jeans and blouse became a leather and linen Celtic battle-dress.

She selected her weapons from a hall closet: a sling-staff and a clutch of stones, and a dagger made from ancient bog-blackened wood. At last she took up the hood and rolled it under her arm.

Miranda did not take more than four steps into her garden when she heard someone clear his throat. She spun around, and her dagger flashed out and stopped just short of the trespasser's neck. Only after that did she recognize Paul Turner, since he was not dressed in his centurion's armour, as usual. Instead he was in an ordinary fall jacket, and a beret that bore the crest of the Guardians. He was leaning on the wall of her house, sheltered from the rain by an umbrella and the overhang of the roof.

"Isn't this house of yours a nemeton? Where no violence is allowed?" said Paul, as he tapped the blade of her knife with his finger.

"Aren't you trespassing?" Miranda snorted back.

"I was hoping you would have me as your guest, at least for a few minutes," Paul replied. Then he opened his hands and said, "I have no weapons. I'm not here to fight. I only want to talk."

Miranda evaluated him for a moment. Then she put away her dagger and said, "Very well, you are my guest. Although I can't let you stay long today. There's somewhere I have to go."

"Or is that somewhere the bann-shee has to go?" Paul asked.

"That's a bold thing to say to your host!" Miranda challenged him.

Paul shrugged and said, "I know it was you who helped protect Eric from the rakshasas after his trial. I'm the one who has to listen to your every word through that bug under your lamp. And I just compared the times when I knew you weren't home, to the times when the bann-shee appeared. It was surprisingly easy."

"You're a clever young man," Miranda remarked coldly.

"I know you're the bann-shee. I know you're secretly breaking that bargain you made with El Duce himself– the bargain that keeps Fellwater Grove protected– well, now that I know those things, perhaps you would like to offer me something, so that I'll forget those things?" said Paul.

"Are you trying to blackmail me?" Miranda laughed.

Paul looked around the garden casually. "You know, when I was thinking about you and the bann-shee, and putting two and two together, I said to myself, why not? My silence must be worth something to you. Name your price."

Miranda paced around him as she spoke. "So. You discovered one of my secrets. You found a way to use that secret to threaten me. You chose my own home as the place to tell me all this, where tradition demands that I do you no harm. You grow more clever by the minute."

"Thank you," Paul smirked.

"Yet as I listen to all this, I can't help think to myself: are you sure that you are the only person who knows what you think you know?"

"What do you mean?"

"While we chat here so pleasantly in my back garden, that bug you planted in my house is still there. And you are certain no one else is listening to us right now?"

"Of course I am," Paul asserted.

"No one who would be annoyed that you went behind his back to gain an advantage over me for yourself personally, and not share it with anyone on your team? Not even your boss?"

"Quite sure," Paul asserted again, but Miranda saw the doubt flicker in his face for a moment.

"Just so that we're clear about this, you're totally and completely confident that no one will discover that you're a shameless mercenary, with no loyalty to anyone but yourself?"

Paul's gaze began to shift around the garden uncomfortably.

Miranda bore her gaze down heavily upon Paul's head to make her last point. "So it's safe to conclude that the moment you set foot off my property and you are no longer under my protection as my guest, that no one will be waiting for you to take you anywhere?"

Paul's nervousness became impossible for him to hide. "What makes you think anyone would be?"

"Wait for it," she told him, with an upraised finger. Within seconds, they both heard the sound of several vehicles arriving in Miranda's driveway, and their doors opening and closing.

Paul tried to reclaim his initiative. "That must be the Guardian Auxiliaries. They're here for you, Miranda. They know about how you broke your bargain with El Duce. And they're here to take a bloody payment from you."

"That they may be," she agreed, "but are you certain they are not here for you, too?"

Paul stepped closer to the door to Miranda's cottage, and his fingers touched the wall behind him.

Miranda perked her ears to the sound of a dozen pairs of boots marching about the other side of her house. "Where do you think they might want to take you? Somewhere deep underground, perhaps? Think you might get a trial, first?"

The next sound to reach them from around the house was the sound of voices speaking on two-way radios, issuing orders and directing troop movements. Paul's fingers inched around the handle of Miranda's door.

"Miranda– please help me," he quietly pleaded.

Miranda let a little smile grow on her face. "Interesting to see that you are more afraid of them, than you are afraid of every bann-shee in the world, all of whom will want to mount your head on her wall for what you tried to do to me here today. But I suppose death would be preferable to even one day in

Tartarus."

"You can't let them know I'm here!" Paul begged her.

"Then I propose a new deal between us. I keep my secret, you keep your life," Miranda growled.

Paul could no longer handle the fear. He galloped down to the end of the garden, leapt over the hedge, and ran away.

Miranda watched him run for a moment. Then she walked through the garden gate and down the path, lush with rain-soaked ferns and long tigerlilly fronds, and shadowed by tall cedars. As soon as she rounded the front corner of her cottage, she made a dismissive gesture with her hands. The noises of car engines, marching boots, and radios, faded into silence.

Miranda smiled.

~ 57 ~

Eric's kitchen table was cluttered with teacups, coffee pots, pencils, note pads, and maps. The Fianna sat around it, some in relaxed and thoughtful postures, some still intensely studying the notes and papers in front of them.

"So, everyone is happy with this plan?" said Ciara. Each in their turn signaled their satisfaction.

"I still think it's crazy," Finnbarr joked.

Eric stood and announced, "I think it's the best plan we've got. Ready to go?"

Everyone said that they were ready.

"All right. See you at the starting line in one hour."

Everyone departed in different directions. Ciara took to the air on a flying broomstick. Maread went in another direction on her motorcycle. Finnbarr departed on a city bus. Síle left through a seven league door. Finally, Ildicoe gave Eric an intimate parting kiss.

"Glad to be adventuring with you again, Eric," she told him. Then she leapt off his balcony, and faded to invisibility before she hit the ground.

Eric cradled his cat in his arms, and hoped that he would fulfill his part of the plan as well as his friends expected.

~ 58 ~

Finnbarr boldly planted his two feet on the edge of the square in

Clan Fianna

front of Domus Eleutherios, and belted out his warrior's challenge.

"I am Finnbarr MacBride! The lightning-striker! The stallion of Fellwater! Greatest warrior of Fianna! Greatest of all the Celtic clans of the Hidden World! I've come to challenge your greatest fighter to single combat! Who dares to fight me, man to man! Come, you pasty-skinned pencil-necks! Fight me, or the world will know you as a clan of fat cats and wastrels! I say no Roman can best me in battle. Come and prove me right!"

It was certainly enough to get the attention of everyone in the square. Several DiAngelo centurions dashed out from various doors and surrounded him. They kept their blades pointed at him, but they would not let themselves be taunted by him.

Carlo DiAngelo emerged from the temple, and the centurions confronting Finnbarr parted to let him through.

"So, I see we have a wild young Brigantian who wishes to test his mettle against the proven strength of Rome?"

"I am no Brigantian anymore. I am Fianna! I've no clan, no chieftain, no lands– and no fear!" Finnbarr taunted back.

"A Fianna! Well! If you are no Brigantian, then the peace treaty we have with them does not protect you. This fight to prove your honour shall have to be a fight to the death."

Finnbarr did not step back, nor did he flinch, but he did briefly scan the square with his eyes, in search of his companions, in case he might need help.

Carlo tapped one of his centurions on the shoulder and said to him, "You're up first, Questor. Kill him."

The centurion grinned, and took up a fighting stance against Finnbarr. The other centurions stepped back, and joined a circle of onlookers which was forming quickly around them. Someone emerged from a nearby building carrying a shield for the centurion to wear on his arm. Finnbarr spun his spear around his body and over his head in an impressive display of martial dexterity. The centurion eyed him cautiously, and then jumped into the fray.

Behind the growing crowd that gathered to watch Finnbarr fighting the centurion, two cloaked figures stole inside the front doors of the temple, and three more dashed around the building and into the shadows behind it.

~ 59 ~

Most of the guards posted outside Domus Eleutherios had gone outside to watch Finnbarr sparring with anybody and everybody, so Maread and Ciara had an easier time moving through the temple unchallenged. Ciara wore a Guardians uniform under her cloak, which she had borrowed from Eric that afternoon. Maread wore a plain cotton dress and plain flat shoes, although she added a hooded cowl to cover her hair and face. She had been seen on a wanted poster a few days before, and was worried about being identified.

Once inside, a temple acolyte approached them and said, "Welcome to Domus Eleutherios! You must be new here, so if you don't mind I must ask to see your letter of invitation."

Ciara sternly rebuked the acolyte. "Don't you know who I am?"

"Excuse me?" the acolyte blinked.

"I am a special emissary from House Tolstoy! Here to negotiate the entry of my house into the New Renaissance. My visit has been planned for weeks! If you're not the official reception party, then where the hell is it!" Ciara barked. The acolyte only blinked with confusion.

"Oh, I'm sorry," Ciara continued, "but I suppose you are not important enough to know anything about that. Best if you forget I said anything, and take me to the Patrician's private chambers."

"His *private* chambers?" stuttered the acolyte.

"We have a gift for him," Ciara informed him, and she nodded toward Maread, who lowered her head.

"Oh, I see. A tribute," the acolyte nodded. "You don't mind if I confirm this with the watch officer?"

"I'll tell you what. If you can be discreet about our presence, then House Tolstoy may have a gift for you too. Tonight." Ciara gently caressed Maread's chin with her finger.

"Right this way," the acolyte smiled, and he beckoned them to follow him.

When Maread thought the acolyte could not hear her, she whispered, "What the hell, Ciara!"

"I know it's bullshit. But it's how these people do business."

The main floor of the temple had been fitted with a gladiator's ring. Beneath the solemn eyes of the statue of

Eleutherios, two heavily armoured fighters assaulted each other with sword and fist, while an audience cheered them on. A bookmaker was collecting bets for the next fight on the program, and tallying the odds on popular fighters. Women in priestess robes threaded through the crowd, refilling people's drinking horns from clay jugs. In the galleries above, the best dressed patrons sipped martinis while watching the fighting or placing bets on roulette tables.

"Now we know where the DiAngelo get their money," whispered Ciara.

Maread pulled the hood over her head a little lower. Ciara did her best to keep a straight face and avoid eye contact with anyone, although she squeezed Maread's hand tightly.

"Just keep walking," Maread whispered back.

Carlo's private chambers in the temple resembled a hotel suite. Two couches faced each other across a coffee table; a flat-screen television and writing desk filled one wall, and well-stocked bar filled the other. A pair of double doors opened to a bedroom, and another pair of doors opened to a balcony. On the wall above the bar hung a fresco of the transfigured saviour, floating over the defeated bodies of his brothers, while a crowd of amazed worshippers looked on.

As soon as the acolyte was gone, Ciara and Maread rushed to the balcony. First they signaled the darkness with flashlights, to let Ildicoe, Síle, and Eric know where they were. When they saw the answering signal, Ciara opened her briefcase and took out two coiled mountain climbing ropes with grappling hooks. She and Maread threw them down the side of the temple and fixed them to the balcony railing, for their friends to climb. Then they scurried back into the room.

"Now we have to find the cup before Carlo gets here," Ciara reminded Maread.

"That's if it's in here at all," Maread warned.

"The sooner we get out of here, the better," Ciara replied.

~ 60 ~

Finnbarr and Questor fought each other to a stalemate. Every thrust from both fighters was parried, every slice was blocked, and every swing was dodged. Finnbarr salted his fighting style with mocking laughter and unnecessarily showy flourishes.

Questor began to tire, and at the same time rage: he had not landed a single blow on Finnbarr at all. Seeing Finnbarr win admiration from the crowd was humiliating.

In an act of desperation he charged directly toward Finnbarr, screaming a battle-cry. Finnbarr saw him coming, and with a a swift step to the side, Questor found himself flipping upside-down and crashing to the stones of the square on his back, the tip of Finnbarr's spearhead above his throat.

"To the death, you say?" Finnbarr taunted Carlo. "Let's see your thumbs. Up for mercy, down for the kill. Come on!"

Carlo only folded his arms. "You can defeat one man in single combat. That doesn't make you a great warrior."

Most of the onlookers laughed, their thumbs pointed down.

Finnbarr glanced at the windows of the temple for any sign of his companions. Seeing none, he turned to Carlo.

"Send me two more."

Carlo smiled.

"Castor, Pollux, it's your turn."

The two centurions leapt up without hesitation, and flung themselves at the Celt.

Finnbarr was prepared. He took Questor's sword and grasped it point-down with his shield arm, to use as a blocking weapon. He circled around his two attackers, keeping one in front of the other, so that he would have to deal with only one of them at a time. When once the two centurions managed to catch Finnbarr between them, Finnbarr was able to duck and dodge and roll out of the way, such that the they almost struck each other. Finnbarr kept them moving and kept them working, until they too began to tire, and to fume with frustration.

Finnbarr saw an acolyte approach the scene, and whisper something in Carlo's ear, and guessed that Carlo now knew about the intruders in his chambers. The next stage of their plan was about to begin. He changed his fighting style from flamboyant moves that kept his opponents guessing, to a more efficient style which disarmed both of them quickly.

With a combination of footwork and swordplay, both of the centurions landed on their backs on the ground beside Questor. With one foot on the chest of a fallen centurions, he raised his spear to the sky and roared.

"I am Finnbarr MacBride! The stallion of Fellwater! Greatest warrior of all the Hidden World!" To shame his

Clan Fianna

defeated opponents, he held his sword with the hilt in his groin and the tip in the air, and pretended to milk it. Some of the onlookers sneered with disgust, while others laughed.

Carlo snapped his fingers. "Sword. Now," he grunted at a nearby centurion. The startled man unsheathed his sword. Carlo had it in his own hand before it was fully out of its scabbard.

Finnbarr readied himself to face his new opponent. Carlo strode forward confidently, and his sword lashed out. Finnbarr saw his spear fly into the air and clatter on the flagstones some distance away. He switched to his sword, but Carlo quickly disarmed him with another expert flourish. Finally, Carlo pressed forward and struck Finnbarr's head with the flat of his blade. Finnbarr stepped back, dazed from the blow, and tripped on one of the fallen centurions. Now Carlo had his foot on Finnbarr's chest, and his sword at Finnbarr's neck.

"Finnbarr MacBride, mare of Fellwater! Go back to your friends and boast about how you faced me in single combat, and I did not kill you."

Heart pounding, Finnbarr scuttled away, first to grab his sword, and then to quit the scene. The audience laughed as he departed, but as he staggered down the path through the trees, still dazed from Carlo's last blow, he turned and checked the windows of the temple.

~ 61 ~

Síle, listening at the door of Carlo's suite, suddenly stood up.

"I think he's coming!"

She and Maread took positions on either side of the door, and unsheathed their swords. Ciara stood front and centre, so that she would be the first thing Carlo would see when he opened the door.

Carlo entered, followed by his acolyte.

"Greetings from House Tolstoy," smiled Ciara.

"House who?" asked Carlo. He recognized Ciara. "Wait a minute. You're a DeDannan!"

Maread immediately slammed the door shut again and locked it. Síle knocked the startled acolyte unconscious with a blow from the hilt of her sword.

Maread pointed the tip of her blade to Carlo's throat. He dodged and drew a dagger of his own, but Síle and Ciara were pointing swords at him as well.

Carlo smiled patronizingly, holding out his weapon for one of them to collect.

"Very well. I surrender, and I salute your audacity," he told them. "Perhaps you would like me to put my hands up now?"

Ciara pulled Carlo's hands behind his back and tied them with a zip cord. Then she pushed him into the couch, while Síle and Maread kept their weapons ready.

"So, the young man outside was a diversion? Very clever!"

The balcony doors opened. Eric strode in, full of confidence and pride, and sat across from Carlo.

"Oh ho!" Carlo laughed. "Young master Laflamme! So you are the mastermind of this operation!"

"It's a team effort, actually." Eric smiled.

"Interesting," Carlo mused. "Now that you have me at your mercy under my own roof, what will you do?"

"I'm going to enjoy the moment, first," Eric gloated. "It seems not so long ago, I was the one tied in the chair, and you were standing over me."

Carlo turned to Maread, who was standing nearest him, and said, "It's like I always say: give any man a taste of real power, he soon turns into an asshole."

"Shut it!" Maread warned him.

In his hands, Eric held an object under a cloth. He removed the cloth and revealed the Cup of Cormac the King. The animals and gods carved on its face were alert and anxious, as if prepared to fight or to flee.

Carlo eyed it and understood what Eric wanted. "I see. You're here for a re-trial." he whistled.

Ciara produced a digital recording device from her pocket, turned it on, and placed it on the table next to the chalice.

"We're also here for the record," she added.

"It seems I have no choice but to answer your questions," Carlo admitted, "at least until my people notice that I'm missing."

"First question," said Eric, ignoring Carlo's implied threat. "Did you visit Fellwater Grove four nights ago?"

"I did," Carlo answered truthfully. The chalice remained intact.

"Why," Eric asked next.

"To meet with Livia Julia McManus, a relative of mine."

"Did you send her to meet with me, to ask me about the fire at your house?"

"I did."

"What did she tell you?"

"She said you didn't do it."

"Do you believe me now, when I tell you myself, standing here in front of you, with this chalice, that I did not do it?"

Eric tapped the table next to the chalice when he posed that last question. The chalice did not break.

Carlo sniffed at the chalice. "This artifact is not a judge of anything. It is only a curiosity of history. Think about how easily it was bent to serve my truth, rather than yours."

"The truth is the truth," Eric asserted. "It's neither mine nor yours."

"You're confusing truth with fact. A sophomore mistake," Carlo countered with a patronizing grin. "Facts are things you can read about in schoolbooks or see in a microscope. They change all the time; they can't be trusted. But truths: they are the rocks on which I build my temple. A thing is true because my integrity depends on it. Because there is no alternative that I can accept. And that truth is, it doesn't matter who lit the match that started the fire, and who didn't. You were there when it happened, you did nothing to stop it, so you are responsible. And I will have my justice."

The chalice vibrated a little bit in response to Carlo's words, but did not break.

"Katie and Tara are dead now, because of you," Eric growled. "So you've already had your justice."

The chalice vibrated again.

"Eric," said Ciara, and she gestured in a way that reminded him to calm down and get on with the job.

So Eric moved to his next question. "Did you poison Livia DiAngelo?" he asked next.

"No," Carlo answered.

The chalice still did not break. The three Fianna women looked at each other with disappointment.

Ciara stepped forward and said, "What about the person who met Livia in the arboretum that night. Was that you?"

"No," Carlo replied. Again, the chalice remained whole. Tension returned to Eric's shoulders, and he looked to the others for suggestions.

"Really? It wasn't you?" Eric flustered.

"Well, do you believe that trinket of yours, or not?" Carlo shot back.

"So if you didn't do it, who did?" Eric asked.

Carlo sighed like a tired teacher. "You're a smart fellow. Figure it out."

Eric glowered at him, but his mind began working.

"It can't have been Heathcliff. He was locked in the dungeon in Hallowstone," Eric reasoned.

"It can't have been anyone else at the feast that night. They were all too drunk," Ciara reminded him.

"It can't have been that person I saw in the woods that night, either," added Síle. "Because when he left, Livia was still healthy."

"He didn't go to the ambassador's camp to do the deed, or I would have seen him," Maread contributed.

"Maybe one of Kendrick's own soldiers did it," Eric theorized.

"That's not very likely," said Ciara.

"The only other person who could have done it is– oh! Of course. I never considered him at all," Eric finished.

Carlo leaned forward. "Why not?"

"Because he's her husband." Eric replied.

"Sure, they have a perfect marriage," Carlo condescended.

"No, they don't. Livia herself told me so."

"If you really must know," said Carlo, "the night Livia was poisoned she and her husband were arguing about who she might have seen. In the dark, in the woods. Need I say more, Eric? But I didn't stay to listen. I got what I came for, so I left."

"So she was having an affair," Eric wondered aloud. "That's all. I was thinking that the poisoner's motive was something more, I don't know. Political."

"Well, there's your answer!" Carlo declared. "Now all you have to do convince everyone else of his guilt, and you're home free! And on that happy note, I'll be on my way."

Síle stepped in front of Carlo, her sword at his heart, and demanded, "Who is chopping down the trees in my forest!"

"Some workers hired for the day. How should I know

their names?" Carlo shrugged in reply.

Síle's irritation was growing. "It's a simple question! You know what I mean!"

"I know precisely what you mean. But why should I answer?"

"Because I'm pointing a sword in your chest, you smarmy bastard!" Síle shouted, and she pushed Carlo back into the couch again.

Carlo looked to Eric and said, "This *inamorata* has some fire in her."

"Of course she does!" Eric barked back. "Someone is destroying her home. What do you expect."

"It wasn't my idea to cut down the trees in the grove," Carlo told them. "Although I did find the idea interesting."

The chalice remained in one piece, and Síle shook her head in disappointment.

"Then who's idea was it?" she demanded.

"If you can't figure that out for yourself, you don't deserve to know," Carlo snorted.

Síle let out a frustrated grunt, and let Ciara take her turn interrogating Carlo.

"Are you the one responsible for opening the Tartarus gate, and letting the monsters out?" she questioned him.

"The chthonic gates are opening because they are old and weak. The prisoners are escaping by themselves," Carlo asserted.

The chalice on the table broke into three pieces.

"The chalice, and I, are both witnesses to the contrary," Eric hissed.

"I was just calibrating your lie detector," Carlo smiled to Ciara. "Of course, yes, the chthonic prisons are weakening by design, and not by nature. A little bit of chaos now and then can be a good thing. It helps cut out the deadwood, and open space up for new growth."

The chalice jumped back into one piece again.

Carlo looked to Eric and said, "Eric, I may as well say I am impressed that you were able to escape."

Eric shrugged his shoulders. "People underestimate me all the time."

Carlo's face, however, remained stern. "Don't push your luck with me."

Eric glowered at Carlo, as if willing his adversary to

concede defeat. Ciara tired of their staring contest. She stood between them and pressed Carlo with her question again.

"So are the gates opening by *your* design?"

"In fact I do know who is responsible for that stratagem," Carlo admitted. "But I cannot tell you his name."

Mairead and Síle poked him with their swords. "Tell us, or we'll kill you."

"If you kill me, you still won't have your answers. Instead you'll have my corpse to dispose of. And a temple full of my centurions chasing you." Then he glared at Eric and asked, "You don't have a plan for that, do you?"

Eric said nothing.

Síle pushed her sword point into Carlo's shoulder a little more. "We don't have to kill you to hurt you," she growled.

Carlo tried to sit up straighter. "You misunderstand. Ever wonder why those judges at your tribunal wore those masks? All of El Duce's messengers hide their faces. That way, when you speak to one of them, you don't know whether you are actually speaking to the man himself."

"Humph! Anyone can wear a mask and pretend to be someone he's not," Eric observed. "Siobhan passed herself off as Ildicoe. And Paul Turner pretended to be Amergin."

"The faces worn by his messengers are their calling cards. Gold-plated, jewel-encrusted; they're very hard to counterfeit, very hard to mistake." Carlo informed him.

Ciara wanted to draw the conclusion. "So you're saying that the man who opened the vaults of Tartarus is one of El Duce's personal servants?"

"The leader's emissaries are a little closer to the boss than I am. But I do not know any of their names, or their houses, or how to find them. When you have need of them, *they* find *you*."

Ciara looked to the chalice on the table for a report about Carlo's words, and found that Carlo spoke true.

"He could be that fellow by the door, who you knocked out just now. Or he could be this girl here who never washes her hair!" said Carlo, enjoying himself.

Mairead shoved Eric out of her way and tried to pounce on Carlo, but Ciara pulled her back, saying, "All right, Mairead. You too, Eric. Both of you! He's just trying to get a rise out of you, so that someone will hear us shouting, and come to rescue him!"

Maread roughly pushed Ciara's hands away, but she did step back.

Eric was still annoyed, and confronted Carlo again. "You're the patrician of your House for all Ontario. And a major financial backer for the Guardians. So you should know the name of the man who– oh, I see! You're actually just a middle manager."

"I answer directly to El Duce!" Carlo glowered, but there was something slightly forced about his bravado. Eric decided that he was right.

Ciara put her hand on Eric's shoulder and said, "We've got everything we can get from him. Let's go."

Eric nodded, then picked up the digital recorder on the table, and wrapped the Cup of Cormac in its veil again. "I'm taking this with me," he told Carlo.

Carlo stood up, and easily snapped off the zip-ties around his wrists, and dropped them to the floor. Then he saluted his departing captors. Eric realized that Carlo could have done that at any time, and he felt a flutter of foreboding pass through his heart.

He slid down the rope a little faster, and told his companions to run.

~ 62 ~

The Bann-Shee stood on the roof of a house in Hallowstone, and watched the parade of Heathcliff's centurions rounding up the dissenters and protesters. Though she drew no special attention to herself, she was soon spotted.

"The Bann-Shee!" cried a voice from the village.

The bann-shee lodged a pebble in her sling-staff, and with it she shot Heathcliff's hat off his head.

"Get her down here!" Heathcliff ordered his centurions, and the centurions swarmed the house the bann-shee stood on. By the time they had opened the trapdoor to the roof, the bann-shee had gracefully backflipped off the house and was gone.

The first of the centurions to emerge from the house saw a flash of blue and green, and received a blow to the back of his head. The next one, turning to see where his companion had fallen, felt a blow to his abdomen, and collapsed in a fetal ball.

The bann-shee pounced upon two more, leaving both of them as she had the others. Heathcliff ordered more of his men to chase her, but she leapt into the branches of a nearby rowan tree and vanished into its autumn-painted leaves.

This left Heathcliff with fewer bodyguards, and emboldened the Wessex villagers to protest his return more vigorously.

"Sir, what should we do?" asked one of Heathcliff's bodyguards.

"Push them back, of course," Heathcliff told him.

"Sir, we can't. There's too many of them!"

"These people are not warriors. They won't stand in our way."

"Yes, sir, they will!"

Only then did Heathcliff fully grasp the situation he was in. The smile on his face melted. He stepped out of the ring of guards and addressed the people: "I am still the lawful Lord Protector of Hallowstone!"

In response, the villagers banged on pots and pans with wooden spoons. Someone shouted, "You arrested Algernon! Let him go!" Soon the whole group was shouting "Free Algernon!"

Heathcliff shouted back, "Algernon is a traitor! And so is anyone who supports him!"

Even as Heathcliff repeated his charge, the villagers kept banging on their pots and demanding Algernon's release, and Heathcliff's resignation. When Heathcliff could no longer hear his voice over the din, he stopped, and gazed uncomprehendingly upon the people.

"Sir, we need orders!" said his centurion captain.

Heathcliff hesitated for a breath, and then said, "I should have known these people wouldn't listen to reason. Fall back to the castle."

In the castle courtyard, the centurions who had arrested Algernon opened the gates, only to find the three Nefzawi brothers, their scimitars unsheathed, waiting for them.

"Good morning, can we help you?" Ibrahim mocked them.

The centurions let Algernon go, and fled.

Algernon dusted himself off. "Thank you," he said to the Nefzawi brothers.

Then the centurions returned, this time as part of Heathcliff's entourage retreating from the angry crowd.

"Into the castle again," Ibrahim suggested.

"Won't Heathcliff just follow us in there?" Ghazwan

wondered.

"He will," said Algernon. "We can escape through the catacombs, then shut the gate behind us, and trap him inside."

"Who will keep him from getting out the front door?"

The answer to that question came in the form of more stones from the Bann-Shee's sling–staff, which harrowed the centurions from the top of the castle walls.

"She will," said Algernon told them.

"Right, then," said Ibrahim. He and the Nefzawi brothers darted into the castle. Heathcliff's centurions saw them go, and wanted to follow, but they were themselves being followed by an angry crowd of villagers, and pelted by the Bann-Shee's stones.

"Bar the doors," ordered Heathcliff, once he was inside the castle.

A moment later, Algernon and his companions emerged from one of the catacomb portals a short distance from the castle. With the help of some of the workers at the carpentry shop they barricaded it closed.

The bann-shee was now perched on a rooftop that gave her a good view of the crowd that was filling the castle courtyard and turning Heathcliff into a veritable prisoner in 'his' own castle. Once she saw Algernon emerge from the catacombs safely, she ducked around behind the house, and through some hedges and over a few garden walls, and found where Kuvira was hiding. There she relaxed at last, and removed her hood.

"Is the man with all those soldiers gone now?" Kuvira asked.

"He's trapped in the castle," said Miranda.

Kuvira fearfully ventured a look around the corner of the wall she was leaning on, and saw the crowd in the courtyard, noisily demanding that Heathcliff should face them, or that he should resign, or that he should leave Hallowstone forever.

Then Kuvira rounded on Miranda and howled, "You were supposed to fight that man, and stop him from coming here, or something! You were supposed to win! So why is he still here!"

"I couldn't force him out of the village. Not while he had all those soldiers around him. I did the best I could," Miranda apologized.

"You told me you would help if I ever called on you!" Kuvira pouted.

"He's trapped in that castle now. The people won't let him out," Miranda assured her. But Kuvira stomped away, and dropped the goddess figurine on the ground.

Miranda picked up the figurine and watched Kuvira go for a moment. Then she turned to the scene unfolding in the castle courtyard. Heathcliff's victory parade had become a siege.

~ 63 ~

The Fianna gathered in a pub in downtown Royal Wyndham, not far from Domus Eleutherios. They claimed a booth, and ordered a pitcher of honey–brown beer.

Finnbarr was the most excited. "I actually had a sword fight with Carlo himself! And what can I say? He didn't kill me! I'd say that makes me one of the top fighters in the country!" he bragged.

"Sure it does," Maread doubted him, although she was smiling too.

"Hey, you and Ciara talked your way past the guards and into Carlo's bedroom. That's no small thing!" Finnbarr praised her.

Maread was more circumspect. "It feels like we don't have much to show for it."

Ciara tried to be positive. "We know who the poisoner was."

Eric unfurled Cormac's Cup from under its veil and said, "We also have this." He placed it on the table. The figures on its face lay in restful postures; they were still alert to everyone's words, but it seemed they were happier to be held by the Fianna than by their previous keepers.

"Amergin told me someone stole it," Ildicoe mused, as she took it in her hands and admired it.

"We stole it back," smiled Finnbarr.

"I think it wanted us to steal it. I think the cup lets itself be taken by whoever is supposed to have it," said Síle.

"How do you know?" asked Eric.

"I asked it, and it told me," Síle replied, in a matter-of-fact way.

Maread rolled her eyes. "She's been talking to inanimate objects since she was nine years old," she smiled.

"Don't you start," Síle chastised her sister. "Just because you can't hear the voices of things, it doesn't mean they can't talk."

"I can hear the voices of things," Finnbarr tried to charm her.

Maread swatted him. "No you can't, you smartass," she said.

Finnbarr smiled, but he also sat back in his seat, deflated by Maread.

"So, here's where we stand," said Ciara, taking charge as the de–facto leader of the group. "We still don't know who is letting the dogs out. As far as that goes, we're pretty much back where we started in the library. But we did get out of there with this treasure. Mission accomplished, I say."

"You're right! Let's fill it with beer and have a drink!" Finnbarr suggested.

"Hey!" Síle objected. "This is Cormac's Cup you're talking about!"

"I know," Finnbarr complained. "But we shouldn't just stick it in a museum and never use it."

"We could drop in on a few other people with some questions, like we did to Carlo," suggested Maread.

"People like Donall," Ciara proposed.

"Or Kendrick," Síle added.

"I know who we should talk to," Eric asserted. "The man whose name Carlo said he didn't know."

The other Fianna mused that he was probably right.

"I saw him, actually. Down there. When they were loading the things with the crab claw hands into the train," Eric said.

"I think we all know who it is, now," said Ildicoe, and everyone around the table sounded their agreement.

"This time," said Ildicoe, "I think we shouldn't go to him We should make him come to us."

"Okay, but where?"

"A place he won't suspect is a trap. A place where he'll think he's in control. A place where he'll think we are in more danger than he is. The Tartarus Gate."

"Oh, that's brilliant!"

"I know what we can use for bait, Eric," she added.

Eric perked his eyebrows, and waited for her to tell him. A heartbeat later, he figured it out for himself. He sat back in his chair, and shook his head.

"Can't someone else do it?" he pleaded.

"You're the one they hate the most," Ciara reminded him. "Besides, you had a private moment with Livia that night. And no one knows what she might have told you. What you might threaten to reveal to the world."

"She didn't tell me anything!" Eric protested.

Cormac's cup cracked and split in two. Eric's friends all jumped, and then looked to him for an explanation.

"Sorry. Slip of the tongue. Obviously she did tell me stuff," he told them. "But nothing to do with their Magnum Opus. Nothing we can use."

The cup mended itself, and Eric picked it up before it rolled off the table.

"The point," said Ciara, "is that they don't know what she might have told you. It *might* have been about their big secret plan. That's what will scare them."

Eric saw the logic of Ciara's plan. "All right," he conceded.

"My fellow Fianna, I think we're ready for our next adventure," Ciara declared happily. She took up Cormac's Cup, filled it with beer, and held it high.

"Truth in our hearts!" she proclaimed.

With renewed joy, the Fianna called back, "Strength in our arms!"

"Fulfillment of our oaths!" Ciara sang.

The Fianna clinked their beer cups on Cormac's chalice, and cheered. They were outsiders now, but they toasted their friendship with the cup of a king. They had no chieftain, no land, and no tribe, but they had each other.

~ 64 ~

The people of Hallowstone built a small fire in the centre of the castle courtyard, just before its front doors. About two dozen people stood around it or sat in wooden chairs near its lip, including Ibrahim Nefzawi and his two brothers, and the Bhattacharya family. Some of them were cooking sausages on pokers or on little metal grills. A few children were roasting marshmallows over the fire using wire coat hangers. Once in a while, one of the Wessex-men would shout something at the castle windows, or bang a stick on the door. They taunted the centurions, and sometimes Heathcliff himself, to come out and face them.

"We've sealed up the other entrances to the catacombs, and built barricades across all the other castle gates," Algernon explained to Satya, Ramanujan, and Ibrahim. "Now, the only way Heathcliff can get out is through the front door."

"Through all of us," Satya contributed, with a smile.

"He's probably calling for help, then," Ibrahim guessed.

"If help comes, for him or for us, it won't arrive until tomorrow morning," Algernon informed them.

Ramanujan said, "Until then, well, we have a fire to keep us warm, and good people around us, and a sky full of stars above. There are many in this world who would say we are very blessed. Very blessed indeed."

Algernon chuckled softly. "First I was locked inside my castle. Now I am locked out of it! Irony may well be a force of nature."

Satya looked to the town behind her and said, "The people are saying there's a ban-shee out there, watching over us, protecting us."

Algernon drew a breath full of smoke from his pipe and said, "Inscrutable creature, the Bann-Shee. If we're protected by her then I'm glad of it, but the help of a bann-shee is a mixed blessing. Death always follows them."

A short distance away, Kuvira overheard Algernon's remarks, and said to herself, "I think the bann-shee is no help at all."

On a rooftop some distance away, Miranda kept her vigil over the castle and the people gathered in its courtyard. A hooded cloak wrapped around her, keeping her warm, as well as hidden from the eyes of anyone who might look her way.

The long hood of the bann-shee lay on her lap.

~ 65 ~

"This is a heroic hall!" cried Donall, as he stood before his high seat in the centre of the mead hall. "So where is the harp, and where is the singer? Where is the teller of tales!"

No music filled hall tonight. No hearth fire warmed it, no food and drink cheered it, no stories enlivened it.

A man in blue overalls cleared his throat and said, "I'm afraid I'm just your electrician." Then he closed a breaker panel near the entrance. "I'm all done now. Ready to turn it on? See what it looks like?"

Donall nodded. The electrician threw a big black switch, and the hall was suddenly bathed in the blue– white light of a dozen electric lanterns, fixed on the rim of the loft that encircled the hall.

"It looks good," Donall approved, in a low and unenthusiastic voice.

"No more need to worry that all those candles and torches might start a fire," the electrician remarked, as he packed up his tools. "You'll get my bill in the mail in a few days. But I hear the Guardians are paying for it anyway."

As the electrician departed. Donall lowered himself into the chieftain's high seat, leaning on his walking stick. He sipped his cup of mead, and daydreamed into the cold fireplace. Above him, the shiny new electric lanterns with their spiral-coil lightbulbs banished every shadow in the hall, making the space resemble a school or a hospital. Or a prison.

~ 66 ~

Another black night passed; another grey morning followed.

A standing stone had been erected just outside the new entrance to Fellwater Grove, and Ildicoe poured some whiskey from a flask upon it. A moment later, the stones on the ridge obligingly rolled away, revealing the mossy passage to the interior of the grove. The tree-branch gate peeled itself back to admit her, and the guards watched her pass.

The guards were DiAngelo centurions, in full Roman armour, carrying black carbine guns.

Ildicoe walked no more than ten feet past the gate before her legs no longer carried her; she could do nothing more than stand aghast, arrested by the sight of how the grove had changed. In the spring and summer, the area by the gate was a verdant quilt of vegetable gardens, flower beds, meditation ponds, and leaf-lush trees. Now the gardens were over-run with weeds, or else crushed flat by an earth-moving machine parked nearby. The ponds were black with mud, and their shores were littered with cigarettes. Tall metal pylons were erected along the paths, carrying heavy electric cables, and bright lamps that made little pools of blue-white light beneath them. A platoon of Roman centurions marched by, led by a drill sergeant in tabard that displayed the crest of the DiAngelo. They paid no attention to Ildicoe as they passed, though she choked a little bit as they trampled a field strewn with the red maple leaves of autumn. One of the gate guards whistle at her. She tightened her lips, and willed herself to say nothing.

Kendrick's main tent was busier now. More soldiers marched around it, and various clerks and administrators talked excitedly among themselves about their various projects and plans. Kendrick himself was in the centre of it all, examining a large map of the grove and some of the surrounding lands that was spread on a long table, alongside various documents and several tablet computers. He glanced at Ildicoe briefly, barely noting her presence, and returned to his map, and his discussion with the others standing about the table. When Ildicoe did not leave, he looked down on her and said, "And, you are–?"

"Ildicoe Brigand, of House Voyageur, freelance summoner," she answered him.

"what brings you to my grove?"

"Your grove? You're just an ambassador. Donall MacBride is the chieftain."

"Donall MacBride is the chieftain of the Brigantians. The tribe, that is. The land, however, now belongs to me."

A knot formed in Ildicoe's belly. "To you? I was told that you promised the grove would remain in Brigantian hands."

"And so it *has* remained," said Kendrick. "In *my* Brigantian hands."

Ildicoe's fingers involuntarily clenched into a fist.

"Now state your business," Kendrick told her, before she could say anything more about the matter.

Ildicoe reminded herself to breathe. "I carry a message for you, from Eric Laflamme."

"A man of no significance. I don't care to hear it," Kendrick decided, and he waved Ildicoe away. Some nearby guards stepped toward her, and made it clear by their postures that she would be removed by force if she lingered.

So Ildicoe raised her voice for everyone in the tent to hear. "He says he is willing to confess to the poisoning of your wife."

The discussions around the table stopped. Kendrick looked up again, attentive but expressionless. Ildicoe knew what a poker face looks like: she did not miss the subtle flicker of interest in his eye.

"Well, that's good news," he gruffed. "With the culprit properly punished and permanently exiled, preferably underground, then we can put this unhappy chapter behind us. Was there anything else?"

"He wishes you to know that he will turn himself in to the archons of the New Renaissance, tonight. But only on one condition."

Kendrick met this news with a patronizing chortle. "Eric is an outsider and a criminal. He is no position to make demands," he judged.

"He will tell the world about Phase Three of The Magnum Opus," explained Ildicoe.

Kendrick was completely committed now, but he still kept his poker face. "The Magnum Opus?" he asked.

"Something that your wife told him about, when they were talking together," Ildicoe replied. "He said that the opening of the nearby Tartarus Gate was only Phase Two. But other than that, I have no idea."

"Eric is bluffing," Kendrick declared. "But if he is willing to submit to arrest, then I may as well hear his condition."

"He wants to be arrested by an archon," said Ildicoe.

Kendrick laughed out loud. "By the gods, what an astonishingly high view of himself he must have! Well, he's not going to get what he wants! He's not nearly important enough."

"Nevertheless, that is his condition," Ildicoe informed him. From a pocket she retrieved a sealed letter and handed it to Kendrick. "Here it is in writing, along with information about when and where he will be found. I will be there too: I'm supposed to lead the archon to the place where Eric is hiding."

Kendrick unfolded the letter and considered its contents, and then handed it to an aid. Then he said, "If you were to tell us where he's hiding, right now, I would be very grateful. And you know, my gratitude is very rewarding."

Ildicoe smiled, although with closed eyes. "I'm afraid I don't know where he's hiding. I'm not to be told until the last minute."

Kendrick pretended to be disappointed. "I see. And if El Duce's archon does not come to arrest him?" he asked.

"He made arrangements with some people from his university. Journalism students, political activists, hackers, you know the sort. But they have access to million dollar computer networks. He's given each of them a flash-drive, and told them to post its contents on the internet, unless he sends them a code word before a certain time. He's paying them to do it, actually. I think he spent his whole life's savings," Ildicoe explained.

"Then he's an idiot," Kendrick declared.

"He's also desperate," Ildicoe added. "He's seen the abyss of Tartarus. He knows what might happen to him after his arrest. And he's also afraid of Phase Three, whatever that is."

"It's nothing," Kendrick sniffed. "Is there anything more to his message?"

"No, that's all," Ildicoe replied.

"Then I've got to get back to my work," Kendrick dismissed her, and turned away.

Once again, the guards moved to usher Ildicoe out of the tent. She acknowledged them with a nod, and departed.

~ 67 ~

That afternoon in Hallowstone, a feeble sun shone through a veil of thin clouds, and its grey light fell on a score of Wessex-men, Brigantians, and refugees from other houses, in the protest camp in the castle courtyard. Some had gone to their houses in the village to get food and other materials for the camp; others still slept on their bedrolls on the ground, warmly wrapped in heavy blankets or sheltered under makeshift tents. A pot hung from a tripod over the fire that had been built the previous night, and someone was cooking a stew for everyone's dinner.

Heathcliff stepped on to the castle balcony and faced the people. His centurions appeared beside him, armed with carbines, and wearing gladiator helmets that concealed their faces. The protesters in the camp roused themselves and shouted angry accusations and slogans at him. Heathcliff only smiled and waved, as if he was greeting supporters.

"Thank you, my friends, thank you for such a warm and generous greeting. I bring you good news: A company of centurions from House Sangiovese is on its way, to secure the town against the terrorism of the bann-shee. What is more, I'm offering a bounty of up to a thousand gold clutches to anyone who has information about her. Who she is. Where we can find her."

This prompted more angry shouts from the people below. Kuvira heard Heathcliff's promise of reward, and slipped away from the crowd. She crept beside the centurions who were lined up in front of the castle gates, and said, "I know who the bann-shee really is."

Her father Ramanujan saw her, and stood up to chase her. "What are you doing, Kuvira! Don't go in there!"

The centurion nearest to Kuvira said, "You better get inside, for your own safety."

Ramanujan confronted the centurion. "That's my daughter! You just took my daughter!"

Seeing what just happened, Satya shouted to everyone around her: "They're taking hostages now!"

The crowd grew noisy again. Some of them took up stones to throw. Heathcliff had not been able to see what happened, and he too was curious, although he tried to maintain a strong demeanor. A centurion came up to him from behind and whispered something in his ear, and then his face broadened into a victorious smile.

"Friends, there is light at the end of the tunnel, and the storm is almost over. We shall soon have the bann-shee in our custody. But please, clear the courtyard. You will be safer in your homes. If you have not left the area by the time the centurions arrive, then they will have to remove you by force."

No one left the courtyard.

"Give me my daughter back!" shouted both Satya and Ramanujan. Others in the crowd shouted, "We're not going anywhere!" and "You're a tyrant!" and "We will starve you out of that castle!" Heathcliff waved one last time, and then stepped back into the safety of the castle.

Watching the scene from the rooftop of an empty house some distance away, Miranda considered what to do next.

She saw a runner, in the waistcoat and beret of the Guardians, dashing up the cobblestone street toward the castle. It gave her an idea.

~ 68 ~

The gate to Tartarus was deep underground, at the end of a long railway tunnel, its gate near an abandoned railway station in the countryside between Fellwater Village and its neighbour Thistletown. Stocky brick walls were cracked and decaying now, and large flakes of plaster and concrete littered the nearby ground. What windows were not covered in plywood sheets were musty and broken. Tall weeds filled the spaces between concrete paving tiles on what was once the passenger platform.

Ildicoe paced the platform now, awaiting sundown, and the arrival of El Duce's archon. The atmosphere was still misty, although it had cleared somewhat since that afternoon. As the streetlights flickered on one by one, an orange-white glow permeated the space beneath them, and soon spread to the sky above.

A black limousine arrived, and from it stepped two armoured DiAngelo centurions, followed by Kendrick McManus.

"So the archon is not coming?" Ildicoe asked him.

"He's coming. But he will come in his own way."

A passenger train passed by at speed, and blew its whistle to warn anyone nearby to get off the track. The wake of its passing fluttered and flapped everyone's clothes; Ildicoe held down her hat, and hoped that no one saw what she hid beneath it. When the train passed the station, all could see the archon standing on the opposite platform, with his judicial robes, and his smiling golden mask with its crown of sun rays.

The centurions instantly snapped themselves into a smarter posture, and saluted.

"Magnum Opus Facimus!" the archon greeted them.

"Avete, El Duce!" Kendrick and the centurions replied in unison.

Ildicoe was taken aback by this show of militant solidarity, but she tried not to show it.

The archon addressed Ildicoe and said, "I am here to arrest the infamous outsider, Eric Laflamme."

"Please follow me," Ildicoe told everyone, and she stepped down the cracked flagstone path to the railway marshaling yard. A side spur led to an underground tunnel, dug into the side of a small artificial hill. Normally the tunnel mouth was blocked by a grill of wrought-iron bars, but there were signs that the grill had been opened recently. The rails leading into the tunnel were shiny, not rusty, suggesting that trains were using the track again. Heavy cables, mostly buried in a shallow trench from the tunnel mouth to a nearby hydro-electric substation, followed the tracks underground. The bars bent away with a wave of Ildicoe's hand. The sight made her imagine that the bars were the teeth of some kind of carnivorous, worm-like creature. She did not let the men behind her see her tremble. She lit a flashlight, powered by a spiral-coil lightbulb, and boldly stepped into the tunnel.

Seeing the kind of light Ildicoe used, and recognizing the tunnel, Kendrick hesitated. "Eric is going to meet us in here? But this tunnel leads to–" and then he stopped himself from finishing his statement.

"Is there something special about this tunnel?" Ildicoe asked him innocently.

"No," he lied, and followed her in.

The archon's feelings could not be discerned through his mask. He, too, hesitated, and then followed Kendrick, flanked by the centurions.

When they were only a few steps inside the tunnel, Ildicoe stopped, and waved her flashlight up and down three times. Then in the darkness ahead, another light appeared, and it repeated her motion.

"Eric? It's me!" Ildicoe called out. "The archon is here. Just like you asked. You can come out now!"

"Umm– that will be– a little difficult," Eric's voice returned her greeting, from deep in the tunnel's darkness.

Kendrick gave a wary glance to the archon.

Eric's voice explained himself. "You see, when I came down here to hide–it was dark–I twisted my ankle and fell on something, and now it hurts too much to walk."

"We can carry him," Kendrick said to the centurions, and everyone proceeded deeper into the tunnel.

And as they walked, Ildicoe pretended to make smalltalk. "It's very curious that Eric chose this particular tunnel to hide in."

"Why is that," said Kendrick, although he did not hide the fact that he did not care.

"Because he's an outsider, but he picked a place to hide that's full of the old magic. The old ruined railway station, actually. Eric told me he used to play in it when he was a child. And he told younger kids in the neighbourhood stories he made up about ghosts who haunted it. He used to explore it, looking for signs that the ghost stories he made up might be real."

"Does this story have a point?" Kendrick said.

"When I first came to Ontario many years ago, I could tell there was something powerful about this place. I thought it might have been a freehold, a long time ago, but where all the people left, so the magic faded away. You know how when a sacred place fades away, you can sometimes tell where it used to be? Then I found out that the earth around here is riddled with caves. It happens that this railway tunnel leads to a cave, and the cave leads to another cave, and that cave leads to another cave, and that final cave leads to a Tartarus gate."

Kendrick realized what she had just revealed. "Archon, it's a trap!" he shouted.

It was too late for them. Lights suddenly flared out, blinding the four men and momentarily disorienting them. They raised their hands to protect their eyes. Swords flashed in the light, disarming the centurions and drawing first blood. Battle cries howled in the fray, echoing up and down the tunnel and seeming to come from everywhere and nowhere.

"How many are there!" shouted one centurion.

"I don't know, I can't see!" the other shouted back.

Kendrick drew a gun from under his suit jacket and stepped into a position where he thought he could defend the archon. He was still blinking with the glare from the light that was blasted in his face, and someone easily took his gun away. He grasped the archon's elbow and tried to escort him out of the tunnel, but they were both still too dazed by the glare in their eyes and the ringing in his ears. Someone he did not see punched him heavily in the centre of his ribcage. He wheezed, breathless, and staggered back, and fell into a chair. Before he could get up again a rope was flung over him and around his wrists, and it held him down. The whole affair was finished quickly and professionally, with Kendrick tied to the chair, the two centurions shut inside the cage of an industrial elevator, and the archon's chest and spine feeling the pricks of three swords pressed into his flesh. The six members of the Fianna stood in a circle around their two captives.

More lights came on: and all could now see that they were on the platform of an underground warehouse, with a cavernous rocky ceiling. At one end of the warehouse, where the rail tracks continued deeper into the earth, all could see the ancient Tartarus gate itself: a massive triangular arch of carved stone blocks, grey-blue in the half-light of the cavern. Two rows of stone guardians flanked it, some posed as if to warn travelers away, and some seemingly ready to repel trespassers by force. The apex of the gate bore the head of a draconic creature, whose gaze was judgmental rather than aggressive; this face more than any other made Eric feel watched. Inside the massive arch, all could see the ancient iron doors, propped open by modern steel posts. Bundles of wires and pipes ran from electric transformers and other equipment in the warehouse through the gate and into the deeper cavern beyond.

"You thought to trap us here? We're standing at a gate to Tartarus! A gate that *we* control! This is our land!" Kendrick lectured his captors.

"Are you so sure?" Ildicoe retorted. As the glare retreated from Kendrick's eyes, he could see a number of blood splatter marks on the walls, and on some of the wooden crates and metal containers.

"You will be disenchanted for this!" Kendrick threatened.

"This was caused by a pack of terrabiters, not by us," Ildicoe said, She pointed to a few acid burn spots as proof. "It seems there was a fault in the electricity, and the lights went dark, just as they were being let out of the train. That's what happens when you open a nest full of monsters. You can never really control what comes out."

Kendrick remained defiant. "No matter. You will still be punished for capturing us. A viscount of an important freehold, and one of our leader's own archons! Every fighter in the New Renaissance will be looking for you!"

"We will let you both go, soon enough," said Eric. "First, you, Kendrick, will admit in the presence of this archon, that you poisoned Livia– your own wife –and that you framed me for it."

Kendrick sputtered. "I did nothing of the sort."

From behind him came the sound of a wooden chalice, cracking into three pieces.

Ciara retrieved the fragments of Cormac's Cup from behind the lid of a shipping crate, where it had been hidden in advance. As she laid the fragments in Kendrick's lap, she kept her eyes fixed on the archon, to ensure he saw everything.

"Now tell us, again, who poisoned your wife?" Eric pressed him.

Kendrick looked back and forth between Eric, the archon, and the fragments of the chalice on his lap. When even the archon turned toward him to hear his answer, Kendrick admitted, "I did."

The fragments of the chalice vibrated in place, and then jumped up and reassembled themselves into a single vessel.

The archon gently brushed his fingers on the sword blades that Síle and Maread held on him. They understood he was more interested in Kendrick's testimony now, and they lowered their blades.

"Viscount McManus, explain yourself," the archon commanded.

Kendrick could no longer hide his fear. "She was out far too late. She was only supposed to deliver my invitation to their chieftain, and come right back to me again. But she went on carousing with these barbarians all night. She even went out to meet one of them afterwards, privately, in the forest!"

Síle perked her ears at that statement in particular.

Kendrick continued. "It's not even the first time she flashed her tits at some boy and put her hand between his legs. She has even done this while friends of mine were in the room! And she's a DiAngelo, she's Carlo's cousin, so she can do anything she wants and Carlo will protect her. Our marriage is only a business arrangement. There's no love in it. But a man still has his rights. So I'm teaching her a lesson. Keeping her as sick as a dog for a while. Making her think she caught something from the last man she took to her bed. Stupid woman, she thinks I'm giving her medicine."

As he spoke, the chalice remained intact. The Fianna looked to the archon for a response.

"Eric Laflamme," said the archon, "I hereby dismiss all charges against you. The archons of the New Renaissance shall pursue you no longer."

Eric closed his eyes and breathed deeply, and wiped his forehead and rubbed his eyes. The other Fianna cheered for him, and patted his back, hugged him, and congratulated him. Ciara and Maread kissed his cheeks; Ildicoe kissed his lips. "It's over, it's over, it's over," he whispered. He sat on a nearby shipping crate, took off his glasses, and rubbed his eyes.

"Kendrick McManus," the archon said next, "You will be brought to Domus Eleutherios to stand trial on the charge of poisoning Livia Julia McManus. As this charge carries the presumption of guilt until innocence is proven, I hereby strip from you the title of Viscount Fellwater, and withdraw from you the lordship of the territory of that name."

The Fianna clapped and cheered for the archon. Finnbarr offered to shake his hand, but the archon did not move his arm. So Finnbarr patted him on the arm instead.

"Does that mean the soldiers will leave the grove now?" Síle asked the archon. "Does that mean they'll stop cutting down my trees?"

"The treaty is signed and properly validated, and so remains in force," the archon corrected her. "Fellwater Grove is a vassal territory under El Duce's protection."

"Donall is the chieftain again, right?"

"Donall MacBride remains chieftain of Clan Brigantia. El Duce remains the lord of Fellwater Grove itself. He will soon appoint a new Viscount to rule the grove in his name."

The Fianna grimaced and shook their heads, and a few of them uttered curses. Síle, in particular, vibrated with growing anger. Then she swiftly ducked and spun around behind the archon, and had the edge of a dagger at his throat before anyone could stop her. "Then tear up that treaty! Tell those soldiers to go home and leave us alone! We never did anything to you!" she demanded.

"Síle, no! We need him!" Ciara howled. "We need him to close and lock the Tartarus Gate!"

"I want him to repudiate that stupid treaty first!" Síle cried back.

"It is not in my power to do what you are demanding," the archon stated. "The treaty transfers the sovereignty of Fellwater Grove to the New Renaissance for ever. And I do not hold the key to the Tartarus Gate."

"Yes, you do! Carlo told us!" Maread challenged him.

"No," the archon asserted again. "I do not."

Everyone looked to Cormac's Cup, to see how it measured the archon's words. It remained whole and intact, confirming that he spoke true.

"But Carlo said–" Maread stuttered.

Eric began to smile, and then to laugh. "Oh, that weasel! That clean-shaven smooth-talking weasel!"

"Why, what did he do?" said Maread.

"It's what he did *not* do!" Eric recalled. "He didn't tell us it was the archon! He let us come up with that on our own! Hats off to him, the bastard!"

Maread pursed her lips angrily, then shook her head and kicked a nearby shipping crate when she realized Eric was right.

"Carlo does nothing by accident," Ciara recalled. "He must have *wanted* us to force a confession out of Kendrick in front of the archon."

"Why would he want that?" asked Finnbarr. "Aren't they on the same side?"

"Don't talk about me as if I'm not here, you knuckle-dragging mouth-breather!" Kendrick blurted, as he grew tired of being ignored. "I'll tell you why Carlo made this happen. He wants Fellwater Grove for himself! He's wanted it for years. And with me out of the way now, he'll probably get it!"

Síle took her dagger off the archon's throat and muttered, "Sorry." She attempted to brush off his tabard and straighten it, as a kind of apology, but something about his glare made her stop.

Kendrick made a patronizing chuckle and said, "Looks like none of you had any idea you were being used. I'd say Carlo found manipulating you bull-heads quite easy."

Finnbarr wanted to pummel Kendrick for the insult, but Ciara touched his arm. "Let's just get out of here."

The rest of the Fianna agreed, and they hiked down the tunnel toward the surface again, although some made a last verbal dig at Kendrick on their way.

"Hey! You can't leave me here!" Kendrick pleaded.

"Sure we can," Maread gloated.

Eric looked to the archon and said, "I'm sure you will take care of him?"

"He and his centurions will be coming with me," the archon confirmed. The ropes holding Kendrick to the chair unravelled themselves when the archon gestured toward them. Kendrick stood up and stretched his arms, and then the ropes bound his wrists behind his back. With a similar gesture from the archon, the elevator cage that held the two centurions opened. He and Kendrick stepped on its platform and ascended to the surface.

Eric paused before following his friends out of the cave. "I suppose I should thank you for finding me innocent, at last," he told the archon, while he was still close enough to hear.

"You can thank me when the Magnum Opus is finally complete," the archon replied.

"Come on Eric!" Ciara urged him. Eric saw that all his companions were jogging away down the tunnel toward the entrance. As he turned to join them, he noticed that Ildicoe was also hanging back. She seemed very interested in a control panel of some kind, attached to an electrical transformer, and locked behind a chain-link cage.

"Ildee, we're done here. Let's go!" Eric called to her.

"Not yet. There's one more thing we have to do!" she

called back.

As the other Fianna gathered close to see what she was doing, Ildicoe managed to pick the lock on the cage and open the control panel.

"All the electricity down here flows through this transformer," Ildicoe explained.

"Great! We can use it to close the gate!" Ciara exclaimed.

"Actually, no, we can't," said Ildicoe, "but we can do the next best thing."

"What's that?" asked Ciara.

Ildicoe puffed with pride and said, "Take control of the story!"

"What are you talking about?" Eric said.

"It's like I said before, Eric. Politics is theatre. And the DiAngelo have been writing the script for too long."

Then she ripped out the wires that connected the control panel to the transformer. The cables on the transformer end sputtered and crackled for a moment, and the lights in the ceiling above dimmed and flickered.

"What the hell!" Eric shouted at her.

Ildicoe laughed and said, "Without the lights to keep the creatures down there pacified, they'll all come running to the surface. It will be too many for the Guardians to handle by themselves. All the Hidden Houses will have to come out to fight them. And the Guardians will not be so special anymore!"

"Just stop and think for a minute, Ildee!" said Eric. "Those creatures are dangerous! They'll destroy the village before we catch them all!"

"They might, I know," Ildicoe acknowledged. "But if we can't win this, we can make sure they can't win either. There's no other way."

"There's always another way!" Eric pleaded

"Tell me about it then," Ildicoe challenged.

Eric was at a loss for a moment. "We'll find one. We'll invent one! There's got to be another way that's better than this!"

"I've been searching for a better way for months," Ildicoe told her. "Of course I would rather see these gates closed and locked forever. But the New Renaissance will never do that. They need us to be afraid of something, so that we will look to them for protection! But if the world finds out that they are the ones who opened this gate in the first place, and that they can't close it again, then they will lose everything. And that's how we will win."

"No, we won't win. Everyone will lose. Everyone will lose!" Eric implored her. "We won't even get out of this tunnel alive!"

Ildicoe appeared to think about Eric's words for a moment. She looked down the tunnel, toward the Tartarus Gate, and then to her friends, and then to Eric. She cast her eyes to the floor, and reached for Eric's hands, to pull him into an embrace. Eric believed she had changed her mind, and so he welcomed her into his arms.

"I'm sorry, Eric, but there's no other way," she whispered. Then in a swift spinning motion, she picked the sword out of Eric's hands, and slashed the cables off the electrical transformer.

A shower of sparks and flames shot out of the transformer from the cable ports. Ildicoe was surprised by the violence of the result, and jumped back a few steps, just in time to avoid the rupturing of the transformer's metal shell. The others, similarly shaken by Ildicoe's unexpected move, jumped out of the way of falling glass fragments from bursting lightbulbs on the ceiling.

Then they heard the rumbling of heavy footsteps and the echoes of enraged voices from the darkness of the tunnel. The sleeping giants were stirring. The light which once imprisoned them so agreeably had vanished, and abandoned them to the darkness of reality. They climbed out of their cages, and roared out their fury and their sorrow, bounding toward the only point of light they could still see: the mouth of the tunnel, and the world outside.

Eric looked to all his friends. "Everybody run!"

~ 69 ~

The Fianna sprinted from the mouth of the tunnel, and dodged over to the old train station. As they scrambled around for a place to hide, the groaning and howling sounds from deep within Tartarus grew louder, until the tunnel disgorged a throng of monsters into the world. Some were creatures that Eric had already seen, like the gargantacores and terrabiters, but he had never seen them in such great numbers, nor with such energetic wrath. These were followed by numerous other creatures he had never seen before: reptilian things with bat-like wings, serpentine things with muscular forearms and sharp claws; saber-toothed wolves the size of horses, giant spiders with dragonfly wings, giant birds that left a trail of fire in the air as they flew by. The horde of creatures surged forth, spreading out and filling the rail marshaling yard, setting fire to trees, smashing idle boxcars, and fighting each other.

The Fianna scurried for cover behind the ruined rail station, and carefully watched the throng from around its corner.

"Who knew there were so many!" said Maread, who had to shout to be heard.

Ciara glowered at Ildicoe and said, "You are responsible for this."

Ildicoe, however, said nothing. She watched the throng of monsters from behind everyone, and she slowly slinked backwards, apparently looking for a shadow or a corner to hide in. Yet she also stared transfixed at the horde of monsters she had let loose.

Eric sensed that she did not really know what to expect when she freed the denizens of the underworld, and he reached out to her.

"Eric, I–" she began to say. But no more words came to her. When she saw the judgment on the faces of the other Fianna, she made a quiet whimpering sound, and gasped for breath for a moment as if about to drown, and then she ran away.

Eric called her name and wanted to follow her, but Maread and Ciara restrained him.

"Let her go," Ciara said. "She can run faster than any of us, anyway. You will never catch her."

Eric staggered off in the direction where Ildicoe fled, but then returned to his companions, as he knew that Ciara was right.

"We've got to close the gate!" said Ciara, who had to shout to be heard.

"I'm not going back in there!" retorted just about everyone.

Síle then noticed that the swarm of monsters in the field now seemed to be moving off in a mass, all in the same direction.

"Where do you think they're going?" asked Finnbarr.

Síle spoke slowly. "They think they are going home," she said.

Clan Fianna

"How do you know?"

"Because I can hear the voice that's calling them. It's the same voice that called me, in my forest, all those years ago."

Maread overheard this conversation and asked, "Where is it calling them?"

"It's strange," Síle whispered. "Normally I hear that call coming from the nearest freehold of the mythic age. Places like Fellwater Grove. But these last few weeks, I've been hearing it all over the village."

Eric suddenly realized why. "Because of the light! From those spiral coil lightbulbs, remember? They're in the streetlights. They're following the light!"

Finnbarr was about to panic. "What do we do? We can't just tell everyone to turn off the lights off."

"There's a hydro substation just over there," said Eric, as he pointed to the far end of the rail marshaling yard. "I bet all the power to the village flows through it. So to save the village, we have to shut it down."

"If we do that, then the direcreatures will go to Fellwater Grove!" Finnbarr protested.

"We have to do it!" Eric insisted. "The village is full of people who won't be able to defend themselves. And the grove is full of DiAngelo soldiers. And we don't have time to debate this!"

No one liked Eric's reasoning, but they murmured among themselves that he was probably right.

Ciara said, "It looks like we have to cut off the finger to save the hand."

"I don't like it either," Eric admitted. "But if we are going to do something, we better do it now."

Ciara turned to Síle and said, "Síle, do you think you can work with the ivy that's growing in there?"

Síle saw that some of the equipment in the hydro-electric substation was covered with ivy. "I think so," she replied. She jogged over to the station, and knelt down and touched the earth, and whispered something into the grass. A moment later, the ivy started to stretch and grow. Its tendrils wrapped around the pylons and wires and cables, and engulfed the transformers. The ivy might have grown that way naturally if left to do so for many years. With Síle's encouragement they fit many years of growth into a single minute. And as the Fianna watched, the ivy pulled the wires from their mountings. White sparks flashed where cables snapped and broke. The incessant humming that normally emanated from the transformers suddenly ceased.

Though the mass of wilderlings and direcreatures from Tartarus had mostly moved on, the Fianna could hear them suddenly roar and howl with frustration, and rampage about at random for a moment. Then they slowly but decisively moved off in a different direction. Síle stood up, and looked at her companions with an expression that told them she was very unhappy with that. To Eric, in particular, she glared coldly.

Ciara looked at Síle's accomplishment, and saw the new direction the direcreatures were moving in, and said, "Now, the rest of you have to go to all the allied clans, and get them to help protect the grove. As for me, I have to see Donall."

Instantly, her friends objected. "You can't go to the grove! You'll be killed!" "It's too dangerous!" "Are you seeing what's happening here!"

"I'll be fine," Ciara assured him. "I can open a seven league door from here to the grove. The rest of you have to get help!"

"No shit!" said Maread. "But there's not enough time to run to Hallowstone and back before those– *things*– get to the grove!"

The Fianna argued with each other about flying curraghs, seven league doors, ghost messengers, telepathic sendings, and every other impossible means of transport or communication that they knew, until Eric interrupted them. "You know, it's the twenty-first century now. Don't you have cellphones?"

The others looked at each other with sheepish, apologetic faces.

Maread took Ciara's hands and said, "I'm coming with you, Ciara. I have to know that Aeducan is okay."

Síle stepped forward and said, "I have to see what's happening to my trees."

Finnbarr also stepped forward. "I don't have a cellphone."

Ciara smirked at him.

Actually, Ciara, can you open one of those doors back to my house?" asked Eric. "I need to get something there."

"It better be a weapon, because we don't have time for anything else," she reminded him.

"It's the thing that will take control of the story away from the DiAngelo."

Ciara knocked on the dilapidated front door of the ruined railway station. It swung open, but not into the dusty interior of the station. It opened into Eric's apartment. As Eric stepped through, Ciara opened the door again, this time to the guest house at Fellwater Grove.

~ 70 ~

On the ridge that protected Fellwater Grove from the outside world, the centurion sentries spotted the approaching mass of monsters, and sounded the alarm. Within moments, teams of soldiers armed with carbines stationed themselves in nests at regular intervals along the top of the ridge, and in a short phalanx before the grove's main gate. They heard the monsters coming before they saw them: the tramping of claws and hooves and paws on the earth, the cries of anguished voices from half-human throats. The front wave of monsters crashed through the trees and poured into view.

The centurions opened fire, and the front line of monsters fell. The next line of direcreatures pressed onward, as did every wave to follow: each gaining more ground than the one before it, until the centurion's bullets put them down. But it was not long before the front phalanx of centurions at the gate had to fall back: the first of them died as the monsters shoved them out of the way, or trampled them. The snipers on the ridge did their best to protect the force on the ground, but soon they too were threatened, as the monsters scaled the walls of the ridge. Though the boulders shifted and pummeled them, still they persevered; and if any fell injured and could not continue, more took their place. Some of the direcreatures could fly, and the snipers shot down as many of them as they could, but they could never put down enough. Boulders were dropped on them; fire was vomited on them; claws snatched them from their posts and tossed them high in the air, and let them fall to their deaths. The centurion commanders were compelled to order a retreat, as the ramparts of Fellwater Grove were overrun.

~ 71 ~

Heathcliff stood by one of the windows in the castle, idly

holding back the curtains with his fingers. His gaze alternated between the courtyard below, where his people were blockading him, and the sky above, in the hope of seeing his reinforcements arrive. Kuvira was looking on the same scene from the next window, searching in particular for a glimpse of her parents.

A small commotion grew among the protesters in the courtyard, when some of them spied the bann-shee, looking down on them from the roof of a nearby house. Voices could be heard saying that Heathcliff's time has come, and that the siege would soon be over, and that Heathcliff would find himself in the dungeon again.

"That's only Miranda Brigand, you say?" Heathcliff asked Kuvira.

"I saw her take the hood off," Kuvira confirmed.

"Ha! Carlo's going to love that!" Heathcliff noted. He looked back outside again, and noticed the bann-shee was gone.

A moment later, a scuffle could be heard from the next room, along with some shouting, followed by a loud thump, and silence. Heathcliff closed the curtains and took a step toward Kuvira.

"It's just our soldiers, kicking out some miscreant who broke in through the catacombs," he told her. "Don't worry, we are well protected in here."

"I don't want your protection. I want the money you promised," Kuvira complained.

"You're far too young to handle that much money," Heathcliff said. "I'll keep it in trust for you, until you're older."

Kuvira pouted, and was about to protest, when another sound of some kind of violence issued from the next room. Heathcliff took a step closer to Kuvira, and motioned to her that she should stand behind him, which she did.

A moment later, the door was kicked off its hinges, and the bann-shee entered, wielding a fighting spear.

"Well, good afternoon, Miranda. I know it's you," Heathcliff crooned.

Miranda pulled her hood back, revealing her face and hair, and her cold judgmental gaze. Heathcliff immediately grabbed Kuvira by the arm and pulled her in front of him. With his other hand he whipped out a dagger, and held it to Kuvira's neck.

"Not a single inch closer!" Heathcliff commanded. "Drop your spear!"

Clan Fianna

Kuvira gasped. "Heathcliff! You told me–" she started to say. Heathcliff covered her mouth with his hand, and pushed the tip of his dagger into her flesh a little bit, not enough to draw blood, but certainly enough to be threatening.

Miranda stood still, but did not drop her spear. "It's over, Heathcliff," she told him.

Heathcliff laughed. "For you, not for me! Any minute now, half a legion of centurions will arrive. And then there will be no doubt who is Lord Protector of Hallowstone."

"They're not coming," Miranda said.

"Of course they're coming!" Heathcliff countered angrily. "Hallowstone is one of the largest and most important freeholds in Canada! The Guardians will send any number of men to protect it!"

"They're not coming!" Miranda repeated. "They have been called elsewhere."

"What could be more important than protecting Hallowstone?"

"Protecting Fellwater."

"Fellwater!" Heathcliff blurted. He glanced out the window again, searching for a sign of the reinforcements he was expecting. And he saw no such sign.

"A runner got here not long ago, to tell you that your New Renaissance lost control of the Tartarus Gate, and a swarm of direcreatures escaped."

"So where is he?

"We had a little chat, and we both agreed that it would be better for me to deliver the news. He seemed a little intimidated by the festival in the courtyard. Here's his letter." Miranda then held out for Heathcliff an envelope, with a wax seal bearing the crest of the Guardians.

Heathcliff stepped back, and pressed his blade into Kuvira's neck again. "Read it," he told Miranda.

So Miranda broke the seal, opened the envelope, and read the letter within:

"To His Grace, Heathcliff Weatherby Wednesday, the Lord Protector of Hallowstone: Be advised that Emergency Procedures have been enacted for the territories of Fellwater Village, Domus Eleutherios, and surrounding New Renaissance possessions. His Lordship, El Duce, First Apostle of the New Renaissance, has every confidence in your ability to maintain Hallowstone using the resources that have already been

assigned to you, until such time as the emergency in Fellwater has been–"

"That's enough," Heathcliff interrupted.

"So you see, Heathcliff, it's over," Miranda concluded.

Heathcliff took a step back and said, "What do you want me to do? Just hand the castle back to Algernon, just like that?"

"Just like that," Miranda replied. "Why not. In fact, I was talking to Algernon today, too. We drew up your letter of resignation for you, since it's so important to you that it be legal. All you have to do is sign it." Miranda held out another letter for him to read, but he backed away again. Kuvira squirmed fearfully, but his grip on her head and his threat with his dagger remained firm.

"Don't you understand what will happen if I sign that? Algernon will be Lord Protector of Hallowstone again!" Heathcliff complained.

"Yes, exactly, that's the idea," Miranda agreed.

"He's not strong enough!" Heathcliff shouted. "There are things about to happen– forces at work that even you don't know about– and without the New Renaissance to protect us, we will lose Hallowstone to the outsiders! Do you even understand what I'm saying! We will lose Hallowstone!"

Miranda studied Heathcliff's face carefully. This was the first time she had ever seen him show fear.

"How can your New Renaissance protect us from the outsiders, when it can't protect you from your own people?" She nodded toward the window, and the courtyard outside, where the Wessex-men and their supporters continued to demand Heathcliff's head.

Miranda stepped closer to Heathcliff, as he nervously watched the protesters bringing up a battering ram to the castle gates. "Now you can sign this resignation," she said. "You can step down graciously. Leave the castle peacefully. Continue to serve your New Renaissance in some other way. Or, I can open the castle gates, and let them decide what to do with you. I suspect they will not be kind to a man whose only remaining leverage is a little girl he's holding hostage."

Heathcliff's eyes darted between the resignation letter in Miranda's hands, and the people in the courtyard outside, who were growing increasingly excited about the battering ram they were assembling. Heathcliff let out an involuntary yelp of disgust, and then threw Kuvira across the room and into Miranda's arms. Miranda caught the terrified teenager before she fell out a window. This gave Heathcliff time to dash out of the room and make his escape.

"Miranda, I'm so sorry!" Kuvira cried.

"We'll talk later. Right now, I have to follow him." Miranda dashed after Heathcliff. She chased him through the corridors and chambers of the castle, dodging the tables and chairs that he threw behind him to slow her down. Eventually he broke into a stable, and made his escape on horseback. He galloped through the air, over the heads of the crowd in the courtyard, and around the castle walls and out of sight. Miranda could do no more than watch him go.

That was when her cell phone rang.

~ 72 ~

In the great hall of Fellwater Grove, Donall sat on his high seat by the fire, with an empty mead horn in his hand. The sounds of fighting, killing, and dying, filled the hall from every direction. Donall made no move from his seat to join it, nor to protect himself should his hall be breached. He sat by the fire and contemplated the embers, and the little tufts of ash that fell from the spent coals.

Someone threw back the blanket that covered the door and strode into the hall. The tick-tock of the visitor's footsteps filled Donall's ears, and he closed his eyes, believing that Kendrick or some other rival had come to finish him. It was Ciara's familiar voice that called his name.

"Ciara!" he exclaimed. He saw that Ciara was holding Cormac's Cup in both her hands. In another time she might have seemed like a priestess bearing the wine that heals the sick and welcomes the lonely. Donall recognized that the cup in her hands could also dispense a different kind of wine, and his eyes shifted, and his hands trembled. In a reticent breath he said, "Aeducan told me you left the clan. Joined a Fianna."

"I did," she informed him. And close behind her, the other Fianna entered the hall.

"Why did you do it?" he grieved. "How could you leave me!"

"I had to, Donall. I'm sorry," she told him.

Donall turned away from her, and looked to the embers

in the fireplace again. "I've done a terrible thing. I signed a treaty with the New Renaissance. They are in charge of the grove now."

"I know," Ciara told him.

"It's your fault, you know. All of you! I might not have done it if you were still by my side," Donall accused.

This outraged all of the Fianna. "Our fault! You drove us away!" some of them shouted.

A crack appeared on the side of Cormac's cup, and a few drops of wine dribbled out.

Donall shook his head, to show that he knew they were right, although he did not want to say so. Then he covered his face with his hands.

Ciara roughly pulled him to his feet and manhandled him to the door of the mead hall. Donall tried to resist her, but there was little he could do: the wound at his side was bleeding, and he had no strength. She threw back the blanket that covered the door and forced him out of the hall. Donall tried to cover his eyes with his arm, but Ciara pulled his arm away and shouted, "Look at what's happening! Look at what's really happening! Right now!"

Donall looked. He saw how the land had changed: electric pylons on the paths, trampled gardens by the gates, bloody bodies floating in the ponds. He saw dozens of direcreatures desperately throwing themselves over the ridge and into the grove, each of them with eyes bulging and throats crying. He saw the Wessex cavaliers with their swords, the centurions with their carbines, and the few remaining Brigantians with their spears and swords, fighting a brave but mostly futile battle to repel the direcreatures and protect the land.

"Tell me you didn't know this was happening. Tell me you couldn't have just opened the door yourself and looked outside!" Ciara dared him.

Donall closed his eyes again and said, "As the earth and sky is my witness, I did not know. I did not want to know. Oh my heart, Ciara, I have been a terrible chieftain! I looked away from things I did not want to see. I waited for others to do what I should have done myself. And now this land, our home, is lost!"

The Fianna stood around him, saying nothing, but acknowledging his confession. Ciara let some of the aggression out of her grip, and Donall staggered forward a little, to see more of the battle in front of him.

"This wound at my side is killing me, Ciara," he said next. "But now I know why it would not heal."

"So what are you going to do?" Ciara asked him.

"I am still the chieftain," he replied. "So give me my sword. I am going to do what a chieftain is supposed to do."

Síle had already picked it from the armoury, and she handed it to Ciara, who handed it on to Donall. He raised himself to his full height as best as he was able, though he grimaced in pain to do so.

A giant had just climbed over the ridge and slapped several centurions out of his way with his club. Donall stumbled toward him, with his sword unsheathed, and his battle-scream pouring from his throat. As he hobbled onward his posture straightened, his muscles bulged with battle strength, his pace quickened, and his flesh began to glow with hero-light.

Seeing this, Maread and Síle and Finnbarr let out their own battle-cries and joined the fighting. Each of them quickly found an opponent: Maread faced a gargantacore, Síle fought a lizard–man, Finnbarr fought a thing that was vaguely human but made of stones and mud. Their hero-light blazed out, and their foes fell back. Ciara saw none of this: her attention was fixed on Donall and his hero-light, and she remembered why she loved him.

"That's what he was like, back in the day," she whispered to no one. "He was as bright as the sun, and more full of beauty. And he would dance and laugh every day, even in the chaos of battle, because he loved, he so loved, to be alive."

Donall's giant was weakened by a barrage of sword blows, and it fell to its hands and knees. So Donall leapt forward for his final attack. The giant grasped a nearby fallen tree, and brandished it as best he could, to fend Donall away. Donall, shining with joy, dodged and danced past every move the giant made. Finally, Donall was close enough to thrust his blade into the giant's neck. The giant tried to howl in pain as the blade sunk into his flesh, but only a strained gurgling noise issued from its throat. As the blood poured from its wound, it collapsed to the ground.

Donall pulled his sword out of the giant's neck and pushed it into its heart, with a shout of warrior's defiance. Then he stood back to admire the sight of what he had just done. When he was satisfied that the giant was dead and his work was complete, he looked over to Ciara, and nodded, and smiled.

He clutched his ribs. Blood saturated his tunic and armour, rendering it crimson and black. His hero-light began to fade. He took a few faltering steps, then staggered himself to the earth, leaned his back on the body of the giant, bowed his head, and closed his eyes.

Ciara screamed Donall's name, and rushed to his side. The other Fianna, hearing Ciara's cry, ran with her, and stood in horrified silence at the sight of Donall's unmoving form. But the next wave of direcreatures gave them no time to say goodbye to their friend and former leader. A dozen or more new enemies raced toward them, brandishing clubs and maces forged from discarded machine parts. Finnbarr and Maread urged Ciara to get up and defend herself, but she was too overwhelmed with grief to hear. So her friends formed a protective circle around her, and defended her to the best of their ability.

Aeducan was also close enough to see what happened. He had been leading a small team of Brigantians to defend the stone circle and the paths leading to the well. But when he saw his friends forming a shield wall around Donall and Ciara, he ran to join them.

Around them, when they had a chance to look, they could see that more warriors from elsewhere in the Hidden World had joined them. Fighters from the Orenda Nation, with their bows and tomahawks and long war clubs, fought back a band of misshapen men with skin the colour of frostbite. A troop of DeDannans, in their blue and green kilts, and armed with swords and throwing spears, finished off a pack of were–bears. Fighters from among the refugees who had sought shelter in Hallowstone also joined them. Ibrahim and his Songhai-men, with their curved scimitars, bravely defended the ridge. And exiled kshatrias from House Arjun, with Satya and Ramanujan among them, cleared the main gate to the grove.

Outside the grove, Eric ran towards the battle, and took a position that was a little too close to the fighting than was safe for him. Though he could not swing a sword, and had never handled a firearm in his life, he carried a weapon that could be more dangerous than a bullet or a blade: he carried a cellphone with a video camera.

Intending to capture an image of every Guardian auxiliary who might flee the battle, Eric found a position with a good view of the main gate, and opened his lens on the scene.

Clan Fianna

Three men in Guardians uniforms ran past him screaming in terror, helpless in the face of chaos.

Eric got a glimpse of Livia Julia McManus, wearing long silk pajamas and a flannel bathrobe, wandering confusedly, and calling out Kendrick's name. Eric called out to her, but the jumble of battle obstructed his view. As Eric tried to find her again, he ran into Paul Turner, who was struggling with a lizard-man. Eric immediately reached for his camera to capture the melee. Paul dispatched his foe, and shouted at Eric

"Eric, when this is all over, give Miranda a message for me!"

"What message?" Eric shouted back.

"Tell her my offer still stands. And tell her she's a bitch!"

Eric was about to object, but Paul had to defend himself from another lizard-man, and he jumped back into the battle.

Back inside the grove, the fighting was mostly over. The Fianna could now see the whole field. They saw Miranda, dirtied and bloodied from a hero's portion of heavy fighting, decapitate a gargantacore with one stroke, and then spin around to break the legs of a wendigo. And with that final blade-fall, the battle was won. The Brigantians and their various allies, and the DiAngelo centurions too, had killed or disabled almost all the direcreatures. Those that remained were easily dispatched by the Orenda's arrows or the DiAngelo bullets.

Miranda saw the circle of her friends, protecting Ciara, who was still sitting on the ground next to Donall. She hustled over, and the circle parted for her.

"He died with his hero-light shining," Aeducan told Miranda. "He died doing all of us proud."

"But he still died, he still died!" Ciara lamented.

Around them, the victorious fighters celebrated their victory, with whoops and cheers, and shots fired in the air. Warriors who had been adversaries that morning, now found that they were brothers, and they hugged each other proudly, and celebrated each other's glory.

Miranda had eyes only for those who lay on the ground. Terrabiters and gargantacores, giants and wendigo, and all manner of chthonic monsters, littered the field so thick that there was almost no room to step between them. The flies and carrion birds circled hungrily above them. Beside them lay the bodies of many more, who had died to defeat them. The saffron-yellow of

the Brigantians, the blue and green of the DeDannans, the red
and black of the DiAngelo, and the many stripes of the Orenda,
the Songhai, the Asura, had all been stained with one colour to
mark them as sisters and brothers of one clan and one house.
Around them, the soil of the grove itself was painted the same
scarlet hue.

As Miranda became aware of the scene, she let her
sword fall from her hands. Her legs buckled and failed. She
needed the last of her strength just to remain sitting upright on
the earth, and to pull the hood of her cloak over her head. From
her breast emerged the piercing keen of the bann-shee. It echoed
and rang among the stones, the ridge, the trees, and the cliffs of
the gorge down by the river, and every corner and field in
Fellwater Grove. But she did not care whether it rang from the
clouds above too, or whether the whole world could hear it. The
keening cried through her, and left its wretchedness upon her.
Her friends dared not comfort her nor touch her, for her anguish
also carried the ring of the sacred, and it somehow seemed
wrong to disturb it.

~ 73 ~

Some hours later, Maread sat on the ground near the boathouses,
just where the land sloped down to the riverside. From behind
her, Aeducan strode tiredly, and sat on the grass next to her. She
looked at him, and then looked back to the water again. The
silence between them was understood, and not uncomfortable,
for they were both warriors, and they were both tired of the war.
Yet Aeducan had something he wanted to say.

"I was living in Germany, around when I turned thirty. I
was staying in a small town. I used to go walking in the hills and
forests all around it, with the woman I loved at the time. There
were hilltops where you could look around in every direction,
and see no sign of civilization. Well, one day we sat on a bench
to watch a thundercloud roll by in the distance. A storm came
straight for us, and we were caught in it. We had wind blowing
the tree branches around. Hailstones pelting us. Lightning
everywhere. We could have been killed! We were rescued by
some farmers who were checking the damage to their fields. I
felt embarrassed, because I didn't have the language, so all I
could say was 'danke schön, mein Herr, danke schön'. I felt like
an idiot, just saying those words, the only German words I knew.

Clan Fianna

That night, with the storm still outside, I dreamed that I was back on that hilltop, and saw the storm coming, and I knew I was just one small little thing on the surface of the earth, facing an immensity far greater than me. I felt lonely. I felt scared. But I stayed on my feet. You know what I did? I opened my arms, and I said Yes. The thunder and lightning and wind and hail could blow me down, and kill me. But I said Yes. And that is how I was awakened."

Maread looked into Aeducan's eyes for a moment, and touched his arm and then his shoulder. She knew what Aeducan was really telling her, by way of telling his awakening story, and she was grateful.

"I'm still pissed off at you," she said.

Then she lay her head on his chest, pulled one of his arms around her protectively, and closed her eyes.

~ 74 ~

Síle drifted among the stumps of what had once been her arboretum. But now, most of the trees had been reduced to jagged stumps. The few which remained had lost all their leaves, and stood like claws reaching out of the earth, half-shadowed in a thin autumn fog. A stray wispy breeze cracked and broke the thinner branches, and caused the heavier ones to groan with sadness. A few yearlings and saplings were scattered among them, as the lumberjacks had no use for them; but they too had lost their leaves, and they bowed their crowns in the breeze. The bodies of direcreatures and the warriors who fought them also lay strewn on the earth here, and the crows feasted upon them, and the flies swarmed in black clouds above them. Síle came to the great maple that held her treehouse, and found that it was still standing, but that it was the last tree of its kind in the field. Scorch marks and chainsaw cuts scarred its bark. She examined the damage more closely, and touched her ear to its roots to hear its voice. The tree would live, she decided, but it was dreadfully wounded, the summer of its vitality over.

Finnbarr wandered into the scene, with his hands open. "I'm so sorry about your forest, Síle," he told her. "But new life will soon grow."

Finnbarr's words only made Síle angry. "'New life will soon grow' – That's supposed to make everything okay? As if every kind of evil can be justified, because in the end it all somehow works out for the best! Look around, Finnbarr. Do you not understand what happened here?"

Finnbarr wanted to respond, but all he could think of to say was, "I'm sorry, Síle. I couldn't think of anything else to say."

Síle was no longer listening. She stood on an outcropping stone, raised one of her feet behind her knee, held one hand behind her back, and closed one of her eyes. With her other hand she pointed in the direction of Kendrick's camp, and then she intoned in a deep voice: "The curse of the old gods upon whoever did this to the land! The curse of the darkest and the brightest one– the curse of the Phantom Queen! Havoc upon their houses! Disease upon their flesh! Defeat for all their battles! And their weapons to turn against them! The curse of the old gods! The curse of the old gods upon them!"

The crows which had been pecking at the bodies of the dead now circled and spiraled and swam in the air above Síle, as she repeated the last line of her curse with ever greater ferocity. Finnbarr staggered away. And when he was out from beneath Síle's halo of crows, he ran.

~ 75 ~

Warriors from all the houses that participated in the battle co-operated to remove the bodies of the slain. Those who had once been enemies, but who had fought side by side, showed in subtle ways that respect had been gained. Most simply gazed at each other and nodded with understanding. Some shook hands with each other. A few even hugged each other, helping to carry their wounded to the healing house, where Neachtain tended to everyone, no matter who they called chieftain.

Ciara stood by Donall's mortal remains, and refused to let anyone touch it. When the corpse of the giant that Donall had faced in combat had been removed, Ciara took up a shovel and began digging a hole. Miranda came by and asked why she wouldn't let anyone move Donall's body.

"I want no boat to carry him to the House of Donn the Old. I want him to have a grave, a proper hero's grave, and a proud cairn of stones upon it. I want people to know that this is the place where a great man fell, and I want them to hear his story. I want his shield to hang in a heroic hall, and I want to give his sword to my children–" and then Ciara returned to digging Donall's grave, to stop herself from crying.

Miranda borrowed a shovel from a passing warrior. "Donall was my guard captain, and then he was my chieftain. And more than that, he was my friend. For that, the least I can do for him in return is help you dig his grave."

~ 76 ~

Eric returned to his apartment later that evening, and discovered Ildicoe waiting for him there, and cradling Ganga in her arms. Her feathers unfurled when she saw Eric enter. She wanted to take him into her arms and kiss him, but Eric stood back, and did not let her get too close.

"Everybody's really angry with you, Ildee. A lot of people died today because of you." Eric said.

"I didn't kill anyone," Ildicoe protested. "The direcreatures did."

"You're the one who let them out," Eric reminded her.

She acknowledged it with a nod. "They'll probably banish me for it. But can we please– not talk about it, at least for tonight? I'm scared, Eric. And I just want to not be alone."

Eric took Ildicoe's hands and whispered, "Okay."

Ildicoe pulled herself into Eric's arms.

~ 77 ~

Eric awoke the next morning to find Ildicoe's side of the bed empty. On the pillow next to him lay a single black feather.

~ 78 ~

The leaders of the allied clans gathered at Miranda's cottage in Fellwater village. Eric told them the story of how he discovered that the chthonic prisons had been deliberately opened. Next, Aeducan told the story of what had happened to Donall, and how Kendrick McManus became the lord of Fellwater Grove. Finally, Miranda told everyone about the bargain she had struck with the DiAngelo, which was the reason she could not openly help anyone.

"I think the bann-shee has the right idea. It's amazing what you can do, when no one can see your face," said Síle, and she shared a knowing smile with Miranda.

"So this is what I think happened on that first night," Eric related, as he finished his story. "Livia left the mead hall and went to meet someone in the arboretum. She was followed there by Kendrick, and Síle witnessed the meeting. Kendrick took Livia back to their camp, where Carlo was waiting for them. Carlo thought that I was responsible for the fire that killed his mother– he still thinks that– and when Livia told him I wasn't, he didn't believe her, and left.

"Somewhere in there, Kendrick slips a poison into Livia's drink, to punish her for her perceived infidelity. It was a crime of passion, as people used to say. But it then became a crime of opportunity: it gave him the chance to blame me for her condition, and also put the fear of God into Donall. Then he stole some poisonous herbs from Neachtain's house of healing– remember how he knocked over that cupboard?– and got Maread to plant them in the guest house while she was still hypnotized by that telepathic thing in her head. And then he heard that Finnbarr had seen him carrying Livia to the arboretum, so he had to bribe him with a love potion–"

"He didn't make me drink it!" Finnbarr interjected, and was rewarded with polite laughter.

"–he bribed Finnbarr with a love potion, so that Finnbarr would implicate me, when in fact he had no way of knowing exactly who it was he saw. By then, Kendrick must have been feeling quite safe. But I think he didn't count on Carlo's craving for revenge."

"Carlo didn't count on you having the will to escape from Tartarus. That is something none of us can boast of having done. You should be proud of yourself," Miranda told him.

Eric smiled, and continued. "There are a few empty spaces in this picture that we haven't coloured in yet. We still don't know who, exactly, was responsible for opening Tartarus in the first place, although my money is on Carlo."

"Mine too," said Miranda.

"The last thing we don't know," said Ciara, "is the identity of the third person in the arboretum, the person Livia went to see."

"We have all the important facts now, so it doesn't really matter," said Eric.

Then Eric had to stop, because a sound he did not expect to hear suddenly issued from a nearby bookshelf. It sounded like a wooden vessel cracking, and then falling to the floor. Everyone looked, and saw the Cup of Cormac, sitting on a showcase pedestal, broken into pieces.

A beat of silence passed, in which Eric felt the weight of judgment falling on him. His flesh paled as the blood rushed out of his head, and his knees trembled. He leaned on the back of a nearby chair, and his eyes darted from one face to another, like a cornered animal.

"Eric, what are you not telling us?" said Miranda.

Eric said nothing, and dared not meet anyone's eyes.

"Most everyone here today had to admit something we were keeping a secret. Now it's your turn," Miranda asserted again.

Eric did not look up, but he acknowledged the fairness of Miranda's statement. So he said, "I *do* know who Livia went to meet in secret, in the middle of the night. I've known all along. She had gone to the forest to meet– me."

Soft gasps escaped the lips of most of Eric's listeners. And to certify the truth of Eric's words, two of the three fragments of Cormac's Cup united again.

"The last thing she did before she left the mead hall was ask me to meet her in private, so we could make love," Eric continued. "I knew she was a married woman. I knew she was married to a powerful man. But no one had reached out to me like that in a long time. So when she reached out to me, I reached out to her. I should have said no. But I didn't. I said yes."

The Cup of Cormac mended itself whole again, confirming Eric's truth.

"I suppose everything is my fault, really," Eric rambled quietly. "Sure, I had a lot to drink that night, and so did Livia. But if I had remembered to think with my head instead of with my– well, then maybe none of this would have happened."

Ciara got up. "You're damned right, Eric! It's all your fault! Donall is dead and we have no home anymore because you couldn't keep your dick in your pants!"

Then she tore Eric's glasses off his face and crushed them under her heels. She wanted to do more to hurt him, but Aeducan and Miranda grabbed her arms and restrained her.

"I should go home," Eric concluded. With shoulders downcast and eyes on the ground, Eric collected his coat and left the cottage quietly.

~ 79 ~

Around Fellwater Grove, a dozen towers of noxious black smoke rose from pits where the soldiers were burning the bodies of the dead. Carlo, Heathcliff, and Paul Turner stood on a catwalk on the ridge, to survey their new possession.

"This is what victory looks like, gentlemen," Carlo said. "Fellwater Grove finally belongs to us. Enjoy it. Savour it."

"It looks like a war zone to me," said Paul.

"War is the natural state of human life, my friend," Heathcliff reminded him.

"Don't forget that our ultimate purpose is to transcend the state of nature, and lift up the soul of humanity," Carlo added. "From all this chaos, the New Renaissance will emerge."

Paul sighed. "I don't know. It seems like we've been telling lies, and killing people, to make it happen. I hope it will be worth it, in the end."

Carlo smiled and clapped Paul on the shoulder. "Oh, it will be. I've seen it. It will be."

~ 80 ~

Miranda caught sight of Eric as he was passing in front of the library. She called for him to wait for her, and he did, although he was expecting her to lecture him about the tryst he almost had with Livia. Instead, she handed him his glasses, clean and intact.

"How did you get these fixed so fast?" he asked.

"I have talented friends," she replied coyly, and smiled.

"I suppose you're here to tell me I've been banished again," he said.

"No, you're not banished," she informed him. "You're not the one who opened a can of monsters on us. But there's a few people who are not sure how much they can trust you."

"I'm sure that some of them will never trust me again," Eric sighed.

"I can't say you did right," Miranda said. "But you were honest about what you did wrong, eventually. And you did it from loneliness, not malice. And by earth and sky, I know a thing or two about that."

"It seems like I never make small mistakes in my life. Only big ones," Eric bemoaned.

Miranda took Eric's hands and said, "There's no one

single person to blame for everything that happened, Eric. Carlo played his part, too. And so did Kendrick, and Livia, and Ildicoe. And so did I."

"What did you do?" Eric asked, incredulously.

"I broke a promise," she informed him. "It was a promise I made to an enemy, but it was a promise, nonetheless. I took the law into my own hands, for a while. I told a secret to a child, that I should have told no one. It almost cost that child her life."

Eric sat on the steps of the library, and Miranda sat next to him. Eric leaned into Miranda's shoulder, and Miranda stroked his arm.

"I don't suppose Kendrick or Carlo will ever answer for what they did," Eric speculated.

"They will never apologize for anything. They're too proud," Miranda agreed.

"Ildicoe ran away again. She's afraid the clan will want to banish her," Eric informed her.

Miranda nodded. "A few people suggested it. Nobody wants her around anymore. Eric, I know you love her, and I'm sorry."

Eric sighed. "Yes, I love her. But what can I do? Love is tragedy. Relationships are things that end." With these words said, he looked away.

"Katie and Ildicoe are not the only ones who love you, Eric," said Miranda.

Eric looked up, and was about to ask who Miranda was speaking of, but Miranda changed the subject. "There's good news, too. The clan voted to make me the chieftain again," she reported happily.

"That's great!" Eric smiled. "But is there much of a clan left?"

"Not really," Miranda admitted. "There's Aeducan, Maread, Síle, and Finnbarr, the four best fighters. There's Neachtain the healer, and Ciara will be our summoner. Oh, and there's a few people from other clans who asked to join us, because their own clans joined the New Renaissance. You've already met some of them. And then there's you and me. But that's all. There used to be hundreds of us, in Ontario alone. Now most of our people have left, because of Donall. Who knows where they went. Most of those who stayed are now dead."

Eric bowed his head respectfully. Then he added, "We don't have the land anymore, either."

Miranda nodded. "We kept the direcreatures out of the village. And we posted the video you made to the Hidden Internet. Now everybody can see the Guardians fleeing the battle, saying they can't handle it. People are renouncing their membership in the New Renaissance. Renouncing their treaties with El Duce. He's still influential, but I doubt he'll get his way so easily, now. So, I suppose we can say that we won."

"I suppose," Eric sighed, "Still, it's not a victory I feel like celebrating."

The two friends leaned into each other again. They, like the other warriors, were tired. After a moment, Miranda said, "We also decided we can't call ourselves the Brigantians anymore. Because we lost the grove. A third of us come from other clans anyway. Then some of you gathered here, a few nights ago, and decided to leave Clan Brigantia. You told your stories to each other. You fought your first battle together. You became new clan. So we had to choose a new name."

"So, what are called we now?"

"Clan Fianna," she said.

Eric smiled. "Clan Fianna," he repeated to himself. Then Eric remembered something, and said, "We got our start right here, in this library. You didn't have anything to do with that, did you?"

Miranda only smiled coyly, and held her finger to her mouth, in a playful gesture of secrecy. She laughed.

Eric laughed with her.

Clan Fianna

FIANNA

Clan Fianna

~ Epilogue: Winter in Fellwater Village ~

By day, the log cabin slept. The evergreen bushes in its yard stirred only faintly in the wind, and an untouched mantle of snow surrounded and protected it. Children passing by on their way home from school dared each other to sneak into the back yard and make angels in the snow.

By night, the cabin scrambled with life. Coloured lights flickered in its many curtained windows. Excited voices from within demanded answers, and action. Outside, the coyote and the owl stood on guard.

Those who knew the meaning of such signs whispered among themselves: The Secret People were gathering there. The Secret People were moving.

The Secret People! Women and men from every race and every nation, each of them one out of ten thousand or more, whose wise and potent ancestors were once called the gods. These remnants of mythology, these last and lonely few, answered the summons of a queen whose court was no more grand than a simple log cabin, in a common Ontario town.

Each night, their shadows came and went across the rustic floors. Some came on flying carpets, winged horses, witches' brooms. Some merely stepped out from behind a tree, and some fell out of the sky. Some came in rich and chrome-decked cars with lights that glowed with fireflies. Some came in battered carriages drawn by grizzly bears, or swans. Sometimes footprints appeared in the snow, but not the one who made them. Sometimes a man passed over the snow and left no steps behind him. Swiftly and often they came and they left, staying for an hour, a moment, a week. Some left with heads high, and some with heads down.

But everyone left with a quest.

Brendan Myers

Clan Fianna

~ Notes ~

I feel like I need to apologise to you, dear reader. This was a beastly convoluted book. To paraphrase my editor: of all the books in the Hidden Houses series, this one had the most moving pieces. Some readers and reviewers of a previous edition found it so complex that they gave up in despair. Some also complained that it was too full of typos and errors. These comments prompted me to turn to Kickstarter, to raise funds for a professional editor. The original draft of this book more than 120,000 words, and the editor and I whittled it down to 94,000. In the process, and following his recommendations, I made some *very* big changes to the story, and to the story of the previous book in the series. This required me to change my plans for the rest of the series, too. The result, I think, is a much better book. Although still a complicated one. Nonetheless, I am grateful for his help.

On the front cover: the designer and I wanted to avoid the kind of misogynist tropes that are typical of the genre of contemporary and urban fantasy. Yet we also wanted an image that would catch the eye, and clearly belong to the genre, and exemplify the world of the story. When he searched stock-image websites for pictures with the tag-phrase "female archer", he found lots of images of women with inappropriate footwear. The cover we created, I think, meets our requirements: our heroine is mysterious, powerful, and interesting, and not a trophy wife. Before I embarked on the Kickstarter project to re-design these books, I had only a vague idea how to design a book's cover. I probably still don't know much about design, but I know more than I did before, and I am grateful to my designer for that, too.

Now, let's debrief the story itself. The Irish word 'Fianna' is a curious one. Its root is the old Irish word 'fian', meaning a warrior; its most direct translation from the Irish is 'war band'. But it also suggests a 'band of brothers', a small team of young people solidified into a kind of second family through their shared warrior adventures. Importantly, a band of Fianna were also 'outsiders' or 'wild men', because by joining a Fianna, one effectively becomes no longer a regular member of old Irish society. Fianna bands lived in wilderness camps, and survived by hunting and fishing and trapping, and also from raiding farms and forts. They owned no land, and they often had no formal leaders. It was considered fairly natural, albeit uncommon, for young women and men in Iron Age Irish society to break away from their families and join a Fianna for a few years. During this time they would have some fun, travel the country, fight battles, endure tragedies perhaps, and generally learn some lessons about life and growing up. A few years later, they might rejoin mainstream Irish society, get married, start a farm or a business, and generally settle down. Joining a Fianna was not expected to be a permanent move. The most famous Fianna is of course that which was led by Fionn MacCumhall, and which had thousands of members. Although they were outsiders, they were also elite warriors, and the mythologies describe several tough tests that candidates for membership had to pass. Belonging to the fringes of society, they therefore became implicitly related to the High King, who dwells at the centre. Indeed, the most important cycle of stories about the Fianna describe how the High King employed them to protect Ireland from an invading foreign army. The conception of the Fianna as elite warriors who serve the nation as a whole, not just their own families, survives in modern Irish as the name of the special forces wing of the Irish army: the Fiannóglach, the Irish Ranger Wing.

In the previous book in the series, I borrowed a line from the Fianna hero Oisin, for use as the Brigantian's battle motto. When Oisin was asked by St. Patrick what sustained the people in their lives before they adopted Christianity, he answered: "the truth that was in our hearts, and strength in our arms, and fulfillment of our tongues" (i.e. promises). But as far as I'm aware, there's no suggestion in history or mythology that a Celtic tribe which loses its land automatically becomes Fianna. I've claimed a bit of artistic license on that point, for the sake of telling this story.

Cormac's Cup is mentioned in just one old Irish story. But it has most of the same properties described here: the original cup breaks when it hears three lies, and it mends when it hears three truths. It was said to have been given to Cormac by one of the gods, after Cormac returned from an adventure in the otherworld. I've sometimes wondered if there ever was a real cup which the historical kings of Ireland used to extract the truth from their petitioners, whether by magic or by clever psychological manipulation.

Another piece of Celtic legend I've borrowed here is the figure of the Bann-Shee. This is a faerie-woman who

Clan Fianna

presages a death in certain old Irish families by her howl of lamentation. The name itself is derived from the Irish word for a faerie woman: 'bean sidhe'. I have spelled it as 'Bann-Shee' instead of the more common 'banshee', to give the reader a better sense of how the word sounds in my own mind. 'Bann-Shee', with the accent on both syllables, was how my father pronounced it when he taught stories of the bann-shee to my sisters and I, when we were children. Of course, I've re-imagined the bann-shee a little bit here, under the influence of other mythical female figures like the Furies, the Norns, the Greek Amazons, and some twentieth century feminists whom I admire. If the bann-shee is real, I hope she will forgive me.

I've also borrowed a few things from other heroic societies. For instance, Donall's cry of "Where is the bard?" paraphrases a 10th century Anglo-Saxon poem called The Wanderer. The verbal contest between Aeducan and Livia is an anglo-saxon custom called a 'flything'. A chieftain may prompt a flything when the visitor is someone unknown to him, or when he is uncertain of the visitor's intentions. The exchange between Beowulf and Unferth is perhaps the most famous flything in literature. But there are Irish examples as well: the exchange between Lugh Lamh-Fada and the gatekeeper at the Hill of Tara, for instance. Finally, from a more modern warrior society: a 'reccee' is Canadian army slang for a reconnaissance mission. Since Miranda is a former infantry officer, I imagine she taught the Brigantians some modern military jargon.

The ancient war that Paul Turner mentioned early in the novel is attested in various European and near Eastern creation stories. The Celtic gods, the Tuatha de Dannan, fought a race of monsters called the Fomorians, the Norse gods fought the Giants, and so forth. In the Greek story, the defeated Titans were banished to an underworld prison-realm called Tartarus. The idea that these prisons were weakening had already been introduced to the series in previous novels. But the suggestion that they were opened deliberately follows any number incidents from real world history, not mythology. All governments and armies have enemies, but some of them create their own enemies. They might do so accidentally, as when they hire privateers or mercenaries who subsequently turn on their former paymasters. Or they might do so deliberately, as when they use 'false flag' or 'agent provocateur' gambits to raise public support for their purposes. Paul's remark to Eric about how the great man 'creates his own truth' refers to the latter kind of created enemy. Or, more correctly, the remark refers to the truth that the great man wishes to create, with the aid of an invented enemy that can frighten others into believing it. Paul's words also paraphrase a certain famous American politician, whom I shall not name here.

Hesiod, the main Greek poet-historian who described the imprisonment of the Titans in Tartarus, also described a sequence of five 'ages' of the world. There's a Golden Age, when the world is ruled by a Golden Race of humans (who he calls the Guardians!), and a Silver Age ruled by a Silver Race, and so on. The idea that the history of the world follows a sequence of 'ages' also appears in Hindu mythology, as the cycles of the four Yugas. To some extent it is also discernible in Jewish and very early Christian traditions. More recently, the idea was a central teaching of the Theosophical Society, and from there the idea made its way into the 20th century New Age movement. This is the inspiration for the 'Mythic Age' which most of the Secret People speak of, in all books in the series. It's Hesiod's Golden Age, and comparable ages from other mythologies, which the members of the New Renaissance hope to recover. Whether they are right to do it, of course, is up to you to decide.

The nature of Tartarus, as I've imagined it here, owes something to several philosophical thought experiments, some old and some new. Plato's Cave is one obvious example. John McMurtry's concept of an invisible prison is another: it is just such a prison for the mind that the "audience" of a false-flag political theatre performance end up trapped inside. I was also thinking of Ray Bradbury's "happiness machine", as described in his 1957 novel *Dandelion Wine*, and as reprised by philosopher Robert Nozik in his 1974 book *Anarchy, State, and Utopia*. In both authors' work, we imagine a machine that feeds pleasurable experiences directly into someone's mind. A person invited to enter the machine would decline to do so, or else would enter it but soon wish to leave it, because (according to the argument) people want more than just happiness in their lives. They also want autonomy, agency, a meaningful relationship to reality, and similar things that have little to do with pleasure. As an aside: there have been surveys and practical experiments which invited people to imagine that they're already plugged into such a machine, and which offer people the choice to unplug themselves from it, and return to an unknown reality. They found that most people prefer to remain plugged in. This suggests that what people want is familiarity, not (necessarily) reality, nor even happiness. Curious!

But let's finish the debriefing. The happiness machine I've described in Clan Fianna is not a holiday resort. It's a prison. Its purpose is to enervate people by hypnotizing them with pleasure; and it sits inside another prison which hypnotizes and enervates people with despair. Here I was thinking of something not only philosophical, but also personal. I drew from experiences in my own life, and the lives of others whom I care about, to explore things like truth and lies, justice and revenge, home and belonging, loneliness and exile. I wanted to explore these realms more playfully and intimately than nonfiction philosophy (my usual mode of writing) normally allows. But don't let me pontificate too much in these closing notes. You, dear reader, might have your own experience with Tartarus.

Well, what's next for Eric and Miranda and their new clan-mates? They have some work ahead of them now, if they want to reclaim their beloved home. At this time, I am planning one more novel, to complete the series. I'm also planning various 'spinoff' short stories and novellas, some with new characters, some which raise tertiary characters from the main series to more prominent roles. There are more stories yet to be told about the Hidden Houses, and the Secret People. So please stay in touch! And thank you for reading this many-tangled book.

Brendan Myers
Gatineau, Quebec, Canada
October, 2014

Brendan Myers

~ About the author ~

Brendan Myers loves fairy tales and space exploration. He lives in a library, next door to a forest.

Brendan is a TED speaker, a successful Kickstarter, and the author of fifteen books in fiction and nonfiction. He earned his Ph.D in philosophy at the National University of Ireland, and now serves as professor of philosophy at Heritage College, in Gatineau, Quebec.

Find him on the web at http://brendanmyers.net

Follow him on Twitter @Fellwater